continued . . .

"A surprisingly deep romance." —Bookaholics

Praise for the Second Chance Novels

BACK TO BEFORE

"Big enough to spawn several celebrities but small enough to
be as catty as a high-school clique, [Chances Inlet is] the
perfect setting for a stormy encounter between hunky native
son Gavin McAlister, a wannabe TV star, and Ginger Walsh,
a former ballerina struggling back to the dance world after a
catastrophic injury." —Publishers Weekly

"The first in a new series by Tracy Solheim will thrill con-
temporary romance fans. Striking a great balance between
the plot and the hot sex scenes, Solheim captivates readers
with the depth of her story as well as the overwhelming
passion between the characters. The nod to Solheim's other
series, Out of Bounds, was fantastic." —*RT Book Reviews*

"Solheim is a wonderful storyteller whose characters are
fully formed with all the strengths, vulnerabilities and flaws
of people we meet in real life and whose books leave this
reader sighing with satisfaction. I'm already anticipating my
next visit to Chances Inlet." —The Romance Dish

Sleeping
with the
Enemy

TRACY SOLHEIM

BERKLEY SENSATION, NEW YORK

BERKLEY
SENSATION

An imprint of Penguin Random House LLC
375 Hudson Street, New York, New York 10014

SLEEPING WITH THE ENEMY

A Berkley Sensation Book / published by arrangement with Sun Home Productions, LLC.

ISBN: 978-0-425-28102-4

PUBLISHING HISTORY
Berkley Sensation trade paperback edition / September 2015

PRINTED IN THE UNITED STATES OF AMERICA

10 9 8 7 6 5 4 3 2 1

Cover photo by Claudio Marinesco.
Cover design by Rita Frangie.

Penguin
Random
House

This one is for my favorite NFL owner. I love you, Austin.

ACKNOWLEDGMENTS

It goes without saying that I couldn't do this without the love and support of my family, particularly my husband, Greg, and our two works-in-progress, Austin and Meredith. Love you guys.

As always, thanks to Cindy Hwang at Berkley and my agent, Melissa Jeglinski, for their support—I needed a lot of it for this book!

A big thank-you goes out to my favorite pilot Barry Goldberg, who answered my questions about private jets and flight times. Thanks to his wonderful wife, Kim, who kept me straight on all things Chicago.

Thank you to the women of Talking Volumes book club and the barn moms for helping me taste test different pinot grigio wines. It was hard work, but I appreciate you ladies taking one for the team.

To Melanie Lanham, thank you for always answering the phone and reading what I write.

Thanks to all the wonderful bloggers who've taken the time to promote my books and introduce me to new readers. Many of you have become friends whose kindness I value immensely.

Most of all, I'd like to thank all of you who've taken the time to read one of my books. It's you the readers who make this the best job in the world! A special thanks to two readers—Brandi Swendt and Eric Bluhm—for suggesting that the name of the Blaze cheerleaders be the Sparks.

One

Jay McManus had built his reputation—not to mention his fortune—in business by always keeping his composure and never letting his opponents see him sweat. That cool, ruthless demeanor had propelled him to the top of the dot-com industry before he'd even hit the ripe old age of thirty. It had also earned him enough begrudging respect and money to enable him to become, at thirty-five, the youngest owner of a National Football League team. Right now, though, he was beginning to sweat his decision to go public with his lucrative software company and sink his profits into the Baltimore Blaze.

"Let me get this straight—according to some obnoxious gossip blogger, the Sparks, our team's cheerleaders, are filing a lawsuit suing the team?" With two fingers, Jay pulled at the Windsor knot on the silk tie threatening to strangle him.

"As of this morning, there's only one cheerleader named, but it is a class action suit, which means any of the several hundred women who've cheered for the team during the past decade could potentially join in." Hank Osbourne, the team's general manager, looked way too relaxed for having just dropped a bombshell into Jay's morning coffee. Instead of being the cool one, Jay wanted to strangle someone. "These types of cases are springing up throughout the league," the GM said calmly.

Known as the Wizard of Oz throughout the NFL, Osbourne was a taciturn former military officer who'd been running the day-to-day operations of the Blaze football team for five years and was well respected among the players, the league, and other teams. Jay hadn't given a thought to replacing him when he'd taken over ownership from his godfather the preceding year. The guy had earned his pay and then some since Jay had arrived. As recently as this morning, the GM had been dealing with a kicker who'd been placed on suspension by the NFL after he'd violated the league's alcohol abuse policy one too many times. Unfortunately for the player—and the team—the guy had just been enjoying a beer while on a family vacation. Not that it mattered to the league. Now, besides needing a kicker before the season opener this week, the team was apparently about to get hit with a sensational lawsuit by scantily clad women waving pom-poms.

This kind of bullshit just doesn't happen in Silicon Valley, Jay thought as he stood up from the round table in his large corner office at the Blaze practice facility. He began to pace methodically in front of the room's long picture windows, scattering the dust motes floating in the bright morning sunshine as he did so. "How many people know about this?"

"You know as well as I do, Jay, that this blogger is followed by every media outlet," Hank said. "I spoke with Asia Dupree in our media relations office before I came in here. She's already fielding calls from all the networks and major sports sites."

Jay swore under his breath. The *Girlfriends' Guide to the NFL* had been a pain in the league's ass for over two years now. Unfortunately, most of what the anonymous blogger reported was true. It was the sensationalistic spin she put in her posts that aggravated him—and every other person who'd found themselves mentioned on her site. Lately, it seemed, the Blaze had taken more than its fair share of hits.

"Not only that, but Asia says some women's groups have been calling, too."

He turned to face the other men in the room. "You can't be serious?"

Hank nodded solemnly as the others looked everywhere but at Jay. "Which means the commissioner will likely want to be kept apprised of what we're doing."

Which meant Jay's day had just gone from bad to worse. The NFL commissioner, Reggie Austin, thought Jay was too young and too inexperienced to own the Blaze, and wanted one of his cronies to take over the team instead. But he hadn't had the power or the votes to block Jay's ownership bid. So instead, the man took every opportunity to say "I told you so" to anyone who'd listen. Now, thanks to a cyberbully, this was apparently going to be another one of those opportunities.

"The cheerleader, what do we know about her?" Jay directed his question at Donovan Carter, the Blaze's chief security officer, who was seated at the opposite end of the table. A former college football star, the stocky African-American with the shaved head had once been an agent with NCIS before joining the Blaze staff.

Don scanned his tablet. "Not much yet. Her name is Jennifer Knowles. She was a student at the University of Maryland, but she's not enrolled there this semester. She cheered for the Blaze for two years beginning with the Super Bowl season year before last. The roster doesn't list her as a member now. I have a meeting with Nicki Ellis, the coordinator of the Sparks, at ten. Hopefully she can shed more light on this."

"What does she want?" Jay asked. Someone always wanted something from him. Especially women. Usually it was Jay the women wanted, and if they couldn't have him, they wanted money. Lots of money.

Hank released a long-suffering sigh. "We won't know for sure until Art gets ahold of the complaint being filed." He gestured to the man seated beside him: Art Langford, a tall man sporting a bad combover, who served as the team's general counsel. "We've got someone at the courthouse ready to grab a copy when it reaches the clerk." Hank steepled his fingers and leaned back in his chair. "In all likelihood, she's jumped on the bandwagon of other cheerleading squads who've filed similar suits against their teams. Most have claimed wage discrimination. That argument won't hold up in our house."

"Explain it to me," Jay demanded. He made it a habit to know every detail of each business he owned, but it hadn't occurred to him when he bought the team that he needed to familiarize himself with the operations of the Blaze cheerleaders. Jay was angry at himself for the slipup.

"The Sparks generate their own income in the form of special appearance fees, as well as through other merchandising such as calendars and posters. Last year that amounted to just over one point three million dollars."

Jay's personal assistant, Lincoln Harris, interrupted Hank's explanation with a loud whistle before Jay locked gazes with the young African-American man. Linc quickly dropped his eyes back to his tablet.

"Most teams reabsorb that money into their own coffers, but we use it to ensure the young women are afforded a decent wage—keeping in mind this is only meant to be a part-time job." Hank continued. "The women sign a contract outlining what they're responsible for with regard to appearances, transportation, and practice time. All in all, the Sparks are among the highest paid in the league."

"Yet, according to some malicious blogger, one of them is filing a multimillion-dollar lawsuit against this team." Jay let out an impatient huff as he continued pacing. Something didn't make sense.

The four other men in the room were silent. Art squirmed a bit in his chair.

Jay pinned the lawyer with his gaze. "Out with it."

Art flinched slightly before pulling out a sheet of paper from a folder in front of him and handing it to Jay. "The suits pending haven't all been strictly about wage issues."

Jay scanned the sheet, his pulse squeezing at his neck

despite his loosened tie. He lifted his eyes to the men assembled in the room. "For the love of Christ, tell me there is no one in this organization performing a *jiggle test* on the cheerleaders." Somehow he managed to push the words out through his tight jaw.

"Whoa," Linc said from beside Jay. "Is that really a job? Because if it is—"

Jay silenced his brash young assistant with a glare. Linc had been with him for four years. A three-time all-American wrestler from Duke, Linc had a sharp mind for software that usurped even his prowess on the mat. When Jay went public with his company, he'd intended to leave Linc in place to look after Jay's remaining shares. But Linc was an athlete at heart and the opportunity to work in the NFL was every boy's—and man's—dream, so he'd convinced Jay to bring him along. Up until this moment, Jay hadn't regretted that decision.

Linc gave him a sheepish look. "Not a joking matter. Got it." He went back to his job of taking notes of the meeting.

"Not as long as I'm managing this team," Hank said, his expression every bit as stern as Jay's likely was. "That behavior will not be tolerated."

Jay rubbed the back of his neck, feeling his tight muscles pinch beneath his dress shirt. He really needed a few rounds in the gym with a punching bag. But that would have to wait until this evening. "So how do we prepare and defend ourselves against this crazy case? I really don't want the added negative publicity going into the season. Art, can we hand this off to the league? With so many other similar suits clogging up the courts, surely they have a standard defense prepared."

"That's the problem," Art said. "Cheerleaders are not considered part of the NFL. Each group falls under the purview of the individual team. Even if the league comes up with some standard policy now, it would be too little, too late. The teams are on their own to defend this."

With a harsh sigh, Jay flipped the paper out of his hands and let it drift back toward the table. "Then do your best to make this go away, Art." He picked up his coffee cup for a fortifying sip of caffeine, which he now wished was laced with Scotch. Art deferentially cleared his throat, causing Jay to nearly choke.

Jay arched an eyebrow at the lawyer. Art shot a pleading look at Hank. The coffee went down Jay's throat painfully as he braced himself for what was yet to come, pretty damn sure that it was something he wasn't going to like.

"Art isn't exactly a trial attorney," Hank said unapologetically. "He handles the player contracts, issues with sponsors and the unions, but whenever we've had a trial, we generally hire out."

Swearing under his breath, Jay clunked his coffee mug back down on the table and resumed his pacing. "So we have a specious class action suit looming and—even if we can defend against the claims—I'm going to have to fork out a ransom for outside counsel?"

"Unfortunately, that's the way these things work, Jay," Hank said. "But I've already contacted our local counsel. Stuart and his firm have handled at least a dozen other court cases for the team with great success."

Jay jerked to a halt. "*A dozen other court cases?* How come this is the first I've heard of them? Why weren't they disclosed when I took over ownership last year?" If there was one thing Jay hated, it was being blindsided. He prided himself in having information long before his opponents— much of it information his business rivals wished he hadn't uncovered.

It was Hank's turn to arch an eyebrow. "I believe the words I used were 'with great success.' Stuart is discreet and very astute. He's the one with eyes on the courthouse. In fact, if this case comes to fruition, Stuart already has a partial strategy mapped out, including a whopper of a lawyer to represent the team in court. His firm just merged with a big firm in Boston. The same one that employs Brody Janik's sister. She just successfully defended a small Baltimore company in a major environmental class action suit. Between her trial success rate, her being a woman, and her connection to the team, Stuart thinks we'll have an advantage in the court of public opinion, which is half the battle here."

Jay moved to the large windows overlooking the Blaze campus, putting his back to the other men in the room because he wasn't so sure he could maintain a stoic expression any longer.

"I'm sure you've met Bridgett, at the very least at Brody's wedding this past spring," Hank was saying. "By all accounts, she's as brilliant in the courtroom as she is beautiful."

The tension that had been torturing his neck and shoulders since the meeting began settled uncomfortably in another part of Jay's anatomy as he thought of the "brilliant" and "beautiful" Bridgett Janik. She'd avoided him at her brother's wedding, just as she had every time their paths had crossed in the past eighteen months. Always impeccably dressed in some expensive, figure-flattering outfit, the petite blonde with the light gray eyes hadn't even graced him with a haughty look since he'd taken over ownership of the Blaze. It was as if he was invisible to the woman, while the short hairs at the back of his neck lifted *every freaking time* she entered the same room as him. Given his reaction to her, she couldn't be as immune to Jay as she pretended. He allowed himself a moment to admire her ability to remain aloof—it was a skill he'd cultivated for years. But he needed to discredit her as the Blaze's outside counsel. Because working with the alluring Bridgett Janik would be too much of a distraction for Jay, and he didn't need any more distractions in his life.

His eyes were still focused on the leaves changing color on the trees surrounding the practice facility as he spoke. "I'm sure that's a conflict of interest." He tossed the suggestion out, hoping Hank and Art would latch on to it.

"Actually, no, it isn't," Art piped up. "There's no prohibition on a family member representing another family member in a courtroom. Although, it's not always the best idea. I can quote several cases where it hasn't been effective." Hank cleared his throat and Art continued. "In any case, Ms. Janik will be technically representing you as the owner of the Blaze. Her brother's association with the team is irrelevant."

Great, Jay thought to himself, *the guy can't try a case in court, but he knows all the intricacies of conflicts of interest.*

"With any luck," Hank pointed out, "we won't need outside attorneys, but I think Stuart's plan is a good one. Having Bridgett in our corner will certainly give us some credibility with both men and women."

Jay hoped Hank was right, that this case would die out before the Blaze became the butt of jokes by late-night talk show hosts. More important, he hoped it would settle quickly so that he'd be able to keep his distance from Brody Janik's sister.

"Stuart is sending his team over this afternoon, as soon as they go over the court documents," Hank went on to say. "In the meantime, let's let Don see what he can find out about the Knowles girl. After that, we can come up with a defensive game plan."

He listened as the other men filed out of his office. All the while, Jay was formulating his own game plan on how to ensure Bridgett Janik would quickly recuse herself from the case.

The teakettle whistled with annoyance while Bridgett Janik carefully stirred the ingredients for chai tea into her cup. She tucked the cell phone between her ear and her shoulder and reached for the shrieking kettle.

"I'm sorry, Stuart, but I thought you actually said cheerleaders for a minute there." Bridgett stirred her tea before blowing carefully over the rim.

"That's because I did say cheerleaders, Buffy," the senior partner for her firm's Baltimore office, Stuart Johnson, replied on the other end of the phone. He'd dubbed her "Buffy the Class Action Slayer" two years ago when she'd persuaded the judge to quash half the designated class in a large environmental case weeks before the plaintiffs had even issued subpoenas. "Good to know you didn't leave your hearing over in Italy with all your hard-earned money. How was the shopping spree, anyway?"

Bridgett recognized a redirect when she heard one. And Stuart's were always among the best. It was what made him such a successful trial attorney.

"My trip to Italy was wonderful, Stuart. I slept until noon. I ate bread and pasta and I shopped like I had the money to spend. The best vacation a girl could want after eighteen months on a case. But you already know this because your wife was there for part of my vacation." Elizabeth, her boss's wife, had a bit of a shoe fetish. When Bridgett had mentioned she was headed off for a shopping vacation on the Italian coast, the older woman had looked so enthralled that Bridgett had invited her along. She hadn't minded the company because it gave her an excuse not to invite one of her interfering sisters. "Get back to the subject of stupid cheer-leaders, Stuart."

"You say *cheerleader* as though it's dirty somehow." Stuart's tone was teasing. "Naughty even." He laughed at his words, and Bridgett let out an exasperated sigh as she carried her tea over to the large window in the living room of her condo in Boston's trendy Back Bay area. Sunlight sparkled off the dew still glistening on the rooftops in the early autumn morning. "What have you got against cheerleaders anyway?" he asked.

Bridgett blew on her tea. "Nothing."

"No, your tone says otherwise. Don't tell me you always wanted to be a cheerleader but you just weren't chirpy enough?"

"Funny." She took a sip, letting the chai mingle on her tongue. The Janik girls had all been cheerleaders—all except for Bridgett. She'd tried out, begging her friend Jessica to audition as well. Given that two of her sisters had preceded her on the squad, Bridgett figured she'd be a sure thing. After all, she had the looks and the requisite pom-poms to fill out the uniform. Jessica—the one she'd had to coax into trying out—got picked instead. Stuart was correct. It was the chirpiness. The cheer sponsor and the two captains thought Bridgett was too serious to be an effective cheerleader. Well, she was a serious person. A girl didn't get into Harvard without being one.

Apparently, the decades-old slight went deeper than Bridgett remembered, judging by her reaction this morning. She'd have to examine that little character flaw later, though. "Focus, Stuart. You said we're taking on a case involving cheerleaders. Can you give me more detail than that, please?"

Stuart laughed. "Usually you only get snippy when I mention *conscious uncoupling*. I'll have to add *cheerleader* to the list of words that make Bridgett lose her practiced cool."

Bridgett was glad Stuart couldn't see her bristle at the phrase *conscious uncoupling*. "Hey, Jimmy Fallon, do you want to call me back after you get finished with your monologue?"

He laughed again before sobering up. "I didn't say we were representing the cheerleaders. We get to be the bad guys and defend the party they are suing."

Now, that was more like it. Bridgett took another sip of tea as she considered the possibility of being retained by a school or a university against a bunch of girls in short skirts and ridiculous hair bows. "Oh, please tell me we get to defend against a group of helicopter parents who want their daughters to all win the first-place trophy?"

That got another laugh out of Stuart. "That tune will change when it's your little darling sobbing that some myopic judge robbed her of the blue ribbon."

Bridgett paused with her teacup poised at her lips. She wondered if Stuart was right. But then, she'd never know, would she? Somehow she doubted that, even if she had a child, she'd want him or her not to think they had to be winners all the time. How would that prepare them for life? Life could be cruel. Bridgett knew that firsthand. There was no use sugarcoating it. The point was moot, however, and Bridgett swallowed her tea around the lump in her throat.

"Actually, these are NFL cheerleaders," Stuart explained.

"The NFL has cheerleaders?" Of course there were the Dallas Cowboys Cheerleaders. They were practically icons. But, Bridget wondered, did the other teams have actual cheerleaders? She'd never really noticed.

Stuart was silent for a moment on the other end of the line.

"You can't be serious. Don't you go to your brother's football games?"

Bridgett's younger brother, the baby of the Janik family, was Brody Janik, a Pro Bowl tight end for the Baltimore Blaze and certified heartthrob to women around the globe. He was as much of an icon as the Dallas Cowboys Cheerleaders. In fact, her brother's new sister-in-law had once been on the Dallas squad. "Sure I go to his games, but I don't go to watch the cheerleaders." She mainly went out of family obligation and because Brody was the one member of the Janik clan who understood Bridgett for who she was. The rest of the Janiks wanted to make her over to be more like them: settled. "I didn't think the Blaze had cheerleaders."

"They do," Stuart said just as an ominous feeling settled in the pit of Bridgett's stomach. "And they're suing team management for alleged workplace violations."

"Oh no," Bridgett whispered.

"Oh yes," Stuart said. "And the Blaze have hired us to handle their defense. And you, Buffy, are the perfect person to take the lead. Not only are you a woman—although it would have helped tremendously if you'd been a cheerleader at one time—but you're also Brody Janik's sister. Score one for us in the headlines when this goes public later today."

With a less than steady hand, Bridgett set her tea down on the antique marble side table she'd bought in Florence a few years back. Stuart wanted her to defend the Baltimore Blaze in a class action suit? Against cheerleaders? If that wasn't too insulting, she factored in the team's new owner: Jay McManus. The man was insufferable, arrogant, obscenely wealthy, and sex on a stick. And he made her stomach crawl every time she got within fifty feet of him. She did everything she could to keep her distance from the man at all costs. Working for him on his defense would violate her own personal restraining order and Bridgett couldn't go there.

"I'm sure it's a conflict of interest somehow," she said, adding a silent prayer after the words left her mouth.

"Come on, Bridgett. Second year law school. There's no

conflict here even if the Sparks were suing your brother directly."

Bridgett softly banged her head against the warm window, scaring a pigeon hanging out on the other side. Of course Stuart would have thought this through. He didn't make a move without carefully considering all the options. She tried another tactic. "I don't know. I've been in Baltimore for over two years on the Pressler case. I'd like to hang out close to home for my next case."

"Hang out at home? Bridgett, before you left for Italy, you begged me to staff you on a case that was anywhere BUT Boston. Remember the nagging family whose radar you are trying to fly under? Brody's been married for six months. You're the only single one left. They're gunning for you, Buffy. But hey, if you want to deal with that, I've got an open-and-shut discrimination case filed by some fast-food workers in Worcester you can first-chair."

There's no such thing as an open-and-shut case that involved discrimination. With another headbang against the window, she cursed her entire family, including her not-so-favorite brother, Brody, and her sweet old Grandpa Gus, who had conspired together to marry her off to the first available orthodontist they could find. She'd be a sitting duck if she stayed in Boston.

"How long?" she said, her tone resigned.

"That's the can-do spirit," Stuart said. "I won't know the particulars until we pick up the filing at the courthouse. I sent Dan over there to get it."

Bridgett sighed. Dan Lewis had been her associate on the Pressler case. At least he was a good lawyer.

"That blogger who writes the *Girlfriends' Guide to the NFL* made a vague reference to the case late last night—that's what put it on Hank Osbourne's radar. Since then, the media have run with it." Stuart's chuckle sounded amazed and annoyed at the same time. "Believe it or not, several women's groups have already announced plans for protests of this Sunday's Blaze game."

Bridgett knew of the blogger. Whoever was behind the

poison pen—or in this case, keyboard—had tortured her brother, Brody, last season, nearly causing him to lose his career and the woman he loved.

"I've set up a meeting for three this afternoon at the Blaze headquarters. Hank will be waiting for you. And, Bridgett, I don't have to tell you what a client as wealthy as Jay Mc-Manus could do for this law firm—not to mention your partner earning statements."

"Wait, you said Hank will be waiting for *me*. Just where exactly will you be?"

"On speakerphone. I've got to be in Manhattan to take care another of those conscious-uncoupling cases you love so much. But I'll meet you back at the Baltimore office tonight and we can discuss strategy. Toni has you on the eleven o'clock flight, so you might want to pack those gorgeous Burberry bags of yours and hustle to the airport."

As she hung up the phone, Bridgett gave the window another thump with her forehead. Her options were limited, really. She could stay in Boston and suffer her family's futile attempts at matchmaking or head to Baltimore, where a meeting with the man she'd come to know as the Antichrist awaited her. Every nerve ending in her body screamed that she'd just made the absolute wrong choice.

Two

Dan was waiting for Bridgett at the airport. Instead of heading to the office, they took a detour to G&M restaurant for a working lunch.

"You know me too well, Dan," Bridgett said as their server placed a fresh crab cake in front of her.

"I wasn't sure you'd be happy to be back in Charm City, so I thought I'd sweeten the day with your favorite lunch," Dan said with a laugh.

"Don't worry. Just because I might be here for a few months doesn't mean I'll rescind my offer; my Blaze tickets are still yours to use this season," she told him. "You don't have to stuff me with food." She took a moment to savor the delicious lump crabmeat. "Umm. These are so good, I might be inclined to ask Brody for a sideline pass for you this weekend, though."

Dan had played college football at the University of Delaware and still loved everything about the game. Bridgett had never understood why grown men acted like giddy little boys when they got around professional athletes. Even smart men like Dan fawned over her brother, Brody, as though he were the crown prince of pizza and beer.

"Actually, just between you and me, I'm hoping the exposure to Jay McManus will open a few more doors than just the sidelines." Dan took a sip of his drink while Bridgett's enjoyment of one of her favorite foods evaporated with the mention of the Antichrist's name.

Dan misinterpreted her sigh as displeasure with him. "Oh, hey, I'm going to give everything I have to this case; don't get me wrong. And I love working for the firm. It's just always been my dream to work in the NFL somehow. Did you know the general counsel for the Blaze isn't even a trial attorney? If I play my cards right, maybe they'll place us on retainer and I can fulfill two dreams at the same time."

Bridgett waved him off. "I get it. Trust me, you'll have Stuart's blessing, not to mention a big fat bonus, if you can pull that one off." She didn't mention that she'd rather balloon up two dress sizes before working with a football team—particularly one owned by Jay McManus. "Tell me what you've got so far. What was in the filing?"

Dan pulled the folder out from his briefcase. "It's got all the earmarks of the other cases floating around the NFL: wage discrimination, lack of compensation for appearances, character degradation. Yada, yada. It looks like this woman is out for some publicity and maybe a little blood, too. She's also accusing the team of sexual harassment."

She wilted a little in her seat. Stuart hadn't been short-sighted in naming her as lead attorney. A woman defending against a sexual harassment case was a common legal tactic, but it also put Bridgett in an extremely untenable position. The defense was almost always built on discrediting the supposed victim and her perception of the harassment. She never shrank down from these cases, but she didn't enjoy them either.

"I know I'm going to hate the answer either way, but please tell me there's something substantive to her case."

"The case cites some incidents at the annual calendar photo

shoot in St. Barts this summer. The one named plaintiff claims there wasn't enough security in place and that the women were harassed by sponsors, fans, and—wait for it—a couple of players who also happened to be at the resort."

Bridgett released an exasperated sigh. "Imagine that, players hooking up with cheerleaders."

"Actually, it's in their contract—the cheerleaders', that is—that they're not allowed to fraternize with players, coaches, or any of the staff."

"Is it in the players' contracts that they can't date the cheerleaders?"

Dan looked a little stumped at her question. "Uh, I don't know. But I can check."

"Don't bother. I'm pretty sure I know the answer to that one is a big fat no."

He shrugged. "Most of the girls who sign up for this gig are dancers or aspiring models. I doubt any of them really want to marry an NFL player."

Bridgett arched an eyebrow at him. "At least until they see the number of zeros in the guy's bank account."

"All the same, if this woman can substantiate the sexual harassment charges, it's gonna make headlines."

"Apparently it's already gotten the attention of women's rights activists." Bridgett picked at the rest of her lunch. "What do we know about this woman?"

"Not much yet. I'm hoping the team will have something for us later today, although management of the cheerleaders is actually subcontracted out, so most of the information will come from a third party."

"Wow, and I thought environmental law was complicated," she said, shaking her head. On the positive side, that little tidbit meant she likely wouldn't have to deal with the Antichrist.

Two hours later, she made her way to the Blaze practice facility. Bridgett was glad it was Tuesday and most of the team had the day off. She'd always tried to maintain some anonymity within her large, nosy family and she wasn't sure how she felt about invading her brother's playhouse, as it were. *Stop kidding yourself.* Her anxiety about being in the Blaze head-quarters had nothing to do with Brody and everything to do with seeing Jay McManus again.

Blaze General Manager Hank Osbourne greeted her with a smile and a friendly handshake as he led Bridgett, Dan, Scott Turner, the firm's investigator, and a paralegal, Maureen, toward the large conference room at the corner of the building. Maureen had to be prodded a bit as she openly gaped at the poster-sized pictures of Brody and his teammates that lined the hallways.

"We're glad to have another Janik on our team, Bridgett," Hank said as he pulled out a chair for her across from a wall of windows looking out over the outdoor practice facility. The view had even Scott and Dan gaping now. "Please, everyone help yourself to some refreshments and I'll grab Jay so we can get the meeting started."

An assortment of candies, fruits, and drinks was laid out on a counter next to the conference table. Dan and Scott each grabbed a can of soda while Maureen busied herself setting up her stenotype machine in the corner of the room. Bridgett removed the jacket of her pewter Versace suit and draped it carefully over a chair before taking her seat. She doubted she could eat anything because her stomach was a knot of nerves. Fiddling with the sleeves of her silk blouse, she tried to calm herself down. She hadn't felt this jumpy since her first case out of law school. Stuart was lucky he was participating via a conference call because Bridgett thought she just might strangle him if he walked into the room right now.

Her hands balled into fists at the tall, dark-haired man who did enter the room, however. Looking immaculate in Hugo Boss—*of course*—Jay McManus greeted everyone assembled with a cursory nod before taking a seat at the head of the table. He punched a button on the phone box that connected him with Bridgett's boss.

He and Stuart carried on with their conversation as if the others weren't in the room. That suited Bridgett just fine. She kept her eyes focused on her notes in an effort to avoid the commanding aura that Jay put out, one that made all of her nerve endings tingle. Eventually, Hank and Scott were brought in to discuss how they would try to discredit the claims being made against the team.

"We haven't been able to locate Ms. Knowles," Hank said. "According to her attorney, she's returned to her parents' home in Virginia Beach. Donovan Carter spoke to the manager for the Sparks today and she said that, by all accounts, the young woman had been happy on the squad. Ms. Knowles is trying to break into modeling, so she frequently volunteered for the additional appearances."

"Was the manager with the squad for the calendar photo shoot?" Bridgett spoke for the first time since entering the room, keeping her gaze on Hank.

"I believe she was, yes," Hank replied. "The trip is one of the perks to being on the Sparks. The entire squad goes, all expenses paid."

"We really have no way of knowing whether the manager was a party to the alleged events of that week or not, then. This is going to be one of those cases that boils down to the credibility of *all* the witnesses." She tilted her head toward Scott, who sat beside her. "I'd like our investigator to be able to speak with the manager as well, if that's all right."

Hank nodded. "Of course. I'm sure Don would appreciate the help."

"What do we know about the opposing lawyer?" Jay's question seemed to be addressed to her and there was nothing Bridgett could do except meet his brilliant blue eyes. He leveled a hard stare at her and she had to work to keep from squirming. Jay McManus took no prisoners—especially when it came to his reputation. She knew this firsthand. But his words couldn't affect her anymore. All she needed to do was tell her heart the same thing.

"She's young and eager to make a name for herself," she said. "I've no doubt she fed the information about the case directly to the blogger somehow. The *Girlfriends' Guide to the NFL* has garnered some serious power in mobilizing public opinion, so it doesn't surprise me that opposing counsel would make use of such a broad platform."

Jay eyed her shrewdly. "I still have to wonder what the blogger gets from all this."

"That makes two of us." Hank sat forward in his chair. "That blogger has been a nuisance to this team for two years now. If nothing else, maybe we can compel this attorney to tell us who it is."

"First things, first," Stuart said from the comfort of his seat on an Amtrak train barreling toward Baltimore. "Let's get these charges to go away and then we can continue your quest to unmask the mystery blogger."

A discussion of logistics followed before the meeting finally broke up. Bridgett blew out a slow breath, releasing some of the tension that had been holding her body in check for the past hour. She was a professional, a partner in a law firm, for crying out loud. She could do this. Hank was saying something to Scott about introducing him to the team's security chief, Donovan Carter, while Bridgett shoved her tablet into her red Marc Jacobs messenger bag and reached for her suit jacket. If she was lucky, she could get to her car without having to make any additional eye contact with the Antichrist.

"It's good to see you, Bridgett. Let's get the girls together for a glass of wine while you're in town." Carly Devlin, Hank's assistant, gave her a brief wave from the doorway where she intercepted the team's GM with another apparent pressing problem. Bridgett nodded back. "The girls" she spoke of would be Carly, who was not only Hank's assistant but the wife of the Baltimore Blaze quarterback Shane Devlin; Julianne Connelly, wife of the team's defensive captain, Will Connelly; and Shay Janik, Bridgett's new sister-in-law. While Bridgett considered all the women friends, even the lure of a good glass of pinot grigio couldn't entice her to share an evening with these ladies. Not when all of them would spend the entire time talking about babies.

The familiar lump in her throat that always accompanied the thought of babies and children was painful to gulp down, but Bridgett had become a master of enduring the pain. She'd had to be. Babies were not in her future. Her career was her life. The decision had been made for her years earlier and Bridgett refused to have any regrets about it.

Dan and Maureen were nearly out the door when the Antichrist deigned to speak to her.

"Miss Janik, a word."

It wasn't a request as much as it was a command. Jay McManus was used to his minions heeding his orders. Too bad she wasn't one of those minions. Bridgett had every intention of ignoring his summons and following the rest of her staff out of the door when he hit her with a rusty weapon from his arsenal.

"Please, Bridgett."

She wasn't sure which stunned her more: his uttering the word *please* or her name rolling so easily off his tongue, as though it hadn't been years since he'd spoken to her. Either way, her body froze before she could safely clear the room. Silently cursing her dumb luck for insisting on bringing her own rental car to the meeting, she watched as Dan and Maureen, oblivious to her discomfort, made their way to the elevator. A moment later, Jay closed the door, cutting off her view and her escape route.

Sighing, she dropped her jacket and bag into one of the conference room chairs. If she was going to serve as part of his legal team, it was inevitable that she'd have to carry on a conversation with the man at some point. It was probably best to get everything out in the open sooner rather than later. "That's funny. I didn't think you knew the word *please*." She crossed her arms over her chest. "Or maybe it's just 'I'm sorry' that gets caught in your throat."

He leaned against the door, mimicking her defensive pose as one corner of his mouth lifted slightly, giving her a glimpse of the dimple she'd once loved to trace with her finger and her tongue. She dragged in a rough breath as parts of her body went on alert thinking about not only that dimple but the ones on his very fine ass, too. *Don't go there.* With the futile hope of calming the tremors deep in her belly, she practiced one of her favorite courtroom tricks of looking through the witness.

It didn't work.

Even all these years later, Jay McManus was beautiful. Perhaps more so now that he'd matured. He was definitely sexier. Gone was the tall, loose-limbed, carefree boy with the lazy smile; the guy who always seemed to have her hand in his. The man in his place was now chiseled to perfection, his designer suit barely containing the athletic body that likely rivaled many of the players whose paychecks he signed. His smile was hidden behind a carefully crafted veneer of aloof arrogance. But his blue eyes were nearly her undoing. She remembered the fierce determination reflected in them when he'd been inside of her, when he'd been talking about being with her forever. And then again when he'd left her. That fierceness was in them now, but she refused to be cowed by this man. Not ever again.

"That's exactly the reason we need to have this conversation," he said, that silky smooth voice of his making her insides sit up and take notice. "I need to know if you're professional enough to handle this situation."

Her insides were definitely taking notice now, but not in the same way. The anger and hurt that he'd left with her more than a decade ago roared up her spine, practically jerking her shoulders back and her chin up. "That naïve starry-eyed girl you left at an Italian airport doesn't exist anymore. I won't have a problem handling this case. Or my interactions with you." She didn't need to worry about any lingering attraction for this man. His arrogance had seen to that. Bridgett was relieved to be over him. As long as she ignored the small part of her that was weeping right now.

Jay almost believed her. The key word being *almost*. After years apart, they had inadvertently been thrown together when he'd bought the team her brother played for. She'd been to games, including the Super Bowl, but on every occasion had avoided him like the plague. He'd watch her as she cheered Brody on, safe in the bosom of the large, boisterous Janik family, all the while maintaining her distance, keeping that poised, polished smile solidly on her face as if they'd never been acquainted, much less lovers.

Bridgett was wearing that cool look now. The one that screamed she was untouchable, but made him want to touch her. *Thoroughly.* To familiarize himself again with the soft planes of her body. She was still petite, her frame a little thinner—more brittle—than it had been that summer, when her curves had been filled out with good food and even better wine. Her blond hair no longer hung free down her back, yet his fingers itched to twine through it anyway. Jay couldn't complain about how she wore it now, though. The sleek style only enhanced the classic beauty of her pert chin and gray eyes—eyes that looked like sterling silver when framed by her long, dark lashes. She'd dressed in her uniform of a hip-hugging pencil skirt and a silk blouse that hardly compared to the peekaboo tank tops and shorts she'd favored years ago, yet still the outfit made her look sexy as hell.

"Perhaps it's you who has the problem," she was saying, and Jay suddenly wished her lips were doing something a lot more fun than talking. "If that's the situation, you shouldn't have asked Stuart to put me on the case."

"I didn't."

The truth stung her. He watched—not quite as satisfied as he ought to be—as she flinched slightly at his words. Her reaction was telling. She'd thought he had wanted to work with her. The knowledge spurred him on.

"It was Stuart's suggestion." He took a step toward her and she countered with a step back. He took another step and she was suddenly pressed up against the conference table. "I didn't think you'd want me to tell your boss all the reasons that was the mother of bad ideas." He closed the gap between them, his hips practically pinning her in place.

"Wow, chivalry and the word *please*. This is certainly a red-letter day." She jerked her chin up. "Get to the point, Jay. I have to get back to the office."

Jay had to admire her backbone. The sweet girl he once

loved never would have stood up to him like this. She was the champion of the little guy and she wouldn't have appreciated—or put up with—his bullying. But she'd changed. She'd become more like him. The thought both saddened him and aroused him at the same time. Glancing down, he had a bird's-eye view down her silk blouse, and he saw he wasn't the only one aroused.

Maybe it was this tactic that was the mother of bad ideas. But he had to find out. If she was in fact over him, he'd bury his own lust deep inside and let her take the helm defending him against these ridiculous charges. Stuart was right; it was a brilliant move that made the most sense. But if she reacted to him, he was counting on her turning tail and running. It was what she did, after all. He'd find another lawyer and beat the trumped-up charges, because losing was not what Jay McManus did.

Reaching up, he traced his thumb along the tender skin beneath her jaw. "I'm just wondering why you didn't immediately recuse yourself, Bridgett."

She shivered beneath his touch but her voice was steady. "Why bother? There's nothing between us any longer. I can certainly defend my brother's team against the baseless allegations."

"It's not your brother's team. It's my team. Your brother works for me."

"How naïve I must have been not to notice the arrogant autocrat that lurked beneath your shiny surface."

His thumb moved over her full bottom lip. "That's because you were too busy putting your hands and mouth all over my shiny surface."

Anger flashed in those gorgeous eyes of hers as a soft flush spread over her cheeks. "My hands—not to mention the rest of me—have learned self-control."

"Have they?" His mouth drifted lower and he swore he could taste her.

"Don't even think about kissing me," she hissed as her fisted hands made contact with his chest.

"Babe, I've done nothing but think about kissing you ever

since I saw you again," he admitted before his brain could stop the words from escaping.

"Well, I haven't." She gave his chest a shove, but her pulse had ratcheted up beneath his thumb, and her hips arched toward his. Jay was having difficulty keeping his body in check and his head spun as he inhaled the familiar scent of her. He needed to rethink his strategy here, but his brain didn't seem to be in control any longer. His lips replaced his thumb along her jaw and he finally—*finally*—tasted her. That and the sound of her sighing his name were his undoing. Jay had to know if she still had any power over him. Or if he could let her go again.

His lips found hers and for the first time in years, Jay's brain shut down. All he could think about was sinking deeper into Bridgett and letting her warm, silky mouth wash over him. A soft moan rose from her chest just as her lips parted, and Jay wasted no time. Dragging one hand through her hair, he shifted her head to give himself greater access to her mouth, plundering deeply with his tongue, groaning when her own swept against it. His other hand wrapped around her sweet ass, pulling her in against the part of his body that was suddenly doing all the negotiating.

Even more surprising, she was kissing him back. Bridgett released her fingers from their fists and slid them up his chest and over his shoulders as her hips rolled against his restlessly. Jay had his answer. He needed to end this little experiment before it got out of hand. And he would. In a minute. After he savored her mouth a little longer. A soft keening sound escaped the back of her throat and something snapped inside Jay. He kissed her as if he still had the right to, delving into her mouth and taking what was no longer his.

He nudged her back against the conference table with every intention of taking her there. Fortunately, Bridgett was right about learning a little self-control over the years. With a sudden ferocity, she broke their kiss. They both stood there a moment, avoiding each other's eyes as they tried to tamp down their heavy breathing. This time he took a gentlemanly step back when she pushed at him. Without looking up she snatched her obnoxious red bag and her jacket off the chair and walked, albeit a little unsteadily, toward the conference room door.

"I'll call Stuart and recuse myself," she said, her back to him and her hand poised on the doorknob. "Just . . ." He heard her swallow harshly. "Just stay out of my life. I'm better without you."

She didn't wait for his acknowledgment or his agreement before she purposefully closed the door behind her. Good thing, because Jay's plans had changed dramatically. No way was he going to stay out of her life now. Not after having her in his arms again, after tasting her once more. Jay made few mistakes, but when he did, he never made the same one twice. He'd let Bridgett slip out of his life once before. That wasn't going to happen a second time. Only this time, he wouldn't make the stupid mistake of letting her have his heart.

He punched a button on the intercom. "Linc, call Stuart Johnson and tell him if Bridgett Janik isn't the lead attorney on our case, I'll find another firm to represent us."

It was a gamble, but he knew Stuart wanted the team's business. Jay also knew he wanted Bridgett. Badly.

Three

"Can I say that I truly hate whoever is behind that stupid blog?" Shay Janik reached across the kitchen counter and poured a generous serving of pinot grigio into Bridgett's wineglass. "I honestly don't get what her motivation is."

Coming up behind his wife, Brody Janik wrapped his long arms around her before bending his head down to nuzzle her neck. "Wasn't it your theory that the blogger might not be a she at all, Shannon?" he asked.

Bridgett tried in vain to ignore her brother's PDA. She was beginning to regret her decision to stop by his house, but Carly had already alerted Shay that Bridgett was back in Baltimore. Her sister-in-law had wasted no time texting and inviting her to dinner. Besides, Shay, a PhD in nutrition, was a genius in the kitchen. Brody suffered from reactive hypoglycemia, a condition that affected his blood sugar, but the meals Shay prepared for him were not only incredibly healthy, but delicious, as well. After a month in Italy, Bridgett figured having Shay prepare her meals might be the one upside to being back in Baltimore.

"I did say that, yes." Shay swatted Brody away and began furiously julienning carrots. "But the posts are just too bitchy to be a man. And God help her if I ever find out who she is." Her whiskey eyes narrowed as she concentrated on her task.

Brody carefully edged away from the counter, his trademark grin lighting up his face. "Don't mess with Texas." He winked at Bridgett as he took a seat on the stool next to hers. "Call me crazy, but this is one time I'm glad for her latest installment."

Shay froze with the knife poised in midair. Both women stared at him. Brody shrugged before leaning over to kiss Bridgett on the head. "I missed you. If her nasty words are the reason you're back in Baltimore, then I'm glad." He took a swig from his bottle of water. "Of course, for all we know, *you* could be the blogger and you set this all up just to get away from the wicked wedding planners in Boston."

With an exasperated sigh, Shay shook her head at her husband and went back to cutting carrots as Brody laughed beside Bridgett.

"I guess this makes you unofficially part of the Blaze team," he continued, snatching a sliver of carrot from the cutting board. Bridgett took a fortifying gulp of wine. When she'd arrived back at the office, Stuart had been adamant that he didn't want to listen to any reasons for her recusal from the case. That was probably a good thing, because Bridgett had no idea how she was going to explain herself to her boss.

I just had my tongue down our client's throat? I almost let him take me on the conference room table? Hell, I wanted him to take me. Or, *I gave him my heart years ago and he destroyed it?*

Apparently, the Antichrist had gotten to Stuart first because he'd threatened to fire the firm if Bridgett didn't remain on the Blaze defense team. His logic made no sense. Jay knew as well as she did that they couldn't work together. Their little make-out session in the conference room proved they were still as combustible as oil to a flame. Not to mention the fact that neither one trusted the other. She'd trusted him once. Never again. Of course, Jay believed she was the one who'd betrayed him. Somehow, that part hurt the most.

Her brother's lightning-fast hand pilfered another carrot, distracting her from her painful thoughts. "I'd be careful there, Brody," Bridgett warned. "If Shay slices off your finger, you might have to actually grow up and get a real job."

Brody smiled fondly at his wife. "That threat doesn't scare me as much as it used to. But since McManus would likely castrate me in court for not fulfilling my end of a contract, I'll be a good boy and wait until Shannon puts the knife down."

Shay finished slicing up the vegetables, handing Brody the remainder of the carrot before eyeing Bridgett shrewdly. "Will you be working directly with Mr. McManus, Bridgett?"

Bridgett had been careful over the years to keep her broken heart a secret. No one in her family knew about that summer in Italy all those years ago. None of them were aware of her relationship with Jay McManus and the scars—figurative and real—that had resulted from their affair.

But Shay was perceptive. And smart; smarter than Bridgett if she was being honest with herself. That was a rare find and it was one of the reasons she got along with her sister-in-law so well. But it also made Shay dangerous. The tall, gawky woman with the wild hair saw too much. Shay had sensed there was something not quite right between Bridgett and Jay and had called Bridgett on it more than once. Her brother's house might not be the sanctuary Bridgett had hoped for after all.

"I doubt it." Bridgett was careful to keep her lawyer mask in place. She couldn't afford to slip up in front of Shay. "My associate Dan will be coordinating most of the work on this. I'm going to be handling a big tax evasion case out of Delaware in addition to the Blaze case." It was the one consolation she'd been able to eke out of Stuart. She'd be the lead counsel for the Blaze case only on paper. Instead, she'd focus on defending a bunch of tax-dodging chicken farmers. The subject might be dry, but it beat having to deal with Jay McManus on a day-to-day basis.

"Well, that's got to be a relief for you," Brody said as he stood and made his way to the refrigerator. Both women looked at him questioningly. A flash of panic coursed through Bridgett as she wondered if Shay had confided her suspicions about her and Jay to Brody.

"Yeah," her brother said as he grabbed one of the portioned snacks Shay prepared for him each day. "We all know how you hate cheerleaders, Bridge."

Bridgett slumped her shoulders in relief and it seemed as if Shay let out a breath she was holding.

"I'm with you there, Bridgett. My sister, Teran, excluded, of course," Shay said. "And I agree with Brody. I hate the circumstances that bring you back, but I'm really glad you're here." She toasted Bridgett with her wineglass.

She gave Shay a warm smile in return. Perhaps she'd be safe hanging out here with Brody and his astute wife, after all. Bridgett just wouldn't give Shay anything to go on. Her plan was to stay as far away from Jay McManus as she could while still doing her job. That plan hadn't worked so well today, but now that she knew what she was up against, she'd be extra vigilant.

By seven thirty that night, the weight room at the training facility was deserted. The regular season kicked off that Sunday and most of the team was enjoying their normal Tuesday off before practice began in earnest the next morning. Jay took advantage of the empty room to blow off steam on the punching bag. His plan to keep away from Bridgett had backfired. Not only did he have to deal with finding a kicker before Saturday and a trumped-up lawsuit that was likely a publicity stunt, but his body now craved the one woman who probably hated him the most.

He slammed the bag even harder. A kinder man would have just let her walk away. His right hand struck the bag, swinging it wide out in front of him. Too bad Jay hadn't been considered kind in many years. Steadying himself and the bag, he jabbed it again with a left cross. Instead, he was ruthless; he took what he wanted. And, by God, he wanted Bridgett. Still. Until he'd kissed her today, he hadn't realized how much he craved her. Or how much she still craved him. The two idealistic twenty-somethings who'd shared a passionate summer in Italy thirteen years ago no longer existed, but it seemed the heat still burned between them. He could work with that. All he had to do was convince Bridgett.

"Remind me not to ever piss you off in the blogosphere." Heath Gibson, the newly promoted Blaze offensive coordinator, stepped into Jay's line of sight before he quickly dodged left to get out of the way of the swinging punching bag. Not much younger than Jay, Gibson was only two seasons removed from the gridiron, but he'd proven himself to be one hell of a coach in his first year with the Blaze.

Jay stopped mid-punch. "Did you really just say *blogosphere*?"

Heath laughed. "I should probably let you punch me just for that, but if you damaged the goods, then my wife wouldn't have that terrible crush on you anymore." He seemed to give it some thought before stepping in front of the bag. "On second thought, hit me. I'm sure I've deserved it at one time or another."

The coach was married to the younger sister of Jay's best friend, Blake Callahan, and he definitely deserved more than a fat lip. But that was for something that happened over a decade ago, when Heath and Merrit were in college. Merrit had forgiven him enough to marry the idiot, so Jay figured he'd leave his lip intact.

"Thanks, but I'll pass tonight. You're too valuable to the team to risk you going down with one punch." Jay took a drink from his water bottle. He heard the metal clank of weights being placed on the bar behind him.

"I'm fully recovered," Heath said a little bit defensively.

Jay turned to look at the coach. Dressed in cotton gym shorts and a Blaze T-shirt, his body was none the worse for wear from the ten years of punishing licks he'd taken as a fullback in the league. But it was a hit to the head that had sidelined his career—not to mention his prospects as a broadcaster. He knew Heath was referring to the severe concussion that had lingered for months.

"I know that. Trust me, if you weren't, I wouldn't have you on my payroll," Jay said. "It wouldn't matter who you're married to."

Heath shook his head before leaning back on the bench and sliding under the bar with the weights loaded onto it. "Yeah, I know. It's all about the bottom line with guys like you. I almost feel sorry for those cheerleaders. They won't know what hit 'em."

Jay knew he was perceived as being callous and ruthless. But it was that toughness that had gotten him where he was today. *Mental toughness is just as valuable a commodity as physical toughness,* his stepfather had drilled into Jay. He may not be able to take the beating his players took every week, but he damn sure could outsmart them, and everyone else, in the boardroom.

"Just as long as none of the players are hitting on them," Jay said as he resumed his one-sided sparring.

"Is that what they're saying?" Heath asked as he easily completed a set of chest presses.

"Their list of grievances is a long one and it includes everything from teeth whitening to spray tans. But, yes, one of the complaints involved some alleged sexual harassment by the players."

The bar clinked loudly as Heath lowered it back into its holder before sitting up and wiping his hands and face with a towel. "Teeth whitening? Really?"

Jay looked at the coach sharply. "That's what you got from all that?"

Heath laughed as he lay back down and grabbed the bar for a second set.

"I don't take sexual harassment lightly, Gibson. And neither should you," Jay said. "We have zero tolerance for that kind of behavior in this organization."

With a heavy sigh, Heath sat up again. "I couldn't agree with you more, Jay. But you've got to remember I was a player on those sidelines not too long ago. There's not much opportunity for fraternization between players and cheerleaders. Except for the occasional public appearance. The lines can get blurred easily at some of those events, though." He shrugged. "A lot of these women see this as an opportunity to further their modeling career or land a pro athlete. A lot of the guys will take what's being offered and think about the consequences afterward."

"Are you saying this could be a simple case of a lover spurned?"

"Who knows, man? Women have their own agenda and they aren't above using a man to achieve it."

"Spoken from experience?"

Heath lay back down and grabbed the bar. "First wife. But, trust me, I learned my lesson. Some other young guys on this team might not have, yet. I'll keep my ears open. Of course, now that that damn blogger has whipped the female fans of the league into a frenzy, I'm sure it's all I'll hear about. According to the grapevine, they plan to picket the stadium this weekend." He grunted as he powered through his reps. "Whoever's behind that blog really knows how to hit a team."

Jay gave the bag another thrashing. This wasn't the first case of cheerleaders suing a team, but for some reason the activists championing women had targeted Jay and the Blaze. Of course, this was the first time that damn blog had mentioned one of the class action suits. He was beginning to think Hank was right and whoever was behind the blog had something out for the Blaze.

"She seems to have this team in her crosshairs," Jay said as he wiped down his face. "She even picked on you before she unleashed on DeShawn and Brody last season."

"Oh yeah, she tried hard to screw up my career—not to mention my reconciliation with Merrit." He was breathing a little more heavily as he dropped the bar back into place. "But I think she's been an equal opportunity pain in the ass.

Just ask Blake. He's had more than one client targeted with her venom."

Blake Callahan was the vice president of his father's successful advertising company. But he also managed a small public relations firm that handled elite professional athletes from a variety of sports. Jay tossed the towel in the basket the trainer left out. "You're probably right. I've been so concentrated on my own guys that I haven't noticed who else she's targeted. I should probably recruit Blake to help us out whoever's writing this crap."

"Good luck with that. Blake's got his own sexual harassment problems."

Jay looked at the coach questioningly. He and Blake hadn't spoken for a few weeks. Their most frequent mode of correspondence was text messages ribbing each other over their local sports teams. "He hasn't mentioned that."

Heath grunted again as he lifted the bar. "Probably because most of it is bullshit. He thinks a former employee is trying to smear the firm."

"Grant?" Merrit's former fiancé had been a partner in the Callahan agency until he unceremoniously dumped Blake's sister and stole several clients.

"Who knows," Heath said with a huff. "But even alleged sexual harassment is a stigma a guy doesn't want."

Jay couldn't have agreed more. He knew this case would open up a can of worms. And two could play at using the opposite sex for personal gain. Hell, he was about to launch a war on Bridgett Janik to gain . . . what, exactly? He'd never trust her with his heart again. Jay was just too selfish to allow her to give her own heart—or her body—to anyone else. And that meant possessing her himself.

"Hey, boss."

Linc's voice startled him into nearly missing his mark. Jay steadied the bag and looked up at his assistant, who was still dressed in shirt and tie.

"Did Stuart call back?" Jay asked, surprised at how unsure he felt about how Bridgett would respond.

"He did. Bridgett Janik is still on the case."

Relief surged through Jay. Not wanting to have this conversation in front of Heath, he just nodded at Linc.

"You sure she's the lawyer for the job, though? She looked like she'd rather be defending a serial killer than her brother's football team."

He shouldn't have been surprised that his assistant wasn't as circumspect. "She'll be fine."

"She's not exactly the ball buster I thought she was," Linc went on, ignoring Jay's glare. "I mean, she was kind of emotional when she left your office."

Jay heard the weight bar clank into the stand as Heath dropped it none too gently.

"I thought you were meeting some woman in Fells Point?"

Linc checked his phone. "Yeah, I gotta hit the road. I just wanted to let you know that Princess Charlotte called."

Jay heaved a sigh. "She's in the country?"

"Worse. She's on her way to Baltimore. And she wants to bring some friends to the season opener this weekend. She's pretty insistent that you call her back. Said she wouldn't take no for an answer. Too bad *she's* not a lawyer, because she's the definition of a ball buster."

Charlotte was that and a whole lot more. This day was just getting shittier and shittier.

"Anything else you need tonight, boss?" Linc's look was only slightly pitying.

"No, at least one of us should enjoy himself tonight. Get out of here."

With a wave to both men, he made his way out of the weight room. Jay toweled himself off and was halfway to the showers when Heath spoke.

"A princess, huh?"

Jay didn't bother responding. Let the coach think what he wanted.

"That might be useful to you if she has her own country you can hide out in," Heath went on, his voice quiet but steely. "Because if you're making Brody Janik's sister 'emotional,' he won't care who you are. He'll kill you. Don't even get sucked in by that cheesy smile of his."

"Thanks for your concern, Gibson, but you're way off base." Jay wasn't worried about his glamour boy tight end. He was more worried about what problems Charlotte was going to deposit on the doorstep of his penthouse.

By the time Jay arrived home an hour later, the scent of Charlotte's heavy perfume had already settled like a thick fog over his living room. The doorman informed him that she'd arrived thirty minutes earlier and it had taken everything he had not to hop back into his Jag and head for points unknown. This day was definitely one for the book of all-time crappy days. Ignoring the woman lounging on his leather sofa, Jay headed straight for the liquor cabinet.

"Hard day in the corporate sandbox?" Charlotte asked as she slowly shifted her long legs along the sofa. They were clad in thigh-high leather boots that likely cost more than Jay's doorman made in a month. Apparently it was Jay's lot in life to be surrounded by women who were attracted to the finer things. Since Charlotte was born with a trust fund that rivaled the budget of some small countries, her elitist nature wasn't such a surprise.

The rest of her was wrapped in a blanket of cashmere; the only other apparel visible was the three sterling silver bands that always dangled from her wrist. Her indigo eyes were artfully made up to look like she belonged in a sultan's harem. Long auburn hair—so similar to her father's—flowed over the cushions of the sofa.

"Make yourself at home, Charlie," he said sarcastically before taking a healthy swallow of Scotch. He let his gaze drift over the panoramic view of Baltimore's Inner Harbor. It wasn't the Manhattan skyline or the spectacular view from his home in the foothills of Napa Valley, but the ships bobbing in the water always seemed to soothe him. Tonight, though, he wasn't sure even the Scotch would relax him. "I take it you and your friends are finished running amok in Europe?"

Charlie made a sound of disdain. "Everyone is so on edge there, worried about the economy and the Middle East. It's really put a damper on all the fun I could have been having."

Jay shook his head. *Typical Charlie. Always thinking of herself.* "Good to know nothing has changed."

She sighed and closed her eyes. Jay did a quick double take trying to determine if that was moisture he'd glimpsed on her mink-like lashes. *Charlie crying?* That never happened. Not since her father had died thirteen years ago.

"I thought you'd be happy to see me. I've missed you," she said softly. "Haven't you missed me? Not even just a little bit?"

He squeezed the back of his neck with his hands. It wouldn't be the first time he'd taken out his bad day on Charlie. That was one of the reasons their relationship had deteriorated these past few years. But he refused to accept all the blame. She hadn't been a saint, either.

"Should I not have come home?" she asked.

Jay downed the rest of his Scotch before answering. "I told you that you always have a home here with me."

She sighed again and he wandered back to the bar for a refill.

"Maybe you should pace yourself, Jay. The night's young."

He laughed. "Says the woman who started stealing booze out of the liquor cabinet when she was thirteen."

"I've given it up."

A piece of ice got stuck in his throat and he coughed. "Since when? Don't tell me alcohol has lost its appeal now that you're twenty-one and it's no longer illegal?"

Charlie sat up on the sofa. *Damn, those were tears in her eyes.* "No. I've given up lots of things. For health reasons."

This time when he choked, it had nothing to do with anything clogging his throat.

"Congratulate me, Jay. You're going to be an uncle."

Four

Jay pushed the pieces of omelet around on his plate while Charlie hovered around him. To his credit, he hadn't exploded—yet. It was likely his half sister was expecting a violent outburst at any moment given the way she kept the kitchen counter between them at all times. Her bombshell had knocked him on his ass—literally. He'd collapsed into one of the recliners amid a string of obscenities, the weight of one too many surprises today taking him out at the knees.

"See," she'd said. "I told you that was too much Scotch. When did you last eat anything?" Scrambling to the kitchen, she'd begun preparing him some food. Despite growing up in homes with servants, their mother, Melanie, had insisted both Charlie and Jay learn to fend for themselves in the kitchen. While Charlie had obviously mastered the skill of cooking, Jay paid for someone else to do his.

"Does Mom know?" he asked. His gut seized at the thought of how their mother would react to her twenty-one-year-old, unmarried daughter being pregnant.

Charlie avoided his eyes, wiping the counter with a towel

instead. "God, no. I just found out myself." She shrugged. "It's not like she'll be excited about it, so why bother."

Jay heaved a sigh. For the life of him, he'd never understand the relationship between his mother and sister. Charlotte was the golden child, born to Jay's mother and her second husband, multimillionaire Lloyd Davis, when Jay was fifteen. His mother had been in her early forties while Lloyd had been approaching sixty when his sister arrived. To say that Charlotte had been doted on would be a gross understatement. Unfortunately, the rest of humanity was now paying the price for their family's spoiling of her.

From the moment he'd laid eyes on his beautiful baby sister, Jay had adored her. He'd spent most of his life walking on eggshells around his stepfather, trying to live up to the CEO of the body-armor-manufacturing company's rigid ideals. But Charlie loved her big brother unconditionally. When nothing Jay said or did could please his stepfather, a simple arm fart would send his sister into peals of worshipful laughter. She was the ray of sunshine that allowed him to survive his teenage years living under Lloyd Davis's roof.

And then Lloyd died and everything had changed.

Jay's knuckles were white, he was gripping his fork so tightly. "Who's the father?"

Defiance, pure and strong, was shining in Charlie's eyes. That look didn't faze Jay, though. He'd been dealing with it since his sister had been in her Terrible Twos.

"None of your business."

"I take it that means you actually know who the father is?"

She recoiled as if he'd slapped her and, for an instant, Jay felt like the horrible creature that the business magazines had labeled him as.

"Wow," she said. "You really have become an insufferable ass, haven't you? How dare you ask me that!"

If Charlie had been expecting an explosion from Jay, she was about to be satisfied. He jumped from his stool feeling like his chest was going to rupture. "How dare I? How about how dare you, traipsing around the world with a silver spoon stuck up your ass all these years? You and your jet-setting friends—the so-called beautiful people—partying it up on their daddie's dime like a bunch of lazy, spoiled hooligans," he yelled. "You live in some alternative world from the rest of us, played out on the cover of tabloid magazines and episodes of TMZ, thumbing your nose at your mother, your future, and the freakin' law!"

Charlie had plastered herself against the large refrigerator when Jay began advancing on her. The look of defiance on her face had been replaced by one of horror. "I don't remember much about my father," she whispered. "But I'm pretty sure you've become him."

Jay swore violently. His sister couldn't have picked a better weapon to wound him with. Too bad she was right. He took a moment to reflect on what he'd just shouted at her and realized too late he'd been channeling his dead stepfather. He swore again.

"It's always going to be about the money, isn't it?" she asked.

He raked a hand through his hair and reached for the remains of his Scotch. When Lloyd had passed away suddenly from a brain aneurysm, his will had distinctly favored Charlotte, his only biological child. Their mother was given the majority of Lloyd's shares in the body armor company—after all, she'd been the textile engineer who'd originally designed the suits. But the vast majority of her husband's income was derived from other sources and all of it went to his daughter. Jay was left empty-handed after twelve years of towing the line in his stepfather's orbit.

Jay sucked in a deep breath. "Look around you, Charlotte. Do you think Lloyd's refusal to acknowledge me as his stepson hurt me that much?"

Her hair made a brushing sound against the stainless steel as she shook her head from side to side. "Not in a material way, no. But it did hurt you in ways that can't be quantified: in your heart."

A harsh laugh escaped his lips. "You obviously haven't been reading past your cover photo on the tabloids, little sister. I don't have a heart."

"Yes, you do." A single tear trailed down her cheek. "It's just been roughed up a bit."

He swallowed painfully as he reached over to wipe the moisture off his sister's cheek. "We're one hell of a dysfunctional family."

Charlie's lips twitched. "You need to travel in my circle more often if you think that's true."

"No, thanks. Just look how well it's worked for you." His words brought the defiant scowl back to her face and Jay raised his hands up to his chest in mock surrender. "What's done is done. Let's just move on from here. Do you have a plan?" *Please say you have one that doesn't involve me.*

Her hand moved to rest over her still-flat belly in an innately protective move. An image of Bridgett making the very same gesture years ago filtered through his mind, bringing his heart to a standstill in his chest. *Damn.* Apparently, he was going to need the rest of that bottle of Scotch to get through this night.

"Things are still in flux, right now," she said. "I just need a safe place to land until I can sort things out."

"Meaning sort things out with the baby's father?" Jay had to work to keep his question from coming out as a growl.

"I haven't decided whether the father needs to be involved or not."

Jay slammed his eyes shut and counted to ten.

"Please, Jay," she pleaded. "I need to work this out for myself. I just need you to be a supportive big brother right now. You're all I have."

"You have a mother."

"Please, you know how the Absentminded Professor will react," she scoffed. "She'll behave as if the Earth has fallen out of orbit somehow. She's the last person who needs to know."

While Jay agreed with Charlie's assessment of their mother, he still didn't feel comfortable keeping something so important from her. "This isn't something she needs to find out about on the baby's birthday, Charlie."

A ghost of a victory smile formed on her lips. "I'll tell her soon, I promise. Just let me hang here until I've made some decisions."

Jay sighed. There was never a question that he wouldn't give Charlie anything she asked for. He just hoped that this time, she wasn't dragging him into something that money couldn't fix.

"I so don't want to sit next to you." Bridgett's sister Gwen said as she plopped down into the stadium seat beside her. "I mean, look at you. You're at a football game dressed in Michael Kors while I'm wearing designer Kohl's."

Bridgett glanced over at the oldest sibling in the Janik family. Gwen was pushing forty—a fact that she wasn't afraid of announcing to anyone within earshot. The mother of two kids, she was perpetually unhappy unless she was running someone else's life. Her husband, Skip—a buffoon in Bridgett's opinion—was an orthodontist whom Gwen had put through dental school. Since their father and grandfather were both dentists, Gwen had considered it quite a coup to land one of her own.

Once Skip had established his practice, she'd worked in his office for several years before kids. Now she worked as Brody's personal assistant, a job that enabled her to be home with her children and presumably run roughshod over their little brother's life at the same time. Although, given Brody's recent marriage, that might no longer be the case, which explained why her sister was in a bitchier mood than normal.

"That outfit looks great on you, Gwen." As the middle child of five, Bridgett did her best to keep the peace in the Janik family.

Gwen scoffed. "Puh-leaze, do you know how frustrating it is to be the unstylish sister here? Between you and Ashley, I don't stand a chance." She reached for a nacho off Bridgett's plate and shoved it in her mouth.

Bridgett locked eyes with her sister Ashley, a buyer for Nordstrom department store and Brody's fashion adviser since birth. Ashley was desperately trying to avoid their conversation, taking up a position at the railing of the boxed seats their brother always provided for family and friends. Despite having two kids, Ashley still maintained a successful career. It didn't hurt that her husband, Mark, was a schoolteacher and could help with the kids more than most working fathers. Still, Gwen seemed to resent both women equally. Their youngest sister, Tricia, a nurse, had recently married an Army physician who was stationed in Korea. Asia was a long way to go to avoid Gwen's meddling, but right now, Bridgett was considering it.

Ashley bit back a grimace in response to Bridgett's death glare, reluctantly wandering over to where the two women were sitting. "Bridgett's right, that color really looks fabulous on you," Ashley said as she took a seat on the other side of Bridgett. The stadium crowd cheered when the players took the field for their pregame warm-ups and Bridgett clapped along with them, relieved to have reinforcements. Today had already been grueling enough. The media storm surrounding the Blaze had taken on a life of its own, with women's groups seizing the opportunity to get in front of a camera by protesting in front of the stadium.

The bright midday sun warmed their faces and she relaxed while Ashley deftly changed the subject. "The kids love the books you brought back from Italy, Bridge. The pictures are so beautiful. They missed you at the Cape this summer. We all did. And now it sounds like you'll be here in Baltimore again."

Refusing to be cowed by family guilt, Bridgett sighed. "Both cases will be short-lived, hopefully, and I'll be back by Christmas." She adjusted her sunglasses to avoid having to look at the picture of Jay McManus that had just flashed up on the Jumbotron. Her stomach turned when she recognized his arm candy as none other than Charlotte Davis, the snotty little rich girl who hadn't met a tabloid cover she didn't like.

"I hope so," Ashley was saying. "Remember Mark's college roommate, Jake? He was best man at our wedding. Well, he recently moved back to Boston. He and his wife split up.

Anyone could have seen that coming. She was way too needy for him. I think you would be perfect for him, though."

Gwen snatched another nacho off Bridgett's plate. "Well, Bridgett definitely wouldn't ever be called needy. Wait, isn't Jake the one who tried to surf in the hotel pool with one of the deck chairs the night before the wedding? He ended up with a black eye and chipped tooth in the wedding pictures." She laughed around a mouthful of chips. "Kind of funny considering how many dentists were at the reception."

Ashley let out a snort of disgust. "Kind of funny that it was Skip who led the surfing party."

Bridgett ignored their bickering as she stared at the big screen. Despite her attempts to look away, her eyes were trained on the image of Jay as though he were a magnet. The familiar vibe he and the gorgeous redhead were giving off was so intimate it made Bridgett's mouth dry. She grabbed for her diet drink and took a long pull through the straw, slamming her eyes shut so she wouldn't have to endure any more. It had been five days since she'd seen Jay, much less had her tongue tangled up with his. Just thinking about their kiss in his conference room, her body grew tense with shame and arousal at the same time.

Thankfully, when she opened her eyes Jay was no longer being displayed three stories high. Unfortunately, her sisters were still debating her personal life. Or lack of personal life, to hear Gwen and Ashley tell it.

"Bridgett isn't going to be interested in some car salesman," Gwen was saying.

"Jake isn't a car salesman. His family *owns* a string of car *dealerships*," Ashley argued.

Gwen shrugged. "That's not the same as owning a football team. You should take advantage of the face time you're going to get while defending that gorgeous Jay McManus against those cheerleaders, Bridge. Although, I think they should get paid a lot more for having to wear those skimpy outfits, so maybe you could work some kind of compromise. Especially if it's one where *you* get compromised by the blazing-hot owner of the Blaze."

Ashley's face was aghast as she gaped at Gwen, who was looking pretty proud of her herself and her pun. Bridgett pushed her sunglasses to the top of her head to stare down both of her sisters. "Gwen, as usual, you're being absurd. The man is my client."

"For now." Gwen wiggled her eyebrows. "But you just said the case will be short-lived. You just need to loosen up that bossy-pants personality of yours and make him want you."

"That is so not going to happen," Bridgett stated emphatically.

"Why not? Don't tell me you're too good for him, too?" Gwen leaned closer, lowering her voice. "Or is Skip right? Are you not interested in guys?"

Ashley inhaled a sharp breath as Bridgett groaned in disbelief. *Just another reason to not like Skip.*

Gwen went on, undeterred. "I keep telling him he's wrong. Instead you're just selfish. You don't want to share your money. Or mess up your perfect little body by having kids."

"Gwen!" Ashley practically shouted.

Bridgett was beginning to feel light-headed. Her sister had always been blunt, but her mean streak was new. If Bridgett wasn't so hurt by her sister's words, she might take a moment to analyze what was really troubling Gwen. But right now she didn't care. She shoved her plate of half-eaten nachos onto Gwen's lap and stood up.

"Hey, I'm just telling it like it is," Gwen went on. "You're thirty-five, Bridgett. Stop being so picky or else you'll never know the joys of motherhood." Fortunately, Gwen was quickly distracted. She leaped to her feet and raced to the railing just as one of her little "joys of motherhood" nearly tossed a loaded hot dog over the side and onto some unsuspecting fan below. Her husband, Skip, laughed at his son's antics, but didn't move a muscle to stop him.

"Ignore her, Bridgett," Ashley said. "I think she must be going through the change or something because she's been a mess lately."

"Yeah, whatever. I'm going to the restroom."

Ashley stood, presumably to accompany Bridgett, just as

her own son fell onto the concrete floor. Mark snatched the child up before he'd even shed a single tear, but blood was oozing from both knees. "Crap. They haven't even kicked off for the season and we're already going to the see the stadium medic," Ashley said with a moan. "Don't listen to Gwen. You have the right idea. The joys of motherhood aren't all they're cracked up to be." With that she headed to the exit behind her husband and now wailing three-year-old son.

Bridgett tried to breathe around the boulder in her throat as she made her way out the exit on the opposite side of the box. With kickoff a few moments away, the corridor leading to the luxury boxes and sky suites was relatively empty. A tear escaped her eye and she angrily swiped it away. Her sisters' words had been hurtful in ways even they didn't know. Bridgett's carefully cultivated cool exterior was thirteen long years in the making. It was the only thing that stood between her and a total breakdown.

She leaned against the wall to quell her shaky breathing. Gwen was so wrong. Bridgett wanted children, a baby or two who would love her unconditionally. With the exception of maybe Skip, she was envious of everything Gwen had. Because she would never have that in her own life.

A door opened behind her as Bridgett rubbed away another tear.

"Bridgett?"

She turned automatically at the sound of Jay's voice before realizing he no longer had the power to give her comfort.

"What's wrong?"

"Nothing," she snapped, angry at her traitorous body for wanting him to soothe her. "I have something in my eye."

He muttered something profane and angry before slamming the door behind him and wrapping his fingers around her forearm.

"Hey," she said. "I'm fine. I don't need your help."

Jay ignored her as he pulled her around the corner and punched a code into a keypad located beneath the molding on the wall. A nondescript door that would normally blend in with the wall opened and Jay yanked her inside the room.

Except it wasn't a room, exactly. Instead, it was a cubbyhole located between the owner's box and the skybox beside it. Like the skyboxes, this one opened to seating along the railing, presumably close to where Brody's seats were located. If she stepped out ten yards, she would be visible to anyone in that section, just about three feet below their seats. A band played the first few chords of "The Star-Spangled Banner" and sound filled the small room.

"You're not fine," Jay said after closing the door behind them. "You're crying. What happened?"

Bridgett's head was spinning again. If she wasn't careful, he might trick her into believing that he really cared about her.

"Leave it to you to have a hidey-hole in the stadium," she said, evading his question and his gaze by glancing out toward the field. The stadium shook as a trio of jets sliced through the air above them. "It's almost kickoff. You should probably get back to your guests."

In an instant, she was pinned up against the wall. The cheering of the crowd echoed in her ears as Jay's deep voice rumbled against her breasts. "My guests can go to hell. Who made you cry?" he demanded.

Her nostrils twitched at the distinctive scent of Paco Rabanne cologne. Jay was dressed as casual as he allowed himself these days, in slacks, a Ralph Lauren button-down shirt, and a matching tweed jacket, its silk threads soft beneath her fingertips. His face was so close to hers, she could make out the scruff of his dark beard coming in along the line of his jaw. Bridgett's lips went dry as his hovered just above them.

"Why do you care?" she whispered.

She watched in awe as his eyes dilated a fraction right before his mouth took possession of hers. This wasn't the hungry all-consuming kiss like he'd given her the other day. Today his lips were gentle and comforting. The kiss was sweet, yet it made her toes curl with its intensity. She clutched his jacket with her fingers, trying not to melt along the wall, his mouth was so intoxicating. A whistle sounded in the distance and Jay quickly pulled his lips from hers. He jogged over to the railing and peered out as the crowd roared.

Bridgett steadied herself against the wall, trying to recover her breath and her scattered wits while Jay mumbled something that sounded like *at least the sonofabitch can kick off*. When he turned back to her, his eyes had returned to normal. He took a few steps toward her before apparently thinking better of it. With his hands on his hips, his suit jacket was pushed to the sides, allowing Bridgett to see exactly how uninterested he was in the football game at this point.

"You didn't recuse yourself," he said.

"I wasn't given much choice." She crossed her arms under her chest.

His nostrils flared as his eyes raked over her. "No, you weren't." She wanted to smack the arrogant little grin off his face. Or maybe kiss it.

"I don't understand," she admitted.

"Don't you? The other day. In my conference room. It was eye-opening."

"Eye-opening? What's that supposed to mean?"

A roar went up from the crowd and Jay looked over his shoulder before turning back to her. "You still want me."

Bridgett slammed her head against the wall in frustration. It was hard to refute his words since the other day—not to mention a few minutes ago—she'd had her tongue down his throat and her hips pressed invitingly up against his.

"In case you were wondering, the feeling is mutual," he said. The smug look on his face made her angry.

"Oh really? *If* I was actually as interested as you seem to think, I'd be insulted by the underage party heiress hanging on your arm." Too late, Bridgett realized she'd just given him reason to think she might be jealous. *Stupid, stupid, stupid.* She tapped the back of her head against the wall as Jay took a step closer, his mouth now turned up into a grin that would have looked pleasant on him had it not been so arrogant.

"Good to know. But you have no reason to be jealous of Charlie."

"I doubt Princess Charlotte would appreciate you calling

her Charlie." Her stomach clenched just thinking that the girl
probably let Jay call her anything he wanted and enjoyed it.

"Bridgett," Jay said, his quiet voice refocusing her attention on his blue eyes. "She's Princess Charlotte to the tabloids, but to me, she's always been Charlie."

He studied her face as her mind worked through his statement. "Your *sister* Charlie?"

Jay nodded solemnly. The crowd roared again as the stadium announcer shouted that the Blaze had recovered a
fumble.

"But that's Charlotte Davis, the heir to Lloyd Davis's fortune," Bridgett said as her mind tried to make sense of what
he was telling her. Charlie was a freckle-faced girl with big
blue eyes and Pippi Longstocking–like pigtails. *At least she
had been thirteen years ago.* Jay had carried her picture in
his wallet, proudly showing it off while dragging Bridgett
to various stores, museums, and stalls on the street to find
classic dolls that he'd then send home to his baby sister. "But
Lloyd Davis . . . ?"

"Not my father." He shook his head.

"Wow. Just how many secrets were you keeping that
summer?"

"Do you really want to bring up how both of us evaded
the truth, Bridgett?"

Her body tensed in anger and, truth be told, pain at his
accusation. She gave her own head a little shake, hoping to
clear her jumbled thoughts. "No. In fact, I don't want to discuss anything with you ever again." She pushed away from
the wall headed for the door. Listening to her sisters discuss
her dismal personal life was preferable to trying to have a
conversation with Jay.

"Aren't you forgetting that I'm your client?"

She turned to glare at him as the crowd roared again. "Seriously? Is that why you insisted I take this case? So you could
browbeat me into sleeping with you again?"

Jay had the decency to keep his face in a stoic mask.

"I know how you hate to lose, but you made a gross tactical

error on this one," she informed him. "I don't get involved with clients. Ever."

"And if I weren't your client?"

"I wouldn't sleep with you then, either." She could feel her skin breaking out in a betraying flush just thinking about sleeping with Jay McManus again.

"Too bad your body says otherwise."

Bridgett didn't have an opportunity for rebuttal because the door to their little hideaway flew open and a young man dressed in a Blaze golf shirt and black slacks came charging through the door.

"Whoa," he said, a mischievous grin forming on his face. "Sorry, boss. Security got an alert that someone had opened the door. I'll just leave you two alone." He started to back out the door but Bridgett grabbed it before he could close off her escape route. "Oh hey, boss, did you tell her about the interview with the cheerleader on Tuesday?"

"What interview on Tuesday?" She spun around to face Jay and just as she did, his sneaky assistant closed the door again. Bridgett heaved a frustrated sigh.

Jay crossed his arms over his chest, tucking his hands beneath his armpits, and leaned a shoulder against the wall. "Miss Knowles, the cheerleader. We're meeting with her on Tuesday."

"You can't do that!"

He arched an eyebrow at her. "Why not?"

"Because you're"—*arrogant, intimidating, annoying, and sexy as hell*—"not a lawyer."

"Her lawyer will be there and so will ours. Stuart and I just discussed it. You should have come to my box when you were invited instead of hiding among your family." Bridgett suspected she should have just avoided the Blaze stadium altogether the way this day was going.

"Fine," she snapped. "Stuart can cover your ass and make sure you don't ruin the entire defense." She headed for the door again, only to be stopped by Jay's words.

"I think you're forgetting something, Bridgett."

She glanced over her shoulder, her core heating up at the intensity of his gaze.

"You're the lead attorney for the team's defense. I made that patently clear to your boss and everyone else involved." The crowd behind them was jeering a bad call by the referees.

"I already have a pretrial meeting scheduled for Tuesday," she said, relieved that it was the truth.

Jay stepped away from the wall, one corner of his mouth turned up in a smirk. "Yes, you do. In Virginia Beach. Danny Boy, your earnest associate, can handle the two tax-dodging chicken farmers." He reached for the doorknob behind her, his breath fanning her ear. "My limo will pick you up at seven thirty. We're taking my plane." The crowd roared as the announcer called a touchdown caught by her brother, Brody. "See, here's your opportunity to be a team player like your little brother."

With his hand resting on the small of her back, he guided her out of the small room and into the hallway. Bridgett didn't bother looking back at what was surely his self-satisfied face. Instead she quickly walked away from him—and the warmth of his hand on her body—headed for the insanity that was her family. At the moment, it was the lesser of the two evils tormenting her.

Five

"Tell me what you've got on the two bozos Charlie brought with her," Jay asked Linc sometime during the game's second half. They were seated in the far corner of the owner's box. While the rest of the crowd mingled and ate from the spread of food laid out on the wide tables in the back, Jay and his assistant spoke quietly. Bartenders were hovering with drink refills, discreetly checking for a signal from Jay as to whether one of his guests had imbibed too much and should be cut off. Despite the women waving placards outside the stadium, the mood was festive on the bright, sunny September afternoon.

The Blaze were up by two touchdowns and Jay was feeling relaxed and victorious, not only about the game, but also about his earlier encounter with Bridgett. She'd proven a worthy opponent, dodging him all week while she sent the shiny, eager beaver Dan to do her work for her. But Jay had seen through her tactics almost immediately and countered with the interview in Virginia Beach. Donovan Carter had tracked the Sparks cheerleader down and insisted on a face-to-face meeting. Stuart had practically snorted fire out of his nose when he found out, but since Jay was writing him and his firm a very large retainer check, there was nothing for the lawyer to do but acquiesce. And offer up the lovely Bridgett as a token of his loyalty.

Jay bit back a grin just thinking about having her to himself on Tuesday. Based on the way she'd responded to him a second time, he'd have no trouble convincing her to fall into bed with him. Her mouth may be saying one thing, but her body was definitely speaking his language. He shifted in his seat in an attempt to ease the ache in his jockey shorts.

One thing bothered him more than he wanted it to, though: She'd been crying earlier and Jay hadn't discovered the reason why. Bridgett would never own his heart again, but he still felt uneasy seeing her unhappy. Or for anyone else to be the cause of her sadness. But emotions had no place in what he planned for the two of them, he reminded himself. If they were to rekindle their relationship, Jay was determined to keep it strictly between the sheets. He was pretty sure he could bring her happiness in sixty seconds flat once he got her naked. But that was the only pleasure he was willing to guarantee her.

"Boss, did you hear anything I just said?" Linc asked, redirecting Jay's thoughts back to the more pressing matter of who was the father of his sister's baby.

Jay waved a hand at his assistant. "Sorry, I was listening to what was going on down on the field."

"Uh-huh. It's the end of the third quarter and we're in a TV time-out. Unless you're listening to the Sparks cheer, which I guess is necessary research—"

"You really are mouthy and insubordinate, Lincoln," Jay interrupted him. "Why the hell haven't I fired you yet?"

Linc gave him a face-splitting smile that Jay had seen reduce the women back at McManus Industries into sputtering idiots. "Because I'm so pretty. Not quite as hot as our counsel for the defense, though. And I still say she doesn't like you."

Jay leaned his head back against the wall behind his chair,

working to suppress the grin that threatened. "She likes me just fine."

The kid had the nerve to snort. "That woman looked at you like you were the scum beneath her cute little Manolo Blahnik shoes."

"Her *what*?"

Linc shook his head in what appeared to be disgust. "Shoes, boss. Ms. Janik was wearing Manolo Blahniks. Very expensive, but she was definitely rocking them."

Jay gaped at his assistant, wondering how a mere eight years of age difference could feel like a gulf in the universe. "I'm sure I don't want to know the answer to this question, but how would a guy like you know this?"

"From women. And girls. Heck, old ladies, too. They love shoes. I worked at Barneys in New York city the summer between high school and college."

"Let me guess, in the women's shoe department."

"Boss, it was on my résumé." Linc sounded a little put out that Jay hadn't committed his life history to memory. "Where did you think I got my style from?"

Fortunately, the ref blew the whistle signaling the start of the fourth quarter, bringing an end to this absurd conversation.

"Charlie's swains," Jay said, nudging the file folder in Linc's hand with his knee.

"Sure, boss. Bachelor number one"—Linc nodded toward the guy with sleeves of tattoos on both arms and scruffy blond hair, who'd been nursing the same bottle of beer for the entire second half—"goes by the name of Blaine Porsche."

Jay pinched the top of his nose between his fingers. "Is that even a real name?"

Linc flipped through some papers and handed one to Jay. "According to his Colorado driver's license."

Jay scanned the page. Blaine was twenty-five, scrawny, and, apparently, not a natural blond. "What's his story?"

"Daddy is in oil. Third generation. Lots of money and lots of stepmoms. As best as I can tell, he met Charlotte when they were both at the Dwight School in New York City."

"She was fourteen the year she went there." It was actually the longest she'd lasted at any school. "This guy would have been . . . eighteen." *Jesus.* Jay's temple began to throb. "What does he do with himself now?"

Linc hesitated. Never a good sign. "He's into herb."

"Herb?"

"Legalized marijuana. He actually fronts a chain of stores in the Boulder area. It's a pretty profitable business."

The throb in his temple was close to becoming a full-blown aneurysm. "It's not a business I want my niece or nephew involved in," he said through tightly clenched teeth.

Linc nodded. "Moving on to bachelor number two." He pulled another file from the stack he had in his backpack. Jay glanced over to the smartly dressed dark-haired man seated next to Charlie. She'd been laughing with him all day. It was the first time he'd seen her relaxed since she'd arrived on his doorstep earlier in the week. The guy was friendly enough, for being a pipsqueak. He barely stood tall enough to reach Charlie's shoulder. Although at five foot eleven, his sister towered over a lot of guys. "Spenser Campbell. He comes from Boston money, made from selling steel to shipbuilders during the First World War. His license lists him as being twenty-two. He graduated from Brown in May and works for a Providence real estate firm. They met when they were both at the Gunnery School in Connecticut."

"At least he went to college."

Linc smirked. "Yeah, so did Blaine. He's a University of Chicago grad, just like you."

The crowd groaned as the Blaze's new kicker missed a relatively easy field goal. "Still," Jay said. "Bachelor number two gets my vote so far."

"Yeah, except there's a little bit more to the story."

There always was. "Spit it out, Linc."

Linc shifted in his chair. Jay had never seen the kid look this uncomfortable. "Do you know how many weeks she is?"

Jay shook his head. His sister's pregnancy wasn't something he was comfortable discussing, least of all with Charlie.

"Well, according to Customs, neither of these two has been

out of the country in the past three months. Surely if she's
further along than that, she'd . . . you know"—Linc cupped
his hand over his stomach—"show more. Wouldn't she?"

How the hell would Jay know? It had been twenty-two
years since his mother was pregnant with Charlie. And the
last pregnant woman he'd known . . . He wasn't going there
right now.

"You think neither one of these two is our sperm donor?"
Jay asked Linc.

"If I was a bettin' man, I'd say no."

And that was the reason Jay kept the mouthy pup around:
Linc had great gut instincts. "So who are these two and why
are they here?"

"Friends?" Linc shrugged. "Maybe she's test-driving
step-baby-daddies?"

Jay heaved a frustrated sigh before glancing at the game
clock. He liked to be in the tunnel to welcome the players off
the field after each game and he needed to make his way
downstairs.

"Want me to keep digging?" Linc asked.

"Hell, yeah."

Tuesday dawned cold and rainy. A tropical storm
was headed for the coast of South Carolina later that day, but
Jay's pilot said conditions would be fine for the thirty-five-
minute trip. Jay took a long swallow of coffee as he waited
in the limo outside of the building that housed Bridgett's
temporary condo. He was surprised to see that she was staying only blocks from his penthouse in the Federal Hill neigh-
borhood of Baltimore.

Jay glanced at his watch: seven thirty-nine. She was late.
Women. He'd had about enough of the fairer sex to last a
lifetime. Charlie had been riding a tsunami of mood swings
for the past week, and Jay was pretty annoyed with anyone
sporting breasts right now. He and his sister had argued until
late into the night about telling their mother about Charlie's
pregnancy. She had been adamant that their mother be kept

in the dark until Charlie "had plans in place," whatever the hell that meant. When he'd pressed her about the baby's father, she'd stormed off to her bedroom in a fit of tears.

Not only that, but it seemed the rest of the female population was dogging his every step with threats of protests. He'd been forced to endure a ten-minute dressing-down from the commissioner during the weekly owners' conference call the day before about how women make up nearly fifty percent of the league's fan base. The league wouldn't sit idly by looking like it condoned sexual harassment. If any charges were substantiated against any team, the commissioner threatened, he would level sanctions against any and all teams—and their owners. The implication being that Jay would be the one sanctioned and that pissed Jay off royally.

The door swung open and a gust of wind blew into the car, followed by Bridgett. She smelled like a spring day underneath her gray Burberry raincoat and scarf. Her legs were bare beneath her skirt, and Jay caught a glimpse of her toned inner thigh when she slid across the seat. His annoyance at anyone carrying two X chromosomes faded as he grew hard at the thought of those thighs wrapped around him and her perky breasts in his hands.

His driver, Gerard, closed the door behind her. Bridgett carefully removed her scarf, folding it up and neatly placing it in her garish red briefcase. She tugged at the button of her raincoat and Jay had to resist tugging at the knot on his tie. Maybe he'd get lucky and she'd be one of those women who fantasized about sex in the back of a limousine. Or better yet, an airplane.

Jay needed to say something—anything—to get his mind going in another direction but his brain didn't seem to be functioning all that well right now.

"Nice shoes."

Bridgett's long eyelashes lowered and then rose again quickly, her surprise apparent. Then suspicion must have taken over because those silver eyes narrowed to slits. "What's wrong with my shoes?"

Nothing was wrong with her shoes. He glanced down at

the plum-colored pumps that might have been conservative except for the badass silver studs up the back and the three-inch heels. Just for a moment, he regretted not bringing Linc along just for information about her shoes. But Jay had wanted as much time alone with Bridgett as he could get today. It was pivotal to his plan.

"Can't a guy compliment a woman's shoes without getting his head bitten off?" He gestured to the coffee carafe tucked into the armrest between the seats, but she shook her head. Too late Jay suddenly remembered she was a tea drinker and he cursed himself for not having tea in the limo. Pulling out his phone, he dialed up his pilot. "Ron, can you make sure there's some hot tea on board for Ms. Janik."

Gerard steered the car into the early morning Baltimore traffic as Bridgett let out a little huff. "This isn't a date, Jay."

Jay shoved his phone back into his jacket pocket. "You really are riled up today, woman. What's got you so testy?"

"For starters, I don't appreciate my client forcing me to do things against my will."

He sat forward in his seat so that he was eye to eye with her. "Bridgett, I don't plan to force you to do anything and, believe me, anything and everything you do with me will be by choice."

The air in the limo seemed to evaporate and Bridgett had trouble squeezing a breath through the thin hole that used to be her throat. Jay's eyes were mesmerizing and, for a moment or two, Bridgett thought she'd slipped back in time thirteen years and he was still the man she'd loved with all of her young, unscathed heart. Until she realized he was the Antichrist. Sitting back against the soft leather seat, she slowly crossed her legs, giving Jay a good look at those shoes he seemed to think were so nice—and the calves that Pilates four times a week had toned to perfection. She was pleased to see his eyes dilate slightly. Two could play at this game.

"The only thing I plan 'to do' with you today is question a disillusioned cheerleader and her publicity-hungry lawyer."

She held up her hand as his lips parted in what was sure to be some smooth protest. "I have no plans to break my golden rule of not getting involved with a client. Especially not with you. You can call the shots and lead Stuart around by his wallet all that you want. I'll be at your beck and call for all things legal. But not for anything else. *Never* for anything else."

His mouth settled into a straight line, which he wisely kept closed. But his eyes still held smug challenge in them, and Bridgett was forced to look away before her panties became damp. She heard him settle back against the opposite seat and click on his tablet. They were silent the rest of the way to the airport as Bridgett stared out into the rainy morning, wondering how long she could maintain the fortitude to live up to the words she'd just flung at him.

They arrived at the airport thirty minutes later. The driver pulled the limo onto the tarmac right next to the steps leading up to the sleek Gulfstream jet. Rain pelted her as Bridgett climbed the metal stairs as quickly as she could in her ridiculous shoes. She'd planned to wear her Steve Madden boots in deference to the weather but vanity won out over practicality. Looking her best around Jay gave her a sense of power. The fact that he'd complimented her shoes proved that she'd made the right choice. Until she'd been faced with the elements. *Stupid.*

Bridgett took off her wet coat and laid it over one of the empty seats as Jay closed and locked the door. "I thought Donovan Carter was coming with us," she asked as her eyes darted toward the cockpit, where the pilot was running through whatever preflight checks were needed.

Jay removed his own jacket before he took the seat across from her. "He drove down last night. He had some other business this morning before our meeting."

"Other business?" she said as she adjusted her seat belt. "Not having to do with the case, I hope. Scott is taking the lead on the investigative work. There's no need for anyone from the Blaze to be involved."

He didn't bother answering her, instead adjusting his own

seat belt across his lap and then rolling up the sleeves of his dress shirt.

Bridgett let out a frustrated sigh. "You can't just railroad your way through this case, Jay. That's not how these things work."

Jay looked up at her then, his eyes cool. "Not everything Don does involves this case. But he's a professional. I trust him implicitly."

Which meant that Donovan Carter was likely running around the Virginia coast and mucking things up. She made a mental note to call Scott the second she had a moment alone. "You can't control everything and everyone."

One corner of his mouth turned up, forming that smug smile that annoyed and aroused her so much. "Who says?"

The pilot stepped out of the cockpit then, ending any chance Bridgett had at a rebuttal. "We're sixth in line for takeoff. Unfortunately, with this storm brewing it's going to be a bumpy flight, so keep those seat belts fastened, okay?" He pulled the cockpit door closed behind him as he took his seat at the controls.

He wasn't kidding about the flight being bumpy. They'd been in the air for five minutes and the plane still bobbed and weaved as though it were a rowboat in the middle of the ocean. *Could it really be this bad for thirty-five minutes?* She thought of the emergency Xanax she kept tucked away in her purse, but she couldn't convince her fingers to unclench from the death grip they had on the armrests to go digging for it.

"Bridgett?"

She couldn't pry her eyes open, but the closeness of his voice indicated that Jay was leaning forward in his seat.

"Are you all right?"

"I'm fine." Which, of course, was a lie. Her stomach rolled as the plane took another quick dip. A tremulous moan escaped her lips. Jay swore and then she heard the sound of him unbuckling his seat belt. Bridgett's eyes flew open, growing wide as he moved to the seat next to hers. "The pilot said to keep your seat belt fastened!" she admonished him.

He shot her another of those "I am invincible" smiles and clicked the seat belt around him. Reaching into a cabinet between their two seats, he pulled out a silver flask and offered it to her. "Here. Drink this. It'll help."

Bridgett slammed her eyelids shut as the plane took another sharp dip. "No." She shook her head. "I have a Xanax in my purse." Still, she made no move to reach for it.

"I think you're supposed to take them preflight for it to be effective."

She cracked one eye open and glared at the smug jerk. He peeled her hand off the armrest and wrapped her fingers around the flask.

"Besides," he said. "The Xanax will string you out for the entire day. A swig of this will get you through the rest of the flight with very few aftereffects."

Said the Big Bad Wolf to Little Red Riding Hood. Except he had a point. The metal was cool on her lips as she took a swallow from the flask. She tried not to be a girly girl and cough when the whiskey burned her throat on its way down. The plane lurched up and Bridgett guzzled another swallow before handing the flask back to Jay. Her gaze locked on his as he took a long drink from the flask himself. Closing her eyes again, her fingers dug into the armrest.

She gasped as the plane dipped furiously once again and Jay's big hand covered hers.

"You never did answer my question about why you were crying the other day," he said. He was trying to distract her; she knew that. Still, she wasn't grateful enough to give him the truth.

"I did answer your question. I told you it was none of your business."

She heard him laugh softly. "You're not the same woman you were before."

Bridgett opened her eyes. "I'm pretty sure I already told you that, too."

She wasn't positive, but she thought she saw a look of regret quickly pass over his features. Bridgett closed her eyes again so that she wouldn't have to ponder what might have been. Jay kept his strong hand covering her much smaller one. She hated to admit that even after all these years—after all that had happened between them—she still found it comforting. It was all she could do to not flip her own hand over and intertwine her fingers with his. But then she remembered that he was the enemy—the Antichrist. She may have been forced into representing him on this case, but that didn't mean she was falling into his absurd plans for some sort of affair—no matter how badly her body seemed to want to. That road only led to heartache for her. Jay didn't have a heart. Eventually, the plane settled into a less choppy altitude and Bridgett let whiskey and the warm weight of Jay's hand over hers soothe her. The way her life was going right now, it might be the only few moments of relaxation she'd have all day.

Six

The weather wasn't much better in Virginia Beach, although Jay was glad to be battling it on the ground versus in the air. Don met them on the tarmac, shuffling him and Bridgett to the rental car under cover of a huge golf umbrella. Bridgett appeared to have endured the bumpy plane trip reasonably well. After she'd downed a few swigs of Scotch, she'd closed her eyes and seemed to meditate for the remainder of the flight, drawing from a reserve of inner strength he hadn't known she possessed.

It was true—she had changed. The sweet-natured, bright-eyed activist was gone. Jay's chest grew tight as he realized that perhaps that woman had never existed. Perhaps that version of Bridgett was all just a lie, like the rest of that long-ago summer. But her body had only improved with age and Jay was willing to ignore the twinges in the area where his heart used to be just to get her beneath him again. If there'd been one takeaway from that summer for Jay, it was to keep his heart out of the bedroom. He could have a sexual relationship with Bridgett and not get emotionally involved. After all, he'd been doing the same thing with other women for years.

"Ron is going to rent some hangar space while he waits for you to get back," Don was saying. "The storm took a turn this morning and is projected to make landfall somewhere along the North Carolina coast later today."

Bridgett's eyes grew wide. "Will we be able to fly back?" It was hard to tell whether she was more panicked about getting back in the plane or potentially being stranded at the airport.

"We'll drive back if we have to," Jay said as he slid into the front seat. Don got behind the wheel and drove them out of the airpark. What he really wanted was a few minutes alone with the Blaze security chief so Don wouldn't have to brief him in front of Bridgett, but the timing couldn't be helped. "What did you learn?" he asked quietly.

Don's eyes drifted to the rearview mirror briefly, but Jay nodded for him to speak. "Alesha Warren is divorced with two kids. Dad is on the list of deadbeats who don't pay child support. It's her own shingle out in front of her law firm. She's well respected among the legal community down here, mostly as a public defender. It's likely her stipend from the county for being a PD that's covering the costs for this case, because her credit cards are all entirely maxed out."

"You're digging up trash on the opposing counsel?" Bridgett asked from the backseat.

Jay looked over his shoulder at her. She looked a little rumpled from the weather and the flight, but her face was incredulous.

"Yes," he said. "Do you have a problem with that?"

Her eyes narrowed. "No, I don't. I had Scott looking into her, too." She let out a huff. "You were supposed to be coordinating with him."

Don smiled at her in the rearview mirror. "It was my intention to send him a detailed e-mail, but I decided to wait since you'd be here."

She leaned back against the seat with another little huff. "Fine. You can fill me in just as easily as he can."

"Well, then, you better brace yourself back there, because here comes the stinger," Don said as he pulled the car onto the highway. "Jennifer Knowles is Alesha's sister-in-law. If she can't get the money from the daddy, I'm guessing Alesha figured here was another way to get the money owed to her kids."

All three were silent in the car for a moment before Bridgett spoke. "That's quite a leap. It would be difficult to prove that kind of intent in court. It's not unusual for a family member to represent another family member. I mean, a case could be made that I'm doing exactly the same thing."

"Even if the two women haven't spoken to one another in over five years?" Don asked.

"If you're going to sue someone, why use an attorney you don't like?" Jay asked. "Unless Alesha Warren was the one who came up with the idea in the first place and somehow co-opted her former sister-in-law to play along." He didn't bother to stop the slow grin that was spreading over his face. With luck, this case would never make it to the courtroom.

"That's still all just conjecture, but it certainly gives us a place to start," Bridgett said from the backseat.

The rain was falling harder by the time they arrived at a small office park. Don pulled up outside a brown brick building and the three of them hustled quickly into the lobby. Before they could board the elevator, though, Bridgett reached an arm out to stop them.

"You are not to say anything beyond 'hello' and 'nice to meet you,'" she said to Jay. "Other than that, you're to let me do all the talking. That's what you hired me for. Is that clear?"

Don coughed softly as Jay rocked back on his heels at the fierceness of her tone. "I'm just supposed to sit there?"

"I'd prefer you sit in the car, but since the odds of that happening are nil, I'll take what I can get."

This time Don didn't bother hiding his laugh with a cough and Jay scowled at him over Bridgett's head. "What about Don? Does he get to talk?"

She turned to Don with a serene smile on her face. "Don gets to charm them with his panty-melting grin," she said. "But make sure you keep your gun out of view. It can be a bit intimidating."

After punching the elevator button, she peered into the mirrored doors, patting a stray hair into place. Don exchanged a surprised look with Jay before adjusting his suit jacket to accommodate his holster. When they arrived at the lawyer's office, Bridgett walked in like she owned the place. She cooed to the receptionist about how elegant the space was as if they were in Trump Tower and not some rental office space in an incubator building with furniture from Ikea. Bridgett raved about the tea she was offered despite the fact it was from a yellow box. She was laying it on thick and the staff was eating it up—until they got to Alesha Warren. A woman in her late thirties, she had flawless caramel skin and sleek, long black hair. Her long nails were bloodred, one of them adorned with a shiny stone. Ms. Warren wore her navy power suit well, but it was clearly not of the same quality as Bridgett's soft plum-colored skirt and jacket.

Jay sized up the woman in an instant. Despite the bravado on her face, there was a hint of desperation in her eyes and around her tight smile. For the first time since he'd woken up this morning, he allowed himself to relax. Bridgett may be playing the charming sorority girl from *Legally Blonde*, but he knew from past experience that she could do an abrupt about-face when the need arose.

"Won't Miss Knowles be joining us?" Bridgett asked.

The other woman's chin jutted out. "Not today. If you want to speak to her, you'll have to arrange a time for a deposition."

Don shot forward in his chair. "She asked for this meeting," he said. "She said she had something she wanted to discuss with us."

Obviously his "panty-melting grin" wasn't having any effect on the opposing counsel because the woman eyed Don smugly. "She does, but she'll be doing all of her discussing through me." She slid a piece of paper across the table toward Jay. He reached for it, but Bridgett was faster, snatching it up in her neatly manicured hand. "I'm sure you don't want a lengthy court case, Mr. McManus," Ms. Warren spoke directly to Jay. "This figure will ensure that we can resolve this today."

While Jay would love to resolve this today, he was certain that whatever number the brash lawyer had scribbled on that piece of paper and the one in his head were light-years apart. Bridgett glanced at the paper before handing it to him, her face giving nothing away. Jay was careful not to give anything away, either, keeping his expression stoic while inside he seethed. *Ten million dollars!* The woman had a lot of nerve.

Bridgett made a great show of gathering up her tablet and pen and shoving them in her bag. "Well, thank you for your time, Ms. Warren. We'll be in touch."

"That offer only stands for twenty-four hours," Ms. Warren said quickly.

"I'm sorry." The air in the room seemed to still along with Bridgett as she eyed the other woman. "I didn't realize that you'd made an offer. Instead, I think that you've made a *demand*. A rather outrageous one, in my opinion. I think a judge and jury may have a different number in mind once they get a look at the facts, as limited in scope as they are."

Ms. Warren wasn't as practiced with her poker face as Bridgett because a few beads of sweat had formed on her forehead. "See it however you'd like, Ms. Janik, but this time tomorrow, our willingness to cooperate and keep certain *facts* from being next week's headlines disappears."

Don slid forward in his chair, his aggravation barely leashed. "You mentioned these 'facts' when you set up this meeting, but so far all I'm hearing is a song and dance. How about we cut to the chase and you tell us what you really want."

"Ten million dollars. It's what my client and the rest of the class *deserve*."

"Set up in a trust to be administered by you, I assume," Bridgett asked.

"Through my firm, yes."

That arrangement would net the woman a very nice salary while the settlement was being meted out, especially if her sister-in-law remained the only member of the Sparks cheerleading squad collecting. It was a ballsy move, but, based on the documents he'd already read, the woman didn't have a case to warrant such a settlement. This meant there was something not in play yet and Jay wanted to know what she had. "There isn't anything in the filing to warrant a ten-million-dollar award, so why don't you tell us just exactly what you plan to lead with," he demanded, unable to adhere to Bridgett's command to sit there silently any longer. The tip of one of those dominatrix high heels of hers dug into the instep of his foot and he could have sworn he felt the heat of her bare calf through his pant leg. As arousing as that thought was, he couldn't let it distract him from getting to the bottom of Alesha Warren's legal ploy.

"I'm glad you asked," the other lawyer said. "We'll lead with evidence that the team's owner knowingly fosters a climate of sexual harassment."

Jay didn't move an inch in spite of the fact he wanted to jump across the table and strangle the woman. Don fidgeted on the other side of Bridgett, but she appeared relaxed. "I assume you'll have evidence to back up such an egregious claim?" she asked, coolly.

There isn't any evidence, Jay wanted to scream. At least none that involved the Blaze.

Ms. Warren shrugged. "We wouldn't be here today without it. Mr. McManus left a legacy of sexual harassment accusations at his former company, all of them settled out of court."

Out of the corner of his eye, Jay watched as Bridgett bristled slightly. *Damn.* He knew what she was thinking, but none of those cases was what Warren claimed.

"You can't be serious," Bridgett said. "I'll get a judge to quash those before they even reach the court."

Ms. Warren smiled then, her face seeming to relax as she reeled them in. "You know as well as I do that this won't play out in a courtroom, but rather in the court of public opinion." She glanced smugly at Jay. "The media will eat this up and women's groups all over will demand you be forced to give up the team. It's happened before. Is that what you want, Mr. McManus? To lose a billion-dollar gravy train like the Blaze over this?"

Don swore loudly. "You're in cahoots with that damn blogger, aren't you? You have no intention of proceeding legally in this case."

"No, she doesn't," Jay said, deftly moving his foot so that Bridgett couldn't spear him again, because this time he wasn't sure it would feel so arousing. "This is blackmail. Pure and simple."

"I figured that you'd recognize it for what it was." Ms. Warren sat back in her chair, triumphantly crossing her arms over her chest. "Considering you're so skilled in the art, Mr. McManus."

Jay's mind began to whir. He'd blackmailed many to get where he was today. Most of those involved were scoundrels who deserved to be brought down. But this smelled of retaliation. Barely thirty minutes ago, he'd been hopeful that this case wouldn't be played out in the courtroom. Apparently, he might get his wish. *Except it would get played out in the tabloids instead.* Without so much as looking at his companions, he stood, startling Ms. Warren from her victorious posture. "We're done here." He reached down and dragged Bridgett's chair back from the table as Don stood on the other side of her.

"Thank you for your time," Bridgett said politely, and Jay had to hold back a manic laugh. The other lawyer was a thieving shyster who was bent on being a thorn in his side. He had another phrase besides *thank you* that he wouldn't mind barking out as they departed, but good breeding kept him silent.

"Don't forget, Ms. Janik," Ms. Warren called after them. "I'll expect to hear from you by noon tomorrow."

The three of them quickly made their way back toward the elevator as Don muttered, "Don't hold your breath."

They rode the elevator down to the lobby in silence. Jay could only imagine what was going on in that gorgeous head of Bridgett's. But he didn't have the time or patience to plead his case to her right now. He needed Linc to start digging. Then Jay needed to make his own list. Someone out there had access to his most personal secrets. And if those came out, there would be serious collateral damage.

The rain was still coming down in sheets as they dashed to the car Don had parked in the visitor's spot. With the wind swirling around them, Don opened the door for Bridgett, who quickly ducked into the backseat. Jay slid into the front passenger seat, his cell phone pressed up to his ear just as Linc answered the call.

"Hey, boss. I've got some bad news," Linc began without much preamble. "Seymour is out for the season. Torn ACL."

Jay swore quietly. His premier cornerback had injured himself with a freaking dance move after sacking the quarterback in Sunday's game. Now the Blaze would have to scramble to find a body to fill the secondary before Friday.

"Hank says he has some feelers out," Linc continued. "But it won't be cheap."

Nothing ever was. Jay hesitated a minute. He knew he could trust Don to be discreet and Bridgett had to keep his confidences—she was his lawyer. But that didn't mean he wanted his dirty laundry aired in front of either of them. "Hank can handle that right now, Linc. I need you to gather some data for me."

"If it's about Charlotte's baby daddy, I'm still waiting on some intel from our sources in Europe," Linc said.

Jay pinched the bridge of his nose. He'd forgotten all about his sister in the past thirty minutes, which just demonstrated how screwed up his life was. "No, Linc, I need you to redirect your efforts to something else right now. The other thing can wait."

"Does that mean she's not as far along as we thought?" Linc interrupted him. "Because if we know the conception date, it'll be easier to rule some guys out."

Linc made it sound as if his sister had slept with half of Europe's male population, something Jay definitely didn't want to think about. And no way was he asking his sister how far along she was. Not when choosing a breakfast cereal could reduce her to tears these days. "I haven't got an answer to that one, Linc, but we need to move on. I need you to cull through the HR files from McManus Industries and pull out all the sexual harassment complaints. Particularly the ones involving me."

For the first time in Jay's memory, Linc was silent on the other end of the phone.

"Have them printed and ready for Ms. Janik by the time we arrive back in town this afternoon."

"All of them, boss? Even the ones you settled?"

"All of them."

Linc had the good sense not to argue. "Sure thing, boss."

Bridgett let out an exasperated sigh as Jay ended the call. "Am I going to need a forklift?"

Jay glanced over his shoulder at her. Despite her expensive raincoat, she looked damp and rumpled. And pissed off. Well, she could just join the damn crowd because Jay was none too happy to have to open this can of worms again. The second part of his search would have to take place in Jay's personal files. He didn't dare share that information with anyone. But if his theory was correct, that was where he'd find who was behind this case.

"Your pilot says this weather system is hugging the coast and the tower won't let him take off for another hour or so," Don said. "There's a diner next to the airfield. Maybe we should grab something and strategize what our next move is going to be. I for one would like to find Jennifer Knowles."

Jay nodded his agreement just as his stomach growled. He wanted to get back to Baltimore as quickly as possible, but it wouldn't be fair to make Bridgett endure another bumpy flight. Not when she looked like she wanted to lop his head off with a stick. Hopefully, they sold something stronger than coffee at the diner. They both were going to need it.

Bridgett glanced at herself in the tiny mirror of the diner's ladies' room. She looked a lot like she felt: wrung out. The roller-coaster plane ride followed by the even more turbulent meeting had done a number on her. She should have known there was more to this story. Despite Alesha Warren blindsiding her with her accusations about Jay, Bridgett couldn't say she was surprised. And that disappointed her. Especially since she'd once loved the man.

Soaping up her hands, she ran them under the hot water to warm herself up. Clearly this wasn't going to be an open-and-shut case, no matter what Jay and Hank Osbourne said. She needed to get a media specialist on board as soon as possible before things really got out of control. After drying her hands, she shot a text off to Stuart suggesting he begin interviewing potential candidates this afternoon. With nothing left to keep her in the bathroom, she headed back out to break bread with the Antichrist.

She didn't get very far. Jay was leaning a broad shoulder against the wall next to the men's room. He looked sexy and almost touchable with his hair all tousled from the wind and the rain. His suit jacket was missing and he'd rolled up his sleeves again to reveal his long, tanned hands. Hands that she knew were very capable of bringing a woman immense pleasure. The sight of him warmed her more quickly than the hot water from the tap had. She needed to get out of the close, dark confines of the hallway and back to their table, where Don would be the perfect buffer.

"Wow, is there a line for the men's room? That has to be a first."

He gave her a look as though he didn't quite get the joke, but he didn't move a muscle away from the wall.

Bridgett sighed, motioning with her hands for him to get out of the way. "You're quite the fire hazard here, Jay. Would you mind letting me pass?"

"We need to talk."

"We certainly do, but I'd rather do this sitting down, preferably with a nice hot cup of tea in front of me."

"Privately."

Annoyance made her snap at him. "Out of earshot of Don, you mean? I already told you that any conversations we have from here on out are to be limited to the ongoing case. Anything else is inappropriate."

She stepped forward to slide past him but he moved more quickly, his big body backing her into the ladies' room.

"What the hell are you doing?" she snapped at him again.

"I'm invoking attorney-client privilege." His mouth turned up on one side as though he thought his quip was very amusing.

"I already told you there won't be any *privileges* between you and me, Jay. Especially not in the ladies' room, where someone could walk in at any moment."

He chuckled as he closed the door and turned the lock. "I like the way you think, Bridgett, but unfortunately we really need to talk about the case. And since there are only three other people who were foolish enough to venture out for lunch in this monsoon and all of them are male, I think we'll get more privacy here than the hallway."

Bridgett told herself that wasn't disappointment swelling deep in her belly. Being ravaged by Jay in the ladies' room was the last thing she needed to be doing. The quicker they had their "private" conversation, the better. She considered locking herself in the stall and speaking with him through the metal divider, but that would be childish. So, she took a step farther into the corner of the room, leaning a hip against the porcelain sink protruding from the wall.

"If this is about your string of sexual harassment complaints, save your breath," she said. "Nothing you do anymore surprises me."

His mouth grew hard and his eyes narrowed slightly. "None of those were legitimate."

"That's what they all say."

Jay smiled then. It wasn't a pretty one. "Women will do and say a lot of things to get ahead. I'm rich, good-looking, and I happen to appreciate what the opposite sex has to offer. Unfortunately, a few of those women got a little too attached to my money. Or maybe it was my body; I'm not sure."

It was all she could do not to roll her eyes at him. "It definitely wasn't your ego."

She'd baited him one too many times. He moved away

from the door, prowling toward her, stopping a scant few inches away from her. His body heat radiated off him, warming her damp shoes and body.

"What's the matter, Bridgett? Still can't figure out what women see in me? How a woman might desire me? Love me? Or do you have to constantly remind me that you're the one woman who did walk away from me?"

Tears stung the back of her eyes. That was the one detail he always got wrong. The walking away part. Jay was the one who'd left her all those years ago.

"Again with the ego," she whispered, not trusting her voice as he stirred up memories of their painful past. She didn't have faith in her eyes, either, keeping them focused on the shiny silk of his silver tie.

"Dammit, Bridgett," he whispered. His breath fanned the top of her head before he cupped her face in his warm hands and lifted her chin. Her eyes had no choice but to stare into his and what she saw briefly flickering within them made her breath catch at the back of her throat. "I don't want to travel that road again."

"Then what do you want?"

"I want you." His lips descended, hovering just over hers, making her body tremble with desire. *Damn him.*

"No attorney-client privileges, remember?" She managed to force the words past her lips. As much as her body was screaming in protest, Bridgett was glad that her brain was still in control.

"Hmm," he murmured. His eyes studied her face as if she held the secrets to the universe while his finger traced the line between her ear and her shoulder. "As much as I'd like to dissuade you of that dictate, we have something more important to discuss."

Again the relief that coursed through her didn't feel too much like a reprieve. "Can we get to it? I'm sure my tea is getting cold."

His steely blue eyes went soft, as did his mouth. "I don't know how to tell you this, but I'm afraid that whoever is behind all this has the potential to hurt you, too."

Bridgett was having trouble concentrating when his finger was caressing her neck. His statement confused her. "I don't understand."

"Whoever is doing this has access to my most private information."

Nothing was making sense. Bridgett stared at him as she shrugged her shoulders in bewilderment.

Jay gave her a little shake. His voice was raspy when he spoke. "Bridgett, they'll know about us. And they'll know about Italy. And our baby."

Seven

Bridgett jerked forward at his words, but Jay caught her body against his much larger one. He wrapped his arms around her and all he wanted to do was hold her next to him so that the ugly truth of his life wouldn't touch her. But Bridgett being Bridgett, that wasn't going to happen. She pushed away from him angrily. Her cool demeanor was long gone as she glared at him with flushed skin and silver eyes that were as dark and damp as the rain clouds outside.

"What is that supposed to mean?" she demanded.

This was going to be the tricky part. He didn't want to explain himself to her. Hell, he shouldn't have to. Jay didn't explain himself to anyone. Ever. Lloyd Davis may have left him with a meager legacy but his stepfather's practice of never giving his enemies anything to hang him by was one business tactic Jay practiced day in and day out. That and knowing as much about his enemies as he possibly could, in case he needed that information to use against them at a later date. Unfortunately, someone else had turned the tables on Jay.

As it turned out, he didn't have to say anything to Bridgett. Judging by the stormy look on her face, she was using her brilliant mind to work it all out for herself. "Is this some J. Edgar Hoover thing? Are you keeping files on people? On *me*?"

Jay didn't bother refuting her. He wasn't the type of man who felt guilty about his business tactics. It was called survival of the fittest. The millions in his bank account could attest to the success of his philosophy, not to mention his tactics.

When he didn't answer right away, Bridgett's face crumpled. Jay refused to acknowledge whatever that feeling might be gnawing in his belly. At least he'd warned her of the possibility that she might be dragged through the muck in this rather than let her find out the hard way.

She flung herself at him, her fists pummeling his chest. "You son of a bitch," she cried. "What were you planning to do? Blackmail *me*?" One of her fists made contact with his jaw, but her punch lacked the power of anything his sparring partners had ever hit him with. In an effort to calm her down, Jay captured her hands in his own.

"Stop it!" Jay yanked her hands over her head, bringing her body flush with his. Instead of sinking into him as she had the past few days, she recoiled visibly, her body stiff in his arms. "It was a long time ago," he said. "I hated you, remember?" Hell, he'd hated everybody back then. His stepfather. His mother. But especially Bridgett, for not believing in him. For not loving him enough.

Bridgett's mouth had stopped trembling. "Not as much as I hate you right now."

Her words cracked through the air and Jay sucked in a breath.

"Let me go," she demanded.

Jay hesitated briefly and she tugged at her hands before he finally released his grip. Bridgett took a step back, smoothing down her skirt while she dragged in a ragged breath. "It doesn't matter now anyway. It's not like the information can harm anyone any longer. I no longer work for

Catholic Charities. My parents . . . my parents will be disappointed that I never told them." She swiped at a stray tear that trickled down her cheek. "But in the end, it all worked out for the best." Bridgett jerked up her chin, practically daring him to refute her.

The implication of her words sank in and Jay refused to flinch. He'd realized quickly how little he'd meant to her. He refused to let it bother him now. "Yes, it definitely did," he said smoothly. "But, still, I'd prefer that information be kept private."

"Well, you should have thought of that years ago!" She pressed her fingertips to her forehead. "Believe me, I'm not thrilled about being linked to you in some tabloid headline. Although, it's a sure way to get me off the case."

Her phone buzzed inside her purse.

"Perfect timing. It's Stuart." Her fingers trembled as she pulled the phone out. "This ought to be a fun conversation."

Jay wrapped his fingers around the hand holding the phone, giving her a gentle squeeze. "Don't."

She arched an eyebrow at him.

"I'll do whatever I can to make sure this doesn't come out."

Bridgett hesitated a moment, the phone still vibrating between their hands. "Jay," she said softly. "It's better for everyone if we keep our distance."

Jay knew she was right. But he'd made worse decisions in his career and still come out on top. He couldn't let her go. Not yet. "Twenty-four hours. Give me the same courtesy you gave Alesha Warren."

She narrowed her eyes at him and he figured that she probably liked the conniving lawyer for the Sparks cheerleader better than him right now, but he could deal with that. Her phone stopped ringing and Jay reluctantly pulled his hand away.

"Thank you," he said. "I'll work this out. Trus—"

Bridgett's hand shot up to shush him. "Whatever you do, don't ask me to trust you. Ever."

Well, if that wasn't the kettle calling the pot black. Good to know they shared the same sentiment. Still, her words pissed him off. "I'm paying you and your firm enough money to defend my team in this case. Last time I checked, a lawyer didn't always have to trust her client to earn her pay."

Bridgett had the good grace not to defend her profession. "Then let's get to that part, shall we?" She eyed him and then the door. "If you don't mind, I'd like a minute alone in here to freshen up."

He did mind. Jay minded a lot. Anger and anxiety swelled in his gut when he got next to this woman, but he still hated to let her out of his sight. The image of her walking away from him years ago still speared him in his chest and he loathed that feeling. He swore he'd never be vulnerable to her again. And yet, he was annoyed at himself for having upset her so a few minutes ago. The vortex of emotions flying around in his head was giving him a headache.

"Fine." His hand squeezed the back of his neck. "We'll eat and then head back to Baltimore."

"I'm sorry, Mr. McManus, but it doesn't look like we're going to get out of here tonight," Jay's pilot told them when they'd returned to the small airport two hours later. "The National Weather Service has gone ahead and declared this one a superstorm. It was supposed to make landfall in South Carolina. Instead, it turned north and has been hugging the coastline, picking up strength in the warm waters along shore as it moves. Things are going to be dicey here for the next several hours."

Jay swore as he pulled out his phone. Don had dropped them off and then taken off to follow a lead on Jennifer Knowles. Both he and Jay believed the former Sparks cheerleader was being used as the front for this lawsuit, but Bridgett still hadn't completely bought into their theory. To be honest, she was having trouble thinking clearly about anything today. All she wanted was to be back in Baltimore— no, make that Boston—sitting by the fire and sipping a glass of wine.

"Don is on the other side of the bridge already," Jay said.

"They're closing it to traffic in ten minutes and he doesn't think he'll get through the gridlock to get back before then. The state police are clearing all the roads."

A lick of panic raced up Bridgett's spine. "So you're saying that we can't even drive back?"

Jay shook his head just as a gust of wind shook the metal hangar, sliding several of the smaller planes that weren't tied down. He reached out and wrapped his fingers around her arm, pulling her in next to him. "Obviously, we can't stay here." He yelled toward the pilot, who was furiously helping to tie down the planes. "Ron! We're going to find a place to hole up for the night."

"I'm staying here with the plane, Mr. McManus," Ron said.

"It's only a plane, Ron. No need to be a hero."

Ron grinned at Jay. "You forget I flew planes on an aircraft carrier. This"—he gestured toward the hangar's ceiling, which was currently being pelted by the heavy rain—"is nothing."

With a shake of his head, Jay mumbled something about the Navy as he ushered Bridgett into the office located at the front of the hanger. A woman was pulling on her jacket when they stepped inside.

"We're closed for the day," she started to say, but then her eyes took in Jay and her face softened. Bridgett worked not to roll her eyes at the obvious adoration that took over the other woman's face. "Can I help you?"

Jay flashed his rakish grin at the woman. "It seems we're stranded here for the night. Is there a rental car office nearby?"

"There is, but they closed about an hour ago. As soon as the weather service upgraded the storm."

Bridgett swayed a little on her heels, but Jay's hand on her arm kept her upright. She tried to find the positives in the situation: At least they were safe from the driving rain. Glancing over at Jay, she worked to draw some steadiness of her own from his cool demeanor.

"What about a taxi?" he asked. "We need to get to a hotel."

The woman glanced between Bridgett and Jay, a chagrined

look on her face. "The only motel we have on this part of the beach is the Super Eight down the road. Everything else is on the other side of the bridge."

"Is it on your way?" Jay asked.

With a resigned sigh, the woman nodded to Jay. "It's not much out of the way." She glanced at Bridgett. "It's not the Ritz, mind you."

"As long as it's warm and dry, we'll be fine," Jay reassured her.

He and Bridgett followed the woman out to her car as darkness settled over the area nearly four hours early. The motel was two miles down the road, but it took almost twenty minutes to navigate through the torrential rain. Its parking lot was packed and worry seeped into Bridgett's damp bones that they might not find a room.

Holly—the woman had introduced herself to Jay during the drive over, highlighting the fact that she was divorced—let them out at the front door of the motel's lobby; if it could be called a lobby. The smell of burned coffee assaulted Bridgett's nostrils as they walked into a narrow room that boasted two worn chairs, a metal rack featuring brochures of local attractions, and a reception desk. The Weather Channel blared over a television situated on the Formica desk. Bridgett caught a glimpse of the radar image on the screen.

"Wow," she said. "It's headed right for us."

Jay acknowledged her with a grunt as he tapped his finger on the bell. An Indian woman dressed in a richly colored sari emerged from the back room. "Oh," she said, her bangles jingling as she clapped her hands together. "I didn't hear you come in. This weather, it's so crazy. But you are here and you are wet." She handed each one of them a small towel. "Can I get you some coffee?"

Bridgett's stomach rolled at the thought. "No coffee, thank you," Jay said to the woman.

"Then what can I do for you?" she asked innocently, as if there might some other reason the two of them were standing in the lobby soaking wet.

"We need a room for the night." Jay reached into his pocket, presumably for his wallet.

"Rooms," Bridgett added. He shot her an annoyed look.

The woman in the sari made some sort of tsking sound. "Are you a Super Eight Club member?"

Jay plunked his platinum card onto the counter. "No, but this should do the trick."

The woman frowned. "I have to save my last room for a club member."

"You only have one room left?" Bridgett nearly cried. As much as she wanted to get away from Jay, fate kept throwing them together.

"Yes." The woman nodded.

"Surely you can make an exception," Jay asked. "We're stranded here."

The woman behind the desk contemplated him before shaking her head slowly. "No, it is company policy, sir."

Bridgett glanced around the room as Jay glared at the desk clerk. "Seriously?" Jay's voice shook the walls as soundly as the wind howling outdoors.

Spying what she was looking for, Bridgett pulled a membership form from the brochures in the rack and slapped it down on the counter. She retrieved her Montblanc from her bag and began filling out the paperwork. When she was finished, she tore off the temporary card and handed it to the woman. "I'll take that room, please."

Jay looked at Bridgett with a mix of surprise and admiration as the desk clerk clapped her hands again. "This is perfect. Welcome to the Super Eight Club. You can now have the room." She reached for Jay's credit card. "But your points won't accrue this visit because technically, you aren't in the system yet."

Bridgett tuned the woman out as she explained, in great detail, the terms of the club. The only detail floating around in Bridgett's brain was that she was about to share a room with the Antichrist. The lights flickered briefly and Bridgett's thoughts took a whole new twist.

The desk clerk handed Jay the keys. "If the power does go out," she was saying, "my son, Jagdish, he will bring you a candle."

"You don't have a generator?" Jay asked, his voice incredulous.

"Oh yes." She nodded before waving her arms about the room. "For the office. We will stay up all night and keep you informed in case of an emergency." Funny, but Bridgett didn't find the desk clerk's pleasant nature all that reassuring.

They had to go back out into the rain to find their room. Fortunately for them it was located just beyond the office on the motel's bottom level. Jay opened the door and turned on the lights, only to have them flicker off and back on again. He slammed the door against the wind and the rain as Bridgett walked over to one of the pair of double beds, shooting up a silent prayer of thanks that there were two.

"At least we won't have the roof blow off over our heads," she said, pulling off her soggy raincoat.

"No, but there's a reason she didn't rent this unit. It's at the bottom of a hill. We could be ankle deep in water by morning."

Bridgett glanced over at Jay, who was drying his hair with the hand towel the desk clerk had given him. "Thanks for the reassurance. I hadn't considered flooding."

He chuckled. "You would have figured it out. Nice work on the club membership, by the way." He rummaged through the sparse closet.

"What are you looking for?" she asked.

"An umbrella. Don took the one in the car with him."

"Don't tell me you think the roof is going to leak through two floors?" Bridgett didn't usually panic easily, but today had really worn her down.

Jay actually laughed then. "No. I'm going out."

"Out?" While the thought of sharing a room with him was anxiety provoking, the idea of being alone in the room during this tumultuous storm wasn't exactly the most appealing alternative.

He paused in the act of rebuttoning his overcoat. "I'm not waiting around for Jagdish to bring us a candle. There's a gas station with a convenience store across the street. Lock up behind me. Who knows what other club members are hiding out here." He was out the door before Bridgett could lodge a protest. The lights flickered again and Bridgett lunged across the room to flip the safety lock closed.

Her cell phone vibrated in her purse and Bridgett was glad to have someone to talk to. Gwen had been calling her all day without leaving a voice message. Some days, talking to Gwen was like poking yourself in the eye with a sharp stick, but Bridgett would gladly take the pain right now.

"Hello?"

"Hey there, Buffy."

Bridgett sagged with relief at the sound of Stuart's voice. "Please tell me you're sending the Navy to come rescue me?"

Stuart laughed. "No can do, Buff. You seem to have flown into the eye of the storm—literally and figuratively."

Flopping back on the surprisingly soft mattress, she let out a groan. "I told you Dan should have come instead of me."

"Why? Does he have his own boat?" Stuart was the only one laughing at his quip. "While you're cooling your heels, we're working hard up here. I just hired Mimi Livingston to consult on the potential media fallout involved with this case."

Mimi Livingston was the poster woman of cougars everywhere. Bridgett couldn't stand the gaudy woman's tactics. It was hard to argue with her success rate, though. If anyone could redirect the media, Mimi could.

"I could hear her salivating over the phone when I mentioned the client would be Jay McManus and the Baltimore Blaze," Stuart said.

Bridgett would likely have to spend all of her time peeling the other woman's eyes off Jay's body every time they met. She reminded herself that the twinge deep in her core was *not* jealousy.

Stuart grew more serious. "Did McManus go into any detail about these past cases?"

"He didn't deny them."

"Hmm. That surprises me. I've talked to several colleagues in Northern California who would know if Alesha Warren's claims would be true and no one knows anything about them."

Bridgett ran her finger through her damp hair. "She intimated that many of them were settled."

"Still, my sources would have heard whispers of even that. I'm going to send Scott out there to do some more digging."

She shot up on the bed. If someone had Jay's personal files and knew about their summer in Italy, how easy would it be for Scott to stumble across them? In the ladies' room earlier, she'd told Jay it didn't matter who knew, but that had been a bit of false bravado. The idea of her deepest secret being revealed made Bridgett a bit nauseous. "Jay is having his assistant pull together the files. It sounds as if he has nothing to hide. I wouldn't waste Scott's time on that. We still need to follow up with Jennifer Knowles."

"Don Carter is tracking her down. I'd rather not waste valuable man hours duplicating the work being done by the Blaze. Besides, if it's blackmail this woman is interested in, I'd rather have all the ammunition we can up front. We'll be better able to prepare Mimi this way, as well."

Of course, Stuart was right. Bridgett only hoped that the Antichrist had his stupid files under lock and key. Bridgett's phone beeped and she checked the screen. Gwen again. She'd call her sister back after she finished with Stuart.

"So where are you two riding out the storm?" Stuart asked. "Knowing you, you found the only five-star hotel in Virginia Beach."

Bridgett glanced around the utilitarian motel room. "Hardly. We're at a Super Eight motel next to the airstrip. If you don't hear from me in the morning, I've floated away into the Chesapeake Bay." She didn't bother mentioning that she and Jay had been forced to share a room. Somehow, she didn't think her boss would think the situation was appropriate. Of course, it really wasn't. For all of Bridgett's denial about attorney-client privileges, she'd somehow found herself stranded in a room with a bed and her former lover, who was now her client. She just had to keep reminding herself that he was still—and always would be—the enemy.

Stuart laughed, his deep voice booming over the phone. "Do they still have the massage beds where you put a quarter in and the bed shakes? My brothers and I used to beg my parents to let us do that when we were on a family vacation."

Digging her fingers into the soft mattress, Bridgett forced herself to try not to imagine it vibrating from anything but the thunder overhead. "No, but it would make a nice flotation device if necessary."

"No more joking, Buffy," Stuart said. "You stay safe down there. And don't forget to keep our client happy."

Bridgett bounced back onto the bed again as she clicked her phone off. Rain and wind pelted the window overlooking the dark parking lot and the lights flickered again. In order to keep her mind off the storm—and what things she could do to make Jay happy—she dialed her sister Gwen's number. Gwen picked up before it even rang once.

"Where have you been?" Gwen demanded.

"Well, Gwen, I know it's hard to believe, but I do actually work for a living." Bridgett heard what sounded like a sob come from the other end of the phone. Worried that something might have happened to a family member, she sat up on the bed, softening her tone toward her sister. "Gwen, what's wrong?"

This time there was no mistaking Gwen's distress. "I think . . . I think I need a lawyer."

Her words made Bridgett's pulse jump. While her oldest sister was annoying and overbearing, Gwen was still family and Bridgett would do anything to help her. "Tell me what happened. Why do you need a lawyer?"

"It's Skip," Gwen sobbed. "He's cheating on me."

Bridgett couldn't say she was surprised. Her brother-in-law had proven himself as a rat bastard many times over. But still, she was angry and hurt for her sister and their children. "You're sure about this?" The question was somewhat rhetorical but of course Gwen didn't take it that way.

"Yes, I'm sure!" she yelled through the phone. "He's been doing his assistant Lucy for months now. He thinks he's so discreet but that idiot flaps his mouth as much as he flaps his zipper. Do you know how embarrassing it has been to hold my head up in this town for the past six months?"

"Okay, calm down."

"Calm down? *Calm down!* The bitch was in the gynecologist's office today getting a pregnancy test, Bridgett, while I was getting my friggin' annual exam. I can't calm down!"

The lights flickered again ominously and Bridgett felt that queasiness she'd been battling all day bubble up to the surface. If what her sister was saying was true, it would explain Gwen's testiness the past months. She suddenly felt guilty for not having probed a little deeper to find out what was troubling Gwen.

"Dammit, Bridgett, when are you coming home? I need you," she choked out.

It was the first time in her life Gwen had ever said those words to her and she didn't want to let her down. But she was stranded in a motel during a tropical storm.

"It's going to be a day or so. I'm stuck in Virginia Beach due to bad weather. But I'm going to call the office and get someone working on this right away, okay, Gwen?"

"I don't want anyone else to work on this," Gwen whispered. "I don't want anyone to know. Not Mom or Dad or anyone in the family. Not yet, anyway. It has to be you."

Bridgett's breath hitched at her sister's embarrassed plea. "Gwen, you need to trust me on this, okay? There are people in my firm who are much better at this than I am. They'll make sure you and the kids are taken care of."

"But you're the best lawyer I know, Bridge," she cried. "I can't do this without you. I'm not strong like you are. I don't know what I'm going to do."

Her sister's plea brought tears to Bridgett's eyes. "You're stronger than you think you are, Gwen. And I won't ever let you go through this alone. Just let me get the ball rolling so Skip doesn't do something to catch you off guard. Promise me you'll keep it together until I can get back to Boston?"

Gwen sniffled several times before promising. Bridgett reassured her sister that she'd call her back in a few minutes after she got in touch with Stuart. As soon as she disconnected the phone, the lights flickered again before going out for good.

Eight

Jay was drenched by the time he returned to the motel. His hands were filled with plastic bags so he kicked the door with his foot. The curtain covering the big window moved and a bright light beamed out at him, making him squint. "Open up, Bridgett."

She held the door steady against the wind as Jay hustled inside the now-dark room. Bridgett shined the flashlight on her phone in a wide arc around the room. "Please tell me you got a flashlight or some candles. My cell is about to die and there's no sign of Jagdish," she said.

"There are both in here." He dropped the bags onto the dresser and went in search of the towel to wipe off his wet face and head. Water squished in his shoes with every step. Bridgett's light followed him as he peeled off his sodden raincoat.

"You're soaked."

His stepped out of his shoes before pulling off his suit jacket. "Your parents must be proud of that Harvard education."

With a huff, she redirected her light back to the dresser.

As she rummaged through the bags of supplies, he peeled off his pants that were wet from the calf down.

"Hey!" The beam was shining back on him again. "What are you doing?"

"I'm soaked, remember, Captain Obvious? I'm gonna take a shower."

"In the dark?"

"No, you're going to hand me one of those nauseatingly pumpkin-scented candles and a box of matches first."

The light was obscuring her face, but Jay was sure her eyes were narrowed in annoyance while a sweet pink blush stained her cheeks. He longed to invite her to join him in the shower, but after his admission earlier today, Jay knew he had to tread lightly. He'd win her over eventually; of that he had no doubt. Just not tonight, unfortunately.

She handed him one of the stocky candles and a box of matches. "If you don't like pumpkin, why did you get them?"

Because they were the only damn candles left in the store. "They didn't have mango," he said instead, making his way into the darkened bathroom before he changed his mind and dragged her in with him.

Ten minutes later he emerged from his steamy shower dressed in a T-shirt and his boxer briefs. The room was aglow with the many votives he'd bought. The place smelled like Thanksgiving Day probably did in most of the homes across the country. Bridgett was seated Indian-style on one of the beds, a blanket spread over her lap as her fingers tapped out notes on her tablet. When she looked up, her eyes held a look of profound anguish.

"Hey," he said, sitting on the bed opposite hers, tamping down the impulse to reach for her hand. "We're safe here. The storm should burn out in a couple of hours."

She waved a hand. "I know that. It's just I've had a bit of a family emergency come up and I need to get home. To Boston."

"Nothing life-threatening, I hope."

"Not unless my sister goes all Lorena Bobbitt on her husband, no." She grimaced. "Gwen's husband has been cheating

on her. She wants to divorce—she's *going* to divorce him—
she's just not used to being on her own."

"She's lucky to have you."

Bridgett laughed. "Yeah, kind of funny since she's the one
who made me cry the other day."

"Why?"

She shook her head, the brief glimpse behind the cool
veneer she kept in place closed. Instead she gestured to his
pants, which she'd hung over a chair. "They're still damp at
the cuffs but I squeezed as much of the water out as I could.
You may have to roll them up at the ankles."

He arched an eyebrow at her. "Worried you might not be
able to keep your hands off me without my pants on?"

Her blush was obvious even in the candlelight as she
quickly stood and walked over to the dresser filled with the
food he'd brought back—a can of potato chips, peanut butter
crackers, two apples, and the necessity of women everywhere: a bag of Dove chocolate. He'd also grabbed a couple
bottles of water, a bottle of chardonnay, toothpaste, and two
toothbrushes. The wine wasn't the best vintage, but he knew
they'd both appreciate something a little stronger than water
right about now.

"Thanks for leaving the roller food at the gas station, but
you forgot the corkscrew."

She kept her back to him as he pulled on his pants. He
stepped behind her, reached past her shoulder into his briefcase, and pulled out his pocket knife. Bridgett's breath caught
as his arm brushed over hers. When he clicked a button on
the bottom, a corkscrew emerged. Jay handed it to her and
went into the bathroom to grab the two plastic cups.

"I should have known," she said as she worked the screw
into the cork. "You never went anywhere without one that
summer. Frankly, I'm surprised you went into the dot-com
industry and not the wine business like you'd planned."

"Who says I didn't," he asked, taking the bottle from her
and finishing the job.

Bridgett held the glasses while he poured. "I guess there's
a lot about each other we'll never know."

Her words sounded almost wistful and the warm wine went down rough as Jay swallowed. "Even without being chilled, our chardonnay is definitely better than this."

She sat on the bed, leaning on one arm as she sipped from her cup with the other. "So tell me, how did the guy who wanted to rule the world one bottle of wine at a time end up establishing a major dot-com business instead?"

"There's a lot more money to be made on the Internet than in the vineyards." He sat down on the bed across from her, leaning up against the headboard and crossing his feet at the ankles.

"But wine was your passion."

Jay eyed her over the rim of his cup. "I've learned that it's not always a good idea to be ruled by passion."

Bridgett kept her gaze level with his. "Exactly what I've been telling you all along."

"I didn't say I gave up on passion, Bridgett. I'll never do that."

That got the reaction he was hoping for as she gulped the remainder of her wine and began prying open a package of peanut butter crackers. "With Lloyd Davis as a stepfather, money shouldn't have been an object."

"Lloyd's money was Lloyd's money. And now it's Charlie's." He took another swallow of wine. Everyone always thought Jay should be resentful of the situation, but he wasn't anymore. Perhaps that was the best gift Lloyd had given him: the anger to become a self-made man. Now that he'd accomplished that, the bitterness toward his stepfather had faded.

"She doesn't seem at all like the little girl you described that summer."

Jay snorted. "That little girl died when her father did."

"Your mother . . . is she . . . is? I mean, the tabloids never mention her."

He reached over and took one of her crackers. "My mother is not very maternal. She's the smartest person I know, which begs the question of why the hell she had kids in the first place." He shrugged. "When she's not in the lab or some

ivory tower, she's really very kind, just distracted. She loves
Charlie; they're just from two different universes."

"And you?" Bridgett asked softly. "Does your mother love
you?"

"Yeah. But after my father died, her work became her
one true love. She only married Lloyd so I'd have some sort
of father figure in my life." Too bad Lloyd never saw Jay as
anything but a protégé to be molded, and not a boy who made
mistakes.

"But you and Charlie are still close?"

Jay blew out a breath. "Well, there have been many times
when she's made me mad as hell." He winked at Bridgett.
"But she's never made me cry."

She rolled her eyes at him. "Yet."

He laughed then as his phone buzzed on the nightstand.

"Hey, boss," Linc said. "Can you talk?"

Jay glanced over at Bridgett. There was so much he wanted
to tell her, share with her. But he knew better. He was better
off keeping his own confidences.

He moved to get off the bed, but Bridgett rose instead.

"I'm going to take a bath," she said as she refilled her wineglass and snatched up the bag of chocolates.

"Yeah," Jay said after he'd heard the lock click on the
bathroom door. "What do you have?"

"You're not gonna like it."

Jay was only half paying attention as he heard the water
begin to run and his body reacted to his mental picture of
Bridgett stripping out of her clothes by candlelight. He relaxed
against the headboard, imagining himself in the small bathroom with her pressed up against him. He'd peel her panties
off her and then begin exploring every inch of her with his
hands and his mouth.

"Are you listening, boss? She's gone. Princess Charlotte
has flown the coop."

When Bridgett emerged from her bath, Jay was
agitated and aloof, furiously texting from his phone and then

his tablet when his phone died. Gone was the quiet intimacy they'd shared over the crackers and wine. Bridgett should have been relieved. Except she wasn't. If he'd noticed she'd slipped into the dress shirt he'd left in the bathroom, he didn't mention it. On edge from the overwhelming events of the day, she'd eventually drifted off to a fitful sleep, cocooned in Jay's warm scent.

The storm let up sometime in the middle of the night. The lights suddenly flashed back on at four eighteen the next morning, startling both of them from restless sleep. Jay wasted no time arranging for a car to retrieve them from the motel and take them back to the airfield. When they boarded the plane at six thirty A.M., hot tea, fruit, and pastries were waiting in the small galley. The majority of the town was recovering from the storm, but Jay had managed to make sure she was comfortable. *Again.*

"It should be a much smoother ride this morning," the pilot told them as they took their seats. "We'll be wheels down in Boston by nine."

"Boston?" Bridgett asked as the pilot closed the cockpit door.

Jay looked up from the text he was frantically typing. "You said last night that you needed to be in Boston." One of his eyebrows went up questioningly. "Has something changed?"

Nothing had changed. Gwen had been sending out dire distress texts and e-mails all night. Once the power had returned, Bridgett had responded for her to sit tight, she'd be there by dinnertime. Now it seemed she'd be in Boston in time to make sure Gwen didn't off anyone in the carpool line.

She shook her head. "But what about our noon deadline with Ms. Warren?"

"Call her at eleven fifty-nine and tell her we'll see her in court."

While she'd been all in on that strategy yesterday, Bridgett had some qualms this morning. "And if she decides on a media smear campaign?"

"I can handle it."

"And if it's not just you she's attacking?"

He looked at her then, his blue eyes weary and tinged with what looked like concern. Bridgett's insides twitched at the sexy, rumpled Jay before her. Stubble outlined his jaw and he hadn't bothered to button up his shirt or put on a tie. He looked approachable and lovable. And she suddenly wanted to be back in that motel room with him, and she realized now why she'd been on edge all night: She wanted him. This man who had destroyed her heart still had the power to make her body sing.

"I gave you my word that I'd protect your secret. At least give me a chance to honor it."

She wanted to trust him. Bridgett ached to turn the clock back thirteen years and have him beside her in that hospital room. To have it all turn out differently. She didn't realize she was crying until he reached over and gently wiped a tear off her cheek. "I miss the two people we used to be," she whispered.

His hand found its way behind her neck and he pulled her toward him. Her lips met his without hesitation and she heard his soft groan of pleasure as her tongue tangled with his. Jay allowed her a minute to play before he took control of the kiss, possessing her mouth until every part of her ached for release. He was unbuckling his seat belt and moving to the seat next to hers when the plane began to taxi down the runway.

"This would have been much easier in the motel room, but I like your sense of adventure, Bridgett," he murmured against her ear.

She wasn't sure whether it was adventure, exhaustion, or simple frustration, but Bridgett didn't complain when his mouth found hers again. Leaning the seat back, he lifted up the wide armrest and pulled her body next to his. Her fingers threaded through his thick hair when his mouth drifted lower. His hand slid beneath the waistband of her skirt as he tugged her Dolce & Gabbana blouse free.

The plane left the ground smoothly, quickly climbing to altitude as Jay's hand slid just as smoothly along her rib cage.

A soft sigh escaped her lips and Jay took it as an invitation to explore further. He leaned over her, still plundering her mouth as his other hand made its way up her thigh and beneath her underwear.

The pilot's voice came over the intercom, startling Bridgett. "It's pretty calm up here, so feel free to move about the cabin if either of you need to."

His words were all the enticement Jay needed. He unbuckled them both and quickly pulled her across his lap. She gasped as she came in contact with the hard evidence of his desire. "Jay," she whispered as her mind warred with her body. Bridgett wanted this. She *needed* this. But he was her client. Worse, he was the Antichrist. She hated him. *Most of him, anyway.* But she was so damned tired. Tired of being Bridgett, the perfect one. She wanted to be that girl again, the one she'd been that summer long ago.

As though sensing her dissonance, Jay palmed her breast and nipped at her ear. "Forget all that shit. Let's just be those two people again, Bridgett. It's still good between us. You know it as well as I do," his voice rasped next to her ear.

Bridgett couldn't take it any longer. Digging her fingers into his hair, she tilted his mouth up to meet hers. Jay's hands slid beneath her skirt and pushed aside her panties. He slipped a thick finger inside of her, causing her hips to arch. Both his tongue and his finger picked up the same rhythm, and Bridgett's body began to tighten around him. Moaning, she pulled her mouth free from his, burying her face against his shoulder. Jay's breath caressed her ear as he murmured to her. "Let go, Bridgett. Let go of all of it."

She came in a rush, startling in its intensity, yet not long enough to ease the ache inside of her. Frantically, she stripped her panties off her legs as Jay deftly unzipped his trousers and rolled a condom over his erection. He maneuvered her hips back over top of him and slid home with heavy sigh. Eyes closed, Jay remained motionless a moment as Bridgett stretched to accommodate him. His fingers dug into her hips as he slowly moved beneath her. It was too slow for Bridgett. She tried to rise up on her knees but Jay held her fast, a lazy smile forming on his lips as he opened his eyes. The intensity and possessiveness shining in those blue eyes startled her. "This is real," he said as he moved her over him. "*This* is who we are."

Bridgett didn't have time to contemplate his words because he began to move faster beneath her, and it was all she could do to hold on as her body met his stride for stride. His mouth found her breast and the sensation of his tongue pleasuring her through the silk of her blouse and her bra made her wild. Suddenly his thumb found her sweet spot and her breath seized in her lungs. She threw her head back to scream from the pure pleasure of her climax, but no sound came. Jay stilled beneath her, his face drawn as he watched her come back to earth. Brushing her hair back off her face, he gently touched his lips to hers. Then, with a single thrust, his eyes slammed shut and he breathed her name ferociously as his own release overtook him.

Jay rubbed his hands along Bridgett's back. He was still deep inside her with her body draped over his. The soft, contented breaths she was releasing were making him hard again, but he would die before moving her an inch. The faint scent of pumpkin from her hair mingled with the musky smell of sex that permeated the plane's cabin and he couldn't help but grin smugly. She was his and always would be. While he'd never give her the power to hurt him again, he would possess her, sharing a life with her. They could carve out a relationship that left their hearts intact. They'd have to; because Jay wasn't letting her go again.

His phone buzzed from deep within the pocket of his suit jacket, which was hanging on the seat across from them. Jay ignored it, groaning as Bridgett stirred. She turned her face toward his, her eyes dazed as she began to come to her senses. But Jay didn't want her thinking. A coherent Bridgett was too risky. He tucked a strand of hair behind her ear before leaning in to kiss her back into delirium in hopes of a second round before they landed.

Jay swore against her mouth as Bridgett's phone began ringing seconds after Jay's quieted. She pulled out of the kiss, inhaling a deep breath as she glanced around the cabin. "That'll be Stuart," she said matter-of-factly. "I told him I'd call him at eight."

Bridgett started to climb off him, but Jay didn't want the distance between them to return. "Ignore it," he demanded. Her eyes homed in on his lips and he twitched inside of her, forcing a startled gasp from deep in her throat. Unfortunately, it didn't do the trick because she jumped off him and hightailed it to the lavatory without a second glance his way.

By the time she emerged, all tucked in and buttoned up, Jay had righted his own clothes and was sipping black coffee from a travel cup. She dug into the bowels of the ugly red bag she carried everywhere and pulled out her cell phone. Taking the seat across from him, she checked the screen.

"Stuart is sending our investigator out to San Francisco to check for any potential hot spots that could still be lingering from your sexual discrimination suits," she said without lifting her eyes.

Jay had anticipated such a move, which was why he'd insisted Linc get the files together. "I told you that you can have whatever files I have."

She looked up at him then, worry flashing in her eyes before her cool mask slipped into place. "Scott won't find anything, then?"

He knew what she was asking, but her secret was safe from her firm's investigator. If his suspicions were correct, it would be used to blackmail him instead. Jay didn't bother sharing that tidbit with her, though.

"I'm pretty sure that just before your initiation into the mile-high club I reminded you that I had already given you my word about that. Nothing has changed."

Bridgett fidgeted in her seat, her cheeks a delicious pink as she swiped a finger over the screen of her phone. "I'll put this on speaker so we can both talk to Stuart."

Jay didn't want to talk to her boss. He wanted to unwrap

her from the brittle shield she'd cloaked herself in and have his way with her for the rest of the flight. Unfortunately, Stuart answered on the second ring.

By the time they'd begun their descent, Stuart and Bridgett had mapped out a plan of attack for the day. While Bridgett dealt with her sister this morning, Stuart would be meeting with Mimi Something-or-Other and setting up a prevent defense in case Alesha Warren—or whoever was behind the lawsuit—leaked damaging information to the press or, more specifically, the person hiding behind that damn blog. Jay texted Linc to make the sexual harassment files available to the media specialist since Bridgett would be delayed this morning.

After taxiing the plane up to the small terminal adjacent to Logan Airport, Ron emerged from the cockpit and opened up the outer door. "I'll go check on the car," he said as he hurried down the steps.

Bridgett stood and gathered her things while Jay lounged in his seat, finishing his coffee.

"Is there a taxi stand here or do I have to go to the main terminal?" she asked.

Jay couldn't decide if he was insulted or amused by her demeanor. "The car he's getting is for you."

"Oh." Seeming embarrassed, she shoved her giant bag on her shoulder, clutching her raincoat with the other hand. "Of course. You'll want to head right back. I'll get out of your way, then."

She turned to leave but Jay was quicker. Rising to his feet, he blocked her exit. She took a small step back to avoid coming into contact with his chest, not that Jay would have minded.

"Ron is staying put. He'll fly you back whenever you're ready."

"You're just going to sit around waiting for me?"

"Ron is. I'm not. I'm catching a flight out to Napa in an hour." He reached out and fingered a strand of hair that had attached itself to her cheek.

"To get ahead of Scott?"

"No," he said, easing his body closer to hers. "I told you not to worry about that. It seems, though, that we're both destined to have to rescue our sisters today."

"Is Charlie all right?" Her voice was breathless now as he moved to within an inch of her.

Jay gave a frustrated laugh. "She won't be when I get through with her." He brushed her cheek with his finger, then reached around to pull her in for a kiss, but she quickly pulled away, taking giant step back.

"No," she said, her voice breathless. "No more. We had our walk down memory lane, but that's all it was. We were both tired and overwrought and we lost our heads."

He arched an eyebrow at her. "I have never been nor will I ever be 'overwrought.'"

Bridgett's eyes narrowed and she released an exasperated huff. "No, but you are insufferable. You wore me down once, but it won't happen again. You are a client. Nothing else can or will happen." She jerked her chin up in the air, defying him to argue with her.

Jay felt a grin break out—not to mention a very nice hard-on begin to develop—at her belligerent stance. "That would have sounded a lot tougher if I didn't have your panties in my pocket."

Her eyes went wide and wild as she tried to stomp past him, muttering words that sounded both dangerous and sexy. She didn't get far, though. Jay wrapped his fingers around her arm and maneuvered her back against the wall of the plane, just out of the sight line for the door. She opened her mouth to protest but Jay silenced her words with his own lips. He feasted on her mouth, tasting tea and mint and a well-satisfied woman. She could have resisted him, likely doing serious damage with those weapons that doubled as shoes, but after a token slap on the chest, her fingers curled into his suit jacket and she was putty in his hands. Jay worked his thigh between her legs and she made a sweet sound at the back of her throat that had him agonizingly hard.

Voices on the tarmac brought him back to his senses. As much as they both seemed to want each other, they'd have to wait. The idea of having her naked in a bed soon would have to sustain him through the crazy day he had ahead of him. Breaking their kiss, he ran his lips along her neck as she blew out gasping breaths.

Jay tugged at her ear with his teeth. "We're not done, Bridgett. Not even close. I'm beginning to think we never were. Go. Take care of your family while I go take care of mine. But this *is* going to happen again. Count on it."

He pulled back abruptly and wrapped his fingers around her elbow, guiding her to the metal steps leading off the plane to the tarmac. Ron was waiting to intercept her at the bottom. Jay watched as his pilot led her to the waiting town car. Bridgett walked purposefully toward the car without looking back. Jay bit back a smile, confident that he'd won that round.

Nine

"I should have just done what you did and given up on marriage altogether," Gwen said as she stretched out on the chaise in Bridgett's living room. "I could use a cozy little condo like this to lounge around in and sip wine all day."

Bridgett bit back the ugly retort that bubbled up on her lips, cutting her sister some slack for being bitchy. Gwen did have an excuse. *This time.*

The town car had dropped Bridgett off at her condo an hour ago, long enough for her to shower and change into her business-casual work clothes of wool slacks and a cashmere sweater from Talbots. Gwen had descended on her doorstep just as the teakettle began whistling.

"Unfortunately this 'cozy little condo' costs a fortune and I have to work long hours to maintain it. I don't get much time to 'lounge around and sip wine.'"

"Are you saying I'm afraid of a little work?" Gwen's eyes grew damp and her lip began to tremble.

Apparently, everything Bridgett said was going to be

taken out of context this morning. She took another sip of tea and reached for a tissue for her sister. "Will you stop putting words in my mouth, Gwen? You know that's not what I meant. Just keep in mind that the grass isn't always greener."

Gwen went into mother bear mode at Bridgett's words. "Oh, honey. Do you want to talk about it?" She jumped off the chaise and stood beside the bar stool Bridgett was perched on, wrapping an arm over her shoulders. While distracting Gwen might be the only way to survive the morning, Bridgett knew better than to let her sister in on her secrets.

"I've just had a stressful week, that's all."

"I can imagine. Being stranded in a tropical storm with that hunky Jay McManus had to be traumatic."

Bridgett's head whipped around toward her sister. "How did you know who I was with?"

"That nice lawyer, Adam, mentioned it when he came by with the separation papers this morning."

Lovely. The way her life was going, both the Boston office and the Baltimore staff were gossiping about her trip.

"Don't worry." Gwen gave her shoulder a pat. "I didn't tell him that you don't like men."

"Arghh!" Bridgett shrugged off her sister's arm and trudged over to the sink to rinse out her teacup. Clearly her sister was manic. Because there was no doubt that Bridgett did like men. Especially one man in particular. Grateful that her back was to Gwen, she fanned her flushed face with a dish towel. This morning's little tryst at thirty thousand feet had been amazing. The connection that sizzled between their bodies was stronger than ever. She'd been with men since Jay. But none had ever brought her body to such an intense climax as the Antichrist. *Damn him.*

"We're not done, Bridgett. Not even close," the arrogant bastard had the nerve to declare. *"This is going to happen again. Count on it."* She desperately wanted to prove him wrong. Except her panties were already wet just thinking about it.

With a frustrated sigh, she tossed the dish towel onto the

counter and turned to find her sister scrutinizing her carefully.

"Oh, Bridgett," Gwen finally said. "Who did this to you? Who hurt you so badly that you don't feel worthy of love anymore?"

Bridgett reached for the counter before she could lose her balance and collapse on the floor. Her breath was sawing in and out of her lungs at her sister's startling questions. She tried to formulate a coherent response but words failed her.

Gwen walked over and cupped her hands on Bridgett's face to steady her. "Oh, sweetie. Did you think I didn't know?" She did that tsking thing that always annoyed Bridgett, but right now had her hypnotized. "You came back from your internship in Italy a different person. A woman jaded. With a lot harder shell. I know I say things to annoy you sometimes." A squeak escaped Bridgett's throat. "Okay, most of the time. But it's only because I wanted you to open up. To tell me about your broken heart. You're so self-sufficient sometimes it makes me so damn jealous." Tears were streaming down Gwen's face now. "Yes, I want what you have, Bridge. But not the *things*. I want the resolve that you possess. If I'd had one-tenth of it, I'd have left Skip years ago." She gave Bridgett a little shake. "Please tell me I can do this? Please show me how to survive divorce, because I don't think I'll make it otherwise."

Bridgett pulled her sister in for a tight hug. "Of course you're going to survive," she told Gwen. "You have two beautiful children and a family that loves you. Surviving is the only option. Putting the thumbscrews to Skip will be the icing on the cake."

Gwen laughed through her tears. "There's another thing I admire about you, little sister. You're bloodthirsty."

They spent the rest of the morning crafting the separation agreement that Adam would present to Skip later that evening, and then Bridgett accompanied Gwen to lunch with their parents, where they broke the news of the divorce. Neither parent was surprised, a fact that made Gwen cry yet again. Thankfully, their mother stepped in and took over hand-holding duties for the remainder of the day.

"What was Alesha Warren's reaction when you spoke with her this morning?" Stuart asked later that afternoon. Bridgett was seated at her bistro table, basking in the sun streaming in the French doors as they discussed the case by phone.

"Pretty much as expected. She sounded resigned to the fact that she'd have to play her next hand. I'm starting to agree with the conspiracy theory that Donovan has going. It does look more and more like someone is putting her up to this."

Stuart sighed. "Yeah. I think our client is holding something back here, too. This should be an open-and-shut class action case; one that languishes in the court for years and annoys the team because of the slight tarnish on their image and the never-ending court costs. But I get the feeling there's something more going on here. There's a reason she's going after Jay personally. I just don't know what it is."

A trickle of unease ran up Bridgett's spine. Jay had hinted that whoever's behind this case may be serving a personal vendetta, but she'd hoped that he was just being cautious, if not a little paranoid. Except he'd warned her about their secrets getting out. Who had he angered with his secret files in the past? A Google search had revealed that Lloyd Davis had a lot of enemies. Could Jay have carried on the same business practices? Having Stuart raising suspicions made her nervous, because her boss was like a dog with a bone when he thought there was something out of order. She just didn't want him digging so deeply that he unearthed her secret.

"Do we know if Donovan has located Jennifer Knowles yet?" Stuart asked.

"I assumed you'd hear from Jay when they've found her."

Stuart laughed. "You're forgetting, Buffy, that the man is very clear that you're the lead attorney on this case. He doesn't even take my phone calls half the time. Definitely follow up with him this afternoon. I'd also like for the two of you to meet with Mimi first thing tomorrow. Hopefully nothing will hit the fan—or the web—before then."

"That might be difficult."

"I thought his pilot was prepared to bring you back?"

"Yeah, me." She glanced out the window at the sun reflected in the harbor. "Jay left for Napa after we landed here this morning. Something to do with his sister."

"That or a little blackmail recon," Stuart said. "The Blaze play San Francisco on Sunday. I imagine he'll just stay out there. Which means we'll have to take the mountain to Muhammad. Can you leave your sister in the capable hands of Adam and head west? I'll send Mimi out, too, and the three of you can strategize."

"But what about my other case?"

"Don't worry about the chicken farmers. Dan can handle an easy tax case."

"But, Stuart—"

"No buts, Buffy. Trust me, I know neither one of you is happy about how these cases were assigned, but this is what the client wants. And *I* want Jay McManus's business."

Bridgett debated telling her boss just exactly what Jay McManus wanted; it would definitely get her reassigned. But since she'd been more than a complicit partner earlier this morning, she kept her mouth shut. Besides, sticking close to Jay gave her some reassurance that he'd keep their secrets safe. She just needed to figure out how to keep from sticking too close to her client's body.

Jay stood on the balcony off the master bedroom that overlooked his portion of Napa Valley. Bright red flowers bloomed in the boxes lining the iron railing, but as always, Jay's eyes were drawn to the grapes; rows and rows of them in neat lines from the end of the circular driveway to the Napa River below. Behind the canopy of grapes were the foothills surrounding the valley. Above them, white fluffy clouds floated against the perfect blue sky.

Dressed in jeans, a T-shirt, and bare feet, he breathed in

the aroma of the ongoing harvest. Most of the chardonnay grapes had been picked and crushed in August, but workers were now busy harvesting the cabernet grapes as well as the pinot noir. The weather was mild and Jay relaxed as the breeze blew through his damp hair. Bridgett had been right last night: Wine was his passion. A case could be made that it was in his blood.

His father, Jack McManus, had been a vintner from New Zealand who'd come to the United States to study viticulture and bioengineering at Cornell. It was there that he'd met Jay's mother, a bioengineering student herself. They'd married and continued on to pursue graduate degrees at U.C. Berkeley. Jay's father had died of melanoma the day before his son's third birthday. Two summers spent with his grandfather in New Zealand had solidified Jay's passion for all things wine, from growing the grapes to bottling. Unfortunately, the elder John McManus had been a poor businessman. The vineyards were sold at auction upon his death to cover outstanding debts. Through no small feat of his own, Jay had carried on the family tradition. He hoped the two men would have been proud, but, truth be told, Jay had done it for himself. He'd never really known his father or his grandfather that well. Jay's dream was to have something concrete to pass down to his own child someday.

A flash of pink caught his eye, and Jay watched as Charlie spread a towel over one of the lounge chairs beside the pool before pulling off her wrap and laying her bikini-clad body in the sun. She'd been avoiding him since he'd arrived a few hours earlier, but Jay had been only too happy to give his sister her space. He needed time to regroup after the past thirty-six hours and his mad scramble to locate her after she left Baltimore with no word. This was the second time in a week that she'd holed up in one of Jay's homes as opposed to the seven left to her by her late father. Even more telling, she'd come to California alone.

Deciding he'd put their confrontation off long enough, he made his way downstairs and toward the pool area. The pool was built to look like a tropical lagoon with rocks lining one end of the sea-green water, while a wood pergola hung over its other end. Tall Italian cypress trees shielded the spot from the eyes of the many workers gathering the grapes a few hundred yards away. Grabbing some necessary armor—in the form of a cold beer from the poolside kitchen—Jay stretched out on the lounge chair next to Charlie. Closing his eyes against the afternoon sun, he took a long sip from his beer.

"No wonder you have that awful farmer's tan," his sister said. "Ever think of putting on a bathing suit?"

"You would be the expert in tan lines. According to the tabloids, you've been skinny-dipping in Thailand."

"Don't believe everything you read."

"I wouldn't have to if you communicated with me."

"I'm communicating with you now."

Jay took another fortifying swig of his beer. Charlie was baiting him, angling for a fight, probably thinking it was her best defense to get him to leave her alone. She was wrong.

"What are you doing here, Charlie?"

"What are *you* doing here, Jay?"

Jay swore ruthlessly under his breath. "Charlotte Elizabeth, answer the damn question!"

She flinched beside him. "I'm growing my baby. I'd hoped to do it in private, but since you arrived with your entourage, it seems that won't be the case."

He blew out a frustrated sigh. "If you wanted to be alone, you would have picked one of your own houses. You knew the Blaze are playing here this weekend. I've invited a houseful of people for Saturday night."

"Who says I'm staying until Saturday?"

Jay risked a glance at her then. His sister's face was drawn tight and her eyes were red rimmed and swollen. She looked nothing like a woman aglow with pregnancy. Clearly, she wasn't handling her condition as well as he'd thought she was. Reaching a hand across to her, Jay took her fingers in his. "I had hoped you would stay. These parties are no fun."

"So you want me to share in your torture?" A weak smile appeared on her face. "Why do you even play host if you enjoy them so little?"

"I have an image to maintain."

They both chuckled but neither of them withdrew their hand. Instead, they sat there in companionable silence for a few moments before Linc ambled out from Jay's office.

"Did you have to bring your puppy dog?" Charlie asked, yanking her hand away.

Jay bit back a grin. There wasn't a woman alive who Linc couldn't charm, and Jay suspected his sister liked his affable young assistant more than she let on. Jay tucked that observation away in case he needed it in the future. "Kennels are so expensive these days."

"He's annoying," she said loud enough for Linc to hear as he approached.

"Hmm. He says the same thing about you."

Linc ignored Charlie's barb, instead greeting her with his most mesmerizing smile, turning up the wattage until his sister was forced to look away. "I've arranged for a car to pick up Ms. Janik. They left Boston an hour ago, so she should be arriving here at the vineyard sometime after eight our time."

"More people are coming tonight?" Charlie huffed beside him, sounding a lot like she had when she was eleven.

"Just my lawyer."

"Why can't she stay in town? Some of the state's best B and Bs are there."

"I know," Jay said. "I'm putting the media specialist who's also coming to this meeting up in one."

"Jay," Charlie cried. "I'm in a delicate state here. I'd really prefer not to have to interact with strangers."

He ignored the tears. Years of her crying wolf had toughened him up to her antics. "Don't worry. I'll be the only one 'interacting' with her." With any luck, most of their interaction tonight would be in the king-sized bed in his bedroom. But Jay wanted Bridgett to meet Charlie, too. Throughout that summer long ago, he'd often imagined what would happen when the two people he loved the most met. Too bad the years had erased the people that the three of them once were.

"Fine," Charlie snapped. "But don't expect me to be nice to her."

Linc opened his mouth to add his two cents before wisely thinking better of it. "I have an update, also, when you get a chance," he said instead.

Obviously, whatever it was, it was something Charlie didn't need to hear. While he appreciated Lincoln's circumspection, his jaw tightened in apprehension of what his assistant—and Donovan Carter—had uncovered. "I'll be right in after I finish my beer."

With a nod to Jay, Linc gave Charlie a salute and headed back into the house.

Charlie tsked. "You two are up to no good again. Let me guess: The feminists and the cheerleaders are ganging up on you and burning their bras and pom-poms at Sunday's game?"

"Funny." Jay guzzled the remainder of his beer. "Just boring business matters to take care of. We don't want to put you to sleep." He stood from the chair and turned to walk away.

"Jay," she called. "I really don't feel up to traveling right now, so I guess I'll stay for your stupid party."

Some of the tension he'd been holding in seeped out of his body. He smiled at her. "I'm glad." He took a few more steps before turning back to her. "Listen, I have meetings in the morning, but maybe tomorrow we can head down to Stanford and have dinner with Mom?"

Charlie shot from the chair. "Hell, no! I told you I didn't want Mom to know until I had a plan."

"It's just dinner, Charlie. Not true confessions. It's not like anyone can tell you're expecting."

She glanced off into the setting sun and Jay swore at himself when he glimpsed tears in her eyes again. "It would be a lie of omission."

"Every day you don't tell her is a lie of omission."

Her face was tormented when she finally looked at him. "You're a prick, you know that?"

"I've been called worse." He shrugged. "Suit yourself. I don't even know if Mom is free tomorrow." He marched toward his office, wondering why the hell he even dealt with his sister or his mother. Or women in general. But then his memory drifted back to the mind-numbing sex he'd had with Bridgett this morning and a slow grin spread over his face. Sex was the only form of communication he could handle with women. And tonight he and Bridgett would be conversing between the silk sheets upstairs.

Linc was on the phone when Jay strolled into the office. He signaled for Jay to close the door leading to the patio. "It's Donovan. I'll put him on speaker."

"Please tell me you've found this cheerleader, Don," Jay said as he sat down on the leather sofa across from his desk.

"I wish I could. I really do." Don sounded as defeated as Jay felt. "I just keep coming up against dead ends everywhere I turn. Even her parents have disappeared. According to the church where her mother works, they've gone to Missouri to visit a sick relative."

"She hasn't been on social media since the case was filed a week ago," Linc added.

"I take it you're on your way to Missouri," Jay asked.

Don growled something unintelligible.

"The team doesn't travel out here until Friday night," Jay said. "That gives you forty-eight hours to find this woman. I just want to know who's behind this lawsuit. If it's just her sister-in-law's attempt to finance her own pocketbook, then we'll deal with it in court. But if it's something more, I want to be prepared. This ought to be a cakewalk for you, Don. After all, she's not a hardened criminal."

"Yeah, yeah." Don sighed loudly. "Just don't tell the guys over at NCIS that I'm chasing down cheerleaders, okay?"

Linc laughed. "Good thing your wife works for the team. At least she can't take offense to the hunt for the Blaze cheerleader."

Donovan was married to the team's public relations director, Asia Dupree. "Actually, she may be of some assistance when I do find Jennifer Knowles. She's more likely to open up to Asia than to me."

"If you're asking if your wife can join you on your road trip, that's up to Hank," Jay said. "But I'll be sure to tell him your idea has a lot of merit."

Linc disconnected and glanced past Jay's shoulder out toward the pool area.

"Something on your mind, Linc?"

"Just that for a pregnant woman, your sister still looks hot."

"I've been jonesing to punch someone for two days. One more word and it'll guarantee that it's you."

"I just meant that if we're trying to pin down a time frame for . . . you know . . . when she actually got pregnant, it had to be recent. She can still carry off a bikini without being obvious."

Jay rose slowly from the sofa, but Linc held his ground. "Remember, that's my baby sister you're ogling, Linc. Even if it's under the guise of detective work."

"Sure, boss." Linc reached for a folder on the desk. "By the way, according to the PI following her friend Blaine, he arrived in the area at about noon today. He's staying with a group of friends over in St. Helena."

Swearing beneath his breath, Jay took the folder. "Just as long as he stays away from my house."

"That's the case list you'll need for your meeting with the media consultant tomorrow. I took the liberty of making them each their own copy. She's set to arrive at ten. Is there anything else you need me to do to get ready for that meeting?"

Jay thumbed through the list of outrageous claims made by women once in his employ—some he'd met, a few he'd slept with, but most he'd never even laid eyes on, much less any other part of his body. But if his hunch was correct, there was one person manipulating those claims. And it was the same person likely behind Jennifer Knowles's class action suit and her lawyer's blackmail threats.

"Yeah." Jay walked over to his desk, picked up a pen, and

scratched a name on a piece of paper. "I want you to find this person for me." He handed the paper to his assistant.

Linc eyed the piece of paper before looking up at Jay expectantly. "All I get is a name to go on?"

"Nope," Jay said as he headed out to find his vineyard manager. "You'll find a complete dossier in the file of former employees on the McManus hard drive." He paused before heading toward the winery. "And, Linc, the sooner you can get me their whereabouts, the better."

Ten

The sun had set nearly an hour before, but Bridgett
had no trouble picturing the scenery as the chauffeured car
carefully snaked its way through the twists and turns leading
to Jay's vineyard. She'd avoided this area of California for
this very reason: It would remind her too much of that summer spent in Italy. The headlights illuminated the rows upon
rows of grapes, their rich fragrance signifying that the harvest was in full swing. The car came around another curve
and passed through iron gates. The drive was lined with olive
trees, their craggy trunks wide and twisted, indicative of
their longevity in the vineyard. Landscape lighting lit up a
sprawling house built in the style of an Italian villa, with
multiple terraces and alcoves seated behind a circular drive
complete with a fountain in its center.

The driver parked the car at the front door and climbed
out. Bridgett wasn't able to move as quickly. Her stomach
bottomed out at the overwhelming beauty of the estate surrounding her. *It wasn't fair.* How could Jay live in a place
so steeped in memories of their summer together while she
avoided anything that triggered those thoughts? For the tenth

time in the last four hours, she cursed Stuart for sending her on this errand.

Her door was opened and she was greeted by the sound of the fountain's spray mingling with the chorus of crickets and tree frogs. Bridgett looked up, expecting to see the driver; instead her heart nearly stopped in her chest. Jay was standing in the driveway, waiting to help her out of the car. But it wasn't the cool, buttoned-up Jay who rode roughshod over the business world and the NFL. This Jay was the man she'd fallen in love with all those years ago, looking sexy as hell in his worn jeans, work boots, and a faded Blaze T-shirt.

"Welcome to my vineyard, Bridgett." He held out his hand to help her out.

Bridgett didn't dare touch him. Tears burned the backs of her eyes at the very sight of him. He wasn't supposed to look this calm and unaffected. She wasn't sure if she wanted to kiss him or slug him, and she hated the feeling of being so out of control. It was just that she was exhausted from the long day, she reminded herself. She was here for business, nothing else. Ignoring his hand and the memories of this morning in his jet, she climbed out of the car unaided.

"I told the driver to take me to the B and B where Mimi is staying," she snapped, letting her anger serve as a shield between the two of them.

"Mimi got the last room," he said as he guided her into the lavish two-story foyer.

He was lying; she was sure of it. But when she turned to call him on it, she was stopped by the weariness on his face. Sure, he was dressed as he used to all those years ago, but his face was older, more wary—harder somehow. She recognized it instantly because she felt the same way, deep in her soul.

"Surely there's more than one hotel in this area," she asked with a little less bluster.

A corner of his mouth eased up as if he'd won somehow. "None that would be nearly as accommodating as you deserve."

No, no, no! There wasn't going to be any more "accommodating" or anything else. She was here for a meeting and nothing more. All she had to do was remember that Jay was the enemy. That and keep her panties where they belonged.

"Look, it's been a really long day and I just want a quiet place to get some sleep. If you could just show me to my room now, that would be great."

He looked as if he might say something else, but then he just nodded. "This is Josie Campos. She's in charge of the house. She'll take you upstairs."

Embarrassed that she'd likely come off as a total bitch in front of a stranger, Bridgett turned to find a middle-aged woman with caramel eyes and thick dark hair braided to one side standing quietly near the stairs. She wore a denim shirt, khaki pants, and very bright smile. "If you're on East Coast time, you must be exhausted," she said. "Follow me. I'll show you to your room."

The room Josie took her to was more like a luxury suite, complete with a huge bed and a sweeping wrought iron balcony overlooking the vineyards. A fluffy robe hung from an antique dress stand in the corner of the room. Directly across from it was a beautiful hand-carved table with a basket of fresh fruit, some nuts, and some chocolates. A small glass-door fridge held wine as well as bottled water.

"It's nicer than any hotel in the area," Josie said proudly.

Bridgett didn't doubt that. "Yes, I'm sure it is." She gave the woman a warm smile, hoping to erase her earlier impression.

"The bath is through that door." Josie pointed to a large ornately carved mahogany door that stood slightly ajar. From what she could see, the bathroom was huge and as richly appointed as the bedroom. Suddenly, a soak in a hot tub sounded heavenly to Bridgett. "Mr. McManus says you're a tea drinker. Is there anything else you'd like with breakfast tomorrow?" the housekeeper asked.

She'd have loved a cup of tea right then, but she wanted to be alone with her schizophrenic thoughts even more. Bridgett would make do with a bottle of water and a bath before bed. "Whatever you have will be perfect. Thank you."

When Josie left, Bridgett grabbed her toiletries bag from

her suitcase, suddenly remembering Jay's thoughtfulness in buying her a toothbrush the night before. *And the tea.* That was twice he'd remembered to let his staff know about her preference for tea over coffee. She shook her head fiercely as she reached for the fluffy robe. He wanted her. Jay had made that clear numerous times this past week. These weren't small gestures from a man who cared about her heart. It was the rest of her body he was after.

Ten minutes later, having lit the numerous votive candles surrounding the soaking tub, she sank into the warm bubbly water, rested her head back against the neck roll, and closed her eyes. It had already been a twenty-hour day—and she'd felt every minute of it. The sound of a cork leaving a bottle brought her back to her senses.

"You're awake." Jay stood at one end of the bathroom where he poured white wine into a glass.

"I most certainly am," she hissed. "And have you ever heard of knocking?"

Ignoring her, he ambled over to the tub handing her the glass. "Try it. I'm eager to get your opinion."

"Jay! Do you accost all your guests this way?"

He had the audacity to wink at her. "Not the men." Jay pushed the glass farther toward her. "Take it, Bridgett. I think you'll like it."

Fuming, she took the wine from his outstretched hand. "Fine, but only if you promise to leave."

With a sly grin, he poured himself a glass and leaned a hip against one of the marble countertops, in no hurry to quit the room. Still dressed in his jeans and T-shirt, he'd removed his work boots. The image of Jay standing in his bare feet a yard away from where she sat naked in the soapy water felt very intimate. And erotic. She wanted to hurl the wine at him.

"How's your sister," he asked. The sincerity in his voice confused her already frustrated body even more.

Bridgett sighed. "It'll be a bumpy ride, but she'll be fine." Begrudgingly she took a sip of wine, hoping it would speed his exit. The white was cool and crisp on her tongue. Its full-bodied flavor was fruity and refreshingly creamy when she swallowed. "Pinot grigio," she murmured as her eyes slid closed again. The wine had been their favorite all those years ago. "It's very good," she said before taking another sip.

"Hmm," he agreed. "This is our initial foray in producing the Alsace style. Our first few years, we concentrated on the lighter, less aromatic, lower-alcohol pinots. They're extremely popular here in the United States. But I wanted the richer, more alcoholic version, like the French drink. I think with some decent promotion, it can be just as trendy as the other pinots."

Bridgett glared at him. "So you can get women drunk in the bathtub and seduce them?"

He laughed, damn him. "I think we proved this morning that I don't have to get you drunk." Setting down his wineglass, he reached over his shoulder and pulled his shirt off in one fluid motion.

She hid her gasp behind another sip of the delicious wine. "You are not getting into this tub with me," she declared even though her thighs trembled at the prospect. The tub was large enough to accommodate them both comfortably.

"I've been out in the field for the last several hours," he said. "I don't think you'd appreciate my sweaty body in the tub with you."

Bridgett tried to summon up some gratitude that he wasn't going to be joining her bath, but the effort became short-lived when she saw him head for the glass enclosure housing the large massage shower.

"What are you doing?" she asked.

He glanced over his shoulder at her. "Again with the obvious questions, counselor?"

"Go take a shower in your own bathroom, Jay." Realization hit her as soon as the words left her mouth. This *was* his bathroom. *Double damn.* She watched as his mouth turned up in a seductive, assured grin. "I'm not sleeping with you in that bed," she said, her voice hoarse. She told herself the disappointment she felt was only because she wouldn't be sleeping in the beautiful bedroom.

"Finish your bath and your wine, Bridgett. We can negotiate the sleeping arrangements after my shower." He was infuriatingly arrogant.

"That is so not gonna—"

She was interrupted by a loud crash from somewhere outside the open veranda door. Jay moved quickly through the bedroom as Bridgett heard laugher coming from outside—both a woman's and a man's. A string of profanity rolled off Jay's lips as he sprinted out of the bedroom calling for his assistant, Lincoln.

Bridgett climbed out of the tub and pulled on the robe, tying it securely at her waist just as more commotion from outside drifted through the open door. She made her way outside onto the terrace where she could see a gorgeous pool lit up by dim lights. Suddenly Jay appeared to tackle a man standing in the shadows. A woman screamed.

"Jay! Stop it! You'll hurt him!"

She cringed as she heard some grunting and the sound of fist meeting bone before Linc's voice entered the fray.

"Boss, don't kill him. Let the cops handle this."

"Kill him? Cops?" The woman's voice was shrill in the dark night. "Jay, leave him alone! I invited him here."

The skirmish had stopped. Bridgett could hear the heavy breathing of both men.

"Does he have the right to be here, Charlie?" Jay asked, his tone lethal. "Does he?"

Bridgett didn't understand Jay's question or the charged silence that followed.

"No!" Charlie finally yelled, the word coming out on a defeated-sounding sob.

She heard hushed voices and the sound of shoes crunching on the gravel.

"Do you really think drinking is wise right now, Charlie?" Jay eventually asked.

"For your information, jerk-off, I *wasn't* drinking. I was just giving Blaine a tasting."

Jay muttered something Bridgett had trouble deciphering

due to the distance. It was something about the vineyard being private property.

"Oh, so what you're saying is that my friends aren't welcome here," Charlie shouted. "I should have just gone to Carmel to my own house. I don't need you playing chaperone for me or my baby!"

Oh my.

"What was I supposed to think, Charlie?" Jay stood with his tender fists clenched on his hips, staring down his sister. Tears of rage were streaming down her cheeks. "There was a strange guy drinking my wine beside my pool at night."

"Oh, come on, Jay," Charlie cried. "You've been angling to punch some guy out about my pregnancy since the moment I told you. Blaine just happened to be in the right place at the right time."

"No, he was in the wrong place. Why is he here? Did he follow you from Baltimore?" Jay's head was aching as badly as his fists right now. "Did you ask him to? If he's not the father, then who is he to you? The guy's a freaking weed dealer, Charlie."

"That's not fair! He doesn't actually sell the stuff himself."

Jay didn't bother responding to her. If the dickhead sold marijuana—even legally—he most likely used it and he didn't want to hear Charlie defend Blaine with more lies. Nor did he want his unborn niece or nephew exposed to drugs. "I may not know a lot about prenatal care, but I'm pretty sure cannabis isn't on the recommended diet."

Charlie staggered back as though he'd actually hit her, too.

Linc emerged from the shadows. "He won't be back."

"Ohmigod! What did you do to him?" Charlie pulled out her cell phone, presumably to call Blaine the Pain.

"Go to bed, Charlie," Jay said as he began walking back toward the house. "You need your rest."

"You're a bastard, you know that? And I'm not going to

bed! I am so *not* sleeping in this house." Charlie all but stomped her foot. "I'm leaving."

Jay's gut told him she wouldn't leave. Charlie had sought him out for some reason. His instincts told him to wait her out. Hell, it was likely his little sister didn't even know the reason she was here herself yet. But she wouldn't take off. Of that he was reasonably sure. Calling her bluff, he continued on toward the house, exchanging a quick glance with Linc. By some slim chance Jay was wrong, he'd have his assistant keep tabs on Charlie. Linc let out an exasperated sigh before nodding his acquiescence to Jay's nonverbal order.

When he made it back to his suite, he was relieved to see that Bridgett hadn't decamped to another room in the house. Wrapped in the fluffy bathrobe, she was seated in one of the wingback chairs with her bare feet tucked beneath her, her glass of wine in her hand. Jay didn't bother speaking—he had no doubt Bridgett had overheard everything. Instead he headed directly for the bathroom and that shower he needed. He was rinsing his bruised knuckles under cold water when she followed him in with a towel filled with ice.

Taking his right hand between her two smaller ones, she laid the ice pack over top. She kept her eyes on her task while she spoke. "So, Princess Charlotte is pregnant."

"So she says."

It was the wrong thing to say and Jay knew it. But the pain from her lie all those years ago still burned. When Bridgett's eyes rose to meet his, they were wide with incredulous fury. Jay flinched when she squeezed the ice over his sore knuckles.

"You're sister's right—you are a bastard."

She started to walk away, but Jay reached out and grabbed the belt of the robe and pulled her against him. "I must be, because after everything that happened that summer, I still want you."

Her fists found his chest and she began to pummel him.

"I hate you. I hate this beautiful house. This vineyard. It's everything we dreamed of. And *you* have it. Without me."

Jay let her pound on him, glad that she didn't pack much of a punch. She was going to think he was an even bigger bastard after he spoke. "If you want it, it's yours, Bridgett. The house. The vineyard. All of it."

"What I want is for you to believe me," she whispered.

He wasn't sure what Bridgett meant by her plea but he was sure he'd never believe or trust her with his heart again. But it seemed that little technicality didn't matter to the parts of his body that wanted her. "Whether I believe you or not doesn't matter anymore."

Tears spilled out of her sad eyes. Jay pressed a finger to her lips to keep her from responding. He was done talking. "This is all that matters," he said, replacing his finger with his lips.

She smelled like the floral bath soap Josie left out for guests. Beneath his tongue, her skin was salty from the tears she'd been shedding. Not wanting to be reminded of her anger or sadness any longer, he urged her mouth open with his own, tasting the creamy, crisp pinot grigio on her tongue as his swept over it. He groaned when her nails scraped along the bare skin of his chest. She'd likely meant for it to hurt him but instead her hands were turning him on even more.

He let her break the kiss but he kept his arms loosely wrapped around her. "I hate you," she whispered as her fist made contact with his chest again.

Jay slid a hand beneath the robe to palm her round ass. She sucked in a breath when his finger traced her wet seam. "I can feel how much you hate me."

She head-butted him in the chest. "That doesn't mean anything."

"It means we're good together, Bridgett," he breathed against her ear as his finger explored a little deeper. "You can come to the vineyard whenever you want. Live here. It doesn't matter to me." She sighed and her body arched

against his. "I don't care if you hate me; I'll give you this"—
he flicked his finger inside of her—"morning, noon, and night
if that's what you want."

Bridgett nipped at his chest and Jay was having trouble
keeping his pants on. He needed to hurry the negotiations
along. "Neither of our hearts ever has to be in play." She stilled
against him and Jay wondered if he'd taken it too far. Losing
wasn't an option, though, so he stroked again, lingering at the
spot that always made her come unglued. "Take what I'm
offering, Bridgett. You know you want to."

She glanced up then and her gray eyes were dark and
heavy. "We can't be those two people again, can we?"

Something squeezed in his chest but he refused to
acknowledge it. "No. Never. They were too innocent to survive." He leaned down and let his lips hover over hers. "This
is what we're left with, Bridgett. Take it."

He kissed her then, his hands leaving her body to tangle
in her hair, damp on the ends from her bath. Her own arms
stretched up over his shoulders in compliance, allowing him
to delve deeper into her mouth. Jay was done with negotiating with his words; it was time to use his body to prove his
point. With his leg, he pushed her robe open and maneuvered her so she was riding his jean-clad thigh. He felt her
moan at the back of her throat and he continued his conquest
of her mouth while she rocked over him.

His lips left hers to explore her neck as he pushed the robe
off her shoulders.

"Jay," she whispered when his fingers found her bare
breasts. "Please."

He bent her over his outstretched arm and his mouth hovered over her breasts. "Please what, Bridgett? Tell me what
you want."

Her fingers dug into his shoulders and she released a
throaty sigh when he blew on her firm nipple. "I want . . ."

Jay let his tongue play with her areola. "What do you
want, Bridgett?" he demanded. His own arousal was painful
and Jay was desperate to get her into his bed. But he found

that he was even more desperate to have her agree to his terms. "Say it."

"I want . . . I want you." She thrust against his thigh when his mouth closed around her other nipple. "Please."

"As long as you know you won't get all of me, Bridgett." He was breathing heavy now as lust rolled through him.

"Damn it, Jay," she cried. "Stop teasing."

Jay scooped her up into his arms and carried her to his bed. Shucking his jeans, he slowly crawled over her flushed body, letting his fingers, his lips, and his tongue touch all the places that were once so familiar to him until Bridgett was writhing beneath him.

"In a hurry, counselor?"

Her fingers dug into his skull when he settled between her legs, his shoulders pressing them wide. His lips trailed over the familiar tiny birthmark on the inside of her left thigh before his tongue found her entrance. He'd wanted to taste her this morning, but their hookup had been frantic— not to mention incredibly arousing—and he never got the chance. Now he took his time using his mouth to slowly let the pleasure build within her. But apparently slow wasn't on Bridgett's agenda today because, like this morning, she came in a rush, her body arching beneath his mouth.

Jay kissed his way along her smooth inner thighs, giving her a moment to relax, but she continued to fidget. He smiled against her skin before going in for seconds. This time he'd make her relax. Bridgett gasped as he teased her sweet spot, bringing her close and then backing off again and again. Her hands clutched at the blankets and she moaned his name before he finally set her free. This time she collapsed onto the mattress, sated and still.

Bridgett's eyes were closed when he braced himself on his forearms above her, and Jay felt a measure of relief. That summer, she had always held him spellbound when they'd made love, her eyes wide-open, giving him a window to her soul. Everything she felt and desired, she let him see. It was heady and humbling all at the same time. But he didn't want that connection tonight—or any night. What they shared from now on would be strictly carnal in nature. This was about sex and enjoying each other's bodies. Nothing more.

Her fingers suddenly wrapped around him, the feel of her not-so-gentle stroking forcing his own eyes closed. Jay nuzzled her neck as Bridgett's hand worked him over, bringing him too close to the edge. Nipping her shoulder, he sat back on his heels. He needn't have worried about seeing that young innocent girl again because the woman staring at him beneath her half-open eyelids was no innocent. She knew exactly what she was doing when she wrapped both hands around him.

Jay's breath caught in his lungs at the picture she presented spread out beneath him, her aroused body flushed from head to toe. Grabbing both her wrists, he reluctantly pulled her hands off his now painful arousal and placed each hand beside her head. Her eyes were wide-open now, daring him to look away but, damn it, he couldn't do it. She watched silently, her chin set at that belligerent angle that she never used to have, as he rolled the condom on.

Leaning back over her, he took her lips in a deep, plundering kiss. Jay's tongue tangled with hers as he slowly slid inside her. Her warmth enveloped him and it felt so good he held himself still and groaned in pleasure. Bridgett wrapped her legs around him, sliding the arch of one foot over his ass before she linked her feet together on his lower back. She sought out his hands and intertwined her fingers with his as he began to move in and out of her. Sucking on his tongue, she rolled her hips to allow him deeper access. Jay couldn't take it any longer. He set a vigorous pace that was rough, erotic, and nothing like the way he'd ever treated Bridgett that summer. She responded with soft sounds of encouragement while their bodies moved as one. Jay felt her tightening around him just as she pulled her mouth from his.

"Oh God, Jay," she breathed. Her neck arched back while a satisfied cry escaped her throat.

Jay couldn't hold on any longer, and as he followed her over the edge, his eyes flew open and locked with hers, wide and damp. He swore.

"I hate that it's so good with you," she whispered. "You've ruined me for anyone else."

A feeling of smug satisfaction came over him. Jay leaned in and placed an openmouthed kiss on the sensitive skin beneath her ear. "Good," he said, completely ignoring the niggling fear that he may be ruining both of them.

Eleven

Bridgett loved to explore the vineyards first thing in the morning. Spying several bikes leaning against one of the utility buildings next to the winery, she hopped on one with a wicker basket on its handlebars. It was large enough to hold her camera. The grapes had all been tied into clusters to form canopies and she wanted to get some pictures of the spectacular Italian countryside to send back home to her family in Boston.

The area was surrounded by the Alps and Dolomites and bordered Austria and Switzerland. Bridgett had been surprised to find the perfect rows of grapes located in the northernmost regions in Italy. According to the family hosting her for the summer, only fifteen percent of the mountainous territory was farmable. And the DiSantis family had been harvesting grapes for wine production for centuries. While the charity she interned for hadn't assigned her to Florence or Milan as she'd hoped, Bridgett knew her sisters would be envious of the scenery at least.

Jetta, one of the family's truffle-harvesting dogs, followed Bridgett down the narrow dirt lane, but stopped once she'd reached the main road leading to the village. Bridgett loved to explore the village's old buildings, which had been built by the Austrians long before the area became a part of Italy. Today she'd take advantage of the bright June sunshine and photograph the centuries-old stone chapel across from the clinic where she was working with a Catholic nun who'd taught her chemistry in high school. She was in Italy for six months while she figured out what to do with the rest of her life and Bridgett figured she'd see everything she could while she had the chance.

Less than a mile into her trek, the chain on her bicycle snapped, causing Bridgett to lurch to a halt. Her right foot landed ankle deep in the mud, caking her brand-new Skechers sneaker as though it were quicksand. She groaned. Her sister Ashley had just sent them and Bridgett loved those shoes.

She was still straddling the bike, trying to figure out a way to get her foot out of the mud without leaving her shoe behind when an old Isuzu pickup truck came over the hill in front of her. The truck stopped a few yards ahead and she was surprised to see a young man dressed in a Green Day T-shirt, faded jeans, and Sorel work boots emerge from the driver's seat. Everything about him screamed American. Loose limbed with an easy smile, he nearly knocked Bridgett off her bike with his gorgeous blue eyes.

"Are you okay?" he asked in perfect English. Genuine concern was in his voice and in his expression.

"I'm just a little stuck," Bridgett said shyly. She was relieved not to have to converse in Italian, since her command of the language was barely passable.

His smile grew more relaxed, if that was even possible, as he glanced down at the broken chain. "That's the sorry thing about bikes—no place for a spare. Not even a spare chain." He crouched down close to her, getting a good glimpse of her leg beneath her cropped shorts, making Bridgett extremely grateful she'd used a razor that morning. "I don't think that can be fixed here. Why don't you climb off and I'll see if there's something in the truck's toolbox to fix it."

Bridgett wiggled her sneakered foot. "It's my foot that's stuck. I'm afraid if I get off, my new shoe will be left behind."

He shook his head but his eyes were laughing at her. "What is it with women and their shoes?" He took a step closer and grabbed onto the bike's crossbar. "Here, put your hand on my shoulder for some leverage and pull. Hopefully the shoe will stay on."

His T-shirt was soft but his shoulder was solid muscle underneath it. Bridgett looked down at her feet in order to hide her embarrassing reaction to his body beneath her hand. She yanked her foot free but, of course, her shoe stayed put. Gripping his shoulder a little harder than she wanted to, she drew her leg over the bike and stood beside him, one foot bare on the road.

Her rescuer handed her the bike before stepping around it and retrieving her muddy shoe from the quagmire beside the road. "Let's take this over to the truck and see if we can fix you both up."

She hobbled over to his pickup and he lowered the back tailgate for her to sit on. He dug through the contents of the back and pulled out a towel that he then used to wipe off her sneaker as best he could. Bridgett went to take it from him but he held it away from her, his eyes twinkling.

"Oh no, you get the full Prince Charming treatment," he said as he leaned down to put her shoe on her foot. "Just don't tell my little sister I played Cinderella with anyone else but her." He winked at her before untying her sneaker and sliding it on her foot. "And it fits." Bridgett nearly melted beneath the glow of his satisfied grin.

He lifted the bike up on the tailgate beside her, carefully handing Bridgett her camera from inside the basket. "I guess I'm going to have to do the work of the fairy god-mother as well and fix your coach. Too bad we're not in a pumpkin patch."

"Really, it's okay. I can walk back to the manor house from here. It's not far." While Bridgett didn't want to incon-venience him any longer, the thought of never seeing him again left an unsettled feeling deep in her belly.

"*Nonsense. Charlie would strip me of my crown if I let you walk back.*" *He dug into the toolbox.*

"*Charlie?*"

"*Hmm,*" *he said, pulling out a wrench.* "*My very own princess of a little sister. She's eight.*"

Bridgett smiled at the thought of this devastatingly handsome guy lavishing all his attention on a younger sister. "*And not a bit spoiled by her older brother, I'm sure.*"

He gave her a wicked grin then and Bridgett felt a stirring deep in her core. "*Hey, what's the use of having a younger sibling if you can't spoil them so they annoy your parents?*"

She thought of her brother Brody, the baby of the Janik family, spoiled rotten by four older sisters.

Turning back to the bike, he began to work on the chain. "*So obviously, given your thick Italian accent, you were born and raised here in Trentino?*"

Her smile grew at his teasing and she relaxed as she watched him work. "*More like Boston.*"

"*Ahh, a chowder girl.*"

Bridgett rolled her eyes at the popular quip. "*How about you, local boy?*"

"*I call lots of places home. Mom's a professor so I grew up in college towns mostly but I spent my teenage years in Manhattan.*"

"*Ah, a worldly prince.*"

The chain broke in a second spot and her rescuer swore under his breath. "*How far did you say that walk was?*"

"*Not far. I'm staying at the DiSantis vineyards. I can certainly manage. You've been very kind, but I won't keep you any longer.*" *She reached for the bike, but he shoved it farther into the truck bed.*

"*Well, Cinderella, this is your lucky day. I'm on my way to meet with the harvest manager there. I'll give you a lift.*" *The wariness must have shown in her face because he extended his hand, a sober expression now on his face.* "*Jay McManus at your service. I swear I'm not an ax murderer.*"

Bridgett glanced at his hand, strong yet elegant. "*Isn't that what they all say right before they chop off the obnoxiously naïve woman's head?"*

He smiled that breathtaking smile again and Bridgett had to work not to fall off the tailgate. *"Yep, you're definitely a tough Boston girl."*

She shook his hand warmly. *"Bridgett Janik, and if something happens to me, I have three sisters and a little brother who'll hunt you down and kill you."*

Jay walked her around to the passenger side of the truck before opening the door and helping her in. *"A big family, huh? My college roommate comes from a large Chicago family. I'm thinking they can take yours,"* he said with a wink.

The five-minute drive to the vineyard was much too short for Bridgett. Jay explained he was in Italy as a summer intern, learning the ropes to growing grapes for wine production. His goal was to open a winery in Northern California. He was visiting the DiSantis vineyard to learn about the process for growing pinot gris grapes in order to make pinot grigio, a wine that was becoming extremely popular in the United States.

"Do you like wine?" he asked, his enthusiasm for the subject making Bridgett smile.

"I'm not a big drinker," she said as he pulled the truck in front of the winery. It was a little bit of a lie, but her college friends mostly drank beer when they weren't pretending to be Carrie and her friends from *Sex and the City* and drinking cosmos. *"So I don't know much about wine, I'm afraid."*

"You're in the heart of wine country and you don't know about wine?" he exclaimed as he cut the ignition. *"We need to change that, Cinderella. Today."*

She spent the rest of the day trailing behind Jay, Vincenzo DiSantis and Giovanni, the master vintner, as they discussed grapes, specifically the deep pink pinot grigio grapes. Bridgett learned that the grigio style was achieved by harvesting the grapes relatively early, in an attempt to retain as much fresh acidity as possible. To retain the freshness and "zing" of the wine, fermentation and storage took place in stainless-steel tanks. If barrels were used, Jay explained to *her, this would add palate weight and sweet vanilla-like aromas, which would take away from the clean, simple style the wine is famous for. He told her that pinot grigio wines were almost always intended for consumption within a year or two of harvest, making long-term cellaring unnecessary.*

Later that afternoon, Jay poured her a glass from a bottle Giovanni had just uncorked. "Tell me this isn't smooth on the palate, Cinderella," he said before saluting her with his own glass and taking a healthy swallow. She watched his expression as he savored the wine. Jay studied her just as intently when she took her own tentative sip. But the wine was delicious, crisp and fruity at the same time. Bridgett took another drink and smiled at him. The heat in his eyes as he returned the smile had her gulping down her first glass of pinot grigio.

They spent the next two weeks in each other's company. Bridgett would spend the day at the clinic, and Jay would retrieve her in his battered pickup and they'd explore the countryside, tasting wine and local cuisine as they went. He told her about his sister, whom he obviously adored, and she told him about her uncertainty over what she wanted to do with her life. Jay teased her about becoming a nun, flirting with her about what he might have to do to dissuade her. Still, it was two weeks before he kissed her. And another week before he slowly divested her of her clothes in an inn outside of Verona and made love to her. Despite her involvement with the nuns, Bridgett hadn't been a virgin. Yet her previous sexual encounters had been bumbling and sophomoric compared to the way Jay brought her body to life. He made her feel like a woman should feel. And Bridgett couldn't help but fall in love with him.

Bridgett awoke with a start, her dream of Italy so vivid she could actually smell the grapes of the DiSantis vineyard in the bedroom surrounding her. It took a moment for her to come to her senses and realize the fragrance she was inhaling came from Jay's vineyard. Another moment later, she remembered she was in his bed. Naked. She slammed her eyes shut and groaned as she flopped back down on the pillow.

"And to think, you used to be a morning person."

She cracked her eyelids open, letting her gaze take in the beautiful room—even more gorgeous in the daytime. Sunlight streamed through the terrace door, open just wide enough to let the fresh morning air permeate the room. Jay was seated at a desk in the far corner, typing out something on his laptop. He wore gray slacks, a freshly pressed white dress shirt, untucked, and his feet were bare. If the casual version of Jay McManus could heat up her insides, the dressed-up version made them positively molten.

Bridgett heard the furious buzzing of her cell phone from deep within her purse on the other side of the room and she suddenly remembered why she was in Napa in the first place. "What time is it?" she croaked out, looking around the room for a clock.

"Don't worry," Jay said, closing his laptop and standing. "It's only eight thirty. Mimi isn't coming until ten." He walked to the pretty table she'd coveted the night before and poured her tea from a gorgeous china teapot. Placing the teacup and some sugar packets on a plate with a spoon, he made his way over to the bed. Bridgett sat up against the wooden headboard, cool against her bare skin, and tucked the sheet beneath her armpits. Her phone buzzed again.

"That'll be Stuart," she said when he placed the tea on the nightstand. "Can you hand me my purse, please."

Jay sat down on the edge of the bed. "Not yet." The lines bracketing his mouth were more pronounced and those blue eyes steely. He reached up and traced a finger along her jawline. "Did you sleep well?"

She'd slept deeply. It was eleven thirty East Coast time and she was still in bed. "You know I did," she whispered.

He leaned in, kissing her soundly. Jay tasted like coffee and smelled like soap and her fingers curled into the sheets in an effort to not tangle through his still-damp hair.

"Jay," she breathed after pulling her mouth away from his.

"We can't do this. We have to get ready to iron out a preemptive media strategy with Mimi."

His lips settled into a firm line. "Actually, it's more of a defensive strategy now."

Bridgett's stomach somersaulted and her phone buzzed again. "Alesha Warren didn't waste any time."

Jay continued to stare at her, his gaze remorseful. "No, she didn't."

"What happened?"

He reached for her teacup and placed it in her hands, gently caressing her fingers as he did so. "Drink this first."

Her stomach was somersaulting into her chest now, and her breathing hitched. The look on his face told her that whatever Alesha Warren had done, Bridgett wasn't going to like it. Jay angled his chin toward her cup, urging her to drink, but Bridgett wanted to get out of bed, get dressed, and get to her phone. "I'd rather discuss this when I've got a little more clothing on."

He all but rolled his eyes, giving her a look that said he knew exactly what she looked like under that sheet, and layers of clothing wouldn't make a difference. "Drink the tea, Bridgett."

The arrogant jerk didn't bother moving out of her way, so Bridgett took a large swallow of Earl Grey, nearly scalding her throat her as it slid down. Jay swore, handing her some ice water from a glass beside the bed. "Tell me," she choked out.

Jay stared at her a moment longer, his face softening when his eyes focused on her lips. "That blogger—the *Girlfriends' Guide to the NFL*—wrote about us this morning."

Bridgett's heart began to pound. "How . . . ? How did she find out? You said you kept everything protected."

"Not about Italy. About us sharing a room in Virginia Beach. She's claiming you came on to me in the motel lobby." He gave her a cheeky grin.

"That's ridiculous! It was the last room during a storm. Nothing even happened."

His smile was sly now. "Yet, according to the blogger, you chased me out to my home in Napa."

She was furious now. "We'll have Mimi refute it. You're my client. That's all."

He arched an eyebrow at her smugly. She smacked him in the chest.

"We're going to make this go away, Jay."

"No, we're not."

Bridgett shoved at him, but he wouldn't budge. "I need to call Stuart. He's probably ballistic by now. This story has to be stopped."

"No." Jay delivered the one word with such force, Bridgett shifted back against the headboard. "The story *is* true, Bridgett. You and I are involved. For once, something that damn blogger wrote has real legs. It's the perfect cover to flush out the person who's behind all of this while still protecting my other secrets."

"So you're going to use me to protect yourself?"

He gave her another one of those smug smiles. "It's not using you if you enjoy it as much as I do. And I'm not only protecting myself here, Bridgett."

She slumped against the pillow. At least she could take solace in the fact that he was shielding her past as well.

"I need to protect Charlie from all of this," he said, his tone fierce. "I don't think anyone in her circle or anywhere else knows about the baby. It's the only reason she would come to my home instead of hers. She knows that my staff can be trusted to keep her private life from playing out in the tabloids."

A lump formed in Bridgett's throat. Of course he was shielding his little sister. Bridgett's career he could sacrifice, but not Princess Charlotte's reputation. It didn't matter if he believed Charlie or not; he would still be there for her. The thought made tears sting the backs of Bridgett's eyes. She jumped as her phone buzzed again.

"I need to talk to Stuart," she said. Her fingers picked at the sheet. "I just have no idea what to tell him."

"Tell him the truth. That we're a couple."

"We're not a couple!" Except she heard the lie in her own words. Walking away from Jay a second time might not be possible. Even if their relationship was based solely on sex this time around, she wasn't sure she had the strength to refuse his offer.

Jay leaned forward and laid claim to her mouth while one hand gently kneaded her breast. "We are very much a couple, Bridgett," he declared as his lips traced the shell of her ear. "As long as we're both enjoying it, there's no reason for our relationship to be otherwise."

This time it was *his* phone buzzing inside his shirt pocket. Bridgett tried to even out her breathing while Jay answered the phone, his heated gaze never leaving her face. "Yeah." He was silent a moment; then both corners of his mouth turned up. "That's the second best thing I've heard all day. I'll be right down." He clicked the phone off. "It seems Don has located our missing Sparks cheerleader. He's questioning her now and we should have some clues as to who's behind all of this. If nothing else, maybe she can lead us to the blogger."

"You said that was the second best thing you've heard all day?"

That sly smile was back and Bridgett felt the burn all the way to her toes when he leaned down to nuzzle her neck. "Mmmm. Don's news is definitely second to the sound of you moaning my name when I'm inside you." He took her earlobe between his teeth and played with it a moment before he pulled away with a groan. "Get dressed, Bridgett. Tell Stuart we're a couple." He rose from the bed, gingerly tucking in his shirttails around his now tight pants. "If he doesn't like it, tell him I'll take my business elsewhere." He picked up a pair of shoes and socks from the end of the bed. "And I'll take his best lawyer with me. There's no need to rush to get ready. I'll tell Josie to have breakfast laid out in an hour."

Bridgett lunged for her phone as soon as Jay closed the door behind him. She had twenty-one texts. She scanned the ones from Stuart, not surprised by his demands that she call him right away. Gwen had called repeatedly, not to mention her other sisters, their mother, and Brody. She glanced at Brody's text first.

WTF??? Call me. Now.

Bridgett rolled her eyes. Her little brother presumed himself to be her protector. She didn't need Brody's protection from Jay. Not much anyway. The next message was from Gwen.

Damn girl. You've been holding out on us. Did you have to make me look like an idiot the other day when I told you to chase after him? Call me! Skip is being an ass. Or are you too busy with your own creative coupling? Haha! ☺

The rest of Bridgett's messages were just as bad. Her mother was doing a happy dance at the beauty salon.

So happy for you. Is his vineyard big enough for a wedding?

Bridgett clicked her phone closed, downed her tea, pulled on the fluffy robe, and headed for the shower. She needed to be dressed for the conversation she had to have with Stuart. Even if it was only going to take place over the phone. On her way to the bathroom, she glanced out onto the vineyards. It was a perfect day in Napa Valley: blue sky, puffy clouds, and bright fall colors. Bridgett sucked in a deep breath of the air fragranced with the smell of cabernet grapes.

Jay didn't make promises lightly. Last night, he'd promised her all of this, the home, the vineyard. All of it in exchange for her body. She was an educated woman with ample means of her own and a great family to support her. So what did it say about her that she was even considering his offer?

Twelve

"Talk to me, Don," Jay said after he punched the button on the speakerphone in his office.

"It's exactly as we suspected. Alesha Warren approached her sister-in-law about filing the lawsuit. According to Jennifer, Warren intimated that there were several other Sparks cheerleaders willing to join the class. Jennifer was surprised when no other cheerleaders were named. She's a little peeved at her sister-in-law."

"Peeved enough to drop the lawsuit?" Jay asked.

"Unfortunately, no. She's still claiming that several Blaze players made her feel uncomfortable at the photo shoot. Jennifer says they crossed the line into sexual harassment several times during the trip. I got the feeling there was more she wasn't telling me, though. But her father wouldn't allow her to elaborate without Alesha Warren present."

Jay swore. "Bridgett will have to depose her as soon as possible. I want to know why Alesha brought the possibility of a lawsuit to Jennifer and not the other way around. Especially if the two hadn't spoken for some time. Any clues there?"

"Not a one," Don said. "She pretty much clammed up when her father gave her the signal. He's likely envisioning a big settlement. The family emergency is legit, though. It looks like Jennifer's grandmother is at the end of her life. I'm thinking I might stick around a little longer to see if Alesha's ex shows up. I might be able to learn something from him."

"Good thinking." Jay paused and glanced out the window overlooking the pool. He was relieved to see Charlie reclining on one of the chaise lounges, a magazine in her hands.

"By the way, Asia has been asking around and she has a list of the players who were at the photo shoot that week. Shall I have her send it along to Bridgett?" Don hesitated when he said Bridgett's name. Don knew the circumstances of Jay and Bridgett's stay at the motel in Virginia Beach and he likely didn't give much credence to the blogger's claims. But Jay needed him to.

"Yeah, e-mail it directly to her. And, Don, if nothing else comes out of this wild-goose chase, I want that blogger found. I won't have mine and Bridgett's relationship talked about all over the Internet."

There was a moment of silence on the other end of the phone before Don spoke again. "Uh, sure thing, boss."

"Call me when you have something," Jay commanded before clicking the speakerphone off. He looked over at Linc. "I take it Charlie stayed put last night?"

Linc looked a little sheepish when he answered. "I talked her into giving it a day."

Jay eyed his assistant carefully. While he liked the kid well enough—he was smart, goal oriented, and savvy—Jay wasn't sure he liked the idea of Linc and his sister together, probably because he didn't want to think about anyone being with his little sister. Both definitely gave off vibes of disliking each other, but all Jay had to do was go up to his bedroom for proof that negative vibes didn't necessarily mean anything. Still, his sister could do a whole lot worse and she was still at the vineyard, so he kept his misgivings to himself. "You didn't talk her into telling you who the father is, too, did you?"

"No, but it's not Blaine," Linc said with a grin. "Apparently, he's in love with one of Princess Charlotte's ladies-in-waiting—the one with the tongue piercing whose daddy is the satellite radio pioneer. They've had a bit of a falling-out and he's being a hangdog putz trying to get her back. He seemed to think she'd be here with your sister."

"Thankfully, Charlie left her entourage in Europe." Jay sorted through some papers on his desk. "Still, I'd like you to keep an eye on her for me. I'm going to be tied up in meetings most of the day."

"With your lawyer?" Linc unsuccessfully tried to stifle the shit-eating grin that spread over his face at the double entendre.

Jay ignored him. "Did you track down that name I gave you?"

Linc sobered up before unlocking the safe in the credenza. He pulled out a file and handed it to Jay. "It's all here, including the current address."

Thumbing through the sheets of papers, Jay bit down on the bile rising at the back of his throat. This was one confrontation he'd hoped to avoid ever having. A fit of conscience had forced Jay to go easy on this person the first time around. Fortunately, Jay never made the same mistake twice. "We'll meet with the media consultant in the dining room," he told Linc as he slipped the file into his briefcase. "I'm just going to have a word with my sister before the day gets away from me."

Linc nodded as Jay made his way out to the pool deck. Charlie didn't bother looking up from the glossy pages of her magazine.

"She must not be that impressive if you had to leave in the middle of boinking her to beat up my friend."

Jay didn't bother responding. His sister was spoiling for a fight of her own and he found it was best not to engage when Charlie was in full princess mode.

Charlie was never able to stand his silence for long and she eventually glanced up. "Damn, not even a fat lip."

"What are your plans for the day?" Jay was still holding

out hope he could persuade her to have dinner with their mother. Perhaps he'd bring Bridgett along, too. Somehow, though, he didn't think the dinner would be everything he'd fantasized about thirteen years ago. Too many secrets would be hovering over the table. But still, he wanted the only three women who were part of his private life to meet.

"I thought I'd throw back a few mojitos, then do some skydiving," she quipped. "From what I read surfing the Internet, I figured you'd be holed up in your suite with your lady lawyer lover. You're awfully dressed up for a day in the sack, though. Unless you two are into some kinky *Fifty Shades of Grey* role-playing." She made a face very similar to one that always used to make Jay laugh when she was kid, but not so much now.

"When you're ready to grow up," he said, "I have a favor to ask."

"I don't do threesomes. Especially not with my brother."

"Can you turn off the snark, Charlie? My favor involves shopping. I know you excel at that."

"Does it involve your lawyer lover?"

Jay flinched at the name the blogger had dubbed Bridgett with. The moniker likely mortified her. "I'd appreciate it if you didn't call her that. She's staying through the game on Sunday and she'll likely need clothes."

"Other than a thong and stilettos?"

He was beginning to regret his decision to involve Charlie, but he wanted his sister occupied. A bored Charlie was a dangerous Charlie. Jay also wanted her to get to know Bridgett. The two would be seeing a lot of each other if his plan came to fruition. It would be a bonus if everyone got along. "I doubt she brought anything to wear to the cocktail party on Saturday night."

Charlie dropped her eyes back to her magazine. "Ah, so I've been replaced as hostess already."

Damn! Why did women always read things the wrong way? Jay didn't have the time or patience to deal with any slight to his sister's feelings this morning, but he didn't want her sulking all weekend, either. "No," he said evenly. "I asked you to help me host, Charlie."

She flipped a page of her magazine. "But your lawyer lover will be there, too."

"Yes."

"Am I spending your money or her money?"

Jay snorted. He doubted Bridgett would be too happy about attending a cocktail party for Blaze sponsors and other NFL dignitaries. She'd be positively furious at the idea of him buying her clothes; of that there was no doubt. "You won't be spending anyone's money. Just showing her where the better stores are." He turned to head back into the house. "And, Charlie, be nice."

"Jay," she called after him. "Is she your lawyer? Because, you know . . ."

He knew what she was asking. Jay had been right when he assumed no one knew about the baby Charlie was carrying. "Yes. The baby is protected under the confidentiality proviso."

She nodded solemnly and went back to her magazine.

"How long has this been going on?" Stuart's normally jovial demeanor was nowhere to be found this morning. Her boss hadn't called her Buffy one time. Bridgett hated lying to him. Then there was the fact that she wasn't lying. One look in the mirror at the disheveled bed behind her and her skin grew warm beneath her Escada suit. She decided to stick as close to the truth as possible.

"Nothing happened in the motel the other night."

Stuart snorted incredulously. "But it is happening now—is that what you're telling me? Damn it, Bridgett, these weren't the type of headlines I envisioned when I put you on this case!"

"I tried to recuse myself but you wouldn't listen!"

She heard the familiar sound of the cracking of marbles. Stuart would work them through his fingers whenever he was agitated. "Fine. Let Mimi handle the media mess that's sure to come of this and whatever else Alesha Warren is planning, and you come back to Baltimore. Dan has already begun interviewing cheerleaders and some of the other staff who were on the calendar shoot. He can take over anything else. I'll have to hold McManus's hand myself."

The words Bridgett had waited to hear didn't bring about the relief she expected. She told herself it was because she knew Jay would use whatever means necessary to make sure she stayed put and it had nothing to do with her reluctance to leave the beautiful vineyard. Or this bedroom. "It's too late for that. He says if I go, he'll take his business elsewhere."

Bridgett held the phone away from her face as Stuart swore. "Well, you've worked yourself out a fine deal, haven't you, Bridgett?"

She cringed as his words. She'd worked hard to achieve the rank of junior partner in her law firm, never letting her reputation become subject to innuendo. Unfortunately, as a woman, she was always at risk for the types of accusations Stuart was making. It was no use arguing because, for the first time in her career, she was guilty.

"I thought you were smarter than this," he said sharply and his words made Bridgett's throat tighten. "It doesn't matter. He has the reputation of being a bit of a playboy. When he's done with you, he'll be done with the firm, too."

Bridgett hated the sound of disgust in Stuart's voice. She wanted to argue with him, but deep down, she knew he was probably right. Whatever it was Jay had proposed last night had been open-ended, and would last only until he grew tired of her. She was a fool for even considering putting herself in that position once again.

But then she glanced in the mirror again. What they had in bed was real. When she made love with Jay, she became her younger self again, the Bridgett who delighted in life and the world around her. The women she'd been pretending to be these past thirteen years was just that: pretend. A thick shell of a lawyer who saw the world in black and white so that she could go through the motions of life. She really didn't like that woman. But it was the only way she'd known how to survive.

"Everything isn't always as it seems, Stuart. I know what my job here is and what the client represents to *our* firm. I'm not about to lose sight of any of that. I'll call you after our meeting with Mimi." She clicked her phone off and stared at the neatly put-together woman in the mirror. "Don't mess this up," she told herself. She just didn't know if she was talking about her job or whatever it was that was happening again with Jay.

She left the sanctuary of the relaxing suite and made her way down to the first floor of the house. The rooms she passed were well appointed with both antiques and cozy, inviting furniture. A soft breeze filtering in through the open terrace doors carried the sounds of workers harvesting the grapes in the vineyards. Bridgett's stomach rumbled and she followed her nose toward the delicious smell of food coming from the large room at the end of the hall.

The dining room was stunning. A huge Swarovski chandelier hung above an oval rosewood table that seated sixteen. The French doors opened to a flagstone terrace complete with sofas, a bar, and a stone fireplace. Behind the terrace was a breathtaking view of the vineyard, framed by the foothills behind it. Viewing the sunsets from that spot had to be amazing.

Bridgett didn't realize she'd spoken the last part out loud until she heard Mimi Livingston's voice behind her. "So you've been too busy doing other things to take in the sunsets, have you?"

She turned to find the media specialist standing beside one of the sideboards, a plate of food in her hand, wearing an Albert Nipon suit, four-inch Jimmy Choos, and enough filler in her face to kill an elephant. Bridgett had worked with the older woman before on a case involving a class action against an Internet provider. The case had been decided in their client's favor, and Mimi had been invaluable in deflecting the negative media away from their defendant.

She'd also been insufferable, condescending, and way too forward with their client, the company's CEO. The last part had bothered Bridgett enough for her to hop on her soapbox and confront Mimi about it. *Damn.* Payback was definitely going to be ugly.

"Good morning, Mimi." Bridgett picked up a plate and loaded it with some fruit that she'd likely pick at, her appetite having suddenly left her.

"Hmm," Mimi said. "I doubt it's a good morning for you, Miss Prissy Pants. Unless you like your dirty little secrets played out all over social media. Or is he just that good in the sack that you're willing to overlook the torpedo to that sterling reputation you've been postulating?"

"Let's save the catfight for the ladies' room, Ms. Livingston. We've got work to do," Jay said as he entered the room, his assistant trailing behind him.

Bridgett wasn't sure which embarrassed her more: Jay's interference on her behalf or the fact that he'd overheard Mimi's comments. She gave him a look of indifference as she took her seat at the table, leaving two open chairs between her and the seat Jay had taken. He arched an eyebrow at her but didn't bother to comment. With a huff, Mimi took the seat directly across from Jay.

"So can we assume the counsel for the Sparks cheerleaders leaked the story about your little tryst with your new attorney in the seedy motel?" Mimi asked.

"For your clarification, Mimi, there was no 'tryst' in a seedy motel," Jay said, his tone even. "Miss Janik's and my long-standing relationship isn't germane to the case."

Mimi flinched at the phrase *long-standing.* "It is now. The question is why and how did the blogger find out about it?"

Jay's assistant spoke up. "Alesha Warren had someone interview the motel's desk clerk."

"How do you know that?" Bridgett leaned forward in her chair to look past Jay at Linc."

Linc glanced at Jay before answering. "Because *we* had someone interview the desk clerk after Alesha's guy was there."

Bridgett glanced between the two men in surprise.

"The spy games part doesn't matter," Mimi said. "I'm actually surprised that she led with this when she alluded to having information about your sexual harassment exploits."

Jay quickly cut her off. "I don't practice sexual harassment and if you've read the case files we've provided you, you'll see that none of those claims were ever substantiated."

Mimi sighed as she flipped open a folder. "Mainly because you paid all these women off. It's a smart way to avoid the court system and a media feeding frenzy, but these things do have a way of cropping back up." She sorted through the papers in front of her before lifting her gaze toward Bridgett. "Some of these cases look like lovers scorned, however. They should be easy to defend in the court of public opinion as long as no one else is going to come out of the woodwork."

A silence settled over the room as Mimi looked from Bridgett to Jay. She knew that Mimi was alluding to Bridgett, but Jay was likely thinking about whoever he thought had access to his most secret files. Bridgett tried not to squirm.

"Nothing else is going to 'come out of the woodwork,'" Jay answered, his tone quiet but lethal. Bridgett hoped he was right, because if the sexual harassment cases had all been settled out of court, Alesha had to have been made aware of them by someone. Bridgett worried her bottom lip as she prayed that whoever it was didn't know all Jay's secrets.

Mimi heaved another sigh. "Let's hope not. For now, we'll start a quiet little campaign to paint these previous cases for what they were—jilted lovers."

Jay's jaw grew taut but he remained silent, not bothering to refute Mimi's perception. Aggravated and annoyed, Bridgett did fidget in her chair this time. Jay shot her a quelling glance that only served to make her more frustrated.

"That way," Mimi continued, "if and when the *Girlfriends' Guide to the NFL* runs with the sexual harassment angle, we'll already have a wave of media outlets who can contradict her."

"Too bad she doesn't have an even bigger story to distract her," Linc said.

Three heads turned to the end of the table to stare at Jay's assistant.

"Be careful what you wish for," Mimi said. "Whoever is behind that blog seems to have a personal vendetta against the team. Or, perhaps, just you, Mr. McManus. Regardless, Stuart wants me to stay close just in case. I'm assuming you'll be remaining in California until after the game on Sunday?"

Jay stood when Mimi did. "Yes, we'll fly back Monday morning. I'm hosting a cocktail party here on Saturday night. Please join us. Linc will give you the details." He nodded at his assistant, and Linc escorted Mimi from the room.

Dropping back down into his chair, Jay released a sigh.

"You agree with Mimi that this is something personal, don't you?" she asked.

"Yeah," he said, leaning his head back and closing his eyes. "According to Asia, the majority of the cheerleaders are happy to be on the Sparks squad. They're paid well for what the job is and they all think they're being treated fairly. They do it for fun. The players allegedly involved in the sexual intimidation are on the practice squad. Hank will cut them immediately if Jennifer Knowles's claim can be substantiated."

"As your attorney, I have to advise you not to settle for Alesha Warren's asking price. Let the case languish in the courts. It'll drop to the bottom of the news cycle pretty quickly if Hank makes a statement that the players are gone and the behavior won't be tolerated. It'll take months to get the class notified, but we'll have a better chance at dismissal if Jennifer Knowles is the only plaintiff."

"I don't plan on giving anyone a dime, Bridgett. But I'm also not going to sit around and let someone use Alesha Warren to slander me. The person behind this isn't going to stop until they reveal all my secrets. This is about payback."

"You know who it is?" she gasped.

Jay's tone was resolute. "I have my suspicions."

"What are you going to do?"

When he didn't answer, Bridgett leaned forward in her chair and whispered. "Jay, don't do anything stupid. I don't care if anyone finds out about the baby. That was years ago."

His face was stoic as he glanced over his shoulder to the sound of a woman's laughter in the hallway. Bridgett recognized it from the night before as Charlie's. "That's not the only baby I'm concerned about here," he said.

"Yes, of course," Bridgett said around the lump that had formed in her throat. She stood, running her hands down her skirt to smooth out the wrinkles. "Just don't do anything stupid. Our firm only handles civil cases. I'll head back to Baltimore this afternoon. As much as Dan is probably enjoying interviewing the cheerleaders, I want to make sure we've got all our bases covered. Mimi can handle whatever media issues arise from here."

"Not so fast, counselor." Jay reached out and wrapped his large fingers around her wrist, pulling her down into his lap.

"Jay!" she cried, frantically looking around to make sure they were alone.

He slid a hand beneath her skirt and cupped her bottom. "You're not going anywhere, Bridgett." She tried to resist him but he had the advantage of surprise when his mouth took hers in a wildly possessive kiss. Bridgett loathed the way her body responded without a trace of resistance to his heavy-handedness. Breaking the kiss, she smacked his chest in frustration at herself as much as Jay.

"I swear I'm going to have to start wearing a flak jacket around you." he murmured against her neck.

"I don't want you kissing me."

She felt his smile against her skin. "I think you do want me kissing you and that's what has you so mad. You like it too much."

"I don't," she breathed as one of his fingers slid beneath the crotch of her panties. "Jay," she gasped when his finger breached her entrance and her body squeezed around it.

"I have to go into the office and then I have a dinner

scheduled," he said as he stroked her. "Otherwise I'd take you upstairs and do this a lot more thoroughly."

Bridgett tried to tell him to stop, that their behavior was unprofessional, but the words never made it past her lips. Instead her breaths became more staccato as Jay flicked in and out of her. Her body began to tighten around his finger just as his mouth covered hers, swallowing up her cry of pleasure.

The room came into focus a moment later. Bridgett was still sprawled out in Jay's lap but his hand was no longer beneath her skirt. He swore softly when she shifted. "Be still a minute," he choked out.

"I can't stay here," she whispered.

His lips brushed her hairline. "Yes, you can. I'm the client. I call the shots and I say you stay here at the vineyard in case I need further legal advice. Or bailing out of jail."

Jay groaned when she jumped off his lap. "You are *not* going to do something stupid!"

She wasn't sure if his grin was one of amusement or pain, but Jay slowly stood to face her. He reached out a hand to cup her face. "I'm not."

"Promise me," she demanded, surprising them both at the ferocity of her tone.

His face softened and he wrapped his fingers around the back of her neck and pulled her body against his. "Promise me you'll be here when I get home tonight, Bridgett. We can spend the day exploring the vineyard tomorrow. I'll even let you bill me at your hourly rate."

She smacked him on the chest again as laughter rumbled up beneath her hand. "I didn't bring anything suitable for a cocktail party."

"I'm way ahead of you. Charlie's agreed to take you shopping."

Bridgett's eyes snapped back up to his. "Your sister?"

"Hmm," he said with grin. "And she's even agreed to be nice."

His lips brushed the tip of her nose and Bridgett sighed.

"Fine. But I'm only agreeing to the weekend, Jay. On Monday, we go back to the way things were."

"Are you sure about that?"

No! If he asked her to run away with him, she'd be sorely tempted, just as his offer last night had tempted her. But she needed to listen to the levelheaded **Bridgett,** who'd been guiding her these past years. It was **the only** way she knew how to survive. "I'm sure."

His mouth took on that self-satisfied grin again. "We'll see."

Thirteen

Everything Bridgett knew of the grown-up Charlie she'd gleaned from the tabloid headlines while standing in the grocery store checkout line. Still, that didn't prepare her for the young woman who met her in the foyer of Jay's home later that afternoon. For starters, his sister was very tall. She wore designer skinny jeans tucked into a pair of riding boots, the look making her legs appear miles long. Her rich auburn hair was tied back in a ponytail and hidden beneath a Baltimore Blaze baseball cap. Charlie had wrapped a fluffy teal scarf around her neck, covering up most of her long-sleeved white shirt. Her only other accessories were three silver bangle bracelets on her wrist.

Bridgett felt positively fuddy-duddy standing next to Jay's gorgeous young sister. She tried not to cringe as Charlie eyed her from head to toe, taking in her outfit of gray slacks, a purple cardigan, and Anne Klein loafers. At least she'd donned her pearls.

Charlie shook her head as she pulled away from the banister she'd been leaning on and headed toward the door. "I'm not sure I know of any stores conservative enough for you, but I'm always up for an adventure," she said, her long strides carrying her out the front door quickly, forcing Bridgett to have to trot to keep up.

"These are my traveling clothes," Bridgett said, unsure why she felt the need to defend herself.

"Whatever." Charlie punched the key fob unlocking the doors to a silver Range Rover parked out front. "The paparazzi won't be expecting me at J.C. Penney, so there's that."

Bridgett climbed into the passenger seat. "I Googled the names of a few boutiques in St. Helena. I'm perfectly happy to go on my own." Getting to know Jay's sister might not be as enjoyable of an afternoon as Bridgett once imagined.

Charlie laughed. "And have you pick out a dress my mother would wear? No way!" She turned the key and started the car. "I love my brother too much to allow that to happen."

They made their way down the winding drive and Bridgett took the opportunity to sleuth a little about Jay and his sister's relationship. "I take it you two are close?"

"Oh no, you don't, lawyer lady." Charlie maneuvered the car along the two-lane road leading to the center of Napa. "I don't dish on my brother and he doesn't dish on me."

"Your life is pretty much an open book," Bridgett couldn't resist saying.

Charlie shot her a grin as the Range Rover merged onto the highway, carrying them north toward St. Helena. "Well, Mrs. Cleaver has teeth."

"Bridgett. My name is Bridgett."

There was a pause before Charlie spoke. "That's actually a very pretty name. It fits you. I'm Charlotte, but you already know that."

"Not Charlie?"

Her tone was sharper than it had been. "My brother is the only one who calls me that."

They were both silent as Bridgett took in the beautiful countryside zooming past. Charlie groaned softly and began digging into the console between the seats, pulling out a package of crackers. "Would you mind," she asked softly. "The alternative is that I barf all over."

Bridgett tore open the package and handed her one. "Would you rather I drive?"

"No, thanks. I get carsick sitting in the passenger seat or the back even when I'm not pregnant." She glanced over at Bridgett while she crunched on the cracker. "Jay assured me that my pregnancy is covered under his attorney-client privilege. Is that true?"

Technically, no, since it wasn't Jay who'd told her, but since Bridgett didn't plan to reveal Jay's sister's condition to anyone, it didn't matter. "You're covered." Bridgett gave her a warm smile. "Do you need something to drink with those? I always found the old standbys of weak tea or ginger ale helped during those first weeks."

Charlie's head snapped around. "You have kids?"

Bridgett wasn't sure how or why the words had slipped out. She was as surprised as Charlie by the admission. "No." She shook her head. "It . . . it didn't work out."

"I'm sorry." Charlie refocused her eyes on the road.

"It was a long time ago," Bridgett said, glancing back out at the vineyards, ending any further discussion of the subject.

They made the rest of the twenty-minute trip in companionable silence, each wrestling with her own secrets. The only sound in the car was the air whistling through the moon roof as they drove through Oak Knoll, Yountville, and Rutherford. The traffic began to slow as they reached the picturesque downtown area of St. Helena, with its charming tree-lined streets and eclectic mix of twentieth-century architecture. Charlie parked the Range Rover on the street in front of the Woodhouse Chocolatier shop. "We may as well start with the fun part," she said with a wide smile.

They each picked out a bag of assorted candies, nibbling on them as they strolled along Main Street and window-shopped. "There are a few fun boutiques up the block here," Charlie was saying, but Bridgett wasn't listening. Her eyes had homed in on a pair of shoes displayed in a store window. The Kate Spade high heels were covered in pieces of crystal that glittered in the afternoon sun. Bridgett looked at the sign above the door: "Foot Candy." She handed her bag of edible treats to Charlie. "Here," she murmured as she pulled the door open. "I've found the candy I want."

Charlie followed her in, chuckling as she did so. "Buying shoes *before* the dress. We just might get along after all, Bridgett."

Two hours later, Bridgett had a pair of Kate Spade pumps, a matching purse, and a royal blue Stella McCartney cocktail dress that would require wearing a backless bra and a very meager set of panties—all of which the salesclerk happily added to the shopping bag. Bridgett doubted Stuart would let her expense the entire ensemble—even if he wasn't mad at her. But the afternoon of retail therapy had definitely lifted her spirits.

Charlie steered the Range Rover back out onto Highway Twenty-nine headed south. "Well, that was more fun than I thought it would be. You're hiding a bit of a wild streak under those conservative duds, lawyer lady." She turned on the satellite radio and a song by Train was playing. "I'm beginning to see why my brother likes you."

Bridgett went to open her mouth to say Jay was just her client, but she bit back the lie. Charlie laughed out loud as though she could read Bridgett's mind.

"Given the way you dress, I'm fairly certain you don't share a bedroom with all your clients. And from what Josie says, he's never brought a woman—other than Mom or me—to the vineyard before," Charlie informed her.

Glancing out at the sun as it dropped lower over the foothills, Bridgett considered what Charlie was saying. There was no denying Jay more than "liked" her body. But as far as anything more, she just wasn't sure if she wanted that. He'd been very clear that any relationship they'd have would be physical and not emotional. She just wondered if such a scenario was even possible. They both were holding on to too much anger from that summer. Neither one trusted the other. Her common sense told her to stick to the plan of staying the weekend, then run. Bridgett just hoped her body was able to listen to her common sense come Monday.

"Hey," Charlie said, interrupting her thoughts. "If I hire

you as my lawyer, you'll definitely have to uphold the whole attorney-client privilege thingy, right?"

"I told you your secret is safe with me."

"I'm not talking about that secret—although you'd better keep that one or that blogger will be the least of your worries." She turned the volume on the radio down to make her point. "I mean an even bigger secret."

Bridgett was beginning to feel very uncomfortable about their conversation. "I'm sure you have quite a team of lawyers representing your trust fund who get paid very well to keep your secrets."

Charlie snorted. "Those old suits? What a bunch of party poopers. I've been trying to establish a nonprofit for the past two years and all I get is gatekeeping. They make too much money off my father's portfolio that they don't want to part with any of it."

"But you do?"

"Well, I don't want to give it all away. That would be stupid. But it can do a lot of good out there in the world rather than in some hedge fund somewhere. I'll certainly never need it all."

Bridgett was stunned by Charlie's words. "Wow. That doesn't sound very Princess Charlotte like."

Charlie shrugged. "You of all people should know not to believe what you read in the tabloids. Or on the Internet." She glanced over and winked at Bridgett. "Although in your case, it looks to be true."

Blushing, Bridgett turned back to the window. "My firm doesn't really handle a lot of nonprofit setup, but I'm sure I can get you a few names of lawyers who'd be happy to help." She knew all about these firms because once, when she was young and idealistic like Charlie, she'd wanted to pursue nonprofit work.

"But you can handle setting up a trust for my baby, can't you? I don't want my father's lawyers involved in my child's life. I need something written out before my condition becomes public knowledge. I'm sure you can knock something out tonight while Jay is at dinner. I'll pay you triple your rate. Hell, I'll take you on a shopping spree at Foot Candy."

"I—"

"Please," Charlie begged. "You already know about the baby, so it's one less person I have to tell."

Bridgett sighed. "Sure. We can draw up the paperwork when we get back."

"Awesome! Now you get to find out who my baby's father is."

"There's no need for me to know that." Bridgett's feeling of unease was growing by the minute. Her intuition was telling her that Charlie was putting her in the middle of something and if the plan was for Bridgett to distance herself from Jay after this weekend, knowing the identity of the baby's father didn't seem like such a good idea.

"Of course it is. But you can't tell anyone. Not even Jay."

A tremor of unease trickled up Bridgett's spine. "Why do I feel like this is some sort of test?"

Charlie grinned again. "Because it is. I need to know I can trust you. Jay doesn't let many people in, but you're here and that has to mean something. I don't want to see him get hurt again."

Bridgett swallowed hard around the lump in her throat. "Again?"

"Yeah." Charlie's face was grim as she navigated the sharp turns on the road leading to the vineyard. "He got his heart broken pretty good years ago when he was in Italy. Some Italian princess or something. My father had just died and I needed Jay, but—but he was different after that summer. Guarded, like he was protecting his heart. He's been that way ever since."

Tears burned Bridgett's eyes and she hid them from Charlie by studying the scenery outside her window. *What happened in Italy had not been her fault.*

"So if he's thinking of opening up to you, I need to make sure you're trustworthy."

"You have it all wrong. We don't have that kind of relationship." *Once maybe, but not now.*

"Says you. All the more reason for me to figure out if you can be trusted with my brother's heart."

Bridgett wanted to scream. It wasn't Jay's heart that had ever been at issue. It was hers. Jay was the one who left her alone and pregnant without even a second thought. "I have no legal reason to need to know the identity of your baby's father," she managed to say through her tight throat.

"But you have every ethical reason to keep it secret now that I've hired you."

"Don't you dare tell me," Bridgett warned, all but plugging up her ears.

Charlie ignored her. "It's patient number Z457."

Anger rolled through Bridgett and it took a moment to absorb what Charlie had blurted out. "What?"

"Yep," Charlie said smugly as the Range Rover passed through the grove of ancient olive trees. "My baby's daddy is a sperm donor."

"I don't understand." Except Bridgett was beginning to think she did.

Charlie pulled the car to a stop in front of the roaring fountain. "I Googled you this morning. You come from a big family. A close family. I want that. Now. Not later. I just told you that Jay has been emotionally distant for years. I have no idea if that will change. And my mother—" She shook her head briskly.

Princess Charlotte wasn't exactly the spoiled little rich girl as much as she was the lonely little rich girl. Bridgett heaved another sigh. "Your child's fortune will definitely need some legal protection if the father ever comes calling, then."

"You see, I do need you, Bridgett. I was assured that the clinic was discreet and word wouldn't get out, but nothing is bulletproof when it comes to the paparazzi these days."

"I'll do my best to provide you both a shield of protection where I can," Bridgett said solemnly. While she didn't want to be involved with Jay's family any more than necessary, she wouldn't leave Charlie and her child unprotected. Clearly, Charlie had no intention of relying on her brother for that protection. He'd be devastated to know his sister had put herself at so much risk. Bridgett would just have to make sure the risk was minimal. "I'll represent you on this."

"Good," Charlie said, her body rigid in the driver's seat. "Because I may need you to defend me for murdering my brother."

Bridgett glanced across the fountain at the foyer where an older woman waved at them. Dressed in a black knit dress and sensible shoes, her shoulder-length ash-blond bob blew slightly in the evening breeze. "Who is she?" Bridgett asked.

"The mother I told my asshole brother I wanted to avoid."

Jay leaned back against the high back of the leather chair in his office at McManus Industries. Housed in San Mateo, the northernmost part of Silicon Valley, the glass-enclosed building overlooked a man-made lake and a tree-lined jogging trail. From his suite on the twenty-second floor, Jay had a great view of the Santa Cruz mountains.

He squeezed at the back of his neck. After four hours of meetings spent getting caught up on the day-to-day operations of his software company, he needed a drink. And a hot shower. Preferably a hot shower with a certain lawyer followed by a smooth glass of Scotch.

He was actually glad his mother hadn't been in the office when he'd called earlier. Instead of meeting her for dinner, he'd left a message inviting her to the cocktail party on Saturday night. At least he'd made the effort. Now he'd let the traffic die down and then head back to the vineyard, where he could lure Bridgett into the tasting room beside the wine cellar. If all went as planned, he'd be tasting more than the wine in a matter of hours.

His cell phone buzzed on his desk. Jay glanced at the screen to see a photo of Blake Callahan rock climbing down the side of a jagged cliff on some island somewhere. Blake was a bit of an adrenaline junkie—a trait Jay had always shared with his friend until Blake had begun taking on extreme sports that involved a lot more risk. Jay suspected there was some deep-seated reason behind his friend's death wish, but so far Blake had been avoiding his probing.

"Mac." His friend called Jay by the nickname he had dubbed him back during their days as college roommates. "You're slipping. You're always bragging about keeping your private life private. First I read about a bunch of cheerleaders suing your ass. Then, every feminist group in the country has you on its most wanted list. There are whispers that the commissioner is considering sanctions. But imagine my surprise when I clicked on my computer this morning." Jay could hear the pounding of Blake's sneakered feet on the treadmill. "So how was it playing the comforting port in the storm for your sexy lawyer? I've seen her at a few fund-raising events in Boston. She's fire and ice all in one designer package. So I gotta know, which one is the real Bridgett Janik?"

"None of your damn business," Jay growled into the phone. No way was he discussing his relationship with Bridgett. Not even with his best friend.

"Whoa," Blake said with a laugh. "Your answer just told me everything I need to know. Don't tell me the guy who vowed during a two-day bender in Las Vegas that he'd never fall in love has finally succumbed?"

That two-day bender had happened a few months after his return from Italy. Not only had he just been cut out of his stepfather's will, leaving his plans of developing his winery uncertain, but the one person who could have made his life's little detour more bearable had betrayed him and broken his heart. "Who said anything about being in love?" What he and Bridgett had was intense chemistry. Jay sure as hell wasn't going to make the mistake of allowing it to become anything more. Not this time.

"You better not be lying to me, Mac. You and I have been on *People*'s Fifty Hottest Bachelors list for nearly a decade. It's actually become a badge of honor. Don't you dare leave me hanging there alone. Every time I turn around, someone is getting married. I'm running out of excuses to avoid all the freaking weddings I'm constantly invited to."

The Callahan family was part of old Chicago money, making Blake the city's proverbial crown prince. The fact that he remained unmarried and ran one of the biggest advertising agencies in the country made him irresistible to society hostesses. They considered him to be the town's biggest catch.

"You love having women throw themselves at you, Blake. Don't lie."

Blake had obviously picked up his pace on the treadmill because his voice was more winded now. "Not when I have no idea whether they're throwing themselves at me or my money."

"Have you looked in a mirror lately? They're all after your money, asshole."

"Screw you," Blake huffed as he ran faster. "Speaking of which, why have you been hounding me all day when according to bloggers, you're entertaining your lawyer lover, who chased you out to your winery?"

"Blogger, not bloggers," Jay said. "And her information is not factually correct."

"So you're not screwing Bridgett Janik? I'm disappointed in you, man. I wouldn't mind getting to know her up close and personal."

Jay shot out of his chair and began pacing the room to calm the surge of anger toward his best friend. "Like hell you will," he snapped. No one was getting to know Bridgett "up close and personal" ever again. She was Jay's now.

Blake laughed heartily. "Damn, Mac, you're so easy. And from the sounds of it, you've got it bad for this woman. I never thought I'd see the day. I'd like to meet her." Jay bristled at the thought of Bridgett meeting the man who'd been named Chicago's Sexiest Bachelor three times in the past five years. "If she hasn't dumped you by then, bring her with you when the Blaze come to play the Bears next month," Blake teased. "You know my mom would love to show her around."

"We'll see." While Jay had no intention of letting Bridgett slip out of his life again, he certainly didn't want to spook her with a weekend in Claire Callahan's clutches. "As interesting as this conversation is, that's not why I left you a message to call me. I have a problem that I might need your help with."

"If it involves the cheerleaders, I'm all in."

"It might involve finding Delaney."

Blake was silent on the other end of the line and Jay could no longer hear his feet pounding on the treadmill. "I thought we agreed we were never going to talk about her again?" his friend finally asked.

This was going to be the tricky part. Once upon a time, Delaney Silverberg had been their third roommate—Blake's lover for over two years. Brilliant and vivacious, she was ambitious as well. The trio had planned to open a winery together, with Jay handling the production component while Delaney, an industrial engineer and software wiz, handled the logistics. As heir to the Callahan Agency, Blake would, naturally, handle all their promotions. The plan, hatched over multiple deep-dish pizzas and beer, had almost become a reality. *Almost.*

"Unfortunately, it might be unavoidable," Jay said.

He heard the beep of the treadmill being stopped before Blake released an explosive sigh. "That woman is toxic, Jay. She destroys everything in her path. Hell, she very nearly destroyed our friendship. I don't want that to happen, and that means keeping her off-limits as a subject of discussion."

Jay squeezed at the back of his neck again. Blake was right—this was an old wound that didn't need to be reopened. But he was sitting on a ticking time bomb and all roads pointed to Delaney.

What had sounded feasible over pizza and beer had proved to be nearly impossible for the very reason that most start-ups never get off the ground: lack of money. Jay had hoped to convince his stepfather to invest in the winery, but when Lloyd Davis died, the trustees overseeing his fortune had emphatically denied the request. Blake landed safely in the boardroom of his father's agency. Jay was offered a job with an investment banking firm in New York, where he would be near Charlie. Delaney would have survived unscathed, too, had her marriage to Blake gone ahead as planned.

"Don't tell me she's in debt again and you're going to bail her out?" Blake asked, his tone harsh.

The problem was, Delaney had a serious gambling addiction, one that had come with dire consequences when two thugs destroyed her car in front of their house one night. Blake had immediately washed his hands of his fiancée, but Jay saw Delaney's dilemma as an opportunity. The woman had a brilliant mind for software development. Instead of taking the job with the investment firm, Jay took the money he'd planned to use for his vineyard and started his dot-com venture. In exchange for paying off Delaney's debts, Jay used her intellect to create his empire.

"The last dollar she ever got from me was a paycheck and that was ten years ago," Jay said.

Delaney's habits were hard to break, and when Jay had caught her trying to sell proprietary information to the Chinese, it had been the last straw. He'd fired her, threatening that if she tried it again, he'd report her to the Feds. In the ensuing years, she'd kept a low profile, presumably hiding from those whom she owed money to. Jay hadn't concerned himself with her whereabouts. Until now.

"Heath told me you'd been hit with a rash of sexual harassment suits lately?" Jay asked Blake.

"My brother-in-law talks too damn much." Blake's anger about their topic was evident in his voice. "Sure. We've had a few at the firm, but all of them were unfounded."

"Were they all directed at you?"

"Hey, screw you, man. I'm not a serial sexual harasser!"

"But someone is making you out to be one." Jay's question was more of a statement, and Blake was silent on the other end of the phone.

"What are you saying, Jay?"

"I've had the same thing happening here. I didn't give it any thought. It was just too coincidental," Jay explained. "But the lawyer representing the cheerleaders claims to have information on all my cases. The leak didn't come from here. I've checked very carefully. Which leads me to believe that she's getting the details from the source."

"Jesus, Jay, you think that Delaney has something to do with this?"

"I don't know. It could be just coincidence. I haven't heard from her in years, but she's the only link between the two of us. I think whoever's behind our recent spurt of sexual harassment suits might be that blogger, too. You know, the *Girlfriends' Guide to the NFL.*"

Blake blew out a whistle. "What makes you think that?"

"Last year, Brody Janik's wife, Shay, pulled together a spreadsheet about who the blogger had been targeting. I had Linc add to it with the more recent data. It's very telling. The majority of her targets are on my team or are players repped by the sports public relations department of the Callahan Agency. The very same firm that you head up."

Jay's statement was met with more silence before Blake answered. "How sure are you?"

"I e-mailed you the spreadsheet. Check it out yourself."

Blake swore viciously. "You never should have bailed her out in the first place."

It had been a brash risk to do so, Jay admitted to himself. But at the time he had been desperate to succeed at something. To show his stepfather that Jay would have been worth an investment—even a small one. What he'd gotten in return from Delaney had been invaluable. Sure, he'd turned the tables and used her but Jay believed in survival of the fittest. Blake wouldn't understand the necessity to prove himself because his father believed in him, supported him, and made room at his company for him.

"Regardless of what I should or should not have done, Blake, I'll take care of it now. She's done hurting those people I care about."

"Bridgett Janik must really be something else if you're willing to go to all this trouble to protect her reputation," Blake said.

Jay's friend didn't know the extent of the damage to

Bridgett's reputation Delaney could do if she put two and two together. He'd told both his friends about his summer affair, the baby, and how it had all ended, but fortunately, he hadn't ever mentioned any names. Given Delaney's monstrous brain, Jay didn't want to take any chances. He had to cut her off before things went any further.

"I'm protecting your sorry ass, too," Jay said. "And don't bother saying 'I told you so.' I know exactly how you feel on the subject."

Blake tsked. "I was going to ask if you needed any help but since you're in Avenger mode, I'll just leave you to it. Just don't do anything stupid, okay?"

"I'm just going to present her with a very good reason to cease and desist."

"Yeah, but she has a bit of a fearless streak. Desperation makes her take risks. Just be careful."

"I'll be sure to call if I need backup," Jay said.

Blake chuckled. "That's your problem. You've been flying solo for so long, you don't even think about depending upon someone else. But I'm here if you need me. Just don't put me in the same room with the woman, because I would probably kill her."

Jay's phone vibrated with an incoming text message. "I'll call you after I've spoken with her," he told Blake. "I'll see you next month when my team comes to put a whupping on your team."

Blake laughed and then hung up, and Jay skimmed the screen to view the text, hoping it was from Donovan with some more news about the case. A small part of him wished that he was wrong and he didn't have to confront Delaney. Unfortunately, the text was from Linc. Jay unleashed a string of obscenities when he read it:

Your mother has arrived at the vineyard.

Fourteen

Jay's mother hugged her daughter tightly as she eyed Bridgett over Charlie's shoulder. "I had no idea you were back in the States, sweetheart."

Charlie scoffed at her mother. "Right. Jay called you, I know."

"Actually, I wouldn't have known Jay was in town had it not been for some gossip blogger," the woman said.

"Oh come on," Charlie said so sharply it made Bridgett cringe. "You don't read anything unless it's a journal or a textbook."

The woman's only reaction to her daughter's harsh accusation was a slight downturn in the corners of her mouth. "Actually, the only way to know if my children are alive is by Twitter and tabloid-stalking them."

A touch of guilt flashed in Charlie's eyes before she hid it behind her usual veil of disdain. "What are you doing here, Mother?"

"I came to speak with your brother, but now I can visit with both my children at the same time. It's been nearly a year since we've all been together." She glanced over at Bridgett.

"Charlotte, where are your manners? You haven't introduced me to your friend."

Charlie rolled her eyes. "If you're reading the gossip blogs, then you know who she is. Dr. Melanie Davis, this is Bridgett Janik, Jay's *lawyer*." Charlie formed little air quotes with her fingers when she said the last word.

Melanie Davis's gaze was shrewd when it landed on Bridgett. "Of course she is." Jay's mother extended her hand. "I've been waiting a long time to meet you, Bridgett."

Bridgett swallowed roughly as she tried not to flinch under the older woman's gaze. So he'd told his mother. Somehow the thought surprised her. The cold way in which he'd abandoned her and their baby didn't mesh with a man who would tell his mother about what was, to him, essentially a summer fling.

Bridgett took her hand, refusing to cower under the woman's gaze. She had nothing to apologize for. It was this woman's son who had perpetrated the wrongdoing.

Charlie stared at them both quizzically. "*Long time?* I thought you guys just started dating?"

Jay's mother arched an eyebrow but fortunately kept her thoughts to herself.

"We're not dating." Technically that was the truth. "My firm is representing his team in a class action lawsuit." Again, technically true.

His sister laughed. "You really do have a courtroom face, Bridgett."

Melanie didn't say a word. She just continued to level a hard glare at Bridgett.

"If you'll excuse me," Bridgett said as she gathered her dress and shopping bag. "I'm just going to put these things away and check in with work. I'll give you two some privacy to catch up."

Charlie shot her a desperate look. "Why don't I ask Josie to get us some tapas and a cool drink by the pool? After all, my mother came all this way to see *you*."

Bridgett detected a little pain behind Charlie's smart aleck attitude. She also saw the panic in Jay's sister's eyes.

From the looks of it, Melanie Davis was unaware of her daughter's condition. Still, none of this was Bridgett's problem. She'd agreed to one weekend; that was all. The less she became involved with Jay's family, the easier it would be to walk away.

"I'm sorry, but I really need to respond to some e-mails before it gets too late on the East Coast." Her statement wasn't actually a lie. Gwen had been texting her the past twenty minutes and Bridgett really did want to find out how things went when Skip was presented with the separation papers today. "It was very nice to meet you, ma'am."

Charlie huffed in annoyance as Bridgett dashed up the stairs. She was glad that she'd asked Josie for another room earlier in the day. Especially if Jay's mother was staying for any length of time. Jay would, no doubt, be furious. But Bridgett needed some space to process the past twenty-four hours—heck, the past forty-eight hours—without his sexy presence intimidating her and clouding her normally good judgment.

Gwen answered on the second ring. "He didn't even deny it," she cried. "The bastard even seemed to be relieved to have gotten caught with his pants down around his ankles."

Bridgett sighed. Sadly, that was the reaction she pretty much expected out of Skip. "I know it's painful, but it would have been worse if he tried to fight you on this, believe me."

"He's already gone." Gwen gulped into the phone. "He didn't even stick around long enough to break it to the kids with me."

"I'm sorry, honey," Bridgett said. And she truly was. Skip was a jerk of epic proportions who didn't deserve to have children. "That had to be difficult."

Her sister sniffed. "Mom and Dad were here with me. They were lovely. Ashley and Mark brought the boys over and Dad just took the kids to Friendly's for ice cream. Apparently, everything will be much better after a cone sundae."

Bridgett smiled to herself. Despite the fact that he was a dentist, Bridgett's father's go-to sympathy ploy always centered around ice cream. "I wish it were that easy for grown-ups, but the kids will be fine, Gwen. You're a good mom. That's not going to change."

"Well, I'm going to be a working mom now. Dad says he has a need for an assistant in his office and I'm going to take him up on that temporarily. At least until I can get my teaching certificate."

Gwen had majored in education, but she'd never pursued that career path. "That's wonderful. I'm so glad you've got a plan."

"Actually, it was Adam's idea."

"Adam?"

"The lawyer you sent."

"Oh, right." Bridgett made a mental note to check the divorce lawyer's relationship status when she got back to the office. The last thing she needed was her sister falling for the first male who paid attention to her—especially one who was getting paid to do so.

She spoke briefly to her mother, who assured her that Gwen was holding up well. When Sybil Janik began to ask pointed questions about Jay, Bridgett quickly ended the call, using the same excuse she'd given to Jay's sister and mother: work. After an hour on the phone with Dan, she learned that none of the cheerleaders were unhappy working for the Blaze. So far he'd interviewed fifty current and former Sparks, and none indicated a desire to join in on the class action suit.

"I'll keep you posted if I hear anything else." There was a hint of bitterness in Dan's voice. "I may not be traveling with the team, but I'm pulling my weight here."

"Don't believe everything you read, Dan," Bridgett cautioned him.

Dan gave a little huff. "Sure. Like I said, I'll let you know if something else comes up."

Bridgett hung up and fielded a few terse e-mails from Stuart. By the time she'd finished, her head was throbbing and her stomach was rumbling. But the thought of confronting Jay's mother and sister made her queasy. Maybe she could talk Josie into letting her fix a cup of tea and a sandwich in the kitchen. She'd made it halfway across the room when the door swung open. A very weary-looking Jay stood at the threshold, still dressed in his Calvin Klein suit, his tie loose and his collar unbuttoned.

He pushed into the room, a look of dissatisfaction on his face. "Did you get lost?"

Bridgett stood her ground. "No. It's a big house. I didn't see any reason we needed to share when this room will do just fine for me."

"Would you like me to demonstrate the most pressing reason why we need to share my bed?"

She kept her eyes away from his sexy mouth. "That won't be necessary."

Jay loosened his tie even further before he dropped down on the bed, laying his head on the pillow and crossing his shiny wingtips at the ankles.

"Make yourself comfortable," Bridgett said sarcastically. "I'm headed to the kitchen for a snack."

He closed his eyes and his face relaxed. "You don't want to go down there. My mother and sister are going at it."

"And you're hiding up here?"

Jay cracked an eyelid. "That's definitely the pot calling the kettle black."

"Shouldn't you be down there refereeing?"

"Hell, no. If I show up, they'll have someone to blame for everything."

Bridgett sat on the edge of the bed. "Your mother doesn't know about your sister's baby."

His sigh sounded beleaguered to her ears. "No. For some reason Charlie feels compelled to keep it a secret even from our mother. Some sort of estrogen power struggle, I suppose."

"But your mother knows about *our* baby?" Bridgett asked. Her stomach knotted up even though she suspected she knew what his answer would be.

Both his eyelids snapped open. "What did she say?"

"She didn't have to say anything."

Jay swore as he pulled himself to his feet. "Don't worry

about my mother, Bridgett. She keeps to herself much of the time."

"Yet she came here today because she wanted to meet me. Or rip my heart out. She's not easy to read, your mother."

"She isn't very maternal. I doubt she'd go all mama bear on you."

"Yet you told her about us. About me. She recognized my name from the blog."

Jay pulled the tie from around his neck and shoved it in the pocket of his suit jacket. "She's the only one I told, if that's what you're getting at."

Bridgett knew that was a lie, but she was tired of rehashing old wounds. She was tired, period. Tired and hungry. "I'm going to find something to eat."

"I've already arranged for dinner. A private dinner for just the two of us."

"Don't be ridiculous. Your mother said she hasn't seen the two of you together for nearly a year. I'm perfectly capable of feeding myself. Go be with your family." She was angry now. Angry at all the emotions pulling at her when she was around Jay. Bridgett just wanted some time alone to think. The little snippets she'd picked up from his sister and mother today were confusing and contradictory to the image of Jay she'd held in her mind all these years. Had his heart been broken? It wasn't possible. Not when he hadn't cared enough to come back to Italy and help her sort out a future.

"Bridgett," he said calmly, making her resent his constant steady composure when she felt like her emotions had been caught up in a cyclone. "My mother and sister need this time alone together. I have no idea how to help their relationship except to provide a neutral territory for them to work things out."

This was the Jay she'd fallen in love with all those years ago. The kind and considerate man who put his family first. Except he hadn't put her first when she needed him the most. Tears burned the backs of her eyes. She didn't want to give him her heart again, but she suddenly realized that he might not have ever given it back to her that first time.

Jay walked across the room toward her.

"Don't," she said. "I don't like you. And I don't want to like you."

He wrapped his arms around her and she, stupid woman that she was, let him. "I told you, this isn't about liking one another, much less loving one another," he murmured against the top of her head. "But I will always treat you with the respect you deserve, Bridgett, in public and in private. We can make this work." His hand slid up and down her back, and Bridgett suddenly couldn't fight it anymore. She pushed her hands beneath his suit jacket and wrapped them around his broad back. They stood there, embracing each other for a few moments, both content to absorb the silence and the warmth of each other's bodies until Bridgett's stomach rumbled loudly.

"That would be the dinner bell," he joked as he stepped back and took her hand. "I promised you a tour of the vineyard. Tonight we start with dinner in the wine cellar."

Jay breathed a sigh of relief when Bridgett allowed him to guide her out of the guest room, down the stairs, and out across the lawn to the winery. Twilight had just settled over the vineyard, and Jay was grateful that his mother and sister had seemingly established some sort of peace accord that would allow them to coexist in one place for the weekend. To say that he'd been surprised that his mother would waylay him at his home was an understatement. He hadn't considered she'd remember anything about Bridgett; he barely remembered the conversation he'd had with his mother himself. Everything about those weeks had been so raw and painful that Jay had blocked the time period out of his memory. It seemed he was destined to relive those days again, though.

He opened the iron gate and gestured for her to precede him through. "There won't be as many spiders as there were in the DiSantis wine cellar," he teased in hopes of lightening the mood.

Bridgett's eyes went wide. "There better not be any spiders."

"I'll protect you," he said, closing the gate behind them. The lights were operated by motion detectors, and each step they took illuminated the stone path in front of them. He directed her to the worn steps leading a half flight down into the cool, stone cellar. Josie had lit the candles in the sconces on the two walls beside the round table, giving the room a soft glow. The table was set for two with food stored in covered dishes on the row of hot plates on the counter.

Jay watched as Bridgett slowly circled the room, taking in the curved stone ceiling, the leather sofa, and the racks of wine. She walked over to the wall to peer more closely at a painting he'd bought in Wyoming. It featured a peaceful scene of buffalo grazing in front of Grand Teton Mountain. With a slight smile and a shake of her head, she fingered the flat-screen TV mounted to the other wall.

"Wow, all you need is a smoking jacket and this would be the perfect man cave," she said.

"The humidor is in the corner—help yourself," Jay replied as he uncorked a bottle of cabernet sauvignon and poured them both a glass.

"I can't stand those things when Grandpa Gus smokes them. I doubt I'd enjoy smoking one myself." She took the glass from him and sipped the wine. "It's delicious. Amazing, in fact. This whole place is amazing, Jay. I don't know how you can stand to live in Baltimore for even part of the year."

He took a sip of his own wine so as not to tell her that he hated being at the vineyard by himself. The winery had been a part of his dream—a dream he'd retooled that long-ago summer to include Bridgett—and he was proud that he'd accomplished it, but he felt empty enjoying the vineyard on his own. Jay didn't dare tell Bridgett that, though. He wouldn't give her that much power over his heart again. Instead he redirected her attention. "Let's have some of Josie's amazing beef Wellington."

Bridgett sat in the chair he'd pulled out for her and Jay

spooned their dinner onto the warm plates. They ate in comfortable silence for a few minutes, both savoring the hearty meal his housekeeper had prepared.

"So how was shopping with my sister?" he asked.

"Enlightening," Bridgett answered, a surprised smile curving her lips.

Jay reached for his wine. "She didn't by chance enlighten you as to who the father of her baby is, did she?"

Bridgett choked briefly before swallowing. "Why would she tell me something like that?"

"She wouldn't. It was just a shot in the dark." Except her mannerisms were telling him it might not have been.

"Hmm," was all Bridgett said as she buttered her roll.

Jay studied her as he took a sip of his wine. She had that evasive lawyerly look about her. Not only that, but she hadn't said that Charlie didn't confide in her. *Damn.* It would be just like his maniacal sister to tell Bridgett.

He swore viciously. "She did tell you, didn't she?"

Bridgett remained silent, her face an impassive mask.

"Damn it, Bridgett, you need to tell me."

"I don't 'need' to tell you anything."

Jay threw down his napkin. "Suppose it's some deadbeat who's only after her money?" He pushed out of his chair and began pacing around the wine cellar, the candles flickering as he stalked past. "She thinks she's mature enough to handle having a kid, but she's only twenty-one. Charlie acts first and thinks about the consequences later. I need to take care of this before it gets out of hand."

"You don't have to worry about the baby's father," Bridgett said quietly.

"What's that supposed to mean?"

"It means I've agreed to protect her legally on that issue."

Her words stopped him in his tracks. "Why would you do that?"

"Because your sister asked me to." Bridgett stood, tossing down her own napkin. Tears were shining in her eyes when she stood. "Believe me, I didn't want to get involved. But I thought—I thought—oh never mind what I thought! Just drop the issue about the baby's father and try to support *her* pregnancy. It's the least you can do."

Jay grew angrier at her implication that he hadn't supported Bridgett's own pregnancy. He couldn't have very well supported her when he knew nothing about their baby. "Don't make this about us," he argued.

"There is no 'us,'" she said, crossing her arms over her chest.

"Like hell there isn't," Jay growled as he reached for her. He didn't want another innocent hug like they'd shared earlier up at the house. Jay wanted more. He wanted to possess her, to have Bridgett be his and only his. She was wrong. They were most definitely an "us" and he wasn't going to let her go until he proved that to her.

"Jay," she gasped as he pulled her into his chest. Her hand landed on his heart and the warmth of her palm through his shirt stopped him. His eyes locked with her damp ones. "A relationship based solely on sex isn't going to sustain us as a couple. Not in the long run."

An aching began in the area of his chest, but he ignored it. He wouldn't give her more, yet he couldn't let her go. "Then let's see how far we can go with it," he said before taking her mouth in a searing kiss. She sighed against his lips, her body arching around his in surrender. Jay wasted no time, parting her lips with his own and delving inside her warm mouth. She tasted like rich cabernet grapes straight from the vineyard. His vineyard. His woman.

Bridgett's hands trailed up his chest to wrap around his neck. She made a little mewling sound at the back of her throat and he was instantly, painfully hard. He backed her toward the leather sofa as he shrugged out of his jacket. Jay eased her onto her back before covering her with his own body, while her efficient fingers undid the buttons on his shirt. Jay feasted on her mouth and she frantically tugged at his T-shirt, finally tangling her hands in the hair on his chest.

He reluctantly left her mouth to savor the delicate skin on her neck. When her finger flicked at his nipple he returned the favor, taking her earlobe between his teeth. Her hips arched toward his in response.

"I'm going to show you how well this can work," he breathed into her ear.

Her lips grazed his cheek. "I'm not denying this isn't good, Jay. I just don't think it's good for us."

"Bridgett, please turn off your argumentative legal mind and let me do this my way."

"Are you going to stop talking and hurry up, then?"

Jay kissed her again, ruthless and demanding. She responded with another thrust of her hips and a sexy moan that nearly sent him over the edge. He reached for the tiny pearl buttons on her sweater, but opening them took too much effort so he shoved his hands beneath the fabric, where he could trace his fingers along the silky skin on her flat belly. Bridgett wrapped a leg around his hips just as his fingers made contact with her lacy bra. He needed to be inside her. Now. He'd show her how well this could work, both now and forever.

"Boss?"

Bridgett stiffened beneath him at the sound of Linc's voice outside the cellar.

"Whoa! Um, sorry, boss." His voice came from within the room, which meant his assistant was likely getting an eyeful. Damn it, he was going to fire the kid. Bridgett shoved at Jay but he didn't dare move before adjusting her sweater.

"Um, boss. Sir. Mr. McManus. Sir," Linc stammered. Fortunately, it sounded like he'd retreated to outside the cellar door again. "Donovan says he has to speak with you right away. It's urgent. Sir."

Bridgett swatted at his chest and Jay rolled off, allowing her to climb off the sofa. Jay remained where he was, painfully frustrated now.

"Boss?" Linc called. "What should I tell him?"

Jay swore as he watched Bridgett right her clothes, her actions doing nothing to calm his body down. "I'll call him from here. Please make sure Ms. Janik gets back to the house safely."

She arched an eyebrow at Jay before picking up his suit jacket and handing it to him. "Am I under house arrest?"

If that was the only way to keep her, Jay might consider it, but he was pretty sure he was winning the battle for her acquiescence. He wrapped his fingers around her wrist, feeling her pulse ratchet up beneath his thumb. "It's dark out there. I just want to make sure you're safe."

Bridgett leaned down and kissed the corner of his mouth. "If Don is calling about the case, be sure you share whatever he says with your lawyer."

Jay grinned. "My goal is to share everything with my lawyer."

She stood up and gently tugged her arm free. "No, Jay. The offer you've made excludes you from sharing everything." Her face was melancholy as she turned and left the cellar. Jay listened to Bridgett's retreating footsteps as Linc followed behind her, mumbling an apology. He slammed his head back against the leather sofa. While he unleashed a swarm of obscenities in which he pretended to fire everyone in his employ, Jay punched up Donovan Carter's number on his phone. Whatever the Blaze chief of security wanted, it had better be important.

Fifteen

"Jennifer Knowles caved as soon as I got her away from her father," Donovan said. "Apparently Jennifer's father has been helping to provide for his grandchildren, but the idea of having the Blaze do the job his own son won't do sounded like a better plan. He bought right into his former daughter-in-law's plot."

"So Jennifer's father green-lighted the whole thing?" Jay fumed as he paced the stone floor of the wine cellar. "What about the alleged sexual harassment at the photo shoot? Did that story change once she got out of Daddy's earshot?"

"She said there was some truth to the accusations, but nothing physical. Alesha took some liberties when she wrote the petition up."

Jay's expletives bounced off the stone walls. "Hank is ready to fire those guys."

"Some disciplining is probably in order, but firing them might be a little drastic," Don said. "Asia thinks if the team issues a blanket apology with all of them up there at a press conference followed by an in-house mandatory sexual harassment sensitivity refresher, the team will be covered."

"The bigger question is whether it will be enough to appease the commissioner and the crazy feminists?"

Don hesitated briefly. "As long as nothing else is leaked out."

He scrubbed at the back of his neck. "Fine. Tell Asia to work out the details with Hank."

"So now what?" Don asked. "Jennifer wants to tell her former sister-in-law to drop the case."

"No!" Jay snapped. "We need her to keep playing along. Alesha Warren is just a cog in a larger ploy, and I still need to flush out who's trying to come after me."

"Actually, Jennifer might be able to help with that."

Jay stopped in his tracks, his breath stilling in his lungs. Could this actually be the last puzzle piece slipping into place? "How?"

"She said that *after* Alesha had begun compiling the case, she reached out to that blogger—the *Girlfriends' Guide to the NFL*—in hopes for some free publicity," Don explained.

"Tell me Jennifer knows how her former sister-in-law did it."

"Even better," Don said, his tone gleeful. "Jennifer has the e-mail address. In her haste to get court papers ready, Alesha accidently cc'd Jennifer on one of her e-mails to the blogger."

Yes! Jay pumped his fist into the air. He hadn't felt this overjoyed since the Blaze won the Super Bowl. Finally, he could put an end to this. "Don't hold back, Don. Give me that e-mail."

"I called in a favor over at NCIS and they're trying to trace back the IP address," Don said. "Whoever this blogger is, he or she has been pretty adept at hiding their path, but maybe we'll come up with something this time."

Jay already had a good idea who the blogger was and where he could find her. He just needed the e-mail address to confirm his suspicions. "They won't be able to come up with anything. She's too smart to leave a trail. Just give me the e-mail and let me deal with it."

Don was quiet for a moment on the other end of the phone. "You mean you know who it is?"

"I have my suspicions."

It was Don's turn to swear. "If I give you the e-mail address, you promise not to 'deal with it' on your own?"

Jay snorted. "I can handle her." He didn't need former Special Agent Donovan Carter witnessing his retaliatory extortion.

"I'm serious. This isn't something you should be handling on your own."

"Donovan, unless you no longer want to work for the Baltimore Blaze, you'll text me that e-mail immediately."

Don mumbled something that sounded less than respectful for one's boss. "I just forwarded you the e-mail."

"Thank you, Don. You and Asia, go home now. Tell Jennifer Knowles to sit tight and play along until we say otherwise. I'll see you when the team arrives tomorrow night."

He ended the call and clicked through to his e-mail. Jay released a breath he hadn't known he was holding when he finally read the address.

"Gotcha."

Jay found Linc in the office.

"Uh, sorry, boss," his assistant said sheepishly.

Jay held up a hand. "Enough. We've got work to do. I've got to take a quick trip to Las Vegas tomorrow. I'll need the plane ready first thing in the morning."

"Sure, boss. When do we leave?"

"'We' aren't leaving. This is a solo trip." Jay pushed aside a panel in the wall to access his safe.

"You're leaving me here? With Princess Charlotte? And your mother?" The look on Linc's face was comical.

"Next time maybe you'll remember to knock."

"But, boss—"

Jay glared at his assistant. "No buts, Lincoln. I need you to hold down the fort in case of some sort of estrogen implosion."

Linc grumbled about his grandmother calling him Lincoln when she was mad at it him, but Jay ignored his assistant. He shoved two file folders into his briefcase, hoping that they contained enough to make Delaney back down for good.

"Fine," Linc finally said. "I'll keep working on the Princess Charlotte problem."

Jay paused in his packing. Bridgett knew who the father of Charlie's baby was. He could probably get it out of her if he tried hard enough, but then again, he didn't really want to. Sure, Jay wanted to know who the jerk was who'd knocked up his sister, but he was surprisingly comfortable with Bridgett holding on to that secret. She could be trusted with it. Bridgett would do right by Charlie.

"That problem has been solved," Jay said as he snapped the briefcase closed.

"What do you mean it's been solved? You know who the guy is?" Linc looked and sounded astonished—almost as though he were nine and his stepfather had just told him to suck it up, Santa Claus wasn't real.

"I have no idea who the baby daddy is. But Bridgett does and that's going to have to be good enough."

Linc slumped back onto the leather sofa in the office. "Seriously? You're going to let it go?"

Jay didn't have the heart to totally burst the boy's bubble. "For now."

"So what am I supposed to do with a house full of women tomorrow?"

"I don't know. Talk about shoes?' Jay headed for the door, eager to finish what he and Bridgett had started in the wine cellar. "Have the plane ready to go at eight tomorrow morning."

Linc was whimpering much like the pup Charlie had accused him of being when Jay strode from the room headed for the stairs. His mother's voice calling his name stopped his forward progress.

"Jayson Michael McManus."

Jay turned on his heel and glanced toward the far end of the family room. His mother sat in the shadows, a glass of wine in her hand, presumably gazing at the stars.

"The trifecta. You haven't used all three names since I was a teenager." Jay wandered into the dimly lit room. Tossing his briefcase on a chair, he headed for the liquor cabinet. A little voice told him that this conversation would go a lot more smoothly accompanied by two fingers of Scotch.

"Yes, well, you haven't been around me enough this past decade to have an opportunity to warrant a full dressing-down."

Jay sipped at his Scotch. "How do you like the chardonnay, Mother?" He gestured at the wineglass dangling from his mother's fingertips.

"It's lovely, but you know that it's my favorite. You send it to me by the caseload." She saluted him with her glass. "Stop trying to avoid this conversation."

He perched on the arm of the upholstered chair across from the sofa his mother was curled up on. "I thought we were having a conversation."

"Really, Jay, you're incorrigible."

He smiled at his mother. "I haven't heard that word since SAT prep."

She shook her head and took a sip from her wine. "I've raised two headstrong, disobedient children."

Jay wanted to take exception to her use of the word *raised* but while his mother was most times too absorbed in her work to notice either of her children, her neglect was always emotional, not physical, and never on purpose. His stepfather used to explain to Charlie that her mother had a brilliant mind, and sometimes that brain didn't allow her to share her time with others—even her children. It was a crappy thing to say to a first grader, but Lloyd Davis hadn't exactly been the role model of a demonstrative parent either.

"What is she doing here?" his mother asked.

Jay was honestly perplexed as to which "she" his mother was referring to. "Charlie? I don't know. She just showed up," he lied. "She's obviously bored with the beautiful people this week so she's hiding out here."

"I wasn't talking about Charlie. Although shame on you for not telling me immediately when she arrived. I worry about her and I'm tired of having to find about her comings and goings from that obnoxious TMZ program."

"And this is my problem, how?"

"It's never been your problem," his mother snapped. "She adores you. Me, she just tolerates. Lloyd should have never allowed his will to be written to give her access to her trust at eighteen. She was too young. Of course she'd rebel against me." She swallowed hard and jerked her chin up. "Never mind. I can wait Charlie out. One day she'll have children of her own and she'll understand how difficult it is to be a mother."

Jay choked on the Scotch he'd just swallowed, trying not spew it all over his mom. *Damn.* Clearly, Charlie hadn't come clean with her.

"I'm talking about Bridgett Janik," his mother continued. "Why is she here after all these years? You loved her and she broke your heart. I watched you nearly self-destruct after she lied about the baby. Don't tell me you're giving her a second chance to do the same?"

Jay coughed now, the lack of air bringing tears to his eyes. Was he giving Bridgett a second chance? At a sexual relationship, yes, but not at his heart. Somehow, he didn't think his mother would understand that, though. "It's business, Mom. Her firm is representing the team in a crazy class action case."

His mother tsked at him. "According to your sister, your lawyer slept in your room last night. With you. That's monkey business if you ask me. And don't you dare disregard those cheerleaders who represent your team as 'crazy.' You'd better be paying those women a decent wage as well as providing them a safe work environment."

He had to smile at his mother's staunch protection of working women everywhere. "The case is specious. By all accounts, the Sparks are not only happy with their pay, but also their working conditions. The truth will win out and the case will be settled very soon."

"Does that mean your 'business' with your lawyer will be over very soon, too?"

Jay's gut clenched at the thought. After years of being apart from Bridgett—of despising what she did—the thought of letting her go again was unthinkable.

His mother sighed. "Never mind. Your face says it all."

"And what does it say, Mother?"

"That you've forgiven her. And you still love her."

He gulped down the rest of his Scotch. "You're wrong on both counts. But we've moved on."

Coming to her feet, she walked over to Jay and cupped his cheek. "For such a smart man, you really don't get it. You'll never be able to move on. Not without forgiving her. And it's impossible to keep your heart out of any relationship, no matter how hard you try. Love just doesn't work that way." She kissed his cheek. "You've been aloof and guarded since that summer, not allowing anyone to get close to you. I want to see you happy, not just involved in a calculated 'business' relationship. That's not healthy, Jay. And no matter how superhuman you think you are"—she tapped his chest—"it's dangerous here."

Jay didn't bother enlightening his mother that he no longer had a heart to risk. He'd left it in Italy all those years ago.

"I'll see you tomorrow?" she asked, standing in the doorway.

"No," he said. "I have business I need to attend to all day."

She sighed again. "All right, then. But I'd like to find some time before the party to speak with both you and your sister together. It's important."

"Is everything okay?" A trickle of unease ran up Jay's spine.

"Everything is fine. I just have something to discuss with you two while I have you both in the same house. That doesn't happen often enough."

The regret in his mother's voice made him even more uncomfortable. But the last thirteen years hadn't been entirely his fault. "I'll have Josie arrange a nice lunch on Saturday."

His mother nodded. "Good night, then."

Jay heard her footsteps disappear up the stairs, but he

remained where he was, staring out at the darkened vineyard.
The stars in the night sky were not as bright as they were in
the valleys of Northern Italy, but Jay still felt a profound
connection to the place that had changed his life.

"Damn it, Bridgett, the condom broke." Jay looked
*across the cab of his pickup truck at Bridgett, her much
calmer face illuminated by starlight as she drove them
toward the airport in Verona.*

*"I know that, Jay. I was there, remember?" She shot him
a cheeky smile before returning her eyes to the road.
"Please don't worry about that now. Your stepfather just
died. You need to get home to your mother and Charlie."*

*"I wish you'd come with me." It was the first time he'd
admitted that to her, but suddenly the thought of leaving
her behind was more painful than the prospect of attending
his stepfather's funeral.*

*She smiled again, but kept her eyes on the road. "I'll be
with you in spirit. Besides, you'll have too much to do to
think about me."*

*His stepfather's sudden death had been a shock. When
Jay's mother had finally reached him, she'd begged him to
hurry home for Charlie, saying that the little girl was under-
standably devastated. She needed her big brother now more
than ever. He was booked on the first flight out the following
morning and Bridgett was making the two-hour drive to get
him there on time. Jay was grateful to have a few more
hours to spend with her.*

*The last seven weeks had flown by while both of them
worked during the days and spent their nights in each other's arms. He'd told her about his family, his friends and
their dream of opening a vineyard. Bridgett had slowly and
irrevocably become a part of that dream, too. Jay couldn't
imagine a life without her.*

*"I'll e-mail you every time I get near a computer," he
told her. "So if anything results from the broken condom,*

you're to tell me right away. I'm not sure how long it will take me to get things organized for my family."

Bridgett's hands gripped the steering wheel a bit more firmly than they had a moment before. "Please don't spend all your time worrying about that. The odds are pretty great nothing will come of it."

"Yeah, I know that, but promise me anyway," he asked her. "Because I want to do the right thing."

She kept her gaze focused over the truck's hood. "You'll be the second to know."

Jay breathed a sigh of relief. "I'm glad you're living with the DiSantis family. They're good people."

"Yes, well, they've only got to put up with me for eight more weeks. Then it's back home to Boston and the rest of my life, wherever that takes me."

You'll be with me, he wanted to shout out. But something held the words in his throat. It was too early. Jay thought she might feel the same way about him as he felt about her. Bridgett's emotions shone very clearly on her face whenever they made love. But still he hadn't told her he loved her. Even though Jay knew deep in his bones that he did.

Standing outside the terminal, Jay didn't want to let Bridgett go. He kissed her deeply, breathing in the scent of her and committing it to memory. "I might not get back here," he whispered. "After I sort things out with my family, I have to go to Chicago to move out of the house I'm sharing with friends."

"Then it's a good thing I'm coming home at the end of September," she said as she tangled her fingers in his hair.

Jay kissed the tip of her nose. "It's a very good thing."

"Go, before you miss your connection in Rome." She shoved at his chest, but Jay could see the telltale dampness in her eyes. "Your family needs you more than I do right now," she said.

"But you'll call me if you need me?"

She gave him a quick nod of her head. "I'll see you in a few weeks."

"I'll send you an e-mail as soon as I can," he said as he made his way into the terminal.

Jay swallowed the dregs of his Scotch. He had sent Bridgett e-mails at first. Long flowing letters describing the events leading up to Lloyd Davis's funeral. In return, Bridgett had sent back messages of encouragement and support. They'd kept him hopeful for the future. But a week later, Jay's world was rocked again when he learned he'd been shut out of his father's will. Looking back now, he hadn't reacted to the situation as well as he should have. He'd been immature, taking everything out on the people around him. And even those loved ones an ocean away. Not that any of his behavior excused Bridgett's. But admitting some culpability made it a lot easier for him to climb the stairs and seek out her bedroom.

Sixteen

Bridgett had just drifted off to sleep when the mattress dipped slightly and Jay crawled into bed beside her. She hadn't for one second believed he wouldn't follow her to the guest room next to his suite, but she hated that he seemed to be calling all the shots. Jay wanted a sexual relationship, free of any emotional entanglements. Bridgett worried that—even with his abrupt betrayal all those years ago—her heart might still be susceptible to him. Even worse, she hated that the rest of her body seemed to be all in with Jay's "sex only" proposal.

She feigned sleep as his body cocooned around hers, the heat of his naked skin warming her through her flimsy nightgown. The rasp of his late-day stubble brushed against her bare shoulder and Bridgett couldn't hold back her tremor of arousal any longer. Jay instantly wrapped an arm around her midsection, pulling her in closer.

When his lips found the delicate skin beneath her ear, she let out a contented sigh. "Do your best, but I'm still not going to tell you who the baby's father is."

Bridgett felt his smile against her skin. "As much as I'd

like to accept that challenge, I've decided to let you keep Charlie's secret."

Startled by his statement, Bridgett rolled over onto her back. "You don't care who it is?"

Jay rolled on top of her, the hardness of his body causing her breath to catch at the back of her throat. "I do care," he growled next to her ear. "I want to know who the little shit is. But she had some cockamamie reason for telling you instead of me. So I have to honor that. Besides, you've only known Charlie for a day. I've known her her whole life and I'm very familiar with her tactics. She'll tell me eventually."

Bridgett doubted that his little sister would confess to Jay, but she didn't bother telling him so, not while she was so thoroughly enjoying what his lips were doing to her earlobe. She trailed her fingers along the knots in his spine. "Your assistant isn't going to barge in with another emergency?"

"Not if he wants to live to see the game on Sunday." His lips toyed with the corner of her mouth, making Bridgett grow restless. "Besides, Don unraveled the whole case."

She reached between them and shoved at his chest. "He did what?"

Jay pushed up to a plank position. His nostrils flared slightly when he caught a glimpse of her breast, which had escaped the confines of her nightgown. Bridgett yanked the garment back into place. "How?" she demanded.

"It seems his theory about Alesha Warren convincing her sister-in-law to file the suit was one hundred percent correct. Jennifer made a full confession."

Bridgett gasped in surprise and Jay covered her mouth with his, delivering a searing kiss that had her hot and wet in an instant. His hips rocked against hers while his tongue plundered her mouth, but Bridgett's brain wasn't ready to shut down yet. "Wait," she breathed, pulling her mouth free. "If Alesha Warren went to so much trouble to set this up, she's not going to give up that easily. What about her threats to divulge the content of the lawsuits against you? Or—or your other secrets?" she whispered.

Jay leaned down to kiss the tip of her nose. "I'm one step

ahead of you. Alesha doesn't have the secrets. The blogger does."

"You know this how?"

"Because I know who the person behind the blog is."

Bridgett's pulse beat erratically as her brain demanded more oxygen so she could keep up with the conversation. "How long? How long have you known?"

Jay's face grew serious. "I've had a gut instinct about it for a couple of days, but Don just confirmed my suspicions."

"Tell me who it is," she demanded.

His only response was to arch an eyebrow at her.

"Ugh!" Bridgett slapped at his chest in frustration. "Of course you won't tell me. Not unless I tell you who fathered Charlie's baby."

Jay sank back into her, his body pinning hers to the mattress as he reached for both of her hands and drew them over her head. His beard scraped her neck while his tongue traced the shell of her ear. "In this case I think it's best if we both keep our secrets to ourselves."

An ominous feeling settled in Bridgett's stomach. "Why?" she asked. "What are you planning on doing? As your lawyer, I have to tell you to turn her over to the authorities."

His lips nipped at her collarbone. "And what are they going to charge her with? Cyberbullying?"

She tilted her head to the side to give him better access. "How about blackmail or extortion?"

Jay's mouth drifted lower on her chest. "No. That will just add more publicity, which is what the blogger wants. It's easier if I take care of things myself."

"You're not planning on confronting this person, are you?" Bridgett squirmed beneath him. "I thought we discussed this earlier today?"

He heaved a sigh and lifted his face to gaze at her. Passion blazed in his beautiful blue eyes, but Bridgett saw something else in them, too: foreboding. "I'm going to do what I should have done years ago: Deal with the problem once and for all."

Bridgett studied his determined face, finding no clue as to his intentions. "Jay—"

Jay bumped her forehead with his own. "Forget about it, Bridgett. Nothing I do will be as bad as what you're imagining in that pretty head of yours. But I'll have it all taken care of by this time tomorrow."

"Tomorrow?" Bridgett felt a mixture of relief and sorrow. She was grateful their indiscretions in Italy wouldn't be all over the Internet. But her chest felt heavy with the decision she was going to be forced to make. As much as her body wanted to continue with this relationship, Bridgett knew she needed to get out before she got hurt again. And given the feelings about Jay that had been reemerging this past week, she would get hurt. She wouldn't take him up on his proposal. She just couldn't.

"I should get back to Boston, then," she whispered.

Jay swore as he rolled off her and flopped over onto his back. "No. You gave your word."

She pulled the sheet over her body, which had quickly grown cool without the warmth of his skin.

"I said I'd stay through the game on Sunday, but there's no reason for me to be here as your lawyer if—"

"You're not here as my lawyer and you damn well know it."

Bridgett bristled at the truth in his words. Sure, Jay had manipulated it so that she was on the case and even so she'd be staying at his home. But she could have said no last night. And she should have locked her door tonight. Yet, she hadn't. The trouble was she was still dancing like a puppet on that fine line between loving and hating this man, and her body was pulling all the strings. No matter which side of the line she ended up on, the potential existed that her heart would be devastated. She tried telling herself that the Jay she'd fallen in love with that summer didn't exist. Perhaps he never really had. Bridgett had simply been blinded by a passion so intense and overwhelming, it still burned between them today.

But she wasn't ready to go yet. Bridgett didn't have the strength to leave this place, so similar to the vineyard that they'd both dreamed of. She told herself that her desire to stay had nothing to do with the man lying in bed next to her.

It was more that she wanted to be that naïve young girl again, the one who believed in love and happily ever after. Here, at Jay's perfect vineyard, she could still feel the ghost of that girl she used to be.

Jay linked his fingers through hers, lifting her hand to his lips. "You're off the clock, Bridgett. This isn't business. We're two people enjoying one another for mutual pleasure." He gently kissed her knuckles. "It's good with us. Really good. We can make this work."

He was lying, of course. They couldn't make a purely sexual relationship work. But he wasn't lying about the sex being good. *Really good.* She'd leave the vineyard on Sunday as planned, but until then, she'd store up as many memories as she could; enough to last her a lifetime. Bridgett rolled over and straddled Jay.

His mouth turned up in a cocky smile as he slid his fingers beneath her nightgown. "Let the negotiations begin."

Bridgett yanked her gown over her head, watching Jay's chest compress as he sucked in a ragged breath at the sight of her naked body. "No negotiating, Jay. I'm here until Sunday and that's all."

He wrapped his fingers around her hips and rocked his own hips against her core. "You won't be able to live without this," he said arrogantly.

Tears stung the backs of her eyes. "You'd be surprised what I've learned to live without."

A profound loneliness seemed to envelop Bridgett after Jay left. She'd done her best to be upbeat and positive during the long drive to the Verona airport—he'd just lost his stepfather after all—but still, she felt a deep sense of loss of her own. The summer had been idyllic, spent exploring the Italian countryside and each other. She'd come to Italy to find her future path and she'd found her soul mate; she was sure of it. They'd spent long lazy hours discussing his plans to establish a vineyard and her desire to be an advocate for those less fortunate. She'd told him about her crazy, close-knit family and he'd told her everything about his adorable little sister, Charlie. He didn't seem that close to his mother and stepfather, but Bridgett knew some families were like that. It made her appreciate her own love-hate relationship with her siblings and parents.

The fact that neither one had declared their love wasn't important, she told herself. They'd shown each other in many ways. Still, she couldn't help the troubled feeling that began that night she'd left him at the airport, the one that felt like she'd never see Jay again.

The DiSantises had a personal computer in the winery office and Bridgett would wait for the intermittent dial-up access for hours sometimes to send an e-mail to Jay. She knew he was busy with the funeral and his family. But she wanted to be there for him in case he needed her; to send him words of encouragement. Initially, he responded to her e-mails, writing her two or three a day. But as the days slipped into a week, his e-mails became more infrequent, making Bridgett uneasy.

The uneasy feeling turned into queasiness soon after that. Her period was overdue and now Jay's concern about the broken condom began to niggle at her, too. Still, she didn't mention the potential for pregnancy in an e-mail. She needed to deliver that news by telephone. She tried the cell phone number he'd given her, but without international service, she couldn't get through. Her only option was to leave a message on the answering machine at the house he shared with his two roommates. Hopefully one of them would relay the message to Jay that it was urgent that she speak with him.

Bridgett didn't dare test herself at the clinic where she worked. Instead she drove Jay's pickup into one of the other surrounding towns and bought three pregnancy tests. All three gave her the news that would change her life forever. She left another message for Jay, trying not to sound too desperate.

A day went by without an e-mail or a phone call. And then another. And another. Bridgett couldn't imagine what had happened to Jay. It had been two weeks since she'd last seen him and a week since she'd heard from him. Then she began to imagine the worst: that he'd died in an accident and no one had bothered to tell her. Her queasiness turned into genuine sickness and she couldn't get out of bed. Mrs. DiSantis insisted that she be seen by a doctor, who confirmed with a blood test what she already knew.

The DiSantis family was put in precarious position, being devout Catholics and having an unwed, pregnant American woman in their house. The nuns Bridgett was working for weren't too pleased, either. It was agreed that Bridgett would return home as soon as she was able. While the idea of facing her parents was unnerving, she was glad to be returning to the U.S. so she could track down information about Jay.

Not wanting to give up, she tried Jay's home phone in Chicago one last time. Bridgett nearly passed out when a woman answered the phone.

"Hello?"

Bridgett's voice was shaking and the words were difficult to get out. "Yes, hello. I've been trying to reach Jay McManus for several days now. Is he . . . is he okay?"

"Jay? I assume so, but the Cubs are losing, so I doubt he's enjoying being back at Wrigley Field as much as he'd like," the woman said with a laugh. "Of course, they've got beer and a tribe of beautiful women in their box so I'm sure he's not too disappointed."

Jay was alive. And in Chicago. And not returning her calls. The dull ache in Bridgett's lower abdomen that had been bothering her all day squeezed a little harder, making her slide down into a chair. "He's there? In Chicago?"

"Um, yes," the woman said. "Oh, gosh, you must be the girl who keeps calling and leaving messages."

Bridgett sucked in a breath. "Yes. It's urgent that I speak with him. Do you know when he'll be back?"

"Hard to tell. You know Jay. He could be out partying for days at a time. You know how those rich boys like to misbehave."

Apparently, Bridgett didn't know Jay that well because

the Jay she knew didn't seem like much of a partier. And what did the woman mean, rich boys? Jay was a humble graduate student. Her side squeezed again. She desperately wanted to speak with Jay. Her Jay.

"Look, sweetie," the woman on the other end of the phone said. "You sound like you might be a little hung up on Jay. Believe me, it happens all the time. He's constantly leaving a broken heart or two behind when he travels. Then he leaves it to me to deal with their tear-jerking phone calls." She laughed again.

"I'm not—" Bridgett's head was spinning and she was having trouble making sense of her own words, much less the woman on the other end of the phone. "Look, I just need to get a message to him, please. Can you do that for me?"

The woman sighed. "Sure."

"Tell him Bridgett called. Tell him I'm pregnant."

If the woman on the other end of the line said anything at all, Bridgett didn't hear it. All she could make out was the roaring in her ears before everything went black.

When she awoke twenty-four hours later, Bridgett was no longer pregnant. She left Italy as soon as she was released from the hospital and returned to Boston cold, empty, and brokenhearted. In the week since she'd left him that message, Jay had never once tried to contact her.

Seventeen

"You don't follow directions very well," Jay said as he boarded his jet to find Donovan Carter sitting in one of the passenger seats.

"It's my job to protect you." Donovan's voice was a bit raspy, probably from lack of sleep. He would have had to have caught the last flight out to make it to the Marin County airport by eight A.M. Pacific time.

"No, it's your job to provide security for the *team*, not me personally," Jay said as he took the seat opposite Donovan.

"Yeah, well, let's just say I like working for you. I'm not in the mood to break in a new owner."

"But that's all for naught if I fire you on the spot."

Donovan crossed his arms over his chest defiantly. "It's a risk worth taking."

Jay smiled while he shook his head. "Seriously, this isn't going to be like anything you're used to at NCIS. Just a discussion between two people who used to be friends."

"They're not much of a friend if they want to smear your reputation online."

"The friendship went south years ago," Jay said. "But I still have a bargaining chip or two that I can use to get this whole thing to stop."

"You sound as if this is all going to go civilly?" Don sounded doubtful.

"I have every confidence that I won't need a gun-toting bodyguard for this meeting." Jay poured himself a cup of coffee from the carafe next to his seat.

Donovan laughed. "Oh, you're way off base here, boss. I'm not here to protect you from the blogger. I'm here to protect you from Brody Janik."

Jay swore as he burned his tongue on the coffee. "Brody?"

"Oh yeah. He's vowed to take you out himself as soon as he sees you."

"Has he forgotten who signs his paychecks?"

Donovan shrugged. "I doubt that will be a deterrent in this case. He's pretty protective of the women in his life. Don't forget how he tore up that hotel in New Hampshire last year at his sister's wedding."

Jay sighed. "I'm convinced that was just Brody overreacting in that case. And he's overreacting here."

"Yeah, well, I'm not going to take any chances with your former friend or your girlfriend's cranky little brother."

The pilot stuck his head out of the cockpit and Jay gave him the go-ahead to take off. Short of firing the Blaze security chief, who was a team and fan favorite after saving the coach's daughter and Carly Devlin from a crazed stalker a few years ago, Jay didn't have much choice but to let him tag along. He didn't bother taking exception to Don's characterization of Bridgett as his girlfriend. It was as good a word as any to describe his relationship with her.

The real question would be how long their relationship would last. If she had her way, she'd be gone with the team on Sunday. Trouble was, Jay didn't want to let her have her way.

He'd left her bed this morning reluctantly. The only thing getting him out the door was the desire to end the ridiculous efforts to blackmail him. The escapades of the blogger had caused enough collateral damage to players, coaches, and others throughout the league. It was time to put an end to her vendetta against him and Blake.

Don was snoring softly beside him and Jay decided to close his eyes for a moment also. He'd slept intermittently the night before between "negotiations" with Bridgett. He'd definitely need his wits about him this morning.

"What do you mean, there's no money?" Delaney cried.

Jay leaned back against the leather recliner he'd bought at Goodwill when they first found the house in Hyde Park. "Lloyd left it all to Charlie." Jay took a long pull from his bottle of beer. "He left my mother his shares in the body armor company, but not enough to have a controlling interest, the bastard. Not that my mother cares. She says she'd rather go back to research at a university anyway."

"I care!" Delaney's voice was becoming irritatingly shrill and Jay wished he'd kept his buzz up from last night, but Blake was making him sober up. It had been a week since Lloyd's funeral and the bombshell that his stepfather hadn't thought enough of him or his mother to make either one trustee of Charlie's money. Not only that, but Jay's dream of opening up his own winery was indefinitely on hold. He realized now that had Lloyd not died suddenly, he might not have loaned Jay the money anyway.

"We'll open the vineyard," Blake said as he switched Jay's beer for a cup of Starbucks. "My father said he'd help us pull together some venture capitalists to get it started. He believes in you, Jay."

"How long will that take?" Delaney was getting a little twitchy now. She'd seemed a bit jumpy ever since Jay had arrived back from Italy.

Blake shrugged. "These things don't happen overnight. The DiSantises are going to sell you the fermentation formula, right?"

Jay nodded as he took a sip of the bitter coffee. "I'll have to sell the labels to get the money to pay Giovanni, but yeah, they've agreed to sell it to me."

"You can't sell your trademarked wine labels, Mac," Blake said. "They're all you have left from your family legacy."

"How much will they bring in?" Delaney asked.

Blake shot his fiancée a sharp look.

"We can design new labels," Jay said. "The important thing is to get the formula before DiSantis changes his mind. I'll have to move fast, though. I contacted a guy in New Zealand who wants to buy them. My flight is out of O'Hare this afternoon."

"What can we do to help?" Blake asked.

Jay pulled a tattered envelope out of his backpack. "Loan me a stamp?"

"Sending love letters to your Italian girlfriend?" Blake teased.

When Jay had first arrived back in the States, he'd mentioned to his two friends that he'd met someone; someone who was very important to him. But he hadn't felt comfortable going into much more detail—especially since Blake and Delaney's relationship seemed to be deteriorating before his eyes. Besides, he needed to get his crazy life sorted out first before he could go back to Italy and make plans with Bridgett. Knowing that she was waiting for him was the one thing that was keeping him sane.

"She's living with the DiSantises, so I'd rather not send her an e-mail that could be read by anyone else using the vineyard's computer," he explained. "I just want her to know what's going on. After all, she's going to be a part of our venture, too."

Blake's eyebrows lifted in surprise. "Whoa!"

"You're that serious about her?" Delaney asked. "Enough to make her a partner?"

"I'm that serious." A horn honked outside. "That's my cab. Do either of you have a stamp?"

Delaney took the letter from Jay's hands. "No, but I'm

*on my way to the store. I'll get one and mail it out for you."
She kissed Jay's cheek. "Hurry back." Without even a
glance at Blake she headed out the back door.*

*Blake blew out a frustrated breath as he followed Jay to
his cab.*

*"Things gonna be okay with you two?" Jay asked, not
sure he really wanted to know the answer.*

*"Honestly?" Blake dragged a hand through his hair. "I
don't know. She's turning into someone I don't know. But,
hey, you've got enough to worry about right now. Whatever
happens between Delaney and me, it won't keep us from
opening the winery, okay?"*

*It seemed that the world was conspiring against Jay real-
izing his dream of owning a vineyard, but he was determined not to fail. It was his legacy and, more important,
now it was his future with Bridgett.*

Mimi tapped her pen against the table slowly, the
beat reminding Bridgett of a death march. "So can I say you
two are dating?"

Bridgett sipped on her tea and stared out toward the pool,
where Charlie was lounging on a chair and talking on the
phone. "Is it necessary to comment on our relationship at all?"
she asked Mimi.

"So you do have a relationship?" Mimi was like a shopper
at Filene's Basement, digging through the bargain rack for
the best price.

"I'm his attorney. Beyond that I'm not going to comment."

"Oh, come on!" Mimi threw up her pen in exasperation.
"This blogger is making it sound like you two have been an
item for years. Today's post hinted that you met long before
Jay bought the team. Is that true?"

The blogger had come out swinging that morning, report-
ing in the *Girlfriends' Guide to the NFL* that there was more
to Jay and Bridgett's story and details would be forthcoming.
Just as Alesha Warren had warned, the blog had also alluded

to the suspected sexual harassment allegations against the Blaze owner. Other media organizations were already picking up the sexual harassment angle, digging for anything and everything. Jay's assistant, Linc, had been gnashing his teeth all morning between reports on *ESPN* and the *NFL Network,* while Stuart had texted her the link to the *Today* show's feature on it. All were now hinting that possible NFL sanctions against the team were imminent.

Not for the first time, Bridgett wondered who the blogger might be. Like her sister-in-law, Shay, she was convinced that the person behind the secret-revealing column was a woman. Jay had refused to elaborate further last night, but his reluctance to divulge more information just gave Bridgett more clues: The blogger could only be a spurned lover. Bridgett ignored the burst of jealousy that rolled through her belly.

Jay was confident that he could deal with her on his own. Technically, whoever was behind the blog hadn't broken any laws. Nothing she'd printed was libelous—everything written in the titillating column had been true, so far. Somehow, she'd managed to get ahold of secrets those associated with the NFL would prefer be kept quiet. In her brother's case, Brody's secrets were revealed to the blogger by his personal trainer. In this case, very few people knew of Jay and Bridgett's early relationship. Bridgett had told no one in the United States. That meant Jay had done all the talking, despite his insistence that he hadn't. She already knew that Jay had told his mother. The idea that their Italian fling might have been discussed during pillow talk with a former lover made Bridgett's skin burn with embarrassment. And disappointment.

"I think you should concentrate on diluting the sexual harassment allegations by providing quotes from current and former Sparks cheerleaders who are very happy with their working conditions." She tapped the file of e-mails from Dan she'd printed off earlier that morning. "That's the relevant issue here."

Mimi huffed in annoyance. "I've already contacted several

neutral media outlets and given them our side of the story. But TMZ and *Radar Online* want the scoop on you and Jay. The man is a mainstay on *People*'s Fifty Most Eligible Bachelors list. Women want to know if he's officially off the market."

Since Bridgett had no idea how to quantify her relationship with Jay—*enemies with benefits?*—she didn't bother going into detail. "No comment." The vibrating of her cell phone saved her from any further grilling by Mimi.

"Bridgett!" Gwen sounded like she was about to go nuclear. "Do you know what that bastard did? Do you?"

Bridgett wandered out toward the garden area, out of earshot of Mimi. "No, what has Skip done now? You are talking about Skip, right?"

"Of course I am," Gwen snapped. "He told the kids about the baby. The baby he's having with . . . with that woman." Her sister's voice broke on a sob.

This was why Bridgett hadn't gone into divorce law. The thought of dealing with the horrible things spouses did to each other when their marriage ended chilled her. She'd barely gotten over Jay's abandonment all those years ago. There was no way she could emotionally handle watching others go through such pain.

"I'm sorry, Gwen." Her words sounded inadequate even to her own ears.

"The kids were excited," her sister choked out. "They're excited about a baby their father is having with *another woman*. They want to live with the baby. How do I battle that?"

Bridgett's heart sank for her sister. The days and months ahead for Gwen would be difficult. "I'll be home on Monday, Gwen. We'll figure something out. I promise."

Gwen scoffed. "If the tabloids are right, you'll be engaged by Monday."

"I told you, don't believe everything you read, Gwen."

"So you two are not an item? Oh, Bridgett, can't you at least close the deal with a man once in your life?"

"Hey!" Bridgett's tender feelings for her sister were fading quickly.

"I'm sorry, Bridge," Gwen said quietly. "It's just that I really wanted this to be true for you. If anyone deserves a hot torrid affair with a gorgeous millionaire, it's you."

Bridgett heaved a sigh. "It's complicated." That was certainly the understatement of the year.

"It's only complicated if you fall in love with him," Gwen said. "So here's my sisterly advice: Just use him for sex."

"Gwen!" Bridgett had to gulp around the lump that had formed in her throat. She was beginning to think it was too late for "just sex."

"Seriously, Bridge, heed my advice because the falling *out* of love part"—Gwen's voice broke again—"stings something fierce."

She didn't bother telling Gwen that she already knew that kind of pain firsthand.

When Mimi disappeared to parts unknown, Bridgett went to work preparing the necessary documents protecting Charlie's baby from any repercussions from the sperm donor.

"Donors sign their rights away when they leave their sample," Bridgett explained to Charlie later that afternoon. The two were sitting on the verandah overlooking the vineyard. Charlie looked young and fresh, dressed in shorts and a V-neck T-shirt straight from a Gap mannequin, her face makeup free. It would be hard for others to imagine that this beautiful, vivacious young woman could be so lonely, but Bridgett related to Charlie easily. "If you had the procedure in the U.S., you're also protected by HIPAA from any of the medical professionals in the practice where you were inseminated from releasing the information to the public. Of course, that doesn't prevent someone who no longer works there from leaking the news one day."

Charlie groaned. "Yeah, I figured as much. I had the procedure done in New York. The doctor and his nurse were the only people in the room."

"Good. Do you have any information on the sperm donor?"

"No, just the basics, good health, all his teeth, IQ above 120, brown eyes, brown hair. I made sure to pick from the donors who hadn't signed up for the identity disclosure program. I figured that if they didn't want kids looking for them once they were eighteen, they wouldn't be looking for their kids, either."

Bridgett was impressed at her reasoning. "Good thinking."

"I happen to have an IQ over 120 myself," Charlie said.

The smug grin she gave Bridgett was so very much like Jay's that she nearly laughed. She sobered up quickly before she asked the next question, though. "I have to ask if you slept with anyone else during that time period."

Charlie's smile faded and her mouth grew hard. "Contrary to how the tabloids depict me, I'm not some slut who sleeps with a different rock star every night."

"I take that as a no?"

"No!"

"You hired me to do this right for you, Charlie," Bridgett explained. "I wouldn't be doing my job if I didn't cover all the bases."

"Do you like it?"

Her question caught Bridgett off guard. "Like what? My job?"

Charlie nodded.

Bridgett thought carefully about her answer. "I like that things are always black and white. Most of the cases I handle are fairly clear-cut."

"Did you always want to be a lawyer?"

"No. When I was your age, I didn't know what I wanted to do with my life. I liked the idea of helping those who were less fortunate, but in the end, I had to make a living somehow."

Charlie looked wistful as she gazed across the vineyard. "I want to do something where people will take me seriously."

Bridgett was careful to tamp down on the surprise in her voice. "Why don't you?"

She watched as Charlie's hand gently cupped her still-flat belly. "I am."

Somehow, Bridgett didn't think that Charlie's decision to have a baby would get people to take her seriously, but she refrained from saying so. "Well, at least we can make sure your baby's fortune is protected."

"You didn't tell Jay about the baby's father?"

"Of course not."

"Did he ask?"

"You know he did."

Charlie grinned then. "Good. I can trust you. More important, my brother can trust you. He doesn't have too many people in his life he can say that about."

Bridgett didn't bother to comment. It wasn't *her* trust that was at issue between them, unfortunately.

Eighteen

It was nearly midday when Jay's plane landed in a small commercial airfield just outside of Las Vegas. He and Don trudged through the already stifling heat to the car waiting for them on the tarmac.

"You gonna tell me what we might be walking into?" Don asked over the sound of the air-conditioning blowing on high through the vents.

"If you're scared, Don, you should have stayed on the plane."

Don laughed. "I'm not scared. Just being a good Boy Scout. I like to know who I'm up against."

Jay glanced out the window as they sped past rows of neat tract houses lined up like dominoes in the desert on their way into the city. "I'm pretty sure neither one of us has to worry about a thirty-five-year-old woman who's barely a hundred and twenty pounds."

"Damn," Donovan muttered. "It is a woman."

"You're surprised?"

"Nah." He shook his head. "You know what they say about a woman scorned."

"Mm," Jay said by way of agreement.

"What does she want?" Don might as well have given the Final Jeopardy question.

Jay shook his head. "Knowing Delaney, she wants my balls and my heart served up on a platter."

"That must have been a hell of a breakup."

"Yeah, it was," Jay said. "Except the breakup was her engagement to my best friend. I was just the one who nudged it along."

Don let out a little whistle. "In a good way, I hope?"

"Let's just say the wronged party is relieved to have dodged a bullet."

Crowds mingled on the Las Vegas streets as the car traveled along the Strip, passing the replica of a pyramid, a New York City tugboat, the Statute of Liberty, and the Eiffel Tower.

"A gambler's paradise," Don murmured.

"In this case, it's an addict's hideaway," Jay said. The driver pulled into the driveway of the Wynn hotel, where Jay and Don climbed out. "Just follow my lead," he instructed Don.

They walked with purpose through the crowded lobby of the hotel, past ornate gardens of trees, lit up and decorated with huge flower bulb lanterns hanging from the limbs. Jay headed straight for the elevator that would take him to the thirtieth floor. The suite he wanted was strategically positioned at the end of the hallway and he and Don strolled casually toward it, trying not to look too intent as they passed other guests and a stray cleaning crew.

"Here goes nothing," Jay said quietly when he knocked on the door marked thirty thirty-three. A long moment later, the door opened to reveal a young Chinese man.

"Yeah?" His expression became wary as he took in Jay and Don, both of whom looked very official in their business suits.

"We're looking for Delaney," Jay said.

"No one here by that name," the guy said before quickly closing the door.

Don was quicker, however, maneuvering a foot and shoulder between the door and the wall and shoving his way in.

"Told you that you needed me," he grunted as Jay stalked past.

The doorman was grumbling something in Chinese as Jay entered the suite, which was littered with nearly twenty different laptops.

"Well, well, what have you gotten yourself into now, Delaney?"

The years had not been kind to his former roommate. Once upon a time she was a stunning, polished woman with thick, long brown hair and bright brown eyes. Looking at her now, she appeared washed out and haggard. Her addiction had done that to her, Jay reminded himself. He was not responsible for what she'd become. She looked startled, but certainly not surprised to see him.

"It's okay, Li," she said to the man who'd answered the door. "He's not here to report us. Mr. McManus doesn't operate that way. He just gathers intel and uses it for his own purposes. I suspect he's here to make some sort of deal."

Jay scanned the computer screens located throughout the room. All of them had betting odds for that week's upcoming NFL games. "Interesting little business you've got here, Delaney," Jay said as he watched. "Off-site betting on pro football games. I'd say you finally put your two best talents together: gambling and software development. Congratulations."

"A girl's got to make a living somehow, Jay. After all, you destroyed my chances to marry into one of the wealthiest families in Chicago." Her hands went to her hips.

"You destroyed your own chances, Delaney. You were stealing from Blake."

"*Borrowing*, Jay. From my fiancé. It was none of your business."

Jay shook his head. "Actually, it was my business to let my best friend know his future wife had a gambling problem and was already taking him to the cleaners before they even walked down the aisle."

"I told you before, I would have worked it out."

He laughed then. "Before or after the thugs showed up

to rough you up? Face it, Delaney, you were so far in debt you couldn't have 'worked it out.'"

She glanced over at Don, who was furiously snapping photos of the laptop screens. "You'll want to pay attention to this part," she said to Don. "This is where my old friend here claims to be my white knight."

"I bailed you out."

"You blackmailed me," she snapped. "You made Blake fall out of love with me; then you used me yourself. All so you could get rich quick and get your damn vineyard. And a freaking professional football team! What did I get? Nothing!"

"Is that what your little blogger game is about?" Jay demanded. "You think I owe you something?"

Delaney's laugh was harsh sounding. "You wouldn't be where you are today without me."

"And you likely wouldn't be alive without me." Jay's words hung like stalactites in the stale air of the hotel suite.

Her lips formed an angry line but she didn't refute his words. She couldn't.

Jay scrubbed his fingers through his hair. "Look, Delaney, this has to stop. I'm not your enemy."

"No," she whispered. "But you're not my friend, either. I sometimes wonder if you ever were. I loved you, you know. Almost as much as I loved Blake."

"Get help, Delaney. And stop harassing Blake and me with trumped-up lawsuits and that ridiculous blog."

She crossed her arms defiantly against her chest. "Or what?"

"Or we'll turn your ass over to the Feds," Don shouted. "Hell, I'll turn you over to Interpol because I'm sure this is an international operation."

"And here I thought your friend *was* a Fed," Delaney said to Jay before turning back to Don. "You must not know Jay very well, because he'd never turn me in."

Don glanced between Jay and Delaney, a glimmer of confusion in his eyes.

Jay sucked in a breath. "How much do you owe?"

Delaney grimaced and shook her head. "Enough to have me enslaved here for the near future."

"So the blog and the lawsuits are how you've been entertaining yourself while you're in this opulent prison?"

She shrugged. "I needed a diversion."

"Make it stop," Jay commanded as he walked close enough to whisper to her. "All of it. Find another diversion. I'd suggest solitaire but I'm sure you've found a way to cheat at that one by now." He leaned closer so the other men in the room wouldn't overhear him. "Perhaps you could spend your time calculating the interest accruing in that lovely Swiss bank account you have? Tell me, do the goons you work for know you're skimming their profits, Delaney? I wonder how they'd feel about your secret retirement account. Maybe I should set up a blog and write about your creative bookkeeping."

Delaney's eyes grew wide before she narrowed them to slits.

Jay smiled smugly at her discomfort. He had no idea how long she'd been skimming money from the profits, but Delaney's employers likely weren't as smart as Jay was at detecting it. It was what had first alerted him to her backstabbing when she worked for McManus Industries, after all. Knowing Delaney, she was building herself a nice nest egg while she was "enslaved" paying off her debt. If it were anyone else but Delaney, Jay might have been impressed with her acumen.

He turned to Don and signaled him to proceed to the door.

"She won't ever love you, you know," Delaney called after them.

Jay halted, turning around to face her, his chest squeezing when he met her cold eyes.

"Not an honest love, anyway," she continued. "Don't forget how she dumped your ass when she found out you weren't inheriting. Do you really think you can trust her?"

A throbbing started at the base of Jay's skull. He didn't trust Bridgett. But he trusted Delaney less. "To hear you tell it, I don't have a heart, Delaney, so what are you worried about?" The fact that his heart wouldn't be engaged with Bridgett wasn't Delaney's business.

She laughed again. "You may be ruthless and stingy with your money, Jay, but you have a heart. I should know. I've taken advantage of it a time or two."

"Not anymore. Find another diversion, Delaney."

"The same goes for you, Jay. Like I said, she'll never love you."

"Jesus," Donovan muttered when the elevator doors finally closed behind them. "I hope your friend knows how much he owes you for saving him from that."

Jay leaned his head against the back wall and closed his eyes. "I remind him every chance I get."

"Now what?"

"Talk to Jennifer Knowles and get her to go on the record that the case was her sister-in-law's idea," Jay said. "I'll get Hank to get the players to apologize to her and we'll send everyone to sensitivity training. It should all blow over."

The elevator doors opened and they stepped out into the tropical lobby. "Something tells me Alesha Warren won't give up easily."

Jay walked toward the doors leading out into the midday heat. "Alesha Warren can stew for years while the case gets stalled in court for all I care. Mimi has enough to refute any possible crap she leaks to the media."

"And Delaney? Was whatever you threatened her with enough to make her stop blogging?"

Delaney. Jay pulled his sunglasses out of his breast pocket. "She'll stop blogging. It won't be as amusing to her now that I know she's behind it." His threat to out her to her Chinese mafia bosses was enough to end her harassment of both him and Blake. Delaney knew Jay didn't make threats lightly. Of course, that didn't mean Delaney wouldn't find a way to be a pain in his ass once she'd made good on her current debt. She liked messing with his head too much.

She'll never love you.

Delaney thought she was scoring a wound with Jay by

leveling her threat about Bridgett, but she didn't realize how wrong she was. Bridgett had already destroyed his heart. He wouldn't let her do it again. Jay told himself that his uneasiness over Delaney's words had nothing to do with his heart.

"Call for the car, will you?" He handed the valet ticket to Don. "I'm just going to take a walk around the block."

"Sure thing."

The summer heat felt good after nineteen days of winter in New Zealand. Jay jumped out of the cab before it even reached a full stop in front of the Hyde Park house. He was eager to get a shower and get to a computer so he could finally close the deal with DiSantis. Selling the labels had been more agonizing than he thought, but at least now he had the cash for the fermentation formula. He'd take the job with the investment firm and raise the money for the vineyard on his own. His stepfather's death was a setback, but certainly not one that would defeat him. Besides, he'd have Bridgett by his side.

Bridgett. It had been four and a half weeks since he'd last seen her. His cell phone service didn't allow for international calling and finding a computer with AOL access had been impossible in New Zealand. Jay missed Bridgett's soft smile and her sunny, positive outlook. He'd need that and more to get through the next phase in his life. Now that he'd taken care of business, it was time to take care of Bridgett. He couldn't wait for her to return to the States.

The house was nearly empty when Jay bounded through the door. The lease was up at the end of the month and, from the looks of it, Delaney had already moved out, taking with her most of the furniture and likely everything in the kitchen. Jay was surprised to find Blake seated on the only furniture remaining, the old leather recliner. It was midafternoon on a Wednesday, a workday for Blake normally. His roommate had a beer in his hand and was watching the Cubs on a small TV.

"Look who's home," Blake said. "It's the world traveler. I was beginning to think you'd stay in New Zealand."

"Things took longer than I expected." Jay glanced around the room. He took in the boarded-up window in the dining area. "What the hell happened here? Where's your big-screen TV?"

"Delaney happened." Blake took another pull from his beer, but he didn't bother lifting his eyes from the television screen. "You were right. She didn't deny taking the money from me."

Jay swallowed painfully. He'd hated to rat her out to Blake, but he didn't want his friend to go into the marriage without being totally prepared for his wife's imperfections. "Did she tell you what she wanted the money for?"

"Didn't have to," Blake said. "A couple of guys came collecting the other night. They helped themselves to anything that wasn't nailed down. Including my Porsche."

"Holy shit!" Jay sunk down onto the floor. "Did you call the police?"

Blake shot him a look that said, What do you think, dumbass? "Insurance will buy me a new car, but I'm sure that's what Delaney was counting on."

"You don't think she did this on purpose?"

"She's a manipulative bitch with a gambling problem. She's been using us for years. Everything that girl does is on purpose." Blake's whole body radiated anger.

"You don't think they'll hurt her, do you?"

Blake jumped from the chair. "That's not really my problem, is it?" Blake's face was ravaged with bitterness and pain. He'd loved Delaney. Her betrayal had obviously cut him deeply.

Jay struggled to find the right words. "I'm sorry" didn't sound like enough. Despite everything, he was also worried about their former roommate. Delaney was a product of the foster care system with no real family to fall back on for help. She'd obviously gotten in way over her head. He bit back the suggestion he was about to make, the one about them going to look for her, given Blake's demeanor.

"*Look, I've been on planes and in airports for the last thirty-six hours,*" he said instead. "*Let me jump into the shower and then we can go out and grab a beer.*"

Blake shook his head. "*I'm not very good company right now. I've only been hanging out here waiting for you to get back. I've got a place over in Wicker Park. You still headed to New York?*"

Jay nodded. It seemed that his life was changing faster than he wanted. "*Yeah. The job pays well and I'll be close to Charlie.*"

"*Okay, then,*" Blake said. "*Both the Cubs and the Sox are in New York in September. I'll get the corporate seats and we can catch up then. Dad's still serious about lining up investors if you're still serious about the vineyard.*"

"*Hell yeah, I'm still serious.*" Jay had just sold off the only legacy he had from his grandfather in order to make it happen.

"*I'll help with the advertising, but I don't think it would be a good idea for us to be partners.*" Blake swallowed roughly. "*It's just not the same anymore.*"

Jay nodded. Their dream was going to be only his dream, if it worked at all.

Blake clapped him on the shoulder. "*Maybe it's better this way anyway. You and your Italian girlfriend can crush the grapes with your bare feet without me getting in the way.*"

"*I need to call her and let her know I'm still alive.*" He smiled sheepishly. "*It'll be good to hear her voice.*"

"*At least one of us should be happy.*" Blake's words were tinged with bitterness as he headed through the kitchen. Jay followed him out, stopping when he caught sight of an assortment of mail addressed to him that was piled on the kitchen counter. He fingered a letter with a Boston postmark and his gut clenched. Bridgett was the only one he knew from the entire state of Massachusetts. But she wouldn't be home yet. Not unless something had happened. Heart racing, he tore at the envelope.

The handwriting was smudged but it was still lyrical and open like Bridgett herself. Jay suddenly wished they'd *exchanged more letters. But he'd been traveling around trying to secure his lifelong dream and he'd had no real address to give her these past few weeks. He'd explained as much in his only letter to her.*

Dear Jay,

I hope this letter finds you, wherever you may be. I'm sorry to have to tell you this at such a difficult time in your life, but I don't want you to go on believing that our relationship is something more than it actually ~~is~~ was.

He must have made some sort of sound because Blake was suddenly beside him.
"What's up?"
Jay shook his head furiously, forcing his eyes to focus on the words on the page.

I enjoyed our summer together. I really did. But I always thought that being in love with someone would mean I would do anything for them—including living in near poverty to start up a winery. But I find that I might not be suited for that life. I want more. My feelings for you just aren't strong enough and if I've given you the impression that they are, then I'm sorry. To be in love with someone means it hurts to be away from them and while I've missed you these past couple of weeks, I've found I've missed someone else more and I'm returning to Boston to be with him. I hope that someday you'll be happy for me.
I wish you well in your pursuit of your dream.

B.

"No," he whispered. This couldn't be from Bridgett. He didn't believe it. She'd been as enthused about the vineyard as Jay had been, sketching the house they'd live in and the life they would have.

"And she'd never once mentioned a fucking boyfriend," he yelled as he tossed the letter on the counter.

Blake picked it up, scanning the page. *"Damn. They're all alike. Scheming bitches who only want money. She probably heard you didn't inherit."*

Jay's chest squeezed. How could she have? He'd never mentioned Lloyd Davis to her. But DiSantis knew. A roaring began in Jay's head. He reached for the house phone.

"Don't bother. I had it disconnected last week when I moved out," Blake said.

Jay was having trouble forcing the words out. *"I have to make a call. Something's not right here."*

"She's not worth it, Jay. No woman is."

But she was. Or he'd thought she was. Jay didn't understand her change of heart and he desperately needed to. *"I need to call DiSantis,"* he argued.

Blake sighed. *"Yeah, okay. But only to close the deal on the fermentation formula, okay? We're both finished with letting women screw up our lives, Jay."*

They drove to Wicker Park. The air was sawing through Jay's lungs as though he'd run the twelve miles. He snatched the phone out of its base and was dialing before Blake had even shut the door. It took nearly eight rings before someone answered and Jay realized it was likely after midnight in Italy. Vincenzo DiSantis was not happy to be awakened and he sounded even less enthused that it was Jay on the line.

"Where the hell you been, eh?" Vincenzo yelled at him, his accent thick. *"Your* bambolina *needed you!"*

Vincenzo had dissolved into speaking only Italian and Jay was having trouble understanding his rapid tirade.

"Per favore, please, sir, listen to me," Jay tried to interject. *"I was in New Zealand getting the money for the formula. I have it now—"*

The vineyard owner swore violently. *"Is that your only care? The wine? Not your Bridgett? Or your bambino?"*

Jay staggered to a chair and sunk down into it. Baby? What baby?

"I—I'm sorry? Did you say 'baby'?"

Vincenzo shouted another string of obscenities in Italian.
"You want the fermentation formula, you do right by that
bambolina, *Jay. Or else!"*

The line went dead. Jay looked up into Blake's stunned
face. "Holy shit," his friend muttered.

It took him nearly twenty hours to track Bridgett down.
It turned out Janik was a popular name in Boston and he'd
knocked on six doors before he found a relative who could
point him to her parents' home. She hadn't been at home,
but the housekeeper directed him to a coffee shop in Cam-
bridge where she was "meeting a friend." The waitress was
placing the lunch plates on the table when Jay stormed
through the door. The preppy guy she was sitting with looked
up first, his face bewildered as Jay charged toward them.

And then Bridgett's eyes met his, nearly stopping Jay in
his tracks. A look of anguished surprise was reflected in
them. "Jay," she said softly. She looked pale and drawn,
but he refused to feel sorry for her.

"Well, at least you still remember my name."

Her gray eyes narrowed then and her face looked as if
he'd actually wounded her, damn it. He was the one who'd
been wounded. She glanced over at her companion, who
seemed to be considering what to do. Had she actually
thrown him over for this spineless dick? The customers in
the small restaurant were eyeing them and Bridgett threw
down her napkin with a sigh. "I'll be right back, Sean."

Jay glared at Sean the Douchbag, who didn't even bother
to stand up when Bridgett left the table. She led them outside and around the corner, away from the steady stream
of students loitering on the sidewalk.

She turned and studied him critically. "How are you?"

To say Jay wasn't at his best would be an understatement.
He was running on fumes after traveling for more than forty-
eight hours straight, not counting his brief stop in Chicago,
where she'd taken him out at the knees with her Dear John
letter. The thought of that damn piece of paper stoked the
anger in his gut again. Jay didn't have the patience to stand
around and make small talk with the woman who'd just

destroyed his heart. But he also didn't want her to know just how much her breakup had affected him, so he struggled for civility in his tone. "The question is, how are you, Bridgett? More important, how's the baby?" She could try to hide from him, but Jay would not be denied his child. Jay was the last in line of the McManus family and now that the labels were no longer his, this child was the only legacy left.

Her face grew paler, if that was even possible, and she reached out to brace herself against the brick wall while her other hand gently cupped her abdomen. "I'm sorry, Jay, but there isn't a baby anymore," she whispered.

Jay staggered for a moment, eventually supporting a shoulder against the same brick wall. A wave of nausea swept through him. How could she have done this? To him? To their child?

His throat was tight but he managed to get some words out. "Was it easy to just erase the last few months like that?"

Bridgett's eyes glistened with tears and she had both arms wrapped around her middle now but her body still shook. "Wh-what?"

Jay was staring at her through a red haze of anger. "Was it as easy to get rid of the baby as it was to get rid of me?" he demanded. "Hell, was it even mine?"

She surprised him with the force with which her palm connected with his cheek. Tears were streaming down her face. "It was not 'easy,'" she hissed. "But for the first time in the past few weeks, I'm actually grateful, God help me."

Sean had found his man card, apparently, because he was wrapping Bridgett in his arms, leading her back into the restaurant while Jay rocked back on his heels, his cheek, and his pride, still stinging.

Nineteen

Bridgett paused on the verandah outside Jay's office. It was early evening and Josie had put out sangria and tapas by the pool. Charlie and her mother had kept to neutral corners most of the day, with Melanie wandering the vineyards while her daughter camped out beside the pool. Neither one was in sight now, though. Instead, Jay's assistant, Linc, was pacing the office floor while *SportsCenter* droned on in the background.

"More sexual harassment allegations have surfaced today regarding Baltimore Blaze owner Jay McManus, fueling rumors that NFL Commissioner Reggie Austin will sanction not only the Blaze but the team's owner individually," the sportscaster said. "You'll remember that the Blaze are being sued by their cheerleaders, the Sparks, for alleged sexual harassment by Blaze players. While many of these cases are from McManus's tenure as CEO of McManus Industries, some inside and outside the NFL are questioning the timing of these leaks of cases that were settled privately prior to McManus taking the helm of the Blaze."

"Yes!" Linc pumped a fist into the air. "Way to go, Mimi."

Bridgett wandered farther into the office to watch alongside Linc. He winked at her before they both turned their attention back to the screen. A lawyer who specialized in defamation cases was being interviewed by the sportscaster.

"This seems to be a smear campaign against McManus personally," the lawyer was saying. "It's a desperate strategy on the part of the attorney representing the Sparks. The fact that Mr. McManus has been sued before for alleged sexual harassment doesn't mean he's guilty. These cases were settled and are sealed. It's difficult to determine whether they were specious or not. And, it's a stretch to say he's created an environment where this type of activity is tolerated. Let's remember here that only one of the Sparks cheerleaders has come forward as a plaintiff."

"And we've just learned here at ESPN that the plaintiff and the attorney representing the class are former sisters-in-law," the sportscaster interjected.

The lawyer nodded. "There's a lot about this case that stinks and I think that before we all jump on the bandwagon of sanctioning an NFL team and its owner, we should wait to see how the facts play out."

"Hear, hear," Linc cheered.

"Seriously," Bridgett said. "As much as I hate to admit it, that was a brilliant move on Mimi's part to go directly to the sports media."

The topic moved on to a baseball player accused of taking performance-enhancing drugs and Linc lowered the volume on the television. "Do you think it'll be as easy as just discrediting the source?" he asked.

Bridgett shrugged. "It depends on who this person is and what their motivation is." She eyed Linc hopefully, but if he knew who the blogger was, he wasn't sharing.

"Hopefully, that will all be taken care of today," was all he said.

Apparently, she'd have to be more direct. "Is there any news on that front?" Bridgett wandered over to examine another painting on the wall—this one a landscape of Christchurch, New Zealand—while trying to appear nonchalant.

Her curiosity about the blogger's identity and their relationship with Jay had been nagging at her all day. Not only that, but she worried about what Jay would have to do to get the blogger to stop. The Jay she'd once fallen in love with wasn't capable of doing anything violent or nefarious. This Jay, the one whose body she knew intimately but whose heart and feelings were closed off from her, she wasn't so sure about. And it made her very anxious. She wanted to believe in him again, and that desire was becoming very dangerous to her heart.

"I'm sure it went as planned. The boss usually gets what he wants. He and Don are back in San Francisco. Don had some security issues to take care of at the hotel before the team arrives. These women's groups are fired up and say they're going to protest the game again this week." He shook his head in bewilderment. "Don wanted to make sure there won't be any nonsense when the team arrives tonight. Mr. McManus went to his office in San Mateo to finish reviewing the shareholders' quarterly report."

Bridgett felt more let down than relieved. For some reason, she'd hoped Jay would return to the vineyard right away and share with her the outcome of his confrontation with the blogger. She mentally shook herself. *The old Jay would have done that.* The only thing this Jay wanted to share with her was his body. And his vineyard if she accepted the life he was offering. She'd be pampered and her body satisfied, but not her heart. Happiness would be superficial if she found any at all. Bridgett wanted more. This would be one time where Linc's boss didn't get what he wanted.

Her phone buzzed in her pocket and she glanced down at the screen. Gwen. The separation from Skip had made her sister very needy, but Bridgett could empathize with the heartbreak her sister was going through. Worse, she had a sneaking suspicion she'd be going through that kind of raw pain again very soon. Heaving a sigh, she answered the phone.

"Do you think Skip knocked up a twenty-six-year-old because I stopped going to the gym?" Gwen asked. She'd been making outrageous statements like this all day. Their sister Ashley had already texted Bridgett in frustration and concern. It seemed that Gwen was getting more and more manic as the day went on.

"No," Bridgett said calmly. "I think Skip knocked up his nubile young assistant because he's an ass and his common sense is that of a five-year-old." She wandered back out of the office and along the path toward the tasting cellar. "You're beautiful, Gwen. Stop playing this second-guessing game. I know it sounds cliché but it's not you; it's him."

Gwen released a sorrowful-sounding sigh on the other end of the phone. "I'm going to be forty in a few months, Bridgett. And I'm going to be alone."

"It's not that bad. Besides, they say forty is the new thirty and all that. Plus, Skip is going to be forty-one and he's going to have an infant."

Her sister perked up a little at that comment. "Trust me, that's the only thing that has kept me smiling these past few days. Skip hated dealing with all that baby stuff."

Bridgett sat on one of the benches outside the wine cellar tasting room. She took in the view of the sun dipping over the foothills, the late day's light bathing the vineyard in shades of deep yellow and orange. "See, there's always a silver lining. You need to find a way to celebrate this next phase in life; not mourn your marriage. Plan something fun for your birthday. Go on a trip somewhere. Mom and Dad will watch the kids."

"A trip would be wonderful." Gwen finally sounded enthused about something. "Where should we go?"

It took a minute for the "we" in her sister's sentence to sink in. A vacation with Gwen. *Dear God.* "Um." Bridgett hedged. "I don't know. Why don't you think about it and come up with some ideas. Check with Ashley to see what she thinks. Maybe we can go somewhere where Tricia can meet us." No way was she letting her other sisters get out of the trip.

"I will! I'll ask Shay if she wants to come along, too. You're right, this will give me something to look forward to," Gwen said. "Especially since you won't be around to hang out with anymore."

Anymore? Bridgett and her oldest sister hadn't ever "hung out" as far as she could remember. "What are you talking about?"

Gwen snorted on the phone. "All these years you've been single and you wait until I need a wingman to finally snag a guy."

Bridgett rubbed at her temples. "Only guys have wingmen, Gwen. And I haven't snagged anyone. I told you not to believe everything you read."

"Then what do they call a woman's wingman? And please don't tell me you're not trying to snag a rich husband. At least if he cheated on you, you wouldn't have to go work for Dad."

"I told you this three times already today—there's no relationship between Jay and me, so no worries about cheating. And if Dad needs a lawyer, I'll be happy to work with him." Bridgett had tried to keep her voice from sounding terse and aggravated but her sister's silence on the other end of the phone told her she hadn't been successful. She sighed again. "Look, Gwen, it looks like this case will wrap up much more quickly than we anticipated. Either way, I'll definitely be back on the East Coast Monday morning. Hopefully, in Boston. Why don't we plan on dinner next week, okay?"

"I'm sorry," Gwen whispered. "I don't mean to be so selfish. I wanted this thing to be real for you. I honestly did."

Bridgett swallowed around the lump in her throat. "Yeah, I know. But nothing has ever been real between me and Jay. Hang in there, Gwen, and I'll see you next week."

She blew out a cleansing breath as she clicked the phone to off.

"Well, at least you can admit to that."

Jay's mother's voice startled Bridgett into nearly dropping her phone. She looked behind her at the older woman standing in the doorway of the wine cellar. Dressed in designer jeans, a black turtleneck adorned with silver jewelry, and a long, flowing shawl-collared sweater, she glared at Bridgett with the same piercing blue eyes as her son. Whereas Jay's looked at her with undisguised hunger most of the time, Melanie Davis's looked at her with disgust.

Jay had been wrong about his mother. She was definitely going to go "mama bear" all over Bridgett. It was a look she recognized from her own mom whenever someone had harmed her precious Brody.

Bridgett steeled her spine for the worst. "Excuse me?"

Melanie stalked toward her. "'Nothing has ever been real between' you and my son. Isn't that what you just said?"

Ten years as a trial attorney kept Bridgett quiet. Always let the opponent talk and you'll glean something to use as rebuttal to their rambling. Stuart had taught her that.

Jay's mother stopped near the bench. "Was it real when you thought he was wealthy? You thought you could trap him by getting pregnant, perhaps? But then you found out he wasn't inheriting Lloyd's money, was that it?"

Bridgett bristled at her words. *Is that what Jay had thought? That she'd been after his money?* Except he'd never told her about his family. Nothing more than first names. He'd been deliberately vague. The throbbing at her temples grew worse.

"I'll never understand how someone can just throw away a life." His mother's words were laced with disgust, making Bridgett's stomach roll.

After this weekend, she'd likely never see this woman again. Bridgett didn't owe her an explanation. Her head told her to keep her mouth closed, but her heart was beating a mile a minute fueled by anger and despair. "You're supposed to be a scientist," she said quietly.

Her words caught the older woman off guard. "What the heck kind of excuse is that?" she snapped.

Bridgett stood stiffly. "It means don't form a hypothesis without all the facts." Tears were stinging the backs of her eyes and she wanted to get to the safety of her room as quickly as she could before they streamed down her face like they had that day so long ago. She'd cried for Jay and she'd cried for their unborn child. By the time the doctor had told her that her fallopian tube had ruptured and scarred her uterus, she'd had no more tears left to shed. But there was no sense dredging up that pain again just to set the record straight with Jay's mother. The woman wasn't prepared to hear how her son had deserted *her*, not the other way around. How he'd accused her of unthinkable things. What reason would she have to believe Bridgett?

"Jay gave me all the facts years ago," his mother said. "Your relationship was 'real' to him. He was crushed by your betrayal."

Bridgett tried to take a shaky step toward the house, but Jay's mother's glare held her in place.

"It was the first time that I'd seen him cry since his father died. He cried his entire third year, disappointed every morning when he awoke and his father wasn't there. And then, nineteen years later, he was crying over a child he'd never have. And a woman who didn't love him enough to stand by him while he pursued his dream of building a winery in his father's memory. He felt abandoned by a woman who only wanted his money."

Her words were like a knife to Bridgett's belly. She would have stood by Jay. His dream had become her dream. Clearly his mother was mixed up. It was Jay who didn't want to share his life with Bridgett. Jay's version of the events of that summer was dramatically different from the actual ones. How many lies had he told? And why?

Forming a coherent sentence was painful as Bridgett's throat ceased to work properly, but she refused to let this woman see her agony. Bridgett hadn't let anyone see her suffer since that night in the Italian hospital. "It was a long time ago. We've moved on," she managed to choke out.

"Have you? Jay built a company from the ground up just so he could have the money to build this." Jay's mother spread her arms wide as she turned in circle. "It's more beautiful than anything his father and I imagined. And yet, he doesn't enjoy being here. Instead, he buys a football team on the other side of the country. A team *your* brother plays for." She pointed an accusing finger at Bridgett. "He hasn't gotten over you. And if you keep popping in and out of his life, he won't. You said that you're returning to Boston on Monday. I hope to God you're not lying about that, too, because my son doesn't need a woman like you in his life."

Jay made that perfectly clear when he abandoned me in Italy without so much as a word, Bridgett wanted to shout. But she didn't. Jay's mother's rejection stung as much as her son's had all those years ago and speech was now impossible. Instead, she tapped into what remained of her pride and forced her legs to carry her toward the house. She ignored the sound of Charlie calling her name as she climbed the stairs to the guest room. This time, she locked the door.

"What makes you think she's going to stop?" Even with the speakerphone as a filter, Blake's voice sounded a little testy.

Jay watched from his office window as the sun set over the Santa Cruz Mountains. "Delaney has a keen sense of survival. She won't want to jeopardize her financial security. Now that she knows I'm on to her and could out her with her Chinese friends, she'll keep quiet."

"Why the hell was she tormenting us with lawsuits and that crazy blog? Did she tell you?"

"She said she was just bored. My guess is she's lonely and bitter, too."

"Excuse me for not throwing her a pity party," Blake said. "How long have you had this kind of leverage over her?"

"I'd been keeping tabs on her since she started working for me all those years ago." Jay leaned back in his chair, a heaviness settling over his chest.

"That was your first mistake: hiring her to begin with."

"She has a brilliant mind."

Blake scoffed. "Yeah, too bad she's chosen to use it for evil."

Jay unlocked his desk drawer and pulled out an old photo of the three roommates taken at a Cubs game back when they were in college. "Aren't you curious about how she looks? Whether or not she's okay?"

His friend was silent for a few beats on the other end of the line before finally answering. "Honestly, no. Like you said, she has a brilliant mind. She could have chosen a different life."

"She was something to us both at one time," Jay said as he fingered the picture. "Hell, you were gonna marry her."

"Dammit, Mac! Yes, I loved her. Past tense." Blake sighed. "She was using me—us—to support her addiction to gambling. I'm not going to pine over a woman like that. It's been thirteen years. I've moved on. Stop letting her tug at that soft spot you try to hide behind your heartless business demeanor. She'll just use and abuse whatever kindness you offer her. Hell, I don't know why you haven't already turned her over to the Feds."

Jay tossed the picture back into the desk drawer. "Too late for that. She was packed up and out of the hotel in less than thirty minutes. According to my sources, she was on her way to Hong Kong this afternoon."

"Once again, she's dodged a bullet, thanks in part to you tracking her down. If she has any sense at all, she'll lay low, enjoy her ill-gained spoils, and leave us the hell alone."

"Wherever she lands, I just hope she can straighten her life out." Jay didn't bother mentioning his reservations that Delaney would leave the two of them alone.

Blake swore. "There you go caring about her again. She's not worth your time. Delaney is no better than the crazy chick who sent you a Dear John letter from Italy. You wouldn't give her a second chance, would you?"

Jay's chest grew heavier.

"You loved her," Blake continued. "But she was using you just like Delaney was using me. No way you'd keep forgiving that girl like you seem to be doing with Delaney. Get a grip, Mac. Remember who the enemy is here. Neither of those two women deserves even a piece of your heart."

A sweat broke out on Jay's forehead at his friend's words.

He wasn't sure he liked Bridgett being compared to Delaney and that thought bothered him. *"She'll never love you."* Delaney's words echoed in his head. He tried to tell himself that it didn't matter—except Jay was starting to wonder if he could separate his heart from his crotch that easily. Jay still physically desired Bridgett. Big-time. The only thing that kept him from returning to the vineyard earlier that afternoon was Delaney's nagging comments. But her words shouldn't bother him at all, because he didn't want Bridgett's love.

Damn it! A painful pinching began at the base of his neck and Jay reached around to rub it away. *They were good together.* As long as he kept things purely physical and ignored the part about her betrayal. So why was he suddenly having so much trouble with that last part? Jay released an explosive litany of obscenities.

"Yeah," Blake said. "That's exactly how I feel about the opposite sex right now, Mac. We need to go hang gliding over a volcano or maybe wingsuit flying. I guarantee the high you get from either is better than sex."

Jay seriously doubted Blake's claim, but he didn't feel like debating his friend right now. Not when thoughts of Bridgett did strange things to his body—and not just the area around his zipper. "I'll have to take your word for that one, Blake. Neither one of those activities is high on my to-do list right now. I've got to host a party for a bunch of sponsors tomorrow evening and then we're dodging women with placards at a game on Sunday."

"You get a rain check this weekend, Mac, but only because you outsmarted Delaney at her own game. I promised my sister I'd come out to Baltimore to see the baby soon. Let's make plans to grab a beer and some crabs when I'm there."

"Sure," Jay said. He looked forward to seeing his friend again, but he worried about keeping the truth about Bridgett from him. Blake would think he was a chump for hooking up with her again, and that bothered Jay almost as much as Delaney's words.

It was after nine o'clock by the time he arrived back at

the vineyard. Linc and Charlie were playing cards in the great room, but there was no sign of Bridgett or his mother.

"Hey, boss," Linc said. He stood up halfway but Jay waved him back down to his chair. The two had been laughing loudly when Jay walked in and the sound of Charlie's enjoyment of anything was music to his ears.

"Everything okay?" Linc looked at him expectantly.

"It is now." Jay walked over and kissed his sister on the top of her head. "How was your day? I'm glad to see that my house is standing after a day of you and Mom under the same roof."

Charlie snorted. "Mom can't get to me. But she did make Bridgett cry."

Jay halted on his way to the liquor cabinet at the other end of the room. "What?"

Charlie shrugged as she laid a card down on the table in front of her. "The last time I saw her, Bridgett was hiking the stairs two at a time with tears streaming down her face. She hasn't left her room since." His sister glanced over at him, a mulish look on her face. "Just so you know, whatever it is, I'm siding with Bridgett on this one. I like her. She's the best thing that ever happened to you. No matter what our dear mother might think."

Gray spots were floating in front of Jay's eyes. "Where is she?"

"I told you, she's in her room," Charlie said.

"Not Bridgett. Mom."

"She was using her computer in your office earlier," Linc offered when Charlie shrugged again.

Jay was stalking toward his office before Linc finished his sentence. His mother didn't bother looking up from her laptop when he entered.

"I thought I told you that my relationship with Bridgett was none of your business," he said without any preamble.

She tapped out a few more keystrokes before glancing over her readers at him. "Is that what you two have? A relationship?"

"Damn it, Mom. Whatever we have doesn't affect you."

He watched as she swallowed harshly before powering off her computer and quietly closing it. With a sigh, she pushed her glasses on top of her head and stood. "You're wrong, Jay. *Everything* you do affects me. Everything your sister does affects me. I'll be the first to admit I stand at the total other end of the spectrum of helicopter parents; that I've fallen short in many areas of parenting. But not in my love for you both. Never in my desire to see you both happy. Settling for a woman who you can never trust with your love won't make you happy." She swallowed harshly again. "Trust me on this one. But in my case, I did it for you. And I got Charlie out of the deal. Not that she'll ever appreciate me, but that's okay. I'd fight just as hard for her happiness, too."

Jay couldn't get any words to form in his throat. He knew his mother's marriage to Lloyd hadn't been a fairy tale. She'd immersed herself in her work, though, making her appear happy enough. But he was no longer looking at that time period through the lens of a young boy. His mother's comments made him as conflicted as both Delaney's and Blake's had earlier.

She stopped beside him, gently reaching up and brushing back his hair off his forehead. "One day, God willing, you'll be a parent. And you'll know this feeling that I have for both you and your sister. You'll want to battle your children's demons, right their wrongs, and fight tooth and nail for their happiness. I want you to have happiness in your life. Happiness like your father and I had. And I won't give up fighting for it. Neither should you." She kissed him on the cheek. "I'll see you at lunch tomorrow for our family talk."

He stood there mute as his mother quietly walked out of his office. Eventually Jay made his way around to his desk chair, where he sunk down and dropped his head into his hands. He still wanted Bridgett, damn it. His physical need for her was powerful. But the rusty organ deep within his chest kept clenching at the thought of possessing her body only. Fool that he was, apparently he wanted more from the last woman he should trust.

Linc wandered in as Jay was unlocking the safe. "We

have an added guest for the sponsorship party tomorrow night," he announced.

"If it's the father of Charlie's baby, go ahead and shoot me now."

"No, but that actually might be the lesser of two evils," his assistant said sheepishly. "I just got a text from NFL headquarters. The commissioner wants the details so that he can stop by and have a few words with you."

Jay swore silently. The man likely wanted to appear pro-active in front of some of the league's bigger advertisers with a public dressing-down of Jay over the Blaze's current legal situation. Women's rights groups had been hounding the NFL to make someone the scapegoat in all their cheer-leader class action cases by sanctioning a team owner. Apparently, that owner was to be Jay.

With luck, Delaney would heed his warning and all the nonsense surrounding the class action suit would die down. Unfortunately, not soon enough to avoid a visit from the commissioner tomorrow evening, which meant he'd have to suck it up and endure whatever posturing the guy wanted to do before the assembled sponsors. Jay sighed as he trans-ferred the contents of his briefcase into the safe. "When he's here, have him sample the new pinot and arrange to send a case to his wife. She loves the stuff." Hopefully the gesture would take some of the steam out of the blowhard.

Linc chuckled. "Sure thing, boss. The team arrived at the hotel about an hour ago. Mr. Osbourne says everyone is settling in. There were a few women protesting in the lobby, but they left peacefully with a few autographed balls. Mr. Osbourne said the team is scheduled to practice at the junior college twice tomorrow if you want to stop by."

The eager smile Linc shot him told Jay his assistant wanted to "stop by" the Blaze practice. The kid likely deserved it after having to spend the day in the House of Estrogen. An afternoon spent on the sidelines would be a welcome diversion for Jay, as well, given the week he'd been having.

"Change my lunch with my mother and sister to a late brunch and we'll go to the afternoon practice," he said.

"Got it. Is there anything else you need before I turn in?"

Jay shook his head, his eyes suddenly focusing on a yellowed envelope at the back of the safe. He waited until he heard Linc's retreating footsteps before he pulled the letter out of the safe. Sliding back into his desk chair, he flipped the envelope between his fingers, wondering why he hadn't burned the damn thing years ago. He'd kept it as a reminder to be careful who he trusted with his heart, but every time he read the letter he was only reminded that his heart no longer existed. Bridgett's words had seen to that.

I always thought that being in love with someone would mean I would do anything for them.

One look at her letter and the feelings that had been rumbling around in his chest all afternoon quieted. He shoved it into the breast pocket of his suit. Emotions had no place in his life anymore. Jay wanted Bridgett, and he made it a point to always get what he wanted. He'd just keep the letter close as a reminder that what they had would only ever be physical.

By the time he got to the door of the guest room his body was primed and ready for further negotiations over their relationship. But when he tried the door handle, it was locked. Jay swore as he shoved his fingers through his hair. He was seriously considering finding Josie and getting the key but he didn't want Bridgett that way. Jay had promised to treat her with respect at all times in their relationship and he'd honor his word now. Even if it meant he'd be spending the next half hour in a cold shower.

Twenty

Bridgett wrapped the towel around her wet hair and stepped out of the bathroom to find Jay reclining on her unmade bed, his back against the headboard and the morning sun shining on his bare feet. He looked delicious in his faded jeans and khaki button-down. His hair was damp as if he, too, had just come from the shower. She pulled the fluffy robe more tightly around her body so Jay wouldn't detect the slight tremor that came over her at the thought of him naked and wet.

He glanced up from the text he was sending, letting his gaze slowly drift over her body from head to toe. Bridgett couldn't hide her shiver this time; the hunger in his eyes was so intense. Jay gave her one of his knowing smiles and nodded toward the beautiful teapot she'd coveted the other day. "I brought you some scones to go with your tea."

She should have known he wouldn't allow her to stay locked in her room for long. Bridgett had been relieved that he hadn't barged in last night—he obviously had the means. As much as her body had craved comfort after her altercation with his mother, she realized she was becoming too vulnerable to Jay's touch—much less everything else about him. It was time to put something more substantial between them than a locked door.

"The women's rights groups are circling their wagons today," she said as she poured. "I'm going to meet with Mimi to discuss how to use the media to defuse the protest they've got staged for tomorrow's game. There's a room at the B and B and I've already made arrangements to move there."

"No."

Bridgett wasn't surprised at the vehemence in his voice. "You're my client, not my keeper, Jay."

"You promised to stay through the weekend. Not that you've ever been very good at keeping your promises."

The teacup rattled on the plate, she set it down with such force. She hated how he had manipulated their story to make it look like she was at fault for everything. The accusations his mother had thrown at her the day before were untrue and they both knew it. "I never made you any promises, Jay. You might want to remember that when you're telling your mother about me."

Jay swore violently as he rose from the mattress and stalked over to where she was standing. "Is that what this is about? My mother? Ignore her. She won't ever be a part of our relationship."

"We don't have a relationship," she cried out. "Not any-more."

They stared at each for a moment, Bridgett fighting with her body to keep it from leaning into his, until her cell phone buzzed, shattering the tense silence. She tried to step around him to grab her phone, but he blocked her way.

"Ignore it. It's just Brody being a pain in the ass. He texted or called five times while you were in the shower."

Bridgett let out a huff as she shoved at Jay's chest. "Now you're reading my personal messages?" She grabbed the phone and, sure enough, it was a text from her brother demanding that she call him back. She fired off a response telling him she'd call him later before tossing the phone onto the bed.

Turning to Jay, she tried for her best courtroom voice. "I *consented* to remain in Napa this weekend to help with your defense surrounding this lawsuit. As such, I'm going to work with Mimi to mitigate the PR damage from the blogger and the women's groups. I can do that just as easily from a B and B as I can here."

Jay's mouth formed a mulish line. "You 'consented' to sleep in my bed."

Bridgett sucked in a deep breath, trying to muster the strength she needed to walk away from him again. "I can't keep doing that."

"Can't? Or won't?" he demanded.

Tears suddenly clogged her throat making it difficult to speak. "Do the semantics really matter? We can't go back to who we were. Not with everything that's happened between us."

"I know." His arms wrapped around her, pulling her against his hard body. "But we can still have this," he said before his lips captured hers in a deep, drugging kiss.

Bridgett wasn't proud that she couldn't resist this man. She'd contemplate that deep character flaw later. Right now she was exploring the smooth muscles of his back with her fingers as her mouth welcomed the invasion of his tongue. He groaned when her hips pressed restlessly against his tight zipper. Within seconds, his jeans were on the floor along with her robe and his shirt.

His body covered hers on the bed, not wasting any time with preliminaries, which was fine with Bridgett. She wanted him inside her urgently, to the point that she was contradicting her earlier statements by begging him to hurry and take her. Jay complied, burying himself deep inside her with one powerful stroke. Then they were moving as one, just as they always did, their rhythm instinctive and fluid. No words were necessary, just the raw power of their bodies finding release.

Bridgett sighed heavily as she came in a rush, her limbs going weak with contentment. Jay growled something unintelligible as he followed her over the edge, his body sinking into hers on the mattress. Stillness settled over the room, both of them working to get their breathing—and their racing heartbeats—under control. Bridgett tried to commit to memory the feeling of completeness that was pulsing through her. She'd never had the same sensation with any other man and she doubted she ever would. The thought made tears sting the backs of her eyes. But it didn't dampen her resolve to walk away from him.

Jay touched his forehead to hers. "*This* works," he whispered. "This is good. Damn good."

But not good enough. Bridgett kept her thoughts to herself, though. They wouldn't help in her argument with him. He'd vowed never to give her anything more than physical pleasure. Her body may be in sated bliss, but she knew now that her heart—and her head—wanted more. "'This' doesn't change things," she told him. "I'm still going to the B and B."

His eyes fixed hers with a determined stare. "I'll need you here for the party tonight. The commissioner has decided to crash the event and I'd like you to be available to answer any questions about the case if he has them."

She rolled her eyes at his lame excuse for keeping her close but she didn't protest. After all, she did have killer shoes and a dress to wear. "As long as you understand that I'm only attending in my capacity as your lawyer."

His smile was smug as he thrust his hips against hers, causing her to involuntarily clench around his length. She couldn't hold back the contented sigh that escaped her lips.

"We'll see about that." Jay rolled off her and began shoving his legs into his boxer briefs and jeans. Bridgett let out a resigned sigh as the sexy dimples on his ass disappeared, knowing it was likely the last time she'd see them. Her phone vibrated on the bed. "If that's your brother, tell him if he doesn't leave you alone, I'm going to trade his ass to Buffalo."

She wrapped the robe around her body. "I can handle my baby brother."

Jay paused in buttoning his shirt to level a thunderous

gaze at her. "He has as little to do with us as my mother does, Bridgett."

"You seem to keep forgetting, there is no 'us,'" she reminded him.

The smug look was back on his face again as stalked over to where she sat on the bed. "There's an 'us,' Bridgett," he said as he leaned over and nuzzled the skin along her shoulder. "If you'd like more proof, stick around tonight instead of crying off to the B and B with only Mimi to protect you. I promise you'll enjoy the next round of negotiations as much as you enjoyed these."

"Is that what I am? Some prize to be won?" Her throat grew two sizes too small again as she tried to force the words out. "A thrilling business deal to be negotiated? What happens if you get what you want? Will you take off again for the next best thing?"

Anger flashed like lightning in his eyes and that cocky smile morphed into a flat line of irritation. "I'll see you tonight, Bridgett," was all he said before he walked out of the door.

Bridgett hated the fact that she was actually looking forward to seeing Jay later.

"You're what?" Charlie braced herself on the arm of the wrought iron chair to keep from falling out of it. Jay reached over to steady his sister as they both tried to absorb their mother's announcement.

"I'm taking a sabbatical," his mother repeated.

"To do what?" His sister looked as though their mother had just told them she was an alien, and Jay was finding it hard not to laugh at Charlie's reaction. Except his own reaction was only slightly less skeptical than hers. Melanie Davis had let her work define her for over thirty years. It was hard to imagine her outside of a research lab.

His mother threw up her arms. "I don't know yet. Maybe I'll go exploring around the world. You can show me the sights in Europe. Wouldn't that be fun?"

Charlie managed to stop choking on her orange juice seconds before Jay reached over to perform the Heimlich on her. She waved him away frantically. "You want to travel? With me?" Charlie croaked out.

"Sure."

His sister's eyes narrowed to slits. "Is this some kind of punishment or something?"

Jay reached over and gave Charlie's hand a squeeze, trying to stem her overreaction. He knew what was really making her anxious. She needed to tell their mother about the baby. *Tell her,* he mouthed, but she ignored his plea, shaking her head violently before yanking her hand away.

"Of course not," his mother said, her face growing paler. "It's an opportunity for us to enjoy some time together."

"Well, the opportunity for that has long passed, Mother." Charlie stood up jerkily, nearly upending the table. "I don't want or need a babysitter. Or a doting mother."

"Charlie!" Jay called but she had already stormed off. He glanced back over at his mother's face. It was still and drawn, but not defeated. The women in his family possessed the same stubbornness, it seemed.

"Leave her, Jay. I didn't expect she'd jump at the idea. It's going to take some time for her to accept that I want to have a bigger role in her life. In both your lives."

There was that uneasy feeling again, just like the one he'd had both times he'd spoken with his mother this weekend. "What's going on here, Mom? This isn't just about a sabbatical. What's brought this on?"

She stared out at the vineyard spread out below them, the vibrant colors resembling a painting. It was a few moments before she spoke and Jay found he was growing increasingly anxious. "I've shared an office with the same woman for four years now. Brenda Rippen. She was your age, believe it or not."

Jay sighed at his mother's use of the word *was.*

"Mmm," she said. "My answer doesn't have a happy ending. Brenda's husband wanted to start a family, but she kept putting him off. She told him she had plenty of time but she wanted to get a few articles published before she had a baby.

A few weeks ago, she got on the highway to drive home from work and a tractor trailer T-boned her."

"Jesus," he whispered.

"At the funeral, I made the mistake of telling her husband that it was fortunate that they hadn't had children yet."

Jay sucked in a breath as he moved his chair closer to his mother. "You were only trying to be sympathetic."

She rolled her eyes at him. "I was being obtuse. And unfeeling. I thought that if she had children, they would miss their mother. Her husband asked me if my children missed their mother."

He watched her struggle to swallow. "He was coming from a bad place. Grief will make you say crazy things."

His mother turned to look at him, her blue eyes moist. Jay didn't think he'd seen his mother cry. Theirs was definitely not an emotional family. "Don't be coy. I've been an absent mother for years. After your father died, it was easier to bury myself in my work. When I had Charlotte, well, she was Lloyd's from the very beginning. Sometimes I think he resented having to share her. Especially with you." She patted his hand. "But I'm glad she has you."

"She has both of us, Mom. We'll work it out."

Several women holding poster board signs were huddled outside the junior college stadium where the Blaze were practicing. Security guards kept them out while a small horde of television crews filmed it all.

"Great," Mimi said from beside Bridgett in the backseat of the same town car that had chauffeured her from the airport. "A total of five women showed up for a protest"—she made air quotes with her fingers—"and the media outnumber them three to one." The car made its way through the gate. "These days it's no longer 'film at eleven,'" Mimi continued. "Everyone can watch events unfold instantaneously. They don't wait for all the facts. Fans will make up their mind like *that*." She snapped her fingers.

"There are so many other issues more important than

this," Bridgett said as the car parked near the track circling the playing field. "This is supposed to be a game."

Mimi gaped at her. "Wow. For someone so smart, you are naïve. This stopped being a 'game' a long time ago, Bridgett. The NFL is a nine-billion-dollar-a-year industry. Trust me, its image is important to all of those owners, players, and sponsors raking in the dough every week."

Bridgett shook her head as she got out of the car. The whole thing still seemed ridiculous to her. In less than ten days, a potentially specious lawsuit involving cheerleaders— make that one cheerleader—had mushroomed into the lead story on the nightly news.

The sounds of whistles and cleats pounding the turf enveloped them as they walked along the track toward the sidelines. Asia Dupree—the Blaze's director of media—waved at Bridgett. The two had met when Brody signed with the team several years ago, but they'd become friends this past year thanks to Bridgett's sister-in-law, Shay.

"Thanks for meeting with us," Bridgett said after she and Asia exchanged hugs. "This is Mimi Livingston. She's helping us handle some of the media issues relating to the case."

Asia smiled warmly as she shook Mimi's hand. "Unfortunately, this thing has begun to take on a life of its own. Other teams are fighting similar cases, but for some reason that bitchy blogger decided to target us with even more damaging gossip. Not that any of it is relevant." She grinned slyly at Bridgett. "Although, you do have some 'splaining to do, girl. We need to hit the bar after practice so I can get the scoop. The gang back in Baltimore will be jealous that I got the four-one-one before they did."

Mimi snorted. "She claims there's nothing going on. Of course, McManus hasn't taken his eyes off her since she got out of the car, despite the fact one of his players is hunched over on the field."

"A player's hurt?" Asia quickly turned to see who might be injured.

Bridgett glanced farther down the sideline. Sure enough, Jay's stare was fixed on her. He looked imposing behind his aviator sunglasses, his arms crossed belligerently over his chest. Imposing and sexy as hell, especially when the breeze ruffled his hair. But she forced her feet to stay put. She needed to stick to her plan to put distance between them. It was the only way she knew how to survive the rest of this weekend.

"That's just Jervais Stubbing, an offensive lineman," Asia said with a sigh. "He always tries to dog it in practice the day before a game."

The shrill sound of a whistle focused their attention back to the subject they'd come to discuss. "That's the end of practice. The players will shower here before they get back on the buses for the hotel, so we have about twenty minutes or so to discuss your plans." Asia directed them to the first row of seats in the stadium. "Let's go over here."

"Bridgett!" Brody shouted her name before they'd reached the bleachers.

With a sigh, she turned to the other two women and excused herself. Brody had been badgering her for three days and there really was no way to put this conversation off any longer.

"We need to talk," her brother commanded as he stalked toward her. "Privately." He reached out and shackled her wrist with the extra-long fingers that allowed him to be the premier tight end in the NFL. Right now they were likely bruising her wrist as he pulled her toward the tunnel leading to the locker room.

"Let go, Brody." Bridgett tugged to no avail as she tried to keep up with his long strides. "I. Am. Serious. Let me go now or I'll post those pictures of you wearing Ashley's tutu when you were four."

His eyes narrowed to slits as he dragged her into a small office beside the locker room. "You wouldn't dare."

"All it takes is one click of a button on my phone," she said. "Come to think of it, Mimi and Asia would probably be delighted to have that as a distraction to all the other stupid press the team has been getting. Good thing I scanned it in already."

Brody released her wrist, his face incredulous. "Seriously, when did my sisters all turn into hormonal psychos? You used to be the reasonable one." He tossed his helmet on an empty chair. "And don't *even* get me started on Gwen."

She rolled her eyes. "I'm sorry if Gwen's marriage crisis means she can't cater to your every whim right now, little brother, but we all have to grow up sometime."

"Hey, I can take care of myself. And believe me, I'm all in favor of her divorcing that jerk's ass. Skip's lucky I didn't castrate him after the way he talked about Shay last year."

"Okay, well, I'm glad we got that all cleared up." She started for the door. "Believe it or not, I'm working this weekend and I have more to discuss with Mimi and Asia. Who knows what garbage the blogger is going to feed these protesters next. I'll see you tomorrow after the game."

"Whoa!" Brody blocked her path as if she were a defensive lineman trying to get to the quarterback. "You're not going anywhere until you explain what the hell is going on between you and McManus."

"Say the word and I *will* trade his ass to Buffalo, Bridgett."

She looked past her brother's shoulder pad to see Jay leaning nonchalantly against the doorjamb, his feet crossed at the ankles and each hand tucked beneath the opposite armpit. Brody made a growling sound and suddenly she was suffocating from the weight of alpha male egos permeating the small room.

"You can *cut* my ass, for all I care," Brody said, his voice quiet, but lethal. Displaying the fearlessness that made him a Pro Bowl player, he turned and stalked toward the man who held his career in his back pocket. "If you so much as make her sniffle, *your* ass is mine."

"Brody!" Bridgett jumped between the two men, placing a staying hand on her brother's chest while shooting him a quelling look. "Tutu."

Jay's only movement was to arch an eyebrow at his star player. Brody huffed but he came to a stop two feet from Jay, leaving Bridgett sandwiched between them. He leveled his trademark baby blue eyes at her. "Tell me he isn't the one."

Bridgett's mind whirred in confusion. "Isn't the one what?"

"The guy who broke your heart."

She sensed Jay stiffen behind her, but she was glad she couldn't see his face. "I don't understand, Brody," she whispered.

"Damn it, Bridgett, that stupid blogger said this relationship between you two goes way back. I want to know if this jerk's the one who messed you up."

Her chest ached at the fierceness in her brother's eyes and his voice. "Nobody messed me up," she lied. She couldn't have this conversation with her brother. She would not have it in front of Jay.

Brody lifted his eyes to the ceiling, mouthing something to the heavens. His expression was a mix of compassion and uncertainty when he looked back down at her. "I may not have a PhD like my wife, but I'm not stupid, Bridge. I see the way you close up around other couples. I watch you recoil whenever someone brings a baby near you. Sometimes you get that pained look when you're in a room full of happy people as if their joy is crushing you. I hate that haunted expression you get. Someone let you down, destroyed your faith in love. You said as much last year when I was trying to find my way with Shay." He gripped her shoulders. "I'd do anything to take that ache away from you." Brody's face hardened as he pinned his gaze over her head. "Anything."

Bridgett had to work to steady her breathing and keep her tears at bay. She was touched by her brother's words. All this time, she'd thought him oblivious to anyone other than himself. Or his new wife. A small smile escaped at the thought that perhaps her baby brother had grown up after all.

The air grew still behind her. The only indication that Jay remained was a tightening of Brody's jaw. Bridgett didn't like Jay hearing how vulnerable he'd left her after his desertion in Italy. She needed to get her brother out of there. Lifting her hand from his chest, she cupped his cheek. "Thank you, Brody. But this isn't what you think." She tried to muster as much conviction in her voice as she could. "But I love you for your very spirited protection of me." She stretched up on her toes and kissed his cheek. "Get your head back in the game and stop worrying about me. I'm fine."

Brody hesitated before wrapping his arms around her. "I'm not kidding when I say I'll kill him," he whispered.

"I know."

Her brother savagely eyed the man who was technically his boss before sliding past him and out the door, his cleats clicking loudly on the cement. The silence he left in his wake was charged as a maelstrom of emotions coursed through Bridgett. When she finally dared look at Jay it was to find him studying her much like one would analyze a puzzle. He hadn't moved an inch from his original stance, but his contemplative stare was making her uncomfortable.

"I should be getting back to Mimi and Asia," she said.

"We need to talk," he commanded at the same time.

Neither one moved. Bridgett didn't want to talk. Not to this Jay. Her heart ached to speak to the Jay she once knew, but he was long gone, replaced by the über-sexy man who used power and money to get what he wanted. And he wanted her. Correction: He didn't want all of her. Just her body. She needed to keep reminding herself that she deserved more than sex.

Thankfully, they were saved by the arrival of Linc. "Boss, I think you should see this." He shoved his iPad in front of Jay, but Jay kept his eyes fixed on Bridgett. "Boss?"

Jay blinked as if to refocus his vision and his thoughts before glancing down at the iPad.

"Son of a *bitch*!"

Twenty-one

"He's likely set himself up for racketeering charges," Bridgett practically shouted into her cell phone. "Stuart, I'm going to need a little backup here. We're getting into uncharted legal territory for me."

Jay watched as Bridgett paced his office, her cell phone plastered to her ear. She was wearing a dress that hugged every curve and dipped low enough in the back that he almost got a peek at the dimple just above her nice round ass. He shifted uncomfortably in his chair because if he could see that damn dimple, then every other jerk at the party could, too. All the more reason to keep her locked in here with him. Her high heels sparkled in the light when she pivoted to pace back the other way. Jay took a bracing sip of Scotch, trying to quash the heat that shot to his crotch at the thought of her wearing nothing but those damn shoes while she straddled him in this very chair.

"Why are you grinning like a fool?"

He roused himself from his fantasy to find Bridgett had finished up her phone call. She'd stopped pacing and was now standing next to him. Too bad the expression she wore wasn't one that said "I'm going to rock your world."

She'd been on the warpath ever since the latest installment of the *Girlfriends' Guide to the NFL* dropped onto the Internet this afternoon. Delaney had gone for broke, implying that Jay was involved with organized gambling on NFL games. She'd claimed he'd been sighted in the Wynn—a fact that could be easily substantiated via surveillance cameras—where a known gambling ring was operating. As parting shots went, it was a doozy. He'd underestimated Delaney's apparent vendetta and that frustrated him more than having Bridgett strutting her stuff with half of the NFL sponsors two hundred feet away.

"What were you thinking?" she continued. "I told you not to go vigilante on this blogger, but do you listen? No! Now she's implicated you in something much more difficult to defend against. The commissioner is apoplectic and threatening to take away your team. As for the media, they've descended into a feeding frenzy. Seriously, the women protesting on behalf of the cheerleaders are the least of your worries right now. Yet you're sitting here coolly. What do you have to say for yourself?"

Jay stood to his full height, adjusting his tuxedo around his very tight boxer briefs, not wanting to let her know he was anything but cool. "What was your brother talking about earlier today?"

He'd caught her off guard. She blinked those silver eyes a few times, apparently trying to catch up with his quick subject change. "What do you mean?"

"You know exactly what I mean, counselor."

Bridgett shifted uneasily on her heels. "He was just being Brody. It doesn't concern you."

She crossed her arms beneath her breasts and once again Jay was glad he had her all to himself. He didn't want to share her with another man. Ever. But someone had "messed her up" according to her brother and that thought had been consuming him all afternoon, too. Was it the guy she'd sent him the Dear John letter for? Whoever he was, Brody had better hope he got to him first.

Jay reached out and traced a finger along the line of her jaw, shifting it up to tangle in the cascade of stones hanging from her ear. "Everything about you concerns me." It was an admission he didn't want to make out loud, but the words hit the air before he could stop them.

Bridgett sunk her teeth into her lower lip before jutting her chin up defiantly. "I think it's best if we keep things professional from here on out, Jay. I don't want your mind games getting in the way of my mounting a winning defense for you."

"I told you not to worry about my defense. It's all going to work out."

Her eyes widened as her hands shoved at his chest. "For the love of Pete, this isn't something you can buy your way out of, Jay. This is serious."

Jay wrapped his arms around her and did what he'd wanted to do ever since he'd laid eyes on her in that dress: He crushed her to his body. She inhaled sharply when she came in contact with his arousal. "The only thing serious right now is how soon I can get you out of that dress."

"Your arrogance really knows no bounds," she said.

He smiled confidently to himself, though, when she sank farther into his body. "If I didn't know any better, I'd think you actually cared about what happens to me."

She pulled back, eyeing him in what looked like disbelief. Her lips quivered slightly before she reined her emotions back behind the cool façade she wore for everyone else. "You're a fool, you know that?"

Bridgett stepped out of his embrace and the inches separating their bodies suddenly felt like a gulf. Jay silently cursed at himself. He was a fool. A damn fool who, if he wasn't careful, could lose his heart to this woman a second time. There was a loud knocking on the office door and Bridgett took another giant step back.

Jay moved behind the desk. "The cavalry has finally arrived."

The door swung open and Linc charged in. "Boss, the FBI is here." He stepped aside and Jay's friend from prep school, Matt Kovaluk, strode into the room.

"You didn't tell me this shindig was black tie," Matt said. "I could have come dressed as Bond if you'd given me some warning." Matt's eyes darted over to Bridgett and his face relaxed into an appreciative grin. "Damn. And a Bond girl, too. You really have the life, McAnus."

Linc chuckled at the stupid boyhood nickname that Matt never let him outgrow. Jay leveled a look at his assistant and Linc's laugh turned into a cough.

"The commissioner?" Jay directed the question at Linc, but Matt answered for him.

"The director of the field office drew his name. He gets to schmooze with the big celebrities while I get—you." He shot Bridgett one of his smarmy grins, which never failed to help him score in a bar but was bugging the shit out of Jay right now. "Although I must say the view in here is much nicer."

Jay signaled for Linc to close the door behind him on the way out. He didn't want one of his guests—most of whom had shown up tonight in hopes of getting ringside seats to Jay's dressing-down by the commissioner—to overhear their conversation.

"Don't say a word, Jay," Bridgett said, her lawyerly mask firmly in place. But if he wasn't mistaken, her fingers were trembling a bit as she reached for her phone. "If they're going to question you, I want Stuart on the phone, too."

"Whoa there, gorgeous." Matt held up a hand. "The last time I asked this idiot a question, he gave me the wrong answer to a U.S. history test. He actually thought Lewis and Clark were a rock band." Matt laughed and Jay shook his head.

Bridgett narrowed her eyes at the FBI agent, but she didn't loosen her death grip on her phone. "What's going on here, Jay?"

"Bridgett, allow me to introduce you to Not-So-Very-Special Agent Matt Kovaluk. Matt is with the organized crime unit of the FBI. But not because he deserves to work in such a prestigious agency. His mommy made them pick him. She's a federal judge." Matt's pretty smile didn't fade despite the dig. Jay sighed. "Matt, this is my attorney, Bridgett Janik."

"She's your lawyer?" Matt heaved a reverent sigh. "I am seriously on the wrong side of the law." He stretched his hand out to Bridgett, his green eyes twinkling obnoxiously. "Your client isn't under any suspicion here. In fact, he's been doing his civic duty for the past few days. Never mind sanctions. The commissioner will be forced to name a stadium after him when this is all done."

Jay walked over to the bar and poured Matt a drink. "Something tells me he won't like that."

"Could one of you catch me up here, please?" Bridgett was starting to get that testy look—the one Jay loved to kiss off her lips. But he didn't dare touch her right now. Not when he felt the line between sex and emotional involvement was beginning to blur.

Matt took the drink and settled into one of the chairs while Jay leaned a hip on the corner of his desk. He nodded toward the chair beside Matt, but Bridgett shook her head, practically tapping her toe in frustration.

"Jay and the super spy network that he's cultivated throughout his career just helped us nab a Chinese gambling ring known as Sagittarius X. Interpol has been trying to take them down for three years," Matt said as he sipped his Scotch. "It was almost child's play, it was so easy once you came over from the dark side, Jay."

Bridgett's eyebrows went up a hair as she cocked her head. "And just how did he do that?"

"By being a ruthless pain in the ass." Matt saluted him with his glass. "But you owe me fifty-yard-line seats for the rest of the season. I told you she wouldn't take the bait and shut down her blog. Not even for you. Delaney Silverberg seriously has it out for you and Blake Callahan."

"Delaney?" Bridgett's arms dropped to her sides. "*Your* Delaney? She's the blogger?"

Matt snickered. "Technically she was Blake's Delaney.

But Blue Eyes here had a soft spot for her up until the end. Sucker."

Jay rubbed at the back of his neck, trying to make the squeezing stop. He'd really hoped Delaney would make the wise decision. For such an intelligent woman, she wasn't very smart.

"I'm still not following why Delaney is writing the blog and what it has to do with a gambling ring," Bridgett said.

"Do you want to do the honors or shall I?" Matt asked.

Shaking his head, Jay looked over at Bridgett, who was now gripping the back of the chair. "Delaney has always had gambling issues," he began. "It was the reason she and Blake broke up. She owed a lot of money. I bailed her out with the money I was supposed to pay Vincenzo DiSantis for his pinot grigio formula."

Bridgett gasped softly and her fingers dug into the chair.

"First mistake," Matt chimed in sarcastically.

"She has a brilliant mind for software. Without her Mc-Manus Industries wouldn't be where it is today," Jay snapped. "I made the money back in less than two years."

"And you eventually got your winery." Matt spread his arms wide. "Which produces a very fine pinot grigio, I might add."

"There are still a few pieces of the story missing," Bridgett said irritably. "Like how she went from McManus Industries to a Chinese gambling ring, for instance."

Jay slammed his drink down on the desk. None of this was his fault. Except for being an idiot and trusting his former roommate to have more sense than she obviously did. "She has an addiction. One she thought she could outsmart, but apparently not. A few years after the company took off, I caught her stealing funds from one of the accounts. She'd managed to pilfer a little at a time, but by the time I was wise to her she'd socked a million dollars or so away in a Swiss bank account. But instead of using that money to pay off her increasing gambling debts, she stupidly tried to sell some proprietary data of ours to the Chinese. I fired her on the spot."

"You took the money back from the Swiss bank account,

though, right?" Bridgett didn't include the word "chump" at the end of the question, but he heard it loud and clear in her tone.

Matt snickered again and Jay's hands balled into fists. "No. I didn't. I wanted her out of my life and that money was an insurance policy against her having to come back around looking for more. It was a pittance compared to what I made from her designs."

Bridgett shook her head. "So instead of selling the data to the Chinese, she sold herself instead."

"She liked to play the indentured servant, but she's spent the last six years skimming money off the top of their winnings. I kept tabs on the account. The world economy hasn't been that robust that she's earned twenty-five million in interest."

"And now it's all in the hands of Interpol," Matt muttered in disgust.

"So you went to Las Vegas and used that information to suggest she stop blogging?"

Jay wanted to kiss her and her keen mind for catching on so quickly. "Yes."

"Well, that was an epic failure," she said caustically, making Jay not so eager to kiss her anymore. "We learned last year when Brody's trainer was being blackmailed by her to sell out Brody's secret that she was only blogging to get back at someone. Now we know that someone was you."

"And Blake," Matt chimed in, seeming to enjoy the direction the conversation was going. "She used her ill-gotten gains to finance her gossip purchases."

Bridgett crossed her arms beneath her breasts again and Jay watched out of the corner of his eye as his friend sat up straighter to enjoy the view. "She clearly didn't care about money, as you might have noticed if you'd taken *just one second* to think this through." Nope, he definitely didn't want to kiss her now. "A woman scorned isn't going to be satisfied until she gets even."

Jay arched an eyebrow at her, challenging her to say more, but her lips formed a harsh line.

"Exactly what I told you, McAnus, but you had to be a softy and give Delaney one more chance."

Bridgett stiffened at Matt's words. "One more chance?"

"Yeah, he nearly blew the whole thing by warning her off," Matt explained. "But it turned out her desire to prove she still had the upper hand was her downfall. Our tech guys put a wormhole in the blog. If we were lucky enough she'd post from the hotel suite. But in her desperation, she did us one better, and used one of the gambling site's laptops. Right there in the Honolulu airport. It was awesome. She won't be blogging again for a very long time." Matt grinned widely. "The case was broken wide-open on U.S. soil all because Jay was a sucker. I've told you not to be so trusting but you never learn, do you?"

Jay's gut clenched at the haughty look Bridgett was wearing. She thought he was a fool for trusting Delaney, but he'd been a bigger fool for trusting her. He was actually grateful for Matt's reminder. "I believe I've learned my lesson," he said, never taking his eyes off Bridgett. "I won't be giving my trust away freely ever again." He watched as she swallowed harshly and her stance became brittle.

"So this is it, then," she said. The implication in her words wasn't lost on Jay.

"No, there are still some unresolved issues." *Like the fact that Jay's desire for her body hadn't ebbed in the least.* He was aware that Matt was studying them both carefully, but he didn't give a shit. Jay still wasn't ready to let her walk out of his life again.

She snatched her cell phone off of the desk. "I'm fairly certain I'll be able to dispense with the class action suit without too much effort on your part. Mimi can work with Asia to defuse the media circus that currently surrounds you. I'll make sure the commissioner gives them a statement before I leave."

The urge to lunge after her was overwhelming, but Jay remained where he was. He'd let her escape to the B and B, but tomorrow they'd have the discussion they'd been putting off for days now. "My car will pick you up at ten tomorrow."

She paused at the door, tossing another haughty look over her shoulder.

"The Sparks haven't dismissed their suit yet, Bridgett," he told her. "So technically, you're still on the case. And at my beck and call."

Whatever retort she wanted to spew at him, she bit back; most likely in deference to the fact there was an armed agent in the room. It was the first time he was glad Matt had arrived at the vineyard. She nodded regally before gliding out the door.

Matt whistled softly. "My Spidey-sense tells me there's more to your relationship than just attorney-client, McAnus."

Jay moved off the desk to refill his glass. "Is that what they teach you guys at Quantico? Spidey-sense."

"With great power comes great responsibility." Matt was the only one laughing at his own joke. He covered his glass when Jay went to refill it. "Technically, I'm still on duty."

"Good," Jay said. "I have another favor I need from you."

"It's gonna cost you."

"When doesn't it? If we make it to the Super Bowl, I'll make sure you have the entire fan experience."

Matt scoffed at him before he swallowed down the last sip of his drink. "I was thinking more like the phone number of your lawyer after she dumps your ass."

The air stilled in Jay's lungs. This was why he couldn't let Bridgett walk away. The thought of her being with another man made him blind with rage. He needed to treat his dealings with her like any other business deal he ever made: with cool detachment.

"Jay, you still with me?" Matt was standing, waving a hand in front of Jay's face.

"Yeah. If you find yourself in need of an attorney, hire your damn mother."

Matt's laughter echoed around the room. "Blake's right. You've got it bad for that woman."

"Are you going to do me the favor or not?" Jay didn't want to discuss what he did and didn't have with Bridgett with either Matt or Blake, especially when both were doing a good job discussing it among themselves.

"You haven't told me what it is yet," Matt said with a grin.

Jay reached into the top drawer of his chest and pulled out a piece of paper, handing it to Matt.

"Who is this guy?" Matt asked after scanning the paper.

"A deadbeat dad."

Matt leveled a quizzical glance at Jay. "And?"

"And, I want you to find the sonofabitch and make him pay his child support."

His friend waved the paper as if to say "go on."

Jay sighed. "He's the ex-husband of the attorney heading up the Sparks' case. I'm reasonably certain she's only going after the team to pad her pocketbook because this guy doesn't pay."

"You've got to be kidding!"

He kept his face stoic as he stared at Matt, who was still grinning like a fool.

"You're not kidding." Matt swore. "There's got to be something unethical about this."

"What's unethical about making a father pay his child support?"

"Sure, look like a big softy when all the while you're getting your case dismissed." Matt blew out a breath. They both stared each other down for a minute. "The full Super Bowl experience, McAnus. Sideline passes for the halftime show and if Taylor Swift is the halftime performer, I want her to sit on my lap."

Jay eyed his friend incredulously before nodding.

Matt conceded defeat with a sigh. "Fine, I'll get the local boys in Virginia on this and we'll see if we can rattle his cage. But that's all."

"Fair enough," Jay said as Linc slipped back into the room.

"The commissioner wants to make a statement to the press assembled at the end of the drive. The FBI guy says it's okay." Linc looked from one man to the other for confirmation.

"Not without me, he's not," Jay said. "If I'm going to make the commissioner eat crow, I want to stand next to him and watch."

Linc grinned. "That's what I thought."

The three men headed for the door leading out to the terrace.

"Oh, by the way," Matt said quietly. "The Las Vegas bureau found some old letters and stuff among Delaney's things when they were searching her hotel suite. One of them apparently mentions you. I asked for a copy to be e-mailed to me when they get finished with it tonight. Hopefully, it won't turn out to be anything, but I'm happy to let your lawyer take a peek at it tomorrow." He winked at Jay. "Just in case."

Jay couldn't imagine what things of his Delaney might have. He hoped none of it had to do with McManus Industries, but the gruff cadence of the commissioner making his case to reporters distracted his thoughts. "Sure," he said, absently. "Whatever."

Twenty-two

The Blaze were down by three points with forty seconds to go in the first half, but Bridgett was having trouble concentrating on the game. The visitor's box at Levi's Stadium was filled with a crowd of obnoxious revelers who wanted to congratulate Jay on his role in outwitting the blogger. The *Girlfriends' Guide to the NFL* had been a thorn in the side of the league for the past two seasons. The fact that he'd inadvertently had a hand in bringing down an Internet gambling ring only heightened the hero worship of the Blaze owner.

"I think you and the commissioner are the only two people in the stadium who aren't enjoying my brother's added celebrity," Charlie said as she gingerly sat down in the chair next to her. "He's the new hero of the NFL. And he's never even touched the stupid ball."

The crowd cheered when the football was knocked out of Brody's hands just before time expired, ending the half. Jay threw his arms up in disgust as a collective groan sounded in the skybox.

"Ha," Charlie laughed. "Maybe he'll suit up for your

brother in the second half." When Bridgett didn't respond, Charlie sobered up. "So what's up with you two, anyway? You didn't stay at the vineyard last night. Whatever my idiot brother has done, I hope you'll give him a second chance."

Give him a second chance. Charlie's words made swallowing difficult for Bridgett as she worked hard to keep her composure. The suite was crowded with strangers and the last thing she wanted to do was break down. But she was strung out from a sleepless night, one she'd spent pondering second chances. What hurt the most was that he'd given someone like Delaney more than one, but not her. Their "second chance" was to be a sex-only relationship. And that wasn't good enough.

"I know there's something between you two." Charlie continued to badger her. "It's obvious in the way you look at one another. They're smokin' hot, those looks you give each other when you each think the other one's not looking." Charlie fanned herself with a cocktail napkin. "I'd love for a guy to look at me like that."

Bridgett arched an eyebrow at the younger woman. "Men look at you like that all the time, Charlie." She turned away from the crowded room in order to avoid being on the receiving end of a "smokin'-hot look" from Charlie's brother. Bridgett had been avoiding him all day. When the limo had picked up her and Mimi this morning, she was actually relieved to find his mother, Linc, and Charlie already seated inside. The less one-on-one time she and Jay spent together today, the better. Her flight departed two hours after the game, which left little opportunity for him to persuade her to agree to his ridiculous proposal that they be enemies with benefits. Despite the protests from her body, she wouldn't go through with it. She couldn't. Because she still loved Jay.

The revelation wasn't a shock to her. It had arrived in a flood of tears in the early hours of the morning. The only explanation for her being angry and hurt by his willingness to forgive Delaney was because she still loved Jay. But he'd never love her in return. Even if she hadn't had his desertion in Italy as a demonstration, Jay had said as much with his own words. And while he made no secret of his desire for her, desire wasn't the same thing as love. And as much as Bridgett desired him in return, she also wanted his love.

"Sure, men look at me like that all the time," Charlie continued. "But they only see my money. This is a first for my brother. He actually looks like he'd die if he wasn't near you."

"I think you're being overly dramatic, Charlie. Besides, you aren't around him all the time. I'm sure he looks at plenty of women the same way."

Charlie shook her head. "Nope. And I told you, he's never brought a woman to the vineyard before you. That tells me a lot. He likes you." She laughed. "Probably more than he wants to, if I had to guess. He hates not being in control of a situation. It's got to be killing him not to have control over his emotions."

She didn't bother explaining to Jay's sister that, where Bridgett was concerned, he kept his emotions under lock and key; that it was the reason she'd left the vineyard. His refusal to share his heart with her not only wounded her pride, but it was a devastating blow to her own heart. Tears were clogging her throat again at the thought. Bridgett was actually grateful to see Mimi standing next to her.

"I'm feeling a bit superfluous here," Mimi said. "The commissioner's statement last night supporting Jay really took the wind out of the protests the women's groups planned. Not only that, but they actually misspelled the banner flying behind the plane."

The three women looked up at a pink banner floating behind a small plane circling the stadium above the halftime show. The banner read: "Sexual Harasment Has No Place in the NFL." Sure enough, they'd misspelled *harassment* on their sign.

"They give a bad name to women everywhere," Mimi said in disgust. "I'm going for a walk through media alley just to make sure our message is on point."

"A walk actually sounds good." Bridgett quickly stood up to follow Mimi, who right now was the lesser of two evils. "How about you, Charlie?"

Charlie's eyes quickly darted over to where her mother was in conversation with the CEO of a company that sold athletic apparel. The two were vigorously debating the appropriate level of wicking in running shoes. Seemingly satisfied that Melanie was occupied, she shook her head. "Nah. I'm going to sit here and let my lunch settle." She discreetly cupped her belly.

Bridgett leaned down so no one overheard their conversation. "Are you all right?"

"Sure." Charlie eyed her testily. "I just ate something that didn't agree with me, that's all." But Bridgett saw a brief flash of panic in the young woman's eyes. She wasn't sure if it was due to Charlie's concern that her pregnancy remain a secret or something else. "Go for your walk, Bridgett," Charlie commanded.

"I'll see if I can find some crackers," Bridgett said quietly before turning to follow Mimi out of the suite.

They'd made it as far as the door before Jay stalled them.

"Mimi," he said. "I haven't had the chance to thank you for all your help with the media." He extended his hand and Mimi took it with a sly grin. Obviously she thought Bridgett's defection to the B and B meant there was an opportunity now for her. The thought made Bridgett's stomach call for crackers of its own.

"It's been a pleasure," Mimi cooed. "You have a beautiful home. I hope we can work together again sometime."

Jay laughed, nearly taking Mimi out at the knees with his damn dimple. "I'm hopeful that I won't be targeted with any more erroneous sexual harassment cases, but I'll definitely look you up if I am."

"Feel free to look me up anytime." Mimi was nothing if not brazen, patting Jay on the shoulder coyly.

"Bridgett, can I get a word with you? In private," he said.

Mimi pouted as she made her way out of the suite, only to glare at Bridgett from behind Jay's back. Sadly, Bridgett still would have rather gone with the media consultant than have a conversation with Jay. Much less a private one. Her emotions were too raw where he was concerned. They always had been. Suddenly the protective shell she'd erected around her heart seemed very penetrable.

"I'm going for a walk," she said, hoping to discourage him. Surely he didn't have a secret hiding place in every NFL stadium. Unfazed, he gestured for her to precede him out the door. The corridor was crowded during halftime and Bridgett's stomach flipped again as his arm brushed against her shoulder. She tried to put some distance between them but his fingers were suddenly laced with hers. He tugged her to the side and down a corridor to a small balcony overlooking the field.

Bridgett yanked her hand free, wrapping her fingers around the steel railing. "God, you do have secret hideaways everywhere," she mumbled.

He laughed out loud as he leaned a hip against the railing and stared down at her. Bridgett kept her eyes trained on the field. She didn't trust him not to throw her a "smokin'-hot look" that would have her locking her lips with his.

Jay's sigh sounded forlorn and Bridgett's eyes involuntarily tracked to his face. Uncertainty flashed in his own eyes momentarily and his mouth had never looked so unsure. "We can work this out, Bridgett. See where this takes us while the chemistry is so intense." He reached up a finger to trace her cheek but she took a step back. His hand hung in the air a moment before he reluctantly let it drop back to his side. "You said it yourself—it's not this good with anyone else. Does it help to know I feel the same way?"

Finally, an admission of his feelings, but it was still not enough. She should just admit that she loved him. Those words would surely drive him away. Too bad her pride wouldn't let her go all the way with that threat. She shook her head, not trusting her aching throat to let her speak with a steady voice.

Jay swore as he turned to the railing and leaned both forearms on it. A marching band was playing a familiar Neil Diamond tune and the crowd was singing along. "This is a onetime deal, Bridgett. I won't make the same offer again," he said tersely.

Bridgett rocked back on her heels as tears stung her eyes. *A business deal.* That was all she was to him. The band played on as Jay awaited her answer. Still not trusting her voice, she turned from the railing and made her way back to the crowded corridor, thankfully locating a women's restroom. She locked herself in a stall and let the tears fall. Bridgett was angry at Jay for his ridiculous offer, but she was even angrier at her body for its knee-jerk reaction to accept his proposal. The sooner she got to the other side of the country, the better.

"Sweeeeet Caro-line," the audience sang and Jay felt as if his chest was going to explode. His fingers were white-knuckled, he was holding the railing so tightly; all in an effort not to go chasing after Bridgett and beg her to stay with him. "So good, so good, so good," the crowd yelled and Jay wanted to yell something else. Something that would probably land him back in the tabloids. He took a step back and hung his head. She'd left him again. And it hurt just as badly the second time around. Had he really said he'd only make her an offer one time? *Man, what a jerk he was.* Not to mention that his pride stung as much as his chest did right now.

"Boss?"

He tensed up at the sound of Linc's voice, but he didn't bother looking up. No reason for his all-knowing assistant to see the shadows Bridgett had left behind. "Yeah."

"Um, the commissioner wants you to do a photo-op with some of the representatives from the women's groups. He just had a private powwow with them."

Jay unleashed another round of foul words. The damn man wasn't about to let Jay get off scot-free.

"Should I find Mimi?" Linc said warily.

Hell, the last person he wanted hanging all over him right now was Mimi. But the only person he did want all over him had just walked away—for a freaking second time! Mimi would at least be useful navigating any landmines inherent in the photo-op. Jay took a deep breath and stood to his full height. He looked out over the field as the Blaze players trotted out of the tunnel for the second half.

Jay didn't need Bridgett to complete his life. He had his family, his friends, and his team for that. Finding a willing woman wouldn't be a problem, either. Next time, he'd find one who didn't have the power to cut him so deeply.

"Sure," he said to Linc. "Let's get this over with before the second half starts."

He pulled away from the railing and moved on to his own second half. One without Bridgett.

Bridgett rinsed her face in the sink in the now-quiet bathroom. Most of the crowd had made their way back to their seats. Spending the rest of the game in the women's restroom was out of the question, not only because it was awkward, but it was also cowardly. She wouldn't give Jay that much power over her. Bridgett shored up her composure and headed for the exit. The sound of muffled sobbing from the stall closest to the paper towel dispenser caught her attention. Peeking beneath the door, she took in a familiar pair of Steve Madden boots.

"Charlie?"

"Bridgett," Charlie sobbed. "Oh, please, you have to help me."

"What is it? Are you all right?"

"No," Charlie cried. "I'm bleeding."

It took less than five minutes for the stadium paramedics to arrive. Charlie was frantic that she not lose her baby. Bridgett just wanted the EMTs to be discreet. She'd texted Jay the moment she'd found his sister, but he'd yet to respond. Going to the suite was impossible because that would have meant prying her hand out of Charlie's clammy death grip. And Bridgett wouldn't do that.

"Please don't let it be gone," Charlie pleaded with her. Her blue eyes were round in her face, pale even against the white sheet of the gurney as they loaded her into the ambulance.

Bridgett brushed Charlie's hair off her face. "Shh. Let's get you to the hospital so the doctor can examine you and figure out what is going on." Sadly, Bridgett knew what was going on. Her only prayer was that Charlie's was just a simple miscarriage, that she'd be able to have children in the future.

"It's because I didn't love the baby's father, isn't it?" Charlie sobbed. "The baby knew it would only have one parent."

"That's just nonsense, Charlie." Bridgett tried to soothe her while at the same time recounting the HIPAA regulations as they pertained to EMTs. Once they reached the hospital, she'd have a talk with the paramedics, telling them not to breathe a word of what they'd overhead. "That's not the way these things work, sweetheart." She smoothed her palm over Charlie's brow.

"Did you love your baby's father?" Charlie demanded.

Bridgett's breath caught in her throat, but Charlie's blue eyes didn't waver as she waited for an answer. She answered the only way she could. "Madly."

Charlie gulped a sob. "But you still lost your baby?"

"You see, I told you it didn't work that way."

"Then I did something wrong." Charlie was wailing now and the EMT glared at Bridgett as he fiddled with the IV line Charlie was threatening to pull out with her violent cries.

"No!" Bridgett tried to reassure her. "You didn't do anything, either. This is not your fault. You'll see. The doctor will explain everything." She continued to gently stroke the younger woman's forehead in an attempt to calm her fears. Except Bridgett could relate to the emotions rolling through Charlie. She'd suffered from the same anxiety for months after losing her child.

"Why didn't you ever have another baby?"

Charlie's question caught her off guard and it was difficult to stay the tears that were threatening. She shook her head, unable to answer.

"Maybe it's better that there's no father involved," Charlie said, clearly misinterpreting Bridgett's answer. "He can't hate me for losing our child."

Fortunately for everyone involved, they'd reached the ER. Bridgett's phone rang just as the EMTs lifted Charlie from the ambulance.

"I've been in a press conference. I just got your text. Where the hell are you?" Jay barked into the phone.

"We just arrived at the hospital." She hesitated a moment. "You need to come right away. And bring your mother."

"The baby?"

"I don't think there is a baby any longer." The words burned in Bridgett's throat as Charlie cried out for her. "Hurry, Jay."

By the time Jay and Melanie arrived, the nurse had confirmed Bridgett's fears with a sad shake of her head. They'd given Charlie a sedative and she was staring off into space as tears slowly rolled out from the corners of her eyes onto her hair, which was haloed on the pillow.

"Mommy," Charlie whispered as her mother sank down beside her on the bed and wrapped her arms around her daughter. Jay pulled his sister's hand up to his mouth and nuzzled it. His eyes met Bridgett's. The sorrow in them rattled her. She slipped behind the blue curtain cordoning off sections of the ER and made her way to the lobby on legs that were less than steady.

Linc reached for her elbow just as she nearly stumbled. "Is she gonna be okay?" he asked.

"Physically, yes," Bridgett replied. "It might take her a little longer emotionally. She might need to connect with others who've suffered a miscarriage." She grabbed Linc's forearm. "You'll make sure Jay gets her the help she might need, won't you? Please, Linc. Promise me."

Linc nodded empathically as he steered her toward a chair. "I promise. Now, what can I get you? Something to eat or drink? The boss would kill me if he found out you were this upset."

Bridgett hadn't realized tears were streaming down her face until Linc handed her a tissue. She shook her head. "I should get to the airport. Charlie will be fine now that she has her family here."

"I think you should sit a minute. You've got plenty of time before your flight."

"No." Bridgett stood too quickly and Linc had to steady her again. Being in the hospital with Charlie had brought back too many painful memories. She needed air. "I can't go through this again," she whispered.

"Let me get Mr. McManus." Linc's eyes were round with concern.

"No!" Bridgett said it more fervently this time. "My bag is in the limo. I just need to get it and I'll grab a cab out front."

Linc looked like he'd rather streak through a football stadium than let her go, but Bridgett couldn't be around Jay any longer. Especially not after today. And she had to get out of this hospital. "The boss won't like you taking a cab."

"I'll take her."

They both looked up to see the FBI agent from the night before standing beside them. Linc looked at him with relief, and Bridgett remembered that Special Agent Kovaluk and Jay were friends from their boyhood days.

"Jay needs to be here with Charlie," the agent said. He exchanged a look with Linc, who shook his head. "Besides, I have something I need to discuss with Ms. Janik."

He placed a hand on Bridgett's back and began to guide her toward the exit. Bridgett glanced over her shoulder at Linc, and then at the closed curtain at the end of the hall. "Remember what you promised," she reminded him. Charlie would need lots of emotional support these next few months, and while Bridgett had come to care for Jay's sister, she couldn't afford to be that close to his family.

Linc nodded and Agent Kovaluk propelled them out into the sunny day. The world was going on normally, despite the fact that Charlie's baby was no longer living. It had been the same way when Bridgett had lost her baby. The concept had taken her months to accept. It would likely be just as difficult for Charlie.

Agent Kovaluk retrieved her bag from the limousine and stowed it in the trunk of the nondescript Chrysler he drove.

He opened the passenger door for Bridgett and she slid in. Then he was behind the wheel and starting the car's engine. The sportscaster on the radio announced that the Blaze were still trailing by one point in the game.

"It looks like a missed extra point may be the difference in the game," he said.

Bridgett glanced out the window at the afternoon sun as they made their way to the airport. She wasn't in the mood to make small talk, but the agent was doing her a favor. The least she could do was be polite. "I always feel sorry for those guys. They have to have an extra helping of mental toughness to be a placekicker."

"Don't feel too sorry for them. They get paid a hell of a lot more than the rest of us for kicking a ball ten times a week, and they don't even get tackled."

He glanced over at her and his charming smile helped soothe her frayed nerves.

"You do have a point there." She studied his handsome profile. With sandy blond hair, green eyes, and an easy smile, he was the light to Jay's darker persona. Bridgett didn't kid herself for one minute, though. Matt Kovaluk was also a federal agent, and an alpha male personality was practically a requirement to earn a badge. "You said you had something you wanted to discuss with me?"

His lips flattened from a smile to a more somber grin. "I did." His eyes left the road for a brief moment to study her. "I have to ask you if you ever met Delaney Silverberg."

The question surprised her and her legal training unconsciously kicked into gear. "Are you asking for personal reasons or professional ones?"

The corner of his mouth twitched. "Actually, this is just a friendly conversation. I was involved in the case investigating the gambling ring, but only tangentially with Delaney. But some things have surfaced that might come to light in her prosecution, so I'm trying to tie up loose ends."

"What kinds of things?"

Agent Kovaluk paused for a moment, seeming to debate something with himself. "A letter."

"I never sent Delaney a letter. I never met the woman. We had one and only one conversation on the phone thirteen years ago and that was it."

He looked at her out of the corner of one eye before staring back at the highway again. "You seem pretty sure of your facts. And this isn't a letter you wrote. It's a letter Jay wrote to you."

The air seized up in Bridgett's lungs. "Jay never wrote me a letter." She was sure of that fact, too.

"Well, it's his handwriting on the letter and it's addressed to you in Italy. My guess is Delaney intercepted it."

Gray dots were floating in front of Bridgett's eyes and her mouth felt fuzzy. *Jay had written her a letter. What would Delaney have been doing with it?* "Do you have it?" she whispered. "The letter."

"It's part of the evidence file."

An embarrassing squeak escaped the back of her throat.

He sighed. "I have a copy of it on my iPad."

"Please, let me see it."

With another resigned sigh, he switched lanes to pull off at the exit, driving into the parking lot of a fast-food restaurant. He reached into the seat behind her and grabbed his tablet. Bridgett could hear her heart pounding as he powered it up. After punching in a code and opening the file, he handed it to her, pausing before he released it fully. "I have to remind you that you're an officer of the court and what I'm about to show you can't be discussed with anyone."

She nodded, anxious to lay eyes on the letter. The page with the envelope came up first. It was addressed to her, care of the DiSantis villa. She'd have to take the agent's word that it was Jay's handwriting, because they'd never had a chance to exchange so much as a note. Bridgett scrolled down to the next page, gasping when she read the date: It was dated six days before she'd called Jay to tell him about the baby.

"Are you okay?" Agent Kovaluk offered her a bottled water, but she shook her head.

Jay's handwriting was a lot like him—neat, bold, and

dark. She bit back a smile at the sight of it. Her smile turned to tears as she read the letter. He wrote that he was going to New Zealand to sell the rights to the wine labels left from his grandfather's winery. Jay explained that his stepfather had not left him any inheritance. Bridgett was surprised by the lack of bitterness in the letter. But he needed the money to buy the fermentation formula so that they could start their vineyard. His constant reference to them both as a couple robbed her of her breath. Agent Kovaluk seemed to understand and he pushed a button to roll down the window.

Jay asked her to wait for him, explaining that it might take weeks for the process to be completed, and Bridgett gulped down a sob. If only she had known. She would have waited forever.

The final page proved to be her undoing, and her body shook as she read it.

> *I love you. I should have told you that night you left me in the airport. You make me whole, Bridgett. My life is a little unsure right now but the one thing I am sure about is that you're the woman I want to spend the rest of my life with. Please be patient and believe in me. Believe in us. For years, I've dreamed of carrying on my family legacy and passing it onto my children—our children—and I couldn't imagine a more beautiful person to share that dream with. One day we'll walk through our vineyards with them by our side and that dream will be a reality. All because of you. I love you. And I can't wait to hold you in my arms again. Stay out of the mud until I get back. I don't ever want to lose you.*

"Oh my God," she whispered. "He didn't desert me. I just didn't believe in us enough." Her thoughts were scattered, and Bridgett couldn't seem to stop shaking. "Delaney said he was at a Cubs game. But he was in New Zealand. He wouldn't have known about the baby."

Had Delaney ever told him about the baby? But Jay had

been angry when he confronted her in Boston. So he'd known about the baby then. What must he have thought of her? Bridgett gulped another sob as she sank more fully into the seat. No wonder he hated her.

"Maybe I should take you back," Agent Kovaluk said softly.

Bridgett shook her head. "It was a long time ago. It's too late now." It was too late for them. She could no longer blame Jay for not trusting her. She hadn't believed in what they had. Worse still, she was no longer able to give him what he wanted most of all: children. "Please, take me to the airport."

He hesitated a moment before solemnly putting the car into drive and entering the highway.

Twenty-three

They'd taken Charlie into an exam room to do an ultrasound, and when the doctor came out, she confirmed their fears: His sister was no longer pregnant. Jay thought he should feel a tremendous sense of relief—after all, he didn't want her having some deadbeat's child. Instead he felt immense sadness. He hadn't realized how much he was looking forward to having a child running around the vineyard, even if it wasn't his own. The thought of being an uncle had secretly delighted him. And now it wasn't going to happen.

He could hear Charlie's soft sobs from inside her hospital room, but still he remained outside, grateful that his sister was willing to accept comfort from their mother. If their mother was shocked by Charlie's condition, she didn't show it. Instead, she'd quietly offered her daughter unyielding support. Jay was optimistic that if something positive could come out of this situation, it would be the reparation of the rift between the two women in his life.

The two women in his life.

His mother and Charlie. But not Bridgett. Never Bridgett.

Jay was glad that she'd been the one to be there for his sister, but then she'd disappeared. Again.

"Linc, could you stop pacing, please," Jay commanded. "I'm getting a sore neck."

"We ended up losing by eight points," Linc said as he slid into the chair next to him. "Today hasn't been a good day all around. Mr. Osbourne wanted to come by the hospital but I told him it wasn't necessary. I don't think Charlie will be happy that it's on the Internet already."

Jay sighed as he closed his eyes and leaned his head against the wall. "Maybe you should call Mimi. She should be able to help spin this."

Linc nodded. "At least Ms. Janik read the EMTs the riot act already."

His eyes snapped open and he turned to face his assistant. "She did?"

"Oh, yeah. The nurses said it was something to behold. She threatened to sue them, the county, and the state if any of the conversation in the ambulance was leaked."

Jay was suddenly very curious about what was said in that ambulance.

"I underestimated her," Linc said.

"Who?"

"Ms. Janik. I didn't think she was much of a ball buster, remember?" Linc asked. "But she was. She is. As my grandmother would say: She's good people."

Jay swallowed hard. There were so many sides to Bridgett Janik that he wasn't sure which one was the real woman. But Linc was right, she'd been "good people" today when it came to helping out with Charlie.

His mother popped her head out of the door. "We're all done in here."

He was reluctant to go into the room, into the world so obviously female, but he wanted to help reassure Charlie. The doctor was pulling off her gloves when he entered.

"Well, if there's any good news today, it's that this wasn't anything traumatic to your system. You'll be able to conceive both via in vitro again or normally with no problem. Unfortunately, a spontaneous miscarriage happens in fifteen percent of all pregnancies and we don't often know the cause. You're in good health otherwise, but we'll run some blood tests just to ensure nothing is amiss. I'd like to see you back here this week just to make sure you're recovering fully."

"We'll have her back whenever you say, Doctor," his mother said as she gave Charlie's hand a squeeze.

"Good. I want to keep you on IV fluids for a little longer, so you just rest here until I've got the preliminary blood work back from the lab. I'll be back to see you before you're discharged."

Jay waited for the doctor to close the door. "What did she mean 'by in vitro *again*'?"

Both women in the room donned mulish masks. Great, now that the two had made amends, it seemed he was on the dark side of the estrogen triangle.

"Bridgett really didn't tell you?" Charlie asked.

Jay ground his back teeth. "Obviously not."

His sister's face, still splotchy from her tears, softened a bit. "She's a keeper. Whatever you've done to her you need to make up, because you'll never find anyone as nice as Bridgett. She's good for you. Where are you hiding her anyway?"

"She's gone home to Boston," Linc answered from somewhere behind him. He wasn't even aware his assistant had followed him into the room, but he'd deal with Linc's nosiness later. Right now he wanted to get to the bottom of Charlie's pregnancy.

He reached up to knead the muscles squeezing at the back of the neck. "Charlie, are you saying you got pregnant in a *lab*!" His mother shushed him as his sister began to sob again. Jay didn't care—he wanted answers. "Why in the hell would you do something like that?"

"Because," Charlie cried, nearly launching herself off the bed at him. "I wanted something of my own. Someone to love me!"

Jay felt as if the wind had been knocked out of him. He

didn't understand his sister at all. Worse, his mother was looking at him as if he were the villain in this drama. "*I* love you, Charlie." The words stuck in his dry throat. "I've loved you since the day you were born. I don't know how you could have ever doubted that."

Charlie sobbed even harder and Jay felt like he'd been kicked in the head. He seriously didn't understand his sister's rationale. Jay shot his mother a pleading look.

His mother sighed as she held Charlie's head on her shoulder and gently stroked her hair. "It's not about you and I loving her. Your sister was lonely and searching for something to do with her life. You and I both have careers. She chose motherhood for hers." Their mother shrugged, as if it were the most logical answer in the world.

"And I failed at it miserably," Charlie cried.

"Hush," their mother said. "You heard what the doctor said. You'll be able to have children in the future."

"With the emphasis being on 'in the future,' Charlie." Jay was having trouble keeping his tone neutral and his mother shot him a glare that very clearly said, *Now is not the time.* He threw up his hands in frustration.

"I stand corrected," Charlie snapped. "Bridgett is too good for you. I wish that she'd stayed and you'd left!" She buried her face into their mother's shoulder.

"It's just the hormones talking," his mother said quietly over Charlie's head. "She doesn't know what she's saying."

"Yes, I do." Charlie's voice was muffled but no less belligerent. "At least Bridgett could relate to what I'm going through. She lost a baby, too."

Jay stiffened at his sister's words. *How the hell did Charlie know about the baby?* He locked gazes with his mother, whose eyes were wide and confused. She shook her head at his unvoiced accusation. His mother hadn't told Charlie.

"It's not exactly the same thing, sweetheart," his mother said. "Bridgett had an abortion. She didn't lose her baby."

Charlie pulled out of their mother's arms, her face scrunched up with anger now. "Mother! How could you say such a thing? You don't even know Bridgett. She *lost* her baby. She told me so. Bridgett didn't have an abortion." The monitors they had Charlie hooked to began to beep.

"Sweetheart, you need to calm down," their mother said.

"I won't! She was in love with the baby's father. *Madly* in love. She told me. And then he deserted her and she was all alone."

Jay seethed at the revisionist history Bridgett had given his sister. "That's not exactly how it went down."

Realization began to dawn on Charlie slowly and Jay watched her face begin to crumble just as the nurse charged in.

"There are too many people in this room." She pointed at Jay and Linc. "You two—out!"

"I don't believe you, Jay," Charlie whispered. "She loved you and she mourned your child. Damn it, she was still mourning it today. Something isn't right with all this. I know it isn't."

The nurse pinned Jay with an evil look, gesturing for him to leave as their mother settled Charlie back into the bed. Jay woodenly exited the room, Linc at his heels. He stopped inches from the wall and banged his forehead against it. It didn't help.

"Is there anything I can do, boss?"

Jay kept his head pressed to the wall. "Just take my advice and become a monk. Life would be a hell of a lot easier."

The sound of a resigned sigh had Jay turning away from the wall and staring at Matt Kovaluk's familiar mug.

"Not all women are evil, Linc." Matt was talking to Linc, but his eyes never left Jay's face. "And not everything is always as it seems."

A chill ran up Jay's spine at this friend's words. "What's that supposed to mean?"

"Remember last night when I told you they'd found some papers with your name on them at Delaney's?"

Jay's body stiffened in defense of the figurative blow he felt was coming. "Yeah. You said you'd show them to me today."

Matt's eyes darted to his shoes and Jay knew whatever

was coming he wouldn't like. His friend fumbled with his tablet. "They found a letter written by you in Delaney's stuff."

"I don't remember ever writing her a letter. Maybe a postcard or two."

"The letter wasn't addressed to Delaney," Matt said, but Jay didn't hear the rest because suddenly there was a loud roaring sound in his ears.

He slumped down into one of the chairs lining the wall and tried to breathe normally, but that was proving difficult. "She never mailed the fucking letter to Bridgett," he murmured. "Bridgett never saw it."

Matt shifted his stance. "Well, no, not until an hour ago."

Jay's head shot up and he stared mutely at his friend.

"It's in evidence," Matt said sheepishly. "I had to ask her about it. Jay, I'm sorry. Delaney really screwed you both over. I never knew about the baby."

Jay dropped his head into his hands and squeezed tightly. He wanted to block out the doubts and the anguish swirling around inside his mind.

"For what it's worth," Matt continued, "she was genuinely broken up. I got the impression she thought you'd gone off the grid and weren't coming back for her."

His emotions were in the same tailspin as his sister's, and Jay couldn't make heads or tails of what he was feeling. *Could it all have been a simple misunderstanding? One facilitated by Delaney?*

"Where is she now?" he asked through his hands.

"Boarding her plane, I imagine."

Of course she was. She may have been genuinely broken up but not enough to stay with him. *She was in love with the baby's father. Madly in love.* Charlie's words tumbled around in his head. Was his sister telling the truth? Or just something she wanted to believe?

Matt sighed again. "I need to be on a plane back to DC here soon, too. I just wanted to drop off this note she left for Charlie. Bridgett was really concerned about her." Matt dropped a folded-up square of yellow legal paper into the chair next to him before clapping him on the shoulder. "Text me when you're back in Baltimore and we'll grab a beer, okay?"

Jay nodded. Reaching over, he picked up the note Bridgett had written for Charlie. His eyes scanned the handwriting. Something wasn't right.

"Matt!"

His friend stopped and turned around. "This note is from Bridgett?"

"Yeah." Matt took a step back toward him. "Why?"

"You physically saw her write this?" Jay demanded, his voice echoing loudly in the hallway.

"I did, Jay. What gives?"

Jay unfolded the note, not seeing the words, just the smart, neat handwriting that was slanted in the direction of a left-handed author. Bridgett was left-handed. How could he have not recognized that in the Dear John letter? The letter Bridgett obviously didn't write. Rage suddenly blinded Jay and he swore violently. And loudly.

His mother stood at the doorway of Charlie's room admonishing him. "Jay!"

But Jay had Matt shoved against the wall, his arm braced against his chest. "You go to wherever the hell they're holding that bitch and tell her I hope she rots in prison! Because if she ever gets out, she'll spend the rest of her life looking over her shoulder, wondering when I'm going to pay her back for this stunt. And I *will* pay her back, Matt. Count on it."

Matt was relaxed against Jay's hold. "Don't worry. I've got your back on this one, my friend."

He released Matt and took a step back as he struggled to get air through his lungs. Jay saw a security guard out of the corner of his eye and held his hands up at chest level. "We're good," he said despite the fact Jay wasn't good at all. Thirteen years he'd lost with Bridgett. His chest ached at the thought.

Jay reached down and picked up the note he'd dropped on the floor. His mother stared at him wide-eyed and he kissed her on the cheek before going back into Charlie's room. She was quiet on the bed, her eyes red rimmed and swollen. Jay leaned down and pressed his lips to her forehead. "You were right," he whispered. "I've messed this all up. But I'm going to find Bridgett and work it out." He gently wrapped her fingers around the note.

"Jay," her soft voice called after him just before he passed through the door. "Don't screw it up."

It was seven thirty in the morning by the time the cab pulled up outside Bridgett's condo. She was exhausted from flying cross-country all night and it was hard for her to believe she'd only been gone two weeks. As she trudged up the stairs to the third floor, she wondered how she'd live through the *next* two weeks. And the weeks after that. She'd been a fool to think she wouldn't fall in love with Jay again. Hell, she'd been a fool to think she'd ever fallen out of love with him in the first place.

But she couldn't stay with him. Not when she couldn't give him what he really wanted. He'd promised to give *her* everything she ever wanted. The problem was the only thing she wanted was his heart. And, thanks to Delaney, he'd never trust her enough to give her his love again. Bridgett's only hope now was that she could survive walking away from Jay a second time.

"You did it once and you didn't shrivel up and die," she reminded herself as she dragged her suitcase down the hall toward her door. She'd just have to erect that protective shell again, reestablishing herself at work and settling for being the dotty old aunt to her nieces and nephews. Bridgett unlocked the door and wheeled her bag into her foyer. The sound of the kettle whistling made her freeze in terror. Her heart squeezed in her chest when Jay stepped out of her galley kitchen.

"Just in time," he said as though it were perfectly normal for him to be standing in her living room, looking weary and rumpled in charcoal slacks and a black Blaze golf shirt. "Your tea is ready."

She stood and gaped at him as he reached behind her and

pushed the door—*her door*—closed. "What—? How—?"
Bridgett glanced around her apartment. "How did you get
in here?"

Jay dragged his fingers through his already mussed hair.
The lines fanning out from his eyes were a little deeper this
morning. "Simple. Gwen let me in."

"Gwen?"

"Mmm," he said. "I'm on the hook for providing an
exotic locale for her fortieth, but that shouldn't be too hard."
Jay smiled and his dimple nearly did her in before panic
gripped Bridgett yet again. "Charlie?" Surely his sister
hadn't suffered another emergency.

"She's going to be just fine, thanks to you."

Bridgett released a breath she didn't know she'd been holding. His smile never wavered, and those eyes of his were
hypnotizing her. She shook herself. It was just exhaustion
from a four-hour layover in Chicago. Damn it, how was she
going to get over him if he kept showing up when her defenses
were down?

"You shouldn't be here," she snapped. "You wasted a trip."
She stomped into the kitchen and snatched the screaming
kettle off the stove, wanting to scream herself. After reading
his letter, Bridgett had barely been able to get on that plane
last night, and now she was going to be forced to kick him
out of her home. She wasn't sure she could do that. Her hand
shook as she poured, splashing hot water on her finger.
"Ouch!"

Jay was beside her instantly, taking the kettle from her
hand and turning on the cold water before he placed her
finger under the stream. Moving behind her, he took a half
step forward so that her body was cocooned in the warmth
of his. The familiar scent that was uniquely Jay teased her
nostrils, making Bridgett's breath catch in her chest. She
desperately wanted to lean into him and make him forget
that he hated her. Maybe she could survive a loveless relationship after all.

His lips found the sweet spot beneath her ear. "I'm sorry."
Bridgett let her shoulders relax but nothing more as she

turned off the water. Jay's embrace didn't waver, though, and she was left with her back pressed to his chest.

"I'm sorry for what Delaney did to you. To us," he whispered. "I swear she'll be paying for it by spending the rest of her life in prison."

She slumped back against him and his arms wrapped around her more fully as he nuzzled her neck. "I won't be sending her any fan mail," she said.

Bridgett felt his chest rumble before his lips pushed beneath her blouse to trail along her collarbone. "Not unless it's laced with something noxious."

They stood like that for several long moments, each one soaking up the familiar feel of the other's body, and Bridgett thought that maybe—*just maybe*—everything would be okay. Until Jay ruined it.

His breath fanned her ear. "I meant what I said in the letter."

Of course he had. Only Bridgett could no longer give him the children he'd written to her about. She tugged his hands away and stepped out of his embrace. Slowly, she turned to face the man she loved so much. Who, it turned out, returned her love. At least until she told him the truth. He'd run back to his beautiful vineyard then. Her gaze locked with his and she watched as the hope there faded into wariness.

Bridgett sucked in a steadying breath. "I can't give you what you want."

Confusion replaced wariness. "And what is it that you think I want?" Jay gripped her elbows, pulling her in closer. "Besides you."

Getting the words out was harder than she thought. It was a secret she'd never shared with another soul. Bridgett blew out a breath. "I can't—I can't give you children."

The room was silent for a long moment as both their breathing stilled. "And why is that?" he asked eventually.

"I know you think I—I got rid of our baby, but believe me, I would never throw away a part of you." The tears she'd been shedding for days began to flow again, and Bridgett couldn't seem to make them stop.

Jay placed two fingers beneath her chin so his eyes met hers. "I was fed a bunch of misinformation, Bridgett. I know now that most of it was wrong. Tell me what happened."

The profound calm with which he spoke to her spurred her to continue.

"I was afraid to tell anyone I was pregnant, so I didn't go to the doctor right away. I don't know if they would have been able to tell that early anyway, but I always wondered . . ." She thought of Charlie blaming herself earlier and Bridgett cringed. It was so easy to make the fault her own. "The pregnancy was ectopic. By the time I realized it, it was too late. The rupture caused scarring on my uterus. I'll never be able to carry a baby to term."

His arms were around her before she finished her explanation. She shed more quiet tears while Jay hugged her fiercely. His lips brushed the top of her head as he spoke. "You shouldn't have had to go through that alone. I'm so sorry that I wasn't there with you. Jesus, Bridgett, I'm sorry that you've had to live with this alone for all these years."

Jay kissed her then. It was a tender kiss—one filled with remorse. "I love you, Bridgett," he said when his lips finally left hers. "I fell in love with you that first day when I found you stuck in the mud. My appointment wasn't with Vincenzo DiSantis. It was at another vineyard. But I brazened my way in there because I didn't want to have to say good-bye to you yet."

She gasped in surprise as a tenuous happiness began to build inside her.

He remained somber, his unwavering eyes practically boring a hole in her. "Now you listen to me, because this is finally the truth. I don't care if your uterus is scarred or if you're missing a limb or you have some wasting disease. I love you just the way you are. I always have. And I want to spend my life with you, for however long that is. You fill me up and make me whole, Bridgett, and I've spent the last thirteen years trying to feel whole again." He kissed her again soundly and Bridgett's body began to grow warm. "I lied yesterday when I said this was a business deal. I was just fooling myself. I don't want to live without you. Please, tell me you feel the same." The last part came out as a whisper and Bridgett's tenuous happiness exploded into the real thing.

She wrapped her arms around his neck, managing nothing more than a nod before his lips found hers again. Before she knew it, they were a tangle of naked limbs in her bed. The autumn sun streamed in the window as they slowly and reverently made love to each other. Afterward, they lay intertwined—whole, as Jay put it—and Bridgett couldn't hold back the question that nagged at her.

"Why do you think she did it?" she asked as her fingers traced a pattern on Jay's chest.

He sighed wearily. "I wish I knew. Blake and I were never unkind to Delaney. I think some people are just inherently mean. I don't think I wanted to see it in her." Jay squeezed his arm around her. "You have no idea how sorry I am."

Bridgett rolled onto his chest and placed a finger on his lips. "Don't apologize for wanting to believe the best about someone. It's a very noble trait to have." She nuzzled his chin.

But Jay remained still beneath her. "Except I didn't believe the best in you."

She peered into his blue eyes, which were damp with apology. "I never understood why you thought I would abort our child," she admitted.

Jay reached over to the nightstand and pulled out a worn letter from his wallet. Bridgett sat up against the pillows when he handed it to her. Her hands began to shake and her body grew cold as she read the words.

"I didn't write this."

He kissed her shoulder and then her cheek before letting his lips hover next to her own. "I know that. Now."

Bridgett couldn't help the sadness that seeped into her body. "We lost all those years because of one messed-up woman."

Jay rolled on top of her. "In business it's called cutting your losses and making up for lost revenue. That's what we're going to do." The look he gave her was nothing short of toe curling. Bridgett gave him a wily smile of her own as the heat of his gaze melted away the sadness.

He was leaning down to kiss her when a loud pounding sounded at the door.

"Yoohoo! Bridge, it's me, Gwen."

Bridgett groaned. "Oh my God, she really knows no boundaries."

Jay nibbled at her lower lip. "Ignore her. I have her key, remember?"

"Clearly, you don't know my sister that well. She'll stand out there all day until we let her in. She's taking the divorce pity a little too far if you ask me."

He reached back over to the table, this time to grab his cell phone. Jay punched in a text and then tossed the phone back on the table.

"What are you doing?"

Jay grinned slyly. "Wait for it."

"Italy!" Gwen screeched from outside the door. "That's a perfect birthday spot! See you two later. Much later." And then she was gone.

"Now, where were we?" he asked before his lips found her breast.

"We were about to kiss and make up. Again."

"Oh yes, I remember now. We've got thirteen years to make up for, Bridgett," Jay promised as he slid into her. "I hope you're ready for some serious long-term negotiations, counselor."

Turn the page for a sneak peek
at the second book
in Tracy Solheim's Second Chances series

ALL THEY EVER WANTED

Coming from Berkley Sensation
in January 2016!

When he was ten years old, Miles McAlister meticulously and very thoughtfully planned out the remainder of his life. Sitting in the tree house his father had built for him and his four siblings, Miles had put pen to paper and scratched out his future as he saw it: Eagle Scout, All-state track star, high school valedictorian, Duke University, Rhodes Scholar, law school, politics, and, most importantly, President of the United States. Twenty-three years later, he'd revised that list a time or two to include a few things a fifth grader might not have envisioned—like losing his virginity at the national high school debate conference or delaying law school while he backpacked through Europe with his girlfriend. But overall, he was well on his way to executing his carefully mapped-out existence nearly verbatim.

Until life had thrown him a curveball. More than one, actually.

His two brothers and two sisters—as well as the majority of the people in his hometown of Chances Inlet, North Carolina—had dubbed him 'The Ambitious McAlister' with good reason, however. Nothing was going to interfere with the goals he'd set all those years ago. And that was how he found himself on the expansive wrap-around porch of his mother's popular bed-and-breakfast stoically enduring the June heat. With its railings draped in red, white, and blue bunting, a dewy pitcher of lemonade on the wicker side table, and his brother's golden retriever snoring at his feet, the Tide Me Over Inn afforded Miles the perfect backdrop for wrestling back control of what he perceived to be his destiny.

The inn had been his mother's pride and joy for four years now. She and Miles's father had painstakingly restored the 1894 Victorian to all its original splendor, turning it into one of the premiere B and Bs on the Atlantic coast. Situated among lush gardens and centuries-old trees, the sprawling twenty-room home was also walking distance to the ocean and the historical town of Chances Inlet. The B and B's picturesque location, along with a bevy of championship golf courses in the area, guaranteed that the Tide Me Over Inn's ten guest rooms were booked nearly year-round. Today being no exception. A crowd milled about on the verandah scrutinizing Miles's every move.

The late-day breeze blowing inland off the ocean felt refreshing amidst the wilting humidity so typical of the coast. Miles resisted the urge to tug at his shirt collar as the wind gently lifted the skirt of the woman seated in front of him. Rather than fix her hemline, though, she shifted her long legs suggestively, affording him an unobstructed view of a nicely toned thigh, her skin shimmering with perspiration. The smile she gave him lacked even a trace of innocence, however; instead it was outright daring. But then, she wasn't the one with the television cameras trained on her.

"Just a few more questions, Miles. They'll be painless. I promise." Tanya Sheppard, a blue-eyed, bleached blonde former beauty queen who masqueraded as the political reporter from one of Raleigh's affiliate stations, was clearly enjoying her position of dominance in their interview. Miles was sure it was payback for ignoring the hotel keycard she'd slipped into his tuxedo pocket during last year's Governor's Ball.

Pushing out a breath, he forced himself to relax against the old-fashioned glider he sat in. The guests always raved that the damn things were so comfortable, but to Miles the chair felt like he was contorting his six-foot-one, muscular body into the shape of a paper clip. His dress shirt stuck to his back where it was pressed up against the metal chair. He ignored the discomfort, though, bracing himself for whatever questions Tanya decided to throw at him next. They both knew she had been lobbing softballs for the past fifteen minutes.

His campaign for a vacated U. S. congressional seat certainly wasn't sexy enough to warrant the seven-minute segment on the affiliate's weekly political show. Especially since he was running unopposed in a district located in the county where he'd grown up and where his family was still very much a presence. Tanya was here for a bigger sound bite. She wanted revenge with all the trimmings. And that meant discussing the sins of Miles's deceased father.

"How can you expect voters to trust you?" Tanya went right for the testicles. "You've repeatedly stated that you weren't aware of your father's efforts to defraud the bank that financed the two-million-dollar loan for this very inn where we are sitting. Even if you didn't know firsthand of your father's thievery, why shouldn't voters assume that the apple doesn't fall far from the tree, so to speak?"

The ice inside the pitcher of lemonade popped, startling the dog at his feet. Brushing a reassuring hand over its silky head, Miles drew in his own calming breath before launching into the speech he'd been rehearsing in front of the mirror since the mess with his father had been made public the week before.

"*Thievery* is a bit misleading, Tanya." He held up a hand when she began to speak, shushing her before looking directly into the camera lens. "McAlister Construction and Engineering is a privately owned company. If my father moved funds from one account to another, he was misappropriating his *own* money. I don't know what dictionary you use, Tanya, but that's not thievery in my book."

Tanya bristled, uncrossing her thighs and sitting up a little straighter. "There's no *if* about it, Miles. The bank examiner had an airtight case against your father."

And the stress from staying one step ahead of the bank examiner most likely brought on the heart attack that killed Dad. Miles had to work to unclench his hands and appear relaxed. Donald McAlister had been a larger-than-life role model—a dedicated family man who was also a semi-pro athlete, an engineer, a small business owner, and a fixture in the community. Apparently, he'd been so devoted to his wife that he'd bought and refurbished the inn for her while playing fast and loose with the books. Miles had no doubt his father would have made good on the loan if the economy hadn't taken a nosedive right when the balloon payment was due. The enormous weight of the financial burden, along with his attempts to conceal it from his wife and children, certainly put Donald McAlister into an early grave.

The emptiness Miles felt in his chest was still raw. All those years ago when he had carefully crafted his life's roadmap, Miles had never taken into account achieving the goals without his father by his side. It was yet another indication of the short-sightedness of a ten-year-old.

"The fact of the matter is this, Tanya: My father isn't campaigning for a seat in the U.S. House of Representatives. *I am.* He died tragically before any of this could get resolved. But I do know this . . ." Miles looked into the camera lens again. "Whatever my father did, it was out of love for his family. Times have been tough financially for many of us these past several years. Washington has forgotten about small business and the middle class who are living paycheck to paycheck. When I take my seat in Congress, I plan to be the voice for those people. The same people who would do whatever it takes to ensure their family is provided for and that their dreams can become reality. Just as my father did for his own family."

Tanya covered up an indelicate snort before it could be picked up by the microphone. "And the governor? He obviously wasn't too comfortable with having the stigma that now surrounds you tainting his own reelection bid. Isn't it true that rather than keep you as his chief counsel, he put you on leave without pay?"

It was a chore for Miles to appear unfazed by Tanya's goading question despite the anger that was fueling up inside of him, but he miraculously kept his composure. "Governor Rossi's statement was pretty clear on the matter, Tanya. *I* requested the leave of absence. Not the other way around. The leave is so that I can deal with a family emergency here in Chances Inlet. The issue involving my father had nothing to do with it."

At least not in the way she was implying.

She made a show of rustling her notes on her lap. "Of course. Your mother." Tanya brilliantly modulated her voice to sound softer, more serene. Too bad the viewers couldn't see the hard lines still bracketing her mouth. "How is she doing?"

Patricia McAlister had been struck by a hit-and-run driver while riding her bicycle through town ten days earlier. She'd fractured her hip and sustained a concussion along with other minor injuries. But the larger trauma was to her psyche after the secret of Donald McAlister's creative accounting had been revealed on national television.

"She's wonderful." Miles chose to categorize his statement not as a lie, exactly, but more as maintaining his mother's privacy. It was partially the truth, anyway. Her hip would fully heal. "But it's the summer tourist season, the busiest time of the year in Chances Inlet, and until she's back on her feet, she'll need help running the inn. Since my campaign headquarters is located here in town, it made sense to my family that I be the one to help her out."

Again, a partial truth. His younger brother Ryan was a professional baseball player whose contract barely allowed for him to visit their injured mother, much less take three months off during the season. Their youngest sibling, Elle, had two months left in her Peace Corps service. The oldest of the five McAlister children, Kate, was also spending the summer in Chances Inlet. But she and her husband, Alton, were both physicians who operated the beach town's seasonal urgent care clinic. The clinic's hours left them little time to help nurse his mother, much less help with the day-to-day operations of the inn. And then there was Gavin.

His brother had single-handedly carried his father's secret for the two years since Donald's death, mollifying the bank examiner with the charm that had everyone in Chances Inlet eating out of the palm of Gavin's hand. The middle of the McAlister children, Gavin was a natural peacemaker. He'd devised a plan to pay off the debt and preserve their late father's name with no one in the community—or the family—being the wiser. Miles had to concede that it was a pretty damn good plan given the situation. Too bad Gavin had failed to grasp that people always stab you in the back. Always. The past eight years working in politics had taught Miles that.

What peeved Miles the most was that his brother had never thought to confide in him. Born sixteen months apart, they'd grown up in the small town practically in each other's pocket, playing on the same teams, sharing the same bedroom, the same circle of friends. Yet, when push came to shove, Gavin hadn't trusted his older brother to help shoulder the burden their father left behind. To help guard the family name and its legacy. He'd made some lame excuse that he'd kept Miles in the dark to protect his political future, but it felt to Miles as though his brother—and the rest of the McAlisters, for that matter—believed he was so blinded by ambition that he couldn't pull his own weight during a family crisis. And that stung. A lot. So, while his mother had still been in the hospital, he'd taken control of the situation and appointed himself in charge of operating the inn until she was fully recovered. He'd been living at the B and B nearly two weeks now.

"While I'm in town," Miles continued, "I'll have ample time to meet with constituents and take their pulse about which issues are most important to them."

Considering the circumstances that brought him back to Chances Inlet, the situation really had worked to his benefit—even if it meant he had to live alongside the mousey, secretive woman his mother was obviously shelter-ing within the walls of the B and B. Lori—if that was even her name—worked as the inn's maid and cook. While Miles couldn't find fault with her efforts, she was hiding something; he was sure of it. Especially if the smoking hot body she was concealing under her baggy clothes and her shield of artificially dark hair was any indication.

Shifting slightly in the glider, Miles tried to block out the image of a very wet, very naked Lori all soaped up in one of the inn's luxurious two-person showers. Her body was built for a magazine centerfold, full and curvy in all the right places and very definitely X-rated. It was no wonder she kept it under wraps with castoffs from the Goodwill store. He bit back a groan before his microphone could pick it up. Embarrassment, lust, and anger swirled in his gut.

The awkwardness was due to the fact that he'd lingered a moment—okay, maybe two—longer than he should have while he surreptitiously admired the view that day. He'd been checking the air filters in his mother's B and B. It was a job his father always took care of when he was alive and Miles worried was now being overlooked. That day, Miles had unwittingly walked in upon a strange woman showering in a supposedly unoccupied room. Not that anyone would blame him for remaining. He was a red-blooded guy and the shower show was one that would have brought a dead man back to life.

The anger was fueled by the lust that burned through him then and every freaking time he'd laid his eyes on Lori in the four months since. Miles hated the way his body lit up around a woman who was a mystery—a stranger who was very clearly hiding out under his mother's roof. He had no business being turned on by a woman like that. And yet, she mesmerized him with the things he wanted to do with her. She was a distraction he couldn't afford right now. Miles hadn't felt such an intense attraction to a woman since—

"Miles?" Tanya was eyeing him curiously.

He blinked to refocus. *Damn, damn, damn.* Once again Lori had totally derailed his concentration. And she wasn't even within his sight line. In fact, she was probably hiding upstairs just as she did every time someone from the media visited the inn.

Glancing past the television camera Miles's eyes landed on the anxious face of Bernice Reed. The elderly woman had managed McAlister C&E for decades and now worked as the office manager of his campaign headquarters. As usual, she was outfitted like a neon sign, today dressed head to toe in bright pink with an oversized necklace to match. She was staring at him through rhinestone-studded glasses, wide-eyed with her hand to her chest and, knowing her, a "bless his heart" on her tongue. Beside her was Cassidy Burroughs, the teenager who operated the Patty Wagon, his mother's seasonal ice cream truck. Cassidy was holding her cell phone aloft, shooting video of the scene while wearing an expression on her face that clearly said "What the heck?"

"I'm sorry, Tanya." Miles quickly returned his gaze to his other tormentor. "I was distracted thinking of my mother there for a moment." *Jesus, next I'll be invoking apple pie and baseball.* His answer sounded evasive even to his own ears. Miles was tanking the interview all because of a woman who hovered in the shadows of every room but the kitchen. He needed to get her out of his head. Better yet, out of his mother's inn if he could somehow manage that. But for now he just needed to wrap up the sparring match with Tanya.

He looked up to find that Tanya's wide smile had a nasty edge to it. Miles resisted the urge to cross his legs and shield the family jewels. Instead he forced himself to remain relaxed. He was a professional and as such had prepared for anything she could throw at him.

"I asked you whether you and your opponent will be debating one another this summer."

Miles could hear the Atlantic Ocean slamming against the sand across the street, the whirring of the ceiling fans above their heads, and even the gentle hum of the LED lights shining on either side of his face, so he knew he wasn't dreaming. Or dead. He glanced over Tanya's right shoulder at Coy Scofield III, the young flunkie the party had dumped on him as a campaign manager. Coy was twenty-five with the political expertise of a gnat, but that hadn't mattered.

Until now.

The kid was talking a mile a minute into the cell phone glued to his ear, his cheeks flushed with what Miles could only assume was excitement. Coy had been very vocal that he wasn't thrilled to be stuck in a campaign where there wouldn't actually be a contest. He wanted the thrill of the chase. The kid was frustrated because Miles was running uncontested. The opposing party's candidate had withdrawn after being arrested for alleged racketeering violations just days after this spring's primary. Miles carefully pushed the words past his lips so that the audio wouldn't capture the anxiety in his voice.

"From what I understand, Brian Kilpatrick is having a tougher battle with the Treasury Department to worry about debating me. That's why he's no longer running."

"Oh, you haven't heard?" Tanya was practically bouncing in her seat. "Well, I guess that's understandable with your *family crisis* and all. But the opposing party is putting forth another candidate."

"They can't." Miles mentally reviewed the campaign laws. There wasn't a provision. He'd checked. So had the governor and everyone else in the party. The only way they could replace a candidate who'd been put on the ballot via a primary election was if the candidate was ill and could no longer serve the term of the office. The only illness Kilpatrick had was that of a terminal dumbass and the opposing party was out of luck on that loophole.

Tanya leaned back, seductively crossing her legs again as if to say *checkmate*. There was no mistaking the malice in her grin now. She was obviously enjoying the reaction her bombshell had gotten out of Miles. "Technically the party can't add a name to the November ballot. But the voters can."

Son. Of. A. Bitch.

A write-in campaign. There'd been talk of one during the initial days after Kilpatrick's arrest, but the pollsters had assured the governor and the national party bigwigs that Miles's reputation was sterling enough that the opposition wouldn't risk funding another candidate. Instead, they'd spend their time and money on a race that wasn't a shoo-in.

Apparently, with all the talk surrounding his late father these past few weeks, some of the shine had worn off Miles's reputation.

"It's funny how these things work, isn't it?" Tanya was the only one on the verandah who was seeing the humor in the situation.

Determined not to let her—or any of her viewers—see him sweat, Miles leaned back in the stupid glider and smiled back at her. "Well, it's a lot better for the constituents to have more than one candidate. A two-party race offers voters greater opportunities to weigh the issues and make sure their interests will be best represented." Miles was pretty sure he'd read that in a political science textbook somewhere, but at this point he just didn't care. He needed to regurgitate enough bullshit to get him through this train wreck of an interview with his shirt still on his back. "Since you have the inside scoop today, Tanya, do you mind telling me who my opponent will be?"

"Of course. We're headed to Shallotte from here for the big announcement. You'll be facing off against Faye Rich."

"Faye Rich as in the GTO Grandma?" Cassidy blurted out from behind the camera and Miles hoped her words and his wince hadn't been caught on video.

Faye Rich was exactly what her name implied: rich as Croesus. She'd inherited a string of car dealerships from her father and married into more. Her commercials were legendary for their low-budget, smaltzy, down-home humor. Not to mention Faye had appeared in all of them since she was three years old. Now somewhere in her mid-sixties, she was still the voice behind Rich Automotive, occasionally even dressed as the Easter Bunny, the Tobacco Queen, or Uncle Sam. She made it a point to appear at events in her souped-up GTO. Her voter recognition would be off the charts. And then there was the fact her name would be easy to write in.

And just like that, Miles took another curveball right to the chest.

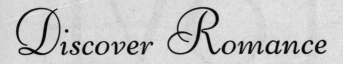